Leslie Waller, a graduate of the Universities of Chicago and Columbia, is a prolific writer of fact and fiction. A member of P.E.N. and Mensa, he has been a journalist and public relations executive, and now works on a free-lance basis. His books *The Banker* and *The Family* have been enormously successful and *The American* follows the footsteps of the central character of these earlier stories. This trip Woods Palmer Jr finds himself entangled with the ruthless kingpins of world crime – and also a beautiful and beguiling woman . . .

Also in Mayflower Books by Leslie Waller

The American

Leslie Waller

Mayflower

Granada Publishing Limited
Published in 1973 by Mayflower Books Ltd
Frogmore, St Albans, Herts AL2 2NF

First published in Great Britain by
W. H. Allen & Co Ltd 1971
Copyright © Leslie Waller 1970
Made and printed in Great Britain by
Richard Clay (The Chaucer Press) Ltd
Bungay, Suffolk
Set in Linotype Plantin

CHAPTER 1

Palmer rolled over on the bed away from Virginia. He reached for his wristwatch, which he held under the night-light. He saw that it lacked five minutes of midnight. He lay on his back then, listening to Virginia's regular breathing and wondering how she had fallen asleep so deeply when he felt so restless.

Thursday seemed to be taking forever. Palmer's flight to Paris was scheduled to leave Friday morning early. But he had begun to doubt if Friday would ever come.

It wasn't just the interminable farewell parties. The one in the bank's boardroom this afternoon had been dull enough but, as chief executive officer, Palmer had been able to cut short the festivities after a suitable interval. The dinner tonight with his three children had gone smoothly enough, too. Since the separation, his wife, Edith, hadn't seen fit to be on hand any of the Thursday nights when he called to take the children out. That source of friction had been spared them both.

Palmer supposed now that it had been Thursday's late-late party, tonight after dinner with the children. Virginia had wanted her farewell to be his final one before the trip. She had some years before bought a small, charming house at the east end of 58th Street overlooking the river and the Queensboro Bridge. It was a place in which the two of them could be quite alone together.

Although they saw a lot of each other now, since the separation, the sexual tension between them still ran high enough so that when Palmer had arrived tonight and found she'd invited another couple for drinks, he'd been both disappointed and impatient. It was true, he remembered now as he lay motionless beside her, that the other two had taken themselves off by eleven o'clock but, until then, the night had dragged.

He turned and propped up his head to look at Virginia. The sheet had slipped away from both of them and she lay slightly turned so as to better silhouette her full breasts and the sweeping curve of her thigh as it flowed into her soft, round buttocks. Palmer smoothed the faintly olive skin along her flank and two

7

the simplest of psychological facts: only the hidden is titillating.

His glance now traced a curved line down Virginia's entirely unhidden body from her eyes, closed in sleep, past the erect roundness of her breasts, their wide brown areolas swelling slightly in the dim light, to her small belly like a smooth hill that had once been a volcano and still had a deep-cut navel to prove it.

He bent down and kissed her navel. As he started to pull back, her knees clamped against each side of his head. 'Whatever gave you the idea you could get off with just a kiss?'

When he glanced up along her body, he could see her smile framed between her swelling breasts. For a girl who was fairly short, he thought, there was a glorious sweep to her from this angle. 'I'd hoped to take advantage of you as you slept,' he mumbled, his mouth pressed against her belly by the pressure of her knees.

She squirmed sideways and he let his head be squeezed, gently at first, between her soft thighs. She increased the pressure and he bit the dark, curly mat as softly as he could.

'Not nice!' she yelped. 'Not even friendly.'

'It was meant in the highest spirit of friendship.'

'That low down a gentleman doesn't bite.'

'A gentleman wouldn't even be this low.'

She relaxed the pressure of her thighs but he remained where he was. 'Better,' he said, planting a short line of kisses.

'You seem to be on some sort of quest.'

'Holy Grail,' he admitted.

'I expect you'll need your miner's hat soon.'

'I brought along my pick, too.'

'At this hour? The noise. The neighbors.'

Later, exhausted, both of them fell asleep. Palmer may have dreamed but when he awoke after a while he couldn't remember any of it. The quality of their relationship still eluded him. Perhaps his worries about it had awakened him. He glanced again at his watch and saw that, finally, Friday had arrived and was, in fact, an hour old.

He tried to sort out why he still felt tense and upset. Perhaps the other couple's being here when he arrived had thrown him off balance. He'd expected to be completely alone with Virginia. Perhaps the disappointment had been deeper than he imagined. Also, the nature of the other two grated on him. The man was

9

chief editorial writer for one of the newspapers. His girlfriend, who had started by staging Off-Broadway plays, now produced documentary films for television.

'They promised to leave by eleven,' Virginia had whispered as she took his coat. She gave him a look that traveled from his mouth to his trouser cuffs. 'I mean this to be a real farewell party.'

But the editorial writer was too intensely curious about Palmer's trip. 'I know it's all off-the-record stuff,' he said several times, petulantly, with a shooing-away gesture as if bothered by small gnats but not very much. 'Sometimes a mere rank outsider layman can give good advice ... off the record,' he added archly, suggesting that he was far indeed from being either mere, rank, or an outsider.

Palmer had found it too boring to explain much about his mission. He'd been recruited for it in such a roundabout way that he assumed it was something secret. He'd been down in Washington, testifying before a House committee on the prime rate as a representative not just of Ubco but of all the commercial banks in the district governed by the Federal Reserve Bank of New York.

A dull economist he knew from having to lecture the man's graduate students at Yale on corporate debt funding invited Palmer for a drink with a stranger who turned out to be the more interesting. He was from one of the larger quasi-public foundations concerned with economic research. Palmer had done military intelligence work throughout most of World War II. His training told him the man and his Foundation for Economic Study were not exactly what they seemed.

The foundation wanted Palmer to undertake a particular mission of major importance related to the dollar drain. It was their hope that an active, knowledgeable banker like Palmer, talking to his counterparts throughout the NATO alliance, could put together a usable plan for redressing the unfavorable balance of payments which was costing the United States billions each year.

Palmer shared their optimism. As he lay beside Virginia now and thought about the mission again, he knew he could do a lot to help. It was the sort of thing that appealed to him these days. The bank had become a dull place even more crammed with intrigue than usual. Palmer's mind could enjoy a general level of internal politicking. But at a certain point, when there was too much of it, he began to lose interest. In any event, it had been harder for him to clear his desk for a month or two that the mission would take than to think creatively about the dollar drain. He felt quite sanguine about the mission's success.

Some of it may have been conveyed as arrogant self-confidence of the editorial writer and his girlfriend. Palmer found it amusing that what passed for conversation in New York these days was often just the naked exploitation of opportunity. The journalist's talk had all been a series of commercials on how he would plug the dollar drain, implying that a banker was the wrong person to send on such a mission. The documentarist's conversation, after a few Scotches, had been limited to what a real groovy now thing a team could do traveling with Palmer and photographing every move he made. Remembering them, Palmer sighed impatiently.

Virginia came instantly awake. She sat up, snapped on the lamp, and lighted a cigarette, her firm breasts glowing warmly in the sudden bath of illumination. Palmer knew her to be forty and yet she seemed destined to have the uptilting breasts of a girl – a well-developed girl – for life. He smiled at her.

'Happy to get away from me for a while,' she said.

'Not at all.'

She ran her fingers through her long, pitch-black hair, getting it out of her face so that she could watch him more closely. 'You need a straight, flat-out vacation from women,' she said then. 'You went right from marriage into this.'

'Then there aren't any women in Europe, I take it?'

One corner of her full mouth quirked up for a moment, then down. 'They'll find you I don't doubt. Is –' She stopped and covered the pause by inhaling smoke and blowing it out in great messy clouds.

Palmer waved it away. 'Will you try giving up cigarettes while I'm gone?'

Virginia laughed and ground out the cigarette. Her face went thoughtful again. 'Are you sure you –' She stopped again. The new pause was even more awkward than the first.

'You'd better just spit it out,' Palmer suggested.

She sighed in exasperation and the upward swell of her breasts excited Palmer all over again. 'It's just this feeling I have. I think you're not telling me all there is to this mission of yours.'

'But I am. I have.'

11

'Then there's more they haven't told you.'

Palmer considered this for a moment. 'Possible. Not probable.'

'They know you as a banker,' she pointed out, 'but somewhere in Washington sits a dossier that says you were once a high-ranking G-2 officer.'

'Nothing that grand. A major in S-2. And let's remember it was twenty-five years ago. That's a quarter of a century where I come from.'

'Don't remind me of the passing of years, darling.' The smile came and went so fast that Palmer almost missed it. She looked grave again. 'It's not beyond the realm of possibility, is it, that there's a dossier on you somewhere in Europe?'

He pulled her to him and began nuzzling her nipples.

CHAPTER 2

Palmer left Virginia's apartment as the sun cleared the tops of the buildings across the river from her house and began to set fire to the upper stories of Manhattan.

He glanced at his watch. His flight left at 9:45 and Jimmy would have the car in front of Palmer's apartment by 8:45 – an hour from now. Palmer walked quickly up an almost deserted First Avenue in the direction of the small furnished apartment he had rented after the separation. The air had a clear smell to it. The trucks and buses and cars hadn't yet poisoned the particular batch that lay over the east side of midtown Manhattan, although a few tractor-trailers were already grinding harshly up the slight incline as they headed northward out of the city.

The chilly modern lobby of his building was deserted as Palmer let himself in. The lobby was under surveillance by closed-circuit television, which was supposed to make up for the fact that the doorman was off somewhere having a nap or a smoke. Palmer got out of the elevator at his floor and started to fit his key into the lock of his apartment. It was then he saw the door stood ajar.

He frowned and took a step backward, balancing unsteadily for a second. Then he placed his hand on the door and stepped sideways as he shoved it open. In the old days they'd called this

12

the Donovan Two-Step, usually executed with gun in hand, and named after Wild Bill Donovan of the OSS.

'Friend,' a voice from inside muttered, almost too low to be heard. 'Come on in, Woody.' It had a familiar sound to it.

Palmer edged around the open door and peered into the darkness of his furnished living room. He could see a small, chubby man sitting in the expensive black glove-leather armchair. Nearer to the door, standing almost at attention, was an impassive young man who allowed Palmer to examine his face in the light of a burnished bronze lamp. The unlined face was devoid of any meaning that Palmer could read, nor did it match the voice that had welcomed him into his own apartment.

He stared at the half-dark in which the chubby man sat. 'Say something else,' he suggested.

The man produced a fuzzy chuckle. 'You always were too damned cautious.'

Palmer walked inside and shut the door behind him. He snapped on a floor lamp that caught the chubby man blinking. 'And you always were too fond of dramatics, Harry.'

The chubby man got to his feet and shook Palmer's hand with both of his. 'Woody, you haven't really changed at all, have you?' he asked, peering into Palmer's narrow face, with its high cheekbones. 'There isn't enough meat on you to shift around, damn it.' He indicated his own belly. 'Unlike a few people I could name.' He brought out the chuckle again. 'Don't look so damned suspicious, Woody.'

'Suspicious? Me?'

Palmer sat down in the sofa across from the leather chair. 'I haven't laid eyes on you in ten years, Harry, and then only socially. Our last professional association was twenty-four years ago. Since then I've entered an entirely different profession. Whereas you are still spying. Me, suspicious?'

Harry's eyes, under furry gray brows, shifted to the young man standing near the door. 'Wait downstairs,' he said. The young man left and the two older ones waited as the elevator door opened and closed outside in the corridor. The pause was a patient one, Palmer noted, as if both of them had all the time in the world.

'My driver picks me up in forty-five minutes, Harry,' he said then. 'Can you possibly get to the point before then?'

'You've guessed it already.' The chubby man sat down heavily in the armchair again.

13

'No. But a friend of mine did. She knows less about this economic mission of mine than I do, but she outguessed me on its purpose. It's a blind, isn't it?'

The chubby man shook his head with firm slowness, in much the way, Palmer noted, that some people who lie accompany their words with an innocent widening of the eyes.

'The mission is bona fide,' Harry assured him. 'I just want to hitchhike a small errand onto it.' The chubby man's voice grew suddenly more forceful. 'I'm in a bind, Woody. I know how you feel about intelligence work. God knows you left me in no doubt ten years ago when I tried to re-recruit you. But –'

'But this is different?' Palmer sighed. 'All intelligence work is the same. If anybody should know that, you do. What are you now, anyway, Number One Spy or something? Or does that title belong to the head of CIA?'

The chuckle began to grate on Palmer's nerves. It occurred to him that he had never liked Harry Bannister, even in the war when he was a civilian liaison officer between the White House and Army Intelligence. Nothing about the man had changed except his girth. He was still what he'd always been, a good spy. Which meant, Palmer told himself, a fairly unpleasant human being. No one called him anything but H.B.

'Woody, let me remind you of a few things,' Bannister was saying. 'Do you know what it takes to get my ass out of Washington these days? I have half a dozen top-ranking people who exist only to perform errands like this one. But I went to a hell of a lot of trouble to get myself up here last night and put in six hours of armchair time waiting while you enjoyed the favors of a certain Miss Clary.'

'A detail your people forgot to give you before you left Washington,' Palmer suggested. 'Still the same old gorgeous lack of coordination, eh, Harry?'

The chubby man shrugged. 'We goof now and then. We're only human. Listen, Woody, this is too big to leave to subordinates. I'm making my appeal direct to you because, for one thing, what I'm asking will create absolutely no problems for you and, for another, you'd have to see this particular contact anyway. He's one of the people you're slated to see in Bonn. I'm only asking you one small favor. After you finish talking to him about your own mission, you simply talk to him about mine. That's all. An additional fifteen minutes. Nothing more. You don't even have to take notes. What he'll tell you can be remembered, it's that simple.'

Palmer shook his head. The light outside the windows had grown stronger as they talked and H.B.'s face was now in shadow again, his form a chunky silhouette. It bothered Palmer that he'd let himself get in this classic interrogation position. He got up and sat on the teak window seat, reversing the position, the light behind him and glaring into Bannister's face.

'When you talk,' he told the chubby man, 'everything's simple. But my experience is different, Harry. My experience tells me this sort of thing is always like flypaper. Venture out onto it for the distance of one step and you're stuck.'

'Wrong.' Bannister blinked confidently up at him. 'I wouldn't do a thing like that to you, Woody, on the level. I'll even give you the full briefing and let you judge for yourself.'

'Full? Don't tell me I've been cleared that high up.'

Bannister tapped his chest. 'It's at my discretion. Never mind official secrets clearance. In here I know you're loyal.'

Palmer's eyes began to feel gritty with lack of sleep. The word 'loyal' had an unpleasant effect on him and he wished H.B. hadn't used it. Loyal was such a meaningless word. 'Loyal to what, Harry?'

'The man you'll see is one of the Bonn government's highest ranking economic officials. He's so respectable that when Willy Brandt came into power he left this man where he is. He's unspectacular, quiet, a good craftsman. He's a credit to whatever West German administration he works for. He doesn't produce a hell of a lot of startling stuff for me. Mostly figures, economic stuff, nothing military.' Bannister raised a thick finger. 'You understand, Woody? Nothing military in this. Purely economic.'

'Why not debrief him in your normal way? You've got a big apparatus in West Germany.'

Bannister heaved his bulky body out of the chair. The interrogation position had begun to tell on him, too, Palmer noted. He began pacing the living room in slow, steady steps, almost like a convict pacing a cell measured by years of practice. Palmer glanced at his watch. His driver would be there in half an hour. Fortunately, he was fully packed except for his suit jackets.

'That's why I'm in a bind,' H.B. began slowly, almost unwillingly. 'My West German apparatus was blown two days ago, Wednesday. The smaller fry are still safe, but the top six people

15

were blown by an article in *Der Spiegel*, fed to the magazine by some bastard across the wall in East Germany, I think.'

'And you haven't got anybody higher than an errand boy to debrief your pigeon in Bonn.'

'That's about the size of it.'

'Harry, I'm not your errand boy.'

Bannister swung on him like a Sherman tank, eyes aiming squarely into Palmer's face. 'You're so goddamned right you're not,' he snapped. 'That's the whole point, Woody. You're a gift from heaven. The opposition people will be watching for one of the small fry in my apparatus to get to Schirmer. They're not even sure Schirmer's my man. It's more likely they're waiting to see which of my small fry contacts what Bonn official. So I badly need somebody out of left field, someone clean who has a reason for being there. I badly need you, Woody.'

'Nonsense.' Palmer got up and walked into the small efficiency bedroom where his bags lay open. 'You set up this whole phony Foundation for Economic Study mission just to get me to Europe. Just to debrief your pigeon.'

H.B. scuttled after him. 'You had this mission offered you months ago, Woody. And the *Spiegel* piece broke only last Wednesday.'

Palmer began folding suit jackets and laying them on the open luggage. 'That could simply be a rare example of your people doing something right for a change, setting me up long before you needed me.'

'Not so.'

Palmer turned to the chubby man. 'What does Schirmer have that you'd waste your time trying to con me into running your errands?'

Bannister sat down on the edge of the bed. 'Economic stuff.'

'What stuff?'

H.B. gestured vaguely. 'You know everything's in an uproar over there. This move of Brandt toward the East has got everyone jumpy as hell.'

'What stuff?'

'I'm getting to it.' The chubby man sighed heavily. 'The cozier Brandt gets with the Eastern bloc, the more embarrassing it is to him to have our military presence on West German soil. But he can't send us packing because we're all the leverage he has in dealing with the East. Do you follow this?'

Palmer nodded. 'It isn't as complex as you imagine, Harry.

16

Let's graduate from kindergarten. Tell me something I don't know.'

Bannister frowned unhappily. 'You don't have to be this difficult, Woody.'

'Possibly.'

'I came to you as an old friend for help in a tight bind. I didn't come to be stuck full of pins and made fun of.'

Palmer closed and locked one suitcase. 'First, we were never friends, much less old ones. You have no friends, H.B., and you know it. Second, the bind you're in is of your own making. Third, by sticking pins in you I'm trying to give you a message. The message is: find yourself another errand boy.'

Bannister sat silently as Palmer began closing the second bag. Then he cleared his throat, simply to break the gathering silence. 'There is a formula,' he said then, 'somewhere in the highest echelons of the Brandt regime, there is a formula or timetable or policy statement – I don't know how it's been expressed formally – that we have to have. It's the timetable of rapprochement between West and East Germany. Or it's their plan of approaches, rejections, agreements, and the like. Or it's a formula for governing the unified nation. Or it's simply an informal agreement among Brandt's top ministers. We have to know the sense of it. Schirmer knows. He won't unload it on anybody except the man who says three words to him. I want you to tell him those three words, listen to what he says and bring it back to me. It's that simple.'

'It's even simpler.' Palmer picked up both bags and carried them to the front door. 'Just have State Department ask Willy Brandt. He's a friend of ours. He'll tell.'

H.B. shook his head with the same slow emphasis. 'You've been out of harness a long time, Woody. Since when do you believe what one government tells another? Or what any government tells the press? What I'm talking about is genuine information, not political hot air. We have to know Brandt's formula or timetable or whatever. Do you have any idea what our military commitment is in Germany? The SAC squadrons? The fighter escorts? The missile bases? Can you imagine how helpless our defense posture would be without our German commitment?'

Palmer glanced at his watch. Jimmy would be downstairs in fifteen minutes. He would come up for the bags. But that would mean another quarter hour of gasbagisms from Harry Bannister.

17

Palmer decided to accelerate his leave-taking. 'Help me down-stairs with the bags?'

H.B. looked horrified. 'I thought we had a little more time. I can't be seen with you, Woody, you know that. If you're going down now, let me get away first. Give me a five-minute lead.'

'Fine.'

'Then you'll talk to Schirmer?'

'When did I promise that?'

Bannister's doughy face went dead. 'You can't let me down, Woody. Too much is riding on this.'

Palmer shook his head. 'Not at all. You'll find another errand boy. We both know that.'

'Woody, you're custom-tailored for the job. It'd take me months to find anyone as qualified. And by then Schirmer could be blown or defected or dead. I need this information within a week. You're on your way to the airport. You're in motion. You're going to Bonn anyway. God, you're even going to talk to Schirmer. By saying three words, you'd do me a tremendous favor. You'd –' Bannister's voice went deeper. 'You'd do your country a tremendous service, Woody. I can't overestimate the value of such a service. And, believe me, the highest people would know what you did for us. I don't mean Cabinet members. I mean the White House, direct. And that can't hurt you. Or your bank.'

Palmer grinned at him. 'You ought to hear yourself. You get that messianic Billy Graham note in your voice and I want to find a hat to start throwing nickels into.'

'You arrogant bastard.'

'Three little words,' Palmer said. 'Are those the three?'

H.B.'s eyes lighted up. 'Operation Overdraft begins.' He stared into Palmer's face. 'Got that? Operation Overdraft be-gins.'

'Forget it, Harry. I was only being funny.'

The chubby man touched Palmer's lapel softly. 'I don't care what you think you were being, Woody. Those are the three words that trigger Schirmer. And Uncle Sam is waiting for the jackpot. It's up to you, now.'

'The hell it is. I –'

Bannister opened the door, stepped out into the corridor and pushed the elevator button. 'Five minutes' lead,' he whispered.

Palmer felt a surge of anger heat his face. He picked up his bags, carried them out into the corridor and double locked the apartment door behind him. 'You get no lead from me,' he said. 'You're assuming too much. You're leaning too hard on old acquaintance. I told you to find someone else. That's my last word.'

'Can't be. You have three more to tell Schirmer.'

The elevator door opened. Palmer shoved his bags inside and stood in the doorway, holding it open. 'To hell with Schirmer and to hell with you.' He let go of the automatic door. It started to close.

II.B. grabbed at the door. 'You know the words,' he said in a desperate undertone, trying to keep his voice down without sacrificing any persuasive force.

Palmer let him get into the elevator, which started down the shaft. Bannister quickly punched the buttons for all the floors between Palmer's and the street. They began a slow descent, opening and closing doors at each floor.

'I didn't make a mistake in calling on you,' Bannister said with deadly earnestness. 'You've still got some spark of interest in helping your country.'

'What makes you think Operation Overdraft will help it?'

'Sh.' Door open, door close. 'It's our considered judgment that the operation is more critical than anything in Western Europe today.'

'Since when did your bunch start using considered judgment, Harry?'

'In fact –' Open. Close. 'In fact, it's no exaggeration to say that what we do in Europe hangs on the information you collect for us.'

Palmer let the next door open and close. 'Big talk, Harry.'

'True talk.'

'Maybe just talk.'

H.B. shook his head solemnly. 'Truth. No lies, Woody. The truth. Our course of action in Europe –' Open. They were at the lobby floor. 'Depends on this.' Bannister stepped out of the elevator. 'On you. Woody, please.' He pointed up at the ceiling. 'Take it back up. Give me five minutes.'

'And fifteen in Bonn.'

The chubby man whirled to survey the lobby. Its only occupant was the young man with the expressionless face. He turned back to Palmer. 'And fifteen in Bonn.'

Palmer stepped back from the door. 'You've got your five, anyway.' The elevator door began to close.

He punched the button for his floor and felt the rising motion. But he knew it was a false feeling of elevation. In the last half hour most of the pleasure of going to Europe had drained out of him. Whether he accommodated H.B.'s request or turned it down, the trip was tainted. People like Harry Bannister had that quality about them, that terrible ability to spoil almost anything they touched, simply by touching it.

Palmer brought his bags back into his apartment and glanced at his watch. His driver would be along in a few minutes. Until then, there was nothing to do but try not to think.

CHAPTER 3

A muted loudspeaker informed the passengers waiting in the first-class lounge, first in French and then in English, that Flight 010 was ready for embarkation.

The tall, thin man put down his copy of the *Times*, glanced at his watch and saw that it lacked ten minutes till his 9:45 A.M. departure. His narrow face, under straight, dark blond hair, looked somewhat grayish with fatigue. His gray eyes seemed slightly bloodshot. He gave the impression of being a successful forty-year-old attorney. Also, there was something rather informal about the way his long, thin legs were crossed, ankle on knee, that seemed not quite New York Establishment. He continued to read as the other passengers boarded the plane.

'M'sieu Palmaire?'

He looked up at the hostess in her pale blue uniform. They were alone in the lounge. 'Palmer,' he responded.

'Zuh aircraft is loading, m'sieu.'

Palmer folded the newspaper and placed it on the low table beside his coffee cup. He stood up and lifted from the sofa where he had been sitting a thin black leather briefcase. He pulled out the case's retractable handles, clenched them in his fingers, and followed the hostess out of the lounge.

The 707's forward compartment held only a few first-class guests this morning. Woods Palmer, Jr., sat in the last seat, accepted a copy of *Figaro*, and proceeded to tax his French to its outer limits as he waited for takeoff.

Palmer was neither an attorney, a New Yorker, nor forty.

20

Originally from Chicago, he was at the age of forty-seven chief executive officer of United Bank and Trust Company, known both as Ubco and as the largest commercial bank in the country, larger even than Bank of America or First National City.

He had not been out of the country for nearly a decade, despite the fact that Ubco's worldwide interests included branches throughout Europe and even an office in Moscow. Palmer's last trip abroad had been with Edith, his wife, on their twelfth anniversary almost a decade ago.

Palmer's eyes flicked unsteadily across the columns of French journalese, but his mind had already switched back in time to that earlier European trip. He and Edith had been handed on from one set of business associates to another like a carefully wrapped package that can never be opened. At the time Palmer had been working for his father's bank in Chicago. As the heir apparent, he had been handled with extreme care. They'd had no real vacation at all, just another form of business trip, the dull Chamber-of-Commerce thing, never once glimpsing what they might have seen.

Palmer knew what they had missed. During and after the war he had operated for Military Intelligence in almost every country of Western Europe, most extensively in France, Germany, and Italy. As he waited for Flight 010 to taxi into position at the end of a runway, he recalled that he had even suggested to Edith a decade ago that they break away from their too-solicitous hosts.

She'd been afraid to. It was entirely possible that this difference between them was merely one of many in those days, but the more readily recalled. Edith had never been what one might call a fearful person. Perhaps his memory of it was flawed by what had passed since then between them. However, he now preferred to believe that her refusal to go on an adventure with him ten years ago had been a strong sign of the eventual death of their marriage.

In the half year since the separation Palmer had spent a good deal of time trying to remember when the marriage had first shown clear signs of going bad. Not that the separation obsessed him, he told himself now. Not that he wasn't getting along even better single than he had married. He missed the day-to-day contact with the children, of course. But being able to avoid the day-to-day contact with Edith somewhat made up for the loss. With all the children in their teens, he knew, he wouldn't have

21

been seeing that much of them at home anyway. Palmer had convinced himself of this.

He had also convinced himself that the separation had nothing to do with Virginia Clary. His relation to her had a life of its own. As important as it was, it had happened long after his marriage to Edith had started to sour.

Palmer glanced out the window at the runway. It was not, he told himself with sudden honesty, for his abilities at self-deception that he had risen in the banking world. No, in banking it was his mercilessly logical mind that had put him so clearly on top. He began to wonder why the only thing he persisted in kidding himself about was the tangled network that lay between him and his wife and his mistress.

In French and English the aircraft's loudspeaker reminded Palmer to fasten his belt and keep his seat in an upright position for takeoff. A stewardess moved slowly down the aisle, making certain her charges had obeyed. A moment later the steward followed her to make sure she hadn't bungled. He had a typical French face, Palmer felt, beaky nose, high cheekbones flushed with horizontal smears of red.

The four fan-jets roared more loudly. The 707 trembled. Palmer picked up *Figaro* and assured himself he was too old a hand at flying to watch another takeoff. During the war he'd flown everything from Mustangs and Thunderbolts to B-17's and B-24's. He'd parachuted out of reconnaissance planes and twice out of gliders. Since the war he'd flown somewhere in the United States at least once a week on business. Now, as chief executive officer, he no longer had to visit problems. They were flown to him.

The 707 began moving forward slowly. Then, abruptly, it put on a burst of speed. Palmer's glance slid sideways from *Figaro* to the window. Flight 010 was still on the ground but moving at well over 100 miles an hour. Suddenly it was off the ground at a wild angle. The ground fell away. The skyline of New York banked crazily.

Palmer's nose was pressed to the window. He watched a narrow sandbar island pass beneath. The seat-belt and No Smoking signs flicked off. The ruddy-cheeked steward was beside him.

'Champagne, M'sieu Palmaire?'

Palmer accepted a tulip glass of the wine. He sipped. There had been too much champagne in the past few days. Even at the boardroom party some bottles had been produced. Palmer

22

hadn't been terribly pleased to sense how happy his officers were to see him leave, even for just a month or so. The younger ones, he suspected, were looking forward to being out from under his intense supervision. The senior officers, Palmer noted, had their own reasons for wanting him temporarily out of the way. He had been particularly hard on them of late, forcing them to make difficult decisions and postpone others. He knew enough about them to smell the beginnings of half a dozen intrigues and plots to end-run his decisions. With him away in Europe, perhaps some of the conspiracies would simply die out.

He'd ordered champagne for himself and his children early yesterday evening. Woody, his oldest, had been drinking wine for several years now. He seemed to be the first to weather the separation and impending divorce. Plodding along, he seemed to have come out the other side of the tensions with something like peace of mind. Of course, Palmer knew, Woody was probably the least intelligent of his children. It was unfair of him to believe this, just as it was unfair to assume Woody felt the breakup of his parents least keenly. But there it was.

Tom, the youngest, was allowed a single glass of champagne. In his typical way – skating over life without ever once sinking into it – Tom had downed the wine as matter-of-factly as he did his Coke. He almost seemed not to know that, in fact, his father no longer lived at home. Tom had always lived on his own plane, insulated from the comings and goings of adults.

It was Gerri, his fifteen-year-old daughter, who had the most wine and created the most trouble for Palmer. She had from the announcement of the separation made it abundantly clear – too often, actually – that she blamed absolutely no one. 'There have to be two sides to the story,' she had repeated from time to time over the past six months, as she had last night over her champagne. 'I don't believe either one, of course, but I'm sure you each have your motives.'

Palmer usually itched to put down this insubordination but, since living away from them, hesitated to leave any of his children with an unpleasant memory of him. This was especially true last night, since he wouldn't be seeing them for a month or two. They had been quite excited about his mission. He had given each of them a copy of his official itinerary – the full one, not the summary published in the *Times* the day before – so that they might write him.

'Or phone me collect if there's a problem.'

'Problem with what?' Gerri had asked.

Palmer had shrugged. 'Teen-age life is one gigantic problem, isn't it? Surely some facet of it will bust loose over the next two months.' He had grinned at her to show her he was teasing.

Gerri had stared at him for a long, unnerving moment. She so closely resembled both Palmer and her mother – and he and Edith looked so much alike – that gazing into her long face with his high cheekbones, gray eyes, and straight, dark blond hair was like staring into a magic mirror, into a mysterious image of the way Edith had looked at fifteen or even the way he had. It was an unsettling experience. It implied something almost biological in Gerri's unspoken understanding of him and his doings.

The way she looked, he knew, was one of the problems when Wasp married Wasp. There was no dearth of different Wasp types. But when two of the tall, thin, blond caricatures of White Anglo-Saxondom mated, the results were all too predictable.

Virginia Clary, now, was a short, dark Celt with the power to see even deeper into him than his own daughter. Sipping champagne now from the Air France tulip glass, Palmer smiled slightly. The last bottle of champagne last night had been opened when he and Virginia had finally been alone.

There was something he hadn't told her or the foundation sending him. Palmer knew it was unlikely he would find anything startlingly new to suggest about redressing the balance of payments. But he could very quickly put together some old ideas in a good new way. This would be leaving him a lot more free time over the next month or so than anyone suspected.

Even that damned sneak Harry Bannister, with his grandiose Operation Overdraft. Palmer was trying to forget the whole sordid scene with Harry. It wasn't possible yet, but it might be in time. Harry was counting on him, but Palmer had no idea if he'd run Harry's 'little errand' or not. In any event he was damned if he would hurry back to New York the moment his work ended. He was damned if New York, with its poisonous air, its wounding noise, its maddening problems and maddened people was going to reclaim him that fast.

He knew what he was suffering from. He'd even given it a name: reverse homesickness. He was sick of home.

As the 707 pushed forward, he felt a great sense of escaping from the old into the new. This was insane, he realized, since it was to the Old World that he was fleeing.

24

But he was determined that once his mission for the foundation ended, his own mission would begin, to get for himself the holiday he so desperately required. Palmer realized he was smiling at the back of the seat in front of him. The smile broadened into a grin.

He relaxed his grip on the slim black leather briefcase and let his chair drop back to a full reclining angle. Flight 010 thundered northeast across the Atlantic.

CHAPTER 4

Flight 010 circled Orly only once before getting the go-ahead for landing. As the plane leveled off and touched the runway, Palmer eyed the collection of modern buildings and half-finished structures. All big airports looked the same, he decided. There was nothing particularly French about Orly, not at this distance, any more than there was something particularly Memphian about the airport at Memphis. All had the same halfway-to-the-stars look about them. Most needed enlarging and were busily trying to catch up. In many of them, Palmer reflected, temporary structures of plywood seemed to dominate the scene. On entering a big city, it was somehow unsettling to have to pass through these huts and lean-tos. But, he supposed, with the way air travel was growing, there would always be temporary structures.

Even before the 707 came to a halt near the international arrival gates, Palmer could spot the man from Ubco. He didn't know his name, had never seen him in his life, but he knew who the crew-cut man was in the olive business suit next to the Mercedes limousine parked on the runway near the movable ramp. He represented Ubco's Paris office and was there to make certain the top brass got triple-A treatment.

It was no good trying to avoid him, Palmer reflected as the plane came to a halt. The man had been given a photograph of Palmer to prevent any slipup in identification.

Palmer stood up, collected his flat briefcase, left behind the perfume and shaving lotion the airline had given him – together with the box of book matches imprinted 'W. P. Jr.' and the two miniature bottles of Cointreau – and left the plane by the front

25

hatch.

He had taken two steps down the ramp when the young man from Ubco raised his arm in greeting, flashed a big smile, and started up the stairs to relieve Palmer of his lightweight briefcase. 'Mr. Palmer, sir. Welcome to Paris.'

Palmer stopped and searched the young face for signs of anything other than extreme enthusiasm. He held onto his black leather briefcase. 'You're from Ubco?'

'Henry Dauber, sir. *May* I take your bag?'

Palmer hid the case behind him. 'It's hardly a bag, Mr. Dauber. Carry on.'

The young man led the way down the ramp and ushered Palmer toward the Mercedes. Overhead an Air France 727 arched skyward and howled out of sight toward the east. Palmer watched it for a moment, then turned to Dauber.

'Nice evening you've turned on.'

Dauber blushed. 'It's rained all week and it's expected to rain all next week. But we've managed to have sunshine for the weekend.'

'Damned efficient.' Palmer eyed the evening sky over Paris. Tiny white cotton-puffs made the blue seem even darker. But to the southwest, over Versailles, a leaden layer of heavy clouds obscured the sunset. Watching this for a moment, Palmer wondered how long the clear weather might last. He'd have to be in town nearly a week before moving on to either Frankfurt or Rome, he couldn't remember which.

He got into the back seat of the car, settled into the dark brown glove-leather upholstery and took note of the fact that a girl with very long legs was sitting across from him on the backward-facing seat of the limo.

Palmer wasn't certain for a moment whether her legs were really that long or, because they were slender and he could see all of them to her upper thighs, they only seemed long.

'Good afternoon, Mr. Palmer,' she said.

He glanced up at her face. She looked to be in her late twenties, with a round doll face whose lines were strong enough to keep her from being doll-pretty. Nevertheless, Palmer saw, she had a certain handsome intenseness, behind her giant-diameter spectacles and low-lying chestnut bangs, that made her much more attractive than a round-faced doll would be.

'Good afternoon.'

'My name i –'

'Mr. Palmer, this is Eleanora Gregorius, your interpreter,' Dauber said as he got into the car and sat beside the girl. Both of them faced Palmer rather solemnly, as if they had bagged an unusual specimen of big game and weren't sure exactly what happened next.

'Miss Gregorius.' Palmer watched her for a moment and saw that her face remained entirely in watchful repose, unlike Dauber's, which betrayed a large amount of uneasiness. Palmer had heard her speak half a dozen words and they had given him very few clues to her nationality. Her English was almost unaccented, but oddly stressed, and the way she pronounced 'Palmer' told him she was not an American or a Briton. The fact that she sounded the *l* tended to indicate that her native language was one of the Germanic ones – or perhaps Spanish – where every letter gets its full due. Her name itself, well, after all, Palmer realized, was Latin and Old Latin at that. Where in Europe could –

'You're Dutch, Miss Gregorius?'

Her dark brown eyes went wide. 'How did you guess?'

Palmer shrugged. He was sorry he'd done it now. It was a trick he had relied on often during the war and, in the past twenty years, almost not at all. But it was a trick one couldn't forget and such a flashy trick that he should never have attempted it.

'I'm not actually Dutch,' she was saying, her smile so full and pretty that it didn't matter that she was exploding his parlor-magic act for him. 'I mean, I wasn't born there. But I lived in Rotterdam for the last five years before coming to Paris.'

Palmer smiled. His luggage loaded, the limousine picked up speed slowly and nosed off the runway area into the main cloverleaf that led to the Paris road. The immense rectangular bulk of the Orly Hilton stood to the left of the expressway like a giant matchbox lying on its side, all window glass. Palmer noted the same kind of expressway overhead signs, in white letters on green and blue backgrounds, that graced the exits of every airport in the U.S. He had a sense of never having left home.

His glance drifted sideways to Miss Gregorius' legs. It was still hard to tell whether they were really that long. He'd have to wait till she got out of the car.

He made himself look out the window. Dauber was talking about something dull and every once in a while a word or a phrase came through without disturbing Palmer's own thoughts. It bothered him that he had no sense of arriving in Paris. Damn it, Paris was something important. And yet he could as easily have been coming into Allentown, or possibly Muncie.

They were passing a section where a great number of very U.S.-looking warehouses lined the highway. The signs told him they were used to store and distribute meats and produce. He had heard the old Les Halles were being torn down. Perhaps...

'... major breakthrough in weather this summer, most Europeans will go mad from too much rain,' Dauber was chattering on.

Palmer wondered why it was that a certain type of upward-mobile executive seemed perfectly capable of talking on at great length about absolutely nothing for as long as necessary to fill what he deemed an awkward pause in the conversation. For that matter, he realized, most Americans seemed able to keep the air filled with talk of a totally inconsequential nature. Everyone seemed vaguely uneasy at a lull. Surely the ever-present transistor radios and the public places awash with loudspeaker music indicated that, while nature might abhor a vacuum, Americans abhorred silence.

The trouble, as Palmer knew, was that if you became a master of trivial conversation, if you learned the knack of going on forever without once touching on a topic of controversy or strong interest, you eventually forgot how to deal with anything of real substance. Palmer was sure that so many of the meetings he called would take half the time they did if those who came were prepared not only to dispense with the endless chitchat but emotionally ready to cope with hard facts.

Take Dauber here, for instance. Obviously frightened at having the Big Cheese on his hands, he had brought along an attractive girl – smart move – and was prepared to gab endlessly until he got a clue from Palmer as to how he wanted to be treated.

That was another annoying thing about Americans, Palmer decided. Together with the bland nothingness of their conversation went an intense desire to feed back to the person opposite them exactly what they felt he'd want to hear. There was a don't-rock-the-boat quality to American conversation, a dread of stirring up anything different, anything that didn't conform to the smooth vanilla-ice-cream surface of life, rich and bland

28

and fattening.

'Tell me, Miss Gregorius,' Palmer said, cutting abruptly into whatever nonsense Dauber was spouting, 'have they really torn down Les Halles?'

Her eyes zeroed in on his, then flicked sideways for a moment to the passing warehouses. 'It's true,' she said. 'Many of the merchants are out here now, as you have noticed.'

Palmer nodded. Handsome and awfully quick, he thought. 'How many languages do you speak?'

'English, French, Italian, German.' She paused and then smiled self-deprecatingly. 'And Dutch.'

Palmer made noises of being impressed. He turned to Dauber. 'Is she on our payroll?'

Dauber, his mouth still slightly ajar, moistened his lips before he spoke. 'Oh yes. Miss Gregorius is normally in our correspondence department at the Place Vendôme office.'

The highway was running between heavier concentrations of houses now. Palmer began to feel that he was, indeed, approaching a big city. But he still had no feeling that the city was Paris.

Miss Gregorius crossed her legs and stared out the window. Palmer shifted his glance and stared out the window opposite hers.

CHAPTER 5

As he glanced around at his suite in the Ritz, Palmer felt pleased that Dauber and Miss Gregorius, without too much urging on his part, had left him alone on his first night in Paris. Dauber had shown an unpleasant tendency toward mother-henning Palmer, but this quickly collapsed when Miss Gregorius seemed to understand Palmer's need for privacy.

While he never enjoyed close supervision of anything he did, Palmer especially wanted to be free of it on this trip. Dauber's vague suggestions of 'a night on the town' sounded too much like an echo of Palmer's earlier European trip, in which he and Edith had been wrapped in velvet and handed on like a crate of eggs from one business associate to another.

Standing in the center of the living room, Palmer eyed his

still-locked bags and wondered how long it would have taken Edith to have unpacked both of them. About things like that, he remembered, she had been unusually good. About more important things. . . .

Palmer unlocked his large suitcase and flight bag to ease the pressure on the clothing within. He glanced at his watch and found that it was not yet eleven o'clock, Paris time. The advantage of taking a daylight flight, if one could waste a whole day, and Palmer could, was that one avoided the grittiness of sleeping en route, or trying to. One also, Palmer knew, more or less successfully bridged the time-zone gap.

Starting to unpack the big suitcase, Palmer regretted not letting the concierge send along a maid for this task. Palmer's almost fanatic desire to remain to himself as much as possible had tricked him into having to serve as his own valet.

By the time he'd unpacked, showered, changed into more informal clothes, and wandered downstairs, the clock over the concierge's counter showed it to be nearly midnight in Paris. Palmer relinquished his key, was told gratuitously that there were no messages for him and started to head out into the Place Vendôme. Then he thought better of it. Everyone left by the front entrance, he decided. The whole purpose of being alone was to do as he pleased.

He reversed direction and moved uncertainly through several empty salons of drapery and chairs until he found a long corridor lined with glass display cases. The hall was easily several New York blocks long and unswervingly straight. It seemed to lead somewhere useful. Along the way, Pamler noted, a variety of merchants and manufacturers, with heavy emphasis on jewelry and perfume, had seen fit to buy display space. At the far end, after some further maneuvering, he found himself on a narrow back street which the enameled plate set high up on a corner building informed him was the Rue Cambon.

He stood there for a moment, trying to sort out his feelings. The air was warm and faintly moist, as if he were near some great body of water, which he knew was not so. He wondered why he had come out the back entrance. He wondered why he had refused any kind of guidance or help. He supposed it was all part of the same thing, and mixed up with his terrible need to leave the United States and especially New York.

Palmer could never understand the expatriates, even the famous ones, who seemed perfectly able to remain Americans

30

without ever living there. He glanced around him. The Rue Cambon took a turn out of sight to the left. Palmer decided to see what was around the bend, if anything. He immediately came upon a branch of the Chase Manhattan and grinned. Like so many Parisian streets, the Rue Cambon's five- and six-story buildings beyond the Chase office remained perfectly impassive and anonymous, a series of limestone or concrete façades pierced by shuttered and curtained windows. Behind them could be anything, Palmer realized. Offices, bedrooms, clubs – the blank anonymity remained intact except for two narrow hotels, the Castille and an establishment calling itself, in English, the Family Hotel.

Imagine, Palmer thought, telling everyone you were in Paris 'and staying at the Family Hotel.' Imagine him cashing traveler's checks at the Chase.

He stopped, turned back, and retraced his steps until he came to the Rue St.-Honoré that led him around the corner to Rue Castiglione and into the Place Vendôme. Standing there amid the confusion of some excavation that had thrown up hoardings and piles of dirt, Palmer watched the façade of his own bank. The Ubco logotype, severe and modern, was outlined at night in bluish light. As he watched, the light snapped off and the façade stood in darkness. He glanced at his watch. Twelve-five. The timing mechanism was off five minutes. Tell Dauber.

Palmer's face twisted in a wry grimace. Tell Dauber nothing. This was not a bank trip. Let the damned Paris office fix its own timer. Or pay the few centimes of extra electricity.

A cab's tires squealed as it rounded the detour past the excavation. Seeing Palmer, it pulled up short. The driver would not, of course, demean himself to ask the obvious question, as he might in New York at this hour. Nevertheless, Palmer waved, opened the door and hopped inside.

'À St.-Germain-des-Prés,' he said.

'Quoi?'

Palmer grimaced again. 'Brasserie Lipp.'

The driver grunted and set the cab in motion. Palmer was not sure why he had told him to go to that particular part of Paris. Montparnasse was associated in his mind with students, existentialist people like Sartre, and such ancient haunts of Bohemia as the Flore and the Deux Magots. It struck him that by now, civilization being what it was, there would probably be no one there but tourists, trampling over one another in their fruitless

31

search for the 'real' Paris.

As he glanced out of the cab windows, Palmer saw that the real Paris seemed to close up early, unlike New York. He supposed the population pressure was simply not as heavy here as back home. There were few parts of Manhattan this deserted at midnight.

He suddenly realized that the building he was passing was the Madeleine. He craned about in his seat to get a better view.

'*Oui*,' the driver grunted, '*c'est ça*.'

The taxi flashed south along the Rue Royale into the empty Place de la Concorde. Dark now and deserted, the spread-out area of trees and shrubbery signified nothing to Palmer. The cab raced past the obelisk, up over the Pont de la Concorde, and across the Seine. Palmer caught a quick glimpse of an immense, glassed-in blaze of light from one of the *bateaux-mouches* sight-seeing boats as it pulled into its dock two bridges to the right. Then the taxi swerved wildly left past the Quai d'Orsay and they were in Left Bank territory, roaring along a deserted Boulevard Raspail toward Boulevard St.-Germain.

Suddenly there were lights and people and traffic. The cab nosed into the midst of a silent jam of cars where more excavations had taken up half the width of the boulevard. Palmer saw the sidewalk sections of the Flore and Deux Magots ahead to the left.

'*Ici est bon*,' he announced.

'*Quoi?*' the driver growled.

'*Ici. Arrêtez-vous ici*.'

There was a grunt. The taxi twisted sideways through traffic to reach the curb. Palmer paid and stepped out into the pedestrian swarm moving like sleepwalkers along the narrow section of sidewalk. The cab was instantly boarded by two nineteen-year-old girls in elephant-leg pants, see-through chiffon blouses, and Indian headbands.

Palmer caught a glimpse across the boulevard of the Brasserie Lipp's stolid dark-wood-and-glass front. It seemed crowded. He realized that he couldn't cross over directly to it because of the excavation. He moved slowly toward the corner past crowded, tiny tables set up in front of the Deux Magots. Two people got up and left a table at the edge of the sidewalk. Palmer found himself sitting down, instantly, thus beating several waiting couples to the table.

He eyed the debris of the previous occupants, a small china

ashtray filled with filter-tip butts, half bearing lipstick, two empty glasses with the remains of ice in them, two empty bottles of orange soda. The cigarettes were American, which might mean nothing, he reflected, but did Parisians really come to the St.-Germain-des-Prés quarter at night to drink orange soda?

The waiter removed the debris after a while, disclosing two one-franc coins. Palmer decided that a forty-cent tip in a place that also levied a service charge had to mean the customers were American.

'Whiskey-soda,' he told the waiter.

'Yes, sir.'

Palmer supposed, as he sat there, that he could never be mistaken for anything but what he was. His accent was poor, he knew, and his clothes – even the sports jacket and loafers he was wearing now – gave him away.

In New York he could be taken for almost anyone in almost any of the professions. Here he could only be one thing: tourist.

He began to watch the back-and-forth strolling of the passers-by. Although this was Sorbonne country, the pedestrians weren't that notably young. Or, at least, not all of college age. There seemed to be a vast number of teen-agers, dressed in what went for high fashion among them these days, buckskin boleros, Ruby Keeler dancing pumps, coats whose hems scraped the sidewalk, yards of fluttering Isadora Duncan tulle, bare feet, grimy with Parisian spittle and coal dust, frizzed hair and vacant eyes.

Occasionally a slightly older couple, either two women or two men, would pass slowly, merchandising themselves with languid strides and excited, fast-sweeping side glances. It wasn't clear to Palmer if they were actually selling. It was more likely, he felt, that they came to be seen for the simple exhibitionist sake of being seen.

Male or female, they had in common the 'poor' look of their age-group's style at the moment, skimpy low-cut jeans, cheap cotton sweaters with scrawny sleeves, thin tank-top shirts, and, in the case of the girls, very little hair. Whether it was a coincidence or something more explicable, they all seemed to Palmer to have immense eyes that devoured the scenes around them as if starving for visual input. In the girls' case, he felt sure, it was a trick of their eye makeup. But even the boys, with their long upper and lower lashes, their small features and thin necks, seemed to have the same hungry, questing quality, strange creatures who fed through the eyes alone.

He watched a cab pull to a halt in front of the Café Flore and disgorge two youngish American men, bellies already hardening into the beer bulge of middle age, with two gorgeous Parisian whores in tow. The girls' eye and lip makeup gave them at fifty feet away the visual impact of a giant movie closeup, Palmer saw. It was as if, unlike the younger strollers who fed on scenes, these girls had, by trade, to be the scenes themselves.

They glanced disdainfully around them as one of their escorts paid off the cab. It was obvious that they were expensive girls and felt they had been taken slumming. The Ritz or the George V was their proper milieu, perhaps, but not this low, student-infested Latin Quarter.

Palmer's waiter arrived with a properly iced glass of Scotch into which he now poured from an oval Perrier bottle, leaving everything in front of Palmer, including the register-receipt bill. Palmer sipped his drink and watched the whores extricate their escorts from the strolling scene and cross the street to a corner establishment whose electric signs proclaimed it 'Le Drugstore.'

As they crossed away from him, they passed Eleanora Gregorius and a man holding her arm. Palmer sat up straighter and squinted over the tops of the traffic to see if he was right. They reached the corner near him and Palmer got a glimpse of her legs, confirming identification. They were long and somewhat lean as he had already noticed. She was tall for a European and, unlike her sisters, most of her seemed to be legs. He watched them continue along a side street out of sight.

Now that, he decided, was an almost incredible coincidence, to meet someone in a foreign city for the first time and then see them again a few hours later in another part of town. He finished his drink quickly, left money on the table, and followed the trail of the two whores to the other side of the street.

Although it was after twelve thirty, he had to wait some twenty minutes for a single table at Brasserie Lipp. He ordered a large mug of their own rich Alsatian beer and resumed his scrutiny of the passing throng.

This side of the boulevard seemed to offer a somewhat more mixed selection of human hors d'oeuvres. There were fewer Americans, it appeared to Palmer, and more French – or at any rate Europeans – of a type he found himself referring to as jet set. All of them in their forties or older, the women were inevitably skinny and tanned to a deep walnut color which they displayed everywhere, including their upper thighs and the surging top halves of their breasts. This was accented on their faces by wan lipstick and fierce black eye shadow. The men, inevitably ever so slightly overweight about the cheeks and paunch, had elaborate bushy sideburns that often merged into mustaches and frequently formed the only hair on their otherwise bald heads. No man of this type that Palmer saw wore a suit as such, or slacks of a solid color. These were invariably striped, checked, or paisley-printed, with thick, wide leather belts of the sort usually worn by sadists for promotional purposes.

As he sipped the Alsatian beer, Palmer began to get a sense of *déjà vu*, not of something that had happened to him before in Paris, but of events that had taken place in New York and in other American cities. He had seen such bizarrely dressed teen-agers wandering the streets of Manhattan. The students in their skimpy garb he had seen in places like Boston and Southern California. And the same jet-set adults inhabited every 'in' bar or club he had been taken to over the past few years in places like San Francisco, Washington, and Chicago. Any time he walked the east side of New York along Movie Row where the art theaters sat in clusters with lines of people waiting in front of each, Palmer saw the same mixture of age-groups, styles of dress, and, in fact, the same strolling-through-life attitude.

That, he decided, was really what gave him a sense of *déjà vu*. The similarity in clothing was easy enough to account for these days, what with the tremendous speed of mass communications by television, films, magazines, and the like. Teen-agers almost anywhere in the Western world knew what their official uniforms were, as did the other age-groups. But Palmer realized now it was their expressions, the bland spectator blankness of their cool, that really tied them in his mind to those he had seen at home.

The captain came for him. Palmer followed him into the Brasserie itself, with its mirrored walls and hard incandescent-bulb lighting. He sat down at a narrow table, ordered another beer, and started reading the menu.

They had fed him well on the plane, but that had been some time ago. Palmer decided on the *choucroute* which he knew – in the same way, he realized suddenly, that teen-agers knew they ought to wear Indian headbands – that the Brasserie Lipp was famous for. Who didn't know the specialty of the Lipp? Obviously, only someone who never thumbed through an American news or photo magazine.

Palmer wondered whether he had really left home at all. Perhaps, horrible to imagine, not only all airports but all big cities were now alike. Perhaps Europe had become a continent-wide imitation of the United States. He sat back with a sick feeling, realizing abruptly how much he had counted on this trip and how depressing it would be if he found he had, indeed, never left home. Palmer swallowed some of the beer. It tasted heavy and common, like tainted water. He had a feeling almost exactly as if his heart had sunk, literally, in his chest.

It just couldn't be, Palmer told himself. There was no sense jumping to conclusions on the basis of a few hours in a strange city. And yet . . .

The waiter held the brown crockery casserole in his serving towel to protect his fingers from the heat. Inside the crock, the sauerkraut, the smoked butt, the pork and the sausage sent up such fragrant steam that Palmer promptly forgot the whole silly idea. The waiter beamed moistly at him as he dished the *choucroute* onto his plate. Palmer dug in.

CHAPTER 6

It was nearly two in the morning when the taxi dropped Palmer in front of the Ritz. He stood for a moment before going in and stared across the Place Vendôme again at the dark façade of the Ubco branch office. He had no idea of his schedule for tomorrow – today, that is – or even if such a schedule existed, but he knew that eventually he would have to set foot in that office, and he dreaded the thought.

In fact, as he walked slowly into the hotel, Palmer had begun to have misgivings about the whole trip. It had been a mistake, he felt sure now, to come over here with any sort of work to be done, even though it was not connected with Ubco. What he ought to have done instead, he told himself, was simply to drop out of sight, more or less, for as long as a month, with only a few people knowing his itinerary. No balance-of-payments mission, no meetings, nothing even remotely quasi-official, just a beach somewhere in the sun and long walks through museums.

He stopped at the desk for his key. A new clerk on duty handed over to him two sealed cablegram envelopes with his name typed on them. Palmer frowned. 'When did these come in?'

The clerk's eyebrows went up slightly. Instead of replying, he pointed to a corner of each envelope where a time stamp in purple ink showed the hour of 11 P.M.

Palmer's frown deepened. 'I'll speak to the manager in the morning,' he said, and walked away to the elevator, tearing open one of the envelopes as he walked.

He tried to understand why he was angry. He had long ago stopped feeling anything but patience for the incompetence of other people. The elevator took him to his floor and he walked along the hall, making no move to open the folded cablegrams.

Inside his suite, he sat down in an easy chair by the large window and stared through the filmy curtains at the street lamps below. The first cable was from Virginia. 'WELCOME TO PARIS. MISS YOU TOO MUCH ALREADY. SOLVE PROBLEMS OF WORLD SOONEST AND GET BACK TO SOLVE MINE. ALL MY LOVE.' Palmer smiled and glanced at his watch. It would be about nine in the evening back in New York. He supposed he might call her now if the circuits weren't busy.

He opened the second cable. 'CHER PAPA, BIENVENUE A PARIS. NOUS SOMMES TRES TRISTE MAIS TRES BON. RETOURNEZ-TOI VITE-MENTE, GERALDINE.' Another female he could call in New York. Palmer wondered if the French grammar and spelling were correct. Gerri was a crack student, but careless when excited.

Instead of reaching for the telephone, however, he sat back in the easy chair and tried to pull his thoughts together. He was usually able to keep his mind on things without too much trouble. Tonight he felt pulled in a dozen directions. Being uprooted and alone in a strange city could not account for his inability to think straight, he told himself. All right, now.

The city first. What had he actually seen of it to depress him so? Palmer settled down in the easy chair and closed his eyes, trying to picture his last time in Paris, not the time with Edith, but the day after the liberation of the city when he and a small Intelligence T-Force swept north of town through Compiègne on the track of some fleeing Gestapo vehicles containing records too valuable to be burned.

He remembered that some of the roads through the Forest of Compiègne had been mined very recently. Aerial reconnaissance had determined that. But had the Germans also mined other roads much earlier, even years before? And more carefully?

Riding the lead Jeep, Palmer was in walkie-talkie contact with a one-engine spotter plane assigned to his T-Force by Artillery. The spotter pilot was ranging up to three kilometers ahead of Palmer's main column trying to make out through the over-hanging trees which routes the Gestapo cars were taking.

'Spotter Charlie to T-Force Six.' The pilot's voice rose and fell in volume through a maze of static.

'Roger, Charlie.'

'Four Mercedes staff touring cars bearing west on Soissons–Reims road. They are running parallel with Aisne River and should be out of forest in about ten minutes.'

'Roger, Charlie. Do you see us?'

'Negative.'

'T-Force is on west-north-west heading on road leading to the armistice monument area.'

'Roger, T-Force Six. Negative visual contact. Hold it.' More crackling of static. 'Staff Mercedes touring cars taking sharp turn due south, direction Pierrefonds. Road extremely narrow and obscured by trees.'

Sitting back in his easy chair, Palmer could visualize the problem of some twenty-five years ago. There was a way of cutting off the Gestapo convoy by getting to Pierrefonds first along a diagonal shortcut through the heart of the forest. But no one knew if the diagonal were mined. His Jeeps were no match in speed for the Mercedes cars. Only the shortcut would work. He remembered the moment of sharp indecision quite clearly. G-2's information was that the valuable Gestapo records were dossiers on informers and other French loyal to the Nazi cause who had been left behind as saboteurs and agents.

Palmer switched on his normal shortwave transmitter and tried to raise Allied personnel assembling at Le Bourget airfield. He had been assured there would be a squadron of P-51's avail-able for strafing missions. It seemed a good time to bring them into the picture. But no matter what wavelength he tried, Le Bourget failed to answer. Finally, he clicked on the walkie-talkie again.

'Spotter Charlie from T-Force Six. Double back and establish visual contact with us. We're going through that southwest dia-gonal and we need eyes upstairs.'

What happened after that was one of the most nerve-racking actions Palmer had ever experienced. Waving back the rest of his vehicles so that they wouldn't get caught in the explosion if his Jeep tripped up a mine, he ordered his driver into the second Jeep and took the wheel of his own. He hit the dirt shoulder on the right and tried to maintain speed even though he was off the pavement. His reasoning was that the mines that had been laid would be toward the center of the road where they could catch a vehicle going either way. It would have been smart of the Germans, however, to take it easier on the routes leading east, since these would be their own escape routes when the time came. He hoped the Germans had been smart.

Twenty minutes later they roared into Pierrefonds at sixty-five miles an hour without having lost a single vehicle. The immense turreted bulk of the chateau, looming right in the center of town, held Palmer's attention for a moment.

'T-Force Six from Spotter Charlie.'

'Go ahead, Charlie.'

'Jerries holed up in a little woods behind the chateau on the southwest perimeter well off the road. They expect you to sweep past on the road without seeing them. I don't know how they know you're on their tail.'

'They're monitoring you, Charlie,' Palmer told the pilot, 'that's how. But thanks, anyway.'

He pulled his column of vehicles in tight and headed around the chateau for the southwest wall, knowing that if the Germans had been listening to the spotter transmission they would break cover and make a dash for it.

The Jeeps and Mercedes touring cars intercepted near the massive stone gates to the chateau. Palmer raked the lead car with a badly aimed burst from his grease-gun submachinegun and the Gestapo answered with Schmeisser semiautomatic fire. Both sides pulled to a halt and dropped behind their vehicles for cover.

It was the bazooka launcher in the third Jeep that finally turned the trick. When the Gestapo saw Palmer wave the bazooka man forward, they began yelling 'cease fire' in English and started coming out with their hands up. The records had been voluminous. They were well worth everyone's trouble. It took Military Intelligence nearly six months to round up every name on the list.

Palmer sat up in the easy chair and reread the cablegrams. 'SOLVE PROBLEMS OF THE WORLD SOONEST AND GET BACK TO SOLVE MINE.'

He smiled and glanced at his watch again. He was feeling

39

better about everything. It was in the nature of memories, he decided, especially recollections of past successes, to make one complacent about present frustrations. Palmer grinned at his own eagerness to soothe himself with memories of the days when he had been able, on his own, to meet and solve almost unbearable problems. A T-Force of more than twenty men could have been wiped out, himself among them, if he'd guessed wrong about the mines. Fascinating memories.

He supposed most men his age had them. In their youth their country had entrusted millions of them with a license to kill. For them, life or death was a daily exercise. Simply to survive was a personal victory. Anything that happened in the years after that was infinitely less important. A quarter of a century had passed for men like him. Some were failures, as the world counted failures. Palmer was a success by those same criteria. But he knew that nothing in this quarter century could compare with the immense success of simply living through the war that ushered in the new era.

He stood up and stretched. Two thirty in the morning. He undressed and got ready for bed. As he left the bathroom, he frowned, remembering something.

Palmer went to the bureau and opened the drawers slowly one after another, staring at the shirts and underwear he had laid out there earlier in the evening. Then he closed the drawers and lifted the slim, black leather briefcase from the top of the bureau. He took it over to the bedside table and switched the lamp up to its fullest illumination.

Fingers working very carefully, Palmer slowly unzipped the three-sided fastener that ran around the edge of the briefcase. The bit of hair, hardly half an inch long, that he had inserted between the metal teeth at the first corner of the zipper, was gone. He had placed it there on his ride to JFK International Airport, some thirty minutes after the scene with Harry Bannister.

The hair he had placed halfway along the handle edge of the briefcase was also gone. The hair he had caught in the far corner was still there. Whoever had opened it while he was out had not had to unzip it completely in order to examine the papers it contained.

These included his schedule for the entire mission, together with names and titles of people he was to see. He noted that a week from now, in Bonn, he was seeing one Gustave Schirmer.

Most of the information, although without such exact dates, had already been printed in the New York *Times* in the story a week before announcing his departure plans. The precise schedule was of interest to almost no one but Palmer himself and the Ubco traffic manager who had booked all his flights and hotels.

Palmer carried the open briefcase into the living room. He stood for a moment in the darkened room. Then he sat back down in the easy chair and switched on the lamp next to it. He read slowly through his schedule. He saw that he did, indeed, have free days tomorrow and Sunday, but solid meetings all next week in Paris until he left on Thursday for Frankfurt and Bonn.

He closed the case and switched off the lamp. So Virginia had been right, after all. She usually was. 'It's not beyond the realm of possibility, is it,' she had asked, 'that there's a dossier on you somewhere in Europe?'

There only remained, Palmer thought, to find out who was holding the dossier. Perhaps it was the CIA or some of Bannister's people. More likely, though, it was someone else.

CHAPTER 7

The telephone next to his bed started ringing in a peculiar way that, as Palmer came awake and reached for the instrument, sounded typically European to him, as if telephones could ring in a foreign language.

'I didn't wake you?' Dauber asked cheerily.

'It's nine A.M. and I wanted to put us at your disposal. We're downstairs.'

Palmer's eyes, open, closed slowly as his heart sank. It would never occur to Dauber that he had gone to bed quite late by Paris time. How to get rid of him?

'Did you come by car?'

'Yes, sir. I've got one of the bank's Buicks here for you.'

'Dauber, are you married?'

'I am. Three kids.'

'Is this any way for a family man to spend Saturday, squiring around the boss? Leave the keys with the concierge. When I come down later, I'll drive myself if I feel like it.' Palmer started to replace the phone in its cradle, but could hear Dauber making noises. 'Yes?'

'It's very decent of you, really. But I'd planned it this way and my wife quite understands.'

'She'll be happily surprised when you show up at home.'

'But, Mr. Palmer?'

'No arguments.'

'What about Miss Gregorius! I brought her along this morning.'

Palmer sighed heavily enough to be heard over the house telephone. 'Ask her if she's had breakfast,' he said.

After a moment Dauber came back on the line. 'She says she doesn't eat breakfast, sir.'

'Fine. Tell her to wait for me at a table in whatever dining room they use for breakfast.'

'Are you sure you don't want me t –?'

'*Allez, allez.*'

There was a tiny pause while Dauber readjusted his thinking. '*Oui mon général. Merci beaucoup.*'

'Talk to you Monday. Good-bye.'

Palmer hung up, showered and shaved, and put on the same sports jacket he'd worn last night in the Latin Quarter. He found his sunglasses after a lengthy search, realizing that if Edith were here, she'd know exactly where to find them. He glanced around the room before leaving it. He'd half expected to have breakfast in bed. It had seemed a Sybaritic enough introduction to Europe.

Miss Gregorius had chosen a corner of the dining room which the morning sun struck with an almost audible force, turning her chestnut hair a vibrating auburn. She got to her feet and held out her hand, not at all like an American woman, Palmer noticed, who would remain seated. What was she? Twenty-six?

'What will you not eat for breakfast to keep me company?' he asked, sitting down.

She smiled. 'Coffee only. I really never eat breakfast.'

'Out of deference to your figure?'

She automatically smoothed down the thin crepe print dress she was wearing. Its zigzag splashes of patterned color were familiar to Palmer – Virginia had one like it – but there was no signature on the fabric, which meant it was an inexpensive imi-

42

tation. The design reminded him of one of those World War I anti-U-boat camouflage dazzle patterns. 'How long have you been with Ubco?'

Her glossy brown eyebrows went up and her round face changed shape slightly.

'Ubco?'

'We usually call the bank by its initials, at least in New York.'

'Ah, Ubco!' she laughed. 'As you can see, I have not been with the bank very long. I think six months, perhaps five.' She frowned. 'Five.'

'And before that?'

She brushed nervously at her bangs and managed to dislodge them slightly. Palmer saw that she had an extremely high forehead which the bangs were designed to hide. He watched her dark brown eyes for a moment. Her glance rested easily on him.

'Before that I worked for UNESCO. All interpreters eventually work for UNESCO. It seems to be a universal law.'

'You're not a translator?'

She shook her head. The sun picked out red highlights in her hair as it swung sideways. 'I deal in the spoken word,' she said. 'Of course, at the bank – at Ubco' – she stopped and grinned mischievously at him – 'I write a lot of letters. But that is hardly translation.'

Palmer turned to the waiter who hovered beside him. 'I think I ought to have a typical French breakfast on my first morning here.'

'Quite, sir. And the lady?'

'Just coffee.'

'As you say, sir.' He left.

'What am I going to get?' Palmer asked Miss Gregorius.

'Just what I don't need. Fattening brioches and croissants and Normandy butter and delicious jellies and marmalades.'

'I don't really need that, either.'

She surveyed him frankly. 'You are quite thin. For you such a breakfast presents no problems. For me . . .' She smoothed down the crepe dress again and Palmer was sure the gesture was unthinking. But it nevertheless led him to see that she was quite narrow through the waist and had rather large breasts. He wondered if he could be as frank in his survey of her. He supposed not.

'Were you up late last night?' he asked then, switching subjects. 'You didn't really need to be here so early.'

43

She gestured airily, as if brushing the whole matter away. 'I get along on very little sleep.'

'What time *does* the St.-Germain quarter close down?'

Her calm brown eyes went wide. She watched Palmer warily for a moment. 'What ... how ... I mean –'

He smiled reassuringly. 'Just a coincidence. I happened to be on my way to the Lipp last night and saw you in the distance.'

'You –' She stopped again.

The waiter's arrival with coffee and hot milk helped her recover her composure. Palmer wondered what had disconcerted her that much and decided it was probably the man she'd been with. Palmer had purposely not referred to her companion and he was glad now that he hadn't. The man was probably married.

'That is quite a coincidence after all, isn't it?' she said then as the waiter poured coffee and milk simultaneously into their cups. Palmer, who usually drank his coffee black without sugar, watched in some dismay. However, he had asked for a typical French breakfast.

'I thought so too,' he said. 'I stayed up a bit late myself to get into the European time zone more readily. It seems to have worked. Did Dauber have any plans for an itinerary today?'

'Oh, you know.' Again the gesture of brushing away. 'The usual Eiffel Tower, ah, Notre Dame, the Tuileries, et cetera. Et cetera.' Her tone made it clear that the itinerary would bore her to tears, but she would be game, if pressed.

'I may get to that tomorrow. Paris is usually emptier on Sunday, isn't it?'

'Quite so.'

He nodded. 'New York, too. I'll keep the car and do my traditional sightseeing on Sunday.'

'Very wise.'

They broke off to watch the waiter dispose about the table baskets of yeast-smelling, brown varnished bakery and pots of orange and strawberry marmalade. Palmer indicated them to Miss Gregorius, who shook her head very gravely.

'I think,' Palmer said then, 'I'll drive us up to Compiègne.'

Again her face changed shape as she wrinkled her forehead. The roundness disappeared and she seemed suddenly to have a much stronger face. 'Why Compiègne?'

'Memories.' Palmer broke the end off a croissant, buttered it, and began eating. 'Do you know Compiègne very well?'

'But not at all.' Her eyes widened to indicate a total paucity of information on the subject and interest in it.

'It has Napoleon's palace and, of course, the Royal Forest.'

She made a faint face of distaste. 'It's an army town, *n'est-ce pas?*'

He shrugged. 'There are a lot of monuments and such around. I suppose there's a detachment of troops on hand for guard duty. And, of course, there's the, ah, *Clairière de l'Armistice,* you know, where the Armistice was signed in a railroad car.'

'Which armistice?'

He eyed her for a moment. 'World War One,' he said, wondering what other armistice she could be thinking of.

'Ah. That war.'

He finished his croissant in silence, then tried a brioche. The rolls were warm to the touch. 'There was no armistice in World War Two,' he remarked. 'Just a surrender. Several of them by several nations.'

'Yes, of course.'

He had the idea she didn't quite have either war firmly in mind and couldn't care less how they had ended. 'You wouldn't recall the second war, would you,' he said then.

'Not really.' She sipped her coffee. The shaft of sunlight had moved sideways and her face was in shadow. 'I was very small.'

'Holland took a lot of punishment.'

There was a slight pause. She glanced up at him, then down, then up again. 'I am not Dutch,' she said then.

'Oh, of course. I made that mistake yesterday.'

'It's not a mistake, actually,' she assured him. 'I am as much Dutch as anything else. I've lived many places. My father's job moved him about Europe a great deal.'

'Which accounts for your amazing way with languages.'

She made a self-deprecating gesture. 'Perhaps. But, why ... what memories does Compiègne have for you?'

He finished the brioche before speaking. 'Some from the last war. We'll see.' The last was the kind of putting-off thing one told a child, but Palmer realized that he might very well not want to tell her anything about his memories of Compiègne. Not that there was much to it, really. A few hours of uncertainty. A tight scrape. Nothing all that glamorous. And, anyway, what business had he looking for something glamorous to tell this girl? Woman.

'It was during the last war,' Palmer heard himself saying.

Her eyes widened slightly. 'You were in France then?'

He nodded. 'The day after the liberation of Paris.' He wondered how he could get himself out of it, now that he had floundered in. 'It's a short, not terribly interesting, story. But it's better shown than told.'

She frowned slightly. 'Pardon?'

'In the U.S. the children have a school exercise called Show and Tell.' He stopped and suppressed an impatient sigh. He seemed unable to extricate himself from this morass of idiotic conversation. 'They bring things to school and show them and tell about them.'

Her face brightened and she nodded vigorously. 'Ah, yes. Quite a good idea.'

He found himself smiling at her. 'I suppose I'm too old for that. I prefer to show and let whatever it is explain itself.'

She started to frown. Palmer noticed that expressions kept flitting back and forth across her face. He had the idea that she was unsure of which to settle on because he had been floundering in personal conversation without giving her much of a clue to it. 'You have children?' she asked then.

'Three.'

'May I see their pictures?'

Palmer's smile widened. 'Is that your experience with Americans?' he asked. 'Do we all produce wallet photos on demand?'

When she smiled her full mouth lost its faintly pouting look. 'No pictures? Not even one?'

Palmer shook his head. 'They're big kids now. The youngest is fourteen.'

'And the oldest?'

'Eighteen. A boy.'

Her face went grave. 'A boy. How –' She stopped for a moment. 'Will he be drafted into the war?'

Palmer broke open a brioche and carefully buttered it before answering. 'His schoolwork is poor, but I think he'll make it into college. His mother –' He stopped now, bit the brioche and chewed for a long moment.

'She is not with you on this trip?'

Palmer swallowed some coffee. 'We're separated.' He began scrambling now to change the subject. The only reason he had brought up Edith was because one of her aunts was married to the president of a small, decent coeducational college in Maine

46

and there seemed a good possibility that Woody could matriculate there, despite his hideous grades. None of this was of interest to Miss Gregorius. 'I don't have a picture of her with me, either,' Palmer said suddenly.

The girl burst out laughing and so did Palmer. Then she reached into her small, brown leather bag and produced a Florentine wallet in green leather with gold embossed scrollwork. From it she drew a small color photograph of a girl about four years old whose round face and chestnut bangs made clear her resemblance to Miss Gregorius.

'This is either you at an early age,' Palmer began, 'or . . .'

'My daughter, Tanya.' She laid the photograph on the tablecloth between them. 'She lives with my parents. She's going to be five in September.'

Palmer never knew what to do with pictures of other people's children, which was why he carried none of his own, not wanting to embarrass people by putting them in the same position he so hated. He picked up the photograph and studied it closely as if teaching a course in portraiture. 'Very pretty little girl.' He put the photograph down near Miss Gregorius.

There were so many things one said to the owner of such a photograph. At business meetings and conventions Palmer had painstakingly learned what most of the clichés were. He used them fairly expertly with men but he had never been called on to use them with women. Better, he thought now, not to use them at all. He had the feeling Miss Gregorius had a built-in cliché detector.

'Do you see her often?' he heard himself ask.

She shook her head and busied herself with putting away the picture. Palmer let the gesture pass, one of many openings he seemed to deliberately fight shy of with this woman.

He watched her replace the wallet in the handbag and then heard her give a tiny cry of exasperation. 'I am so stupid,' she said then, pulling out a sealed envelope with the Ubco trademark on it. 'Mr. Dauber entrusted this to me and I have wasted all this time forgetting to give you it.'

Palmer ripped open the envelope. Inside was a folded sheet of paper torn from the bank's Telex printer. Palmer unfolded the message.

'CONFIDENTIAL WOODS PALMER JR CARE PARIS BRANCH FROM HARRY ELDER MAIN OFFICE NYC.' Palmer glanced up from the cable to Miss Gregorius. Her eyes had been fixed on him. Now they dropped to the table.

'I must apologize,' she murmured. Her face had grown pink. Palmer shook his head. 'No harm done, I'm sure.' He resumed reading the message. 'PEOPLES BANK PROBLEM UPCOMING. OVEREXTENDED LINES MAKE POLICY DECISION NECESSARY WITHIN WEEK. NEED UR AUTHORIZATION TURN ACTION COMMITTEE LOOSE ON SAME. RETWX ME SOONEST.'

Palmer let the message drop to the table. His eyes focused on the words, but his mind no longer took them in. In his experience with Harry Elder this was the most peculiar thing he'd ever seen the man do.

Harry was Ubco's former executive veep for operations, now semiretired to a more or less honorary position as vice-chairman of the board. But he was still active enough in the bank's policy-making. Palmer had always counted Harry in his corner. They tended to think alike even though Harry was now probably seventy years old. Palmer had been helpful to Harry's son, Donny, who was a vice-president of Ubco slated to rise still further.

What made the message so peculiar to Palmer were two things. The first was that the board's action committee needed no authorization from anyone to proceed as it saw fit. That was the entire purpose of the committee, to function on a last-minute basis without the presence of the entire board, or even of the executive committee of ten. The action committee included Palmer – when he was there – but in his absence either Harry Elder or another man was authorized to step in. So it was time-wasting nonsense for Harry to ask for authorization he didn't need.

The second peculiarity of the message lay in the problem of the People's Bank. Originally a small bank in suburban Westchester County, People's had been approached by Ubco for its extensive spread of branch offices. In the long interim between making a purchase offer and having it approved by the State Banking Department, strange but not unusual things had happened to People's. It had been taken over, more or less, by elements of organized crime, functioning through some of the officers of the bank.

Lines of credit had been grossly overextended to builders and other businesses. The mob moneymen had pinched People's so painfully that, to extricate itself, the bank had had to give away huge chunks to representatives of the mob. On the eve of the actual purchase of the bank by Ubco, Palmer had learned most of the unpleasant details. He had tried to get his board to take a position one way or the other on the purchase.

It had been a most difficult decision to make. Any sudden negative move by Ubco – such as reneging on the planned purchase – could have started a run on People's assets and bankrupted it almost overnight. The decision, finally, was to slow the purchase plans down to a crawl and await developments, meanwhile trying to work out with the district attorney and federal law-enforcement people some quiet way of delousing the bank.

Sitting at his breakfast table in the Ritz, Palmer could not visualize any sudden alteration in the status quo that would make it necessary to abandon this policy of calculated delay. Certainly there could be nothing so drastic as to need action committee decisions. And, if there were, the committee had every authority to decide on its own.

He folded the cable and put it inside the breast pocket of his jacket. Then he looked up to find Miss Gregorius watching him with unashamed attention. 'Nothing urgent,' he said then. While he felt there was, in fact, nothing urgent in Harry's message, the queerness of it gave him a feeling of uneasiness he was determined not to mistake for urgency.

'Do you have to make a reply?'

Palmer shook his head. 'Not now, certainly. It's – what? Four A.M.? – in New York now.'

'Sometimes messages are delayed.'

'And it's Saturday. Nobody's there in the head office except a few people on special projects.'

'I see. Then –' She paused as if to indicate, without presuming to do so, that there was nothing to keep them at the table much longer.

'If you'll help me remember,' Palmer said, 'I'll drop by the Place Vendôme office tomorrow afternoon or Monday morning and we'll Telex a message to New York. All right?'

She nodded vehemently. 'I will help you to remember,' she said.

CHAPTER 8

Palmer steered the heavy Buick into the main square of Compiègne and stopped for a moment. A small wedding party had come out of the Hôtel de Ville's big wooden doors to stand on the sidewalk posing for photographs. The city hall itself was the tallest building around, Palmer noted, heavily encrusted with gray sixteenth-century carved stone on its first two floors. The central part of the building kept rising, Palmer saw, through lacier curves and loops of stonework to a cluster of sharply pointed towers and a main clock tower at least six stories off the street.

A wind swept through the square and twisted the bride's veil sideways. Everyone shrieked and helped her rearrange it as the photographer's flash winked whitely in the strong noonday sunlight. The groom grinned.

'He's an off-duty soldier,' Eleanora Gregorius pointed out.

Palmer stared at the bridegroom in his dark business suit and white shirt. 'How so, because the best man's in uniform?'

She nodded. 'So are some of the other men.' She crossed her long legs and pointed to a nearby sidewalk café at the corner of the square. 'And there are more, waving at him. See?'

Palmer watched the married couple hop into a smallish Citroën cab which quit the scene in an immense roar of clashing gears and exhaust and a strident beeping noise, as if leading a long parade.

'This is very good luck,' Miss Gregorius said.

'To see a wedding?'

'Extremely lucky.'

'I'm extremely hungry and thirsty,' Palmer said. 'Let's join those soldiers for a fast lunch.'

They sat down at the only empty table. The harsh noon sun had made the metal chairs uncomfortably hot. Palmer watched Miss Gregorius cross her legs again. He knew women did this for no particular reason except comfort, but he wondered whether women with very good legs did it more often, or whether it just seemed that way.

Both of them had terribly dry ham sandwiches on papery white bread. Palmer drank a beer while the girl had a bottled orange drink. He finished with a bottle of orange, too. The square at noon was deserted now that the wedding party had faded away. A few parked cars stood baking in the sun. From time to time a Jeep-like military vehicle with several soldiers in it would curve through the square. The men would wave at the café waitress and move on. Palmer's body reacted to the stiff cornering of the Jeeps.

'I don't think this café will ever be listed in Michelin,' Miss Gregorius said. 'I noticed around the corner, off the square, a touring inn that seemed to display the shield and insignia of every touring society in Europe.'

'Is that where we should have gone?'

'Certainly not,' she said. 'Those shields mean only one thing: cheap.'

'Then we can forget Compiègne, stomach-wise?' Palmer said. He watched her frown as she assimilated this mocking use of American slang. He realized he was testing her command of the language too stiffly.

'I don't know,' she responded at last, deadpan.

'I didn't think to get the red Michelin. But there can't be much here. Stomach-wise?' This last was a question asked with very wide eyes, as if querying the usage. 'This is an idiom, *par exemple pour* "gastronomically speaking." Yes?'

Palmer nodded sagely, then realized that to give a working interpreter a bad steer on usage would penalize her later in her work. 'It's slang,' he said then. 'In the U.S. we puff up language and twist it around until it loses its meaning. The suffix "wise" is the creature of the advertising people. I intended it only as a joke.'

She nodded vigorously. 'I see.' She didn't.

'Humor-wise, it's nothing much,' he added helpfully. 'Drink-wise this orange beats the beer. Food-wise, the sandwich leaves much to be desired.'

Her face cleared. 'Ah. And dry-wise, the ham was superb?'

'*Exactement!*'

She clapped her hands and smiled. '*Ennui*-wise, Compiègne is the capital of the world?'

'I wouldn't go that far, insult-wise,' Palmer cautioned her. 'We have only seen the town hall and the village square.'

'Square-wise, it is positively cubic.' She shrieked with laughter and covered her face.

The four soldiers at the next table, who had been eyeing her legs for some time, turned to stare boldly at her. There was a directness Palmer found disconcerting. He wondered if this were common in Europe or whether he would have to do something about it. One of the soldiers seemed to sense this and, nudging his comrades, looked away again.

'You must tell me why we are here,' Miss Gregorius said as they got back in the overheated Buick and headed along the banks of the Oise for a few blocks before reaching the confluence of the Aisne.

Palmer turned east and tried to find the road toward the Armistice Clearing. He soon found himself driving along the Soissons–Reims road although he had somehow missed the clearing. It was at this point that he had first established contact with his spotter plane and learned that the Gestapo convoy had made a side run south toward Pierrefonds.

'It's hard to explain,' he told the girl. 'There's been a lot of history around here for France and even a bit for me. You know it was at Compiègne, don't you, that Joan of Arc was captured?'

'Yes?'

'She was guarding the French troops' rear when the Burgundians fell on her.'

'The English didn't mind killing her, though.'

Palmer realized the Buick was speeding almost without his control. He found it odd that he could occupy his conscious mind with details of old French history while his body was responding in an animal way to an entirely different era only a quarter of a century before.

'They minded. They turned her over to the mercies of the Church to make sure the murder was a blessed one. All soldiers are superstitious, I suppose. Nobody wanted to kill an obvious saint unless the Church okayed it.'

He pulled the Buick hard right around a turn at a crossroads and sped south toward the diagonal cutoff for Pierrefonds. Tires squealed wildly.

'Why so fast?'

'Sorry.' He let the car slow down a bit.

He knew she was eyeing him curiously, but for some reason, he wasn't quite ready to tell her his own story. 'Of course,' he said then, 'Napoleon lived here. The imperial palace was his favorite spot, I gather.'

Palmer reached the diagonal cutoff to Pierrefonds and swung the Buick left. There were no mines hidden along the highway, which was as narrow then as it had been in the days after the liberation of Paris, but Palmer kept the Buick on the far right edge of the road, without realizing it. Then a tire slipped into the pebbles of the shoulder and he blinked. Strange, he thought, pulling the heavy car back into the middle of the road. The body is a recording machine that never misplaces a tape.

The vast stretches of the Forest of Compiègne wheeled by and this time Palmer could enjoy the luxury of looking at them. Centuries ago, wide avenues had been cut through the heavy growth of elm, oak, and beech. These green spokes of grassy space flashed majestically past the car. Small lakes glittered in the sunshine. Here and there a forester had felled a tree, sawed the trunk into meter-long pieces and neatly stacked it as firewood for someone. Himself in winter, Palmer wondered.

The French had never bothered to commercialize the Forest of Compiègne with roadside soft-drink stands or hotdoggeries, but there were many things to do in the 15,000 protected hectares.

'A hectare is how much?' he asked the girl suddenly.

'I beg your pardon.' Her legs stirred nervously.

'What is a hectare in the American system?'

'Why, ah, it's a square kilometer, I believe. So there would be an, ah, ten-to-six ratio, approximately. Yes?'

'I don't know,' Palmer said.

'That is, ten hectares equal six square miles. Yes?'

'I still don't know.'

'Obviously,' she said, 'neither do I.'

Palmer laughed. 'This forest is fifteen thousand hectares. That's about nine thousand square miles by your ratio. I sort of doubt it.'

'Why should you doubt it?'

'Because the whole state of New Hampshire's that big. And I know you could hide a few dozen Forests of Compiègne in New Hampshire.'

She frowned. 'Oh, I know!' she burst out. 'The hectare is a square meter. So you must remove two naughts. The forest is ninety square miles.'

'More like it.'

She sighed deeply. 'I feel so much better now.'

'So do I.'

She laughed aloud and again covered her mouth as she did so. Then: 'You are very much the banker, *n'est-ce pas?*' When he didn't answer, she suddenly hurried on. 'I mean to say, that is, with a passion for facts and figures, yes?'

'I've been accused of that.'

'Is your interest in Compiègne to do with banking, then?'

He shook his head, wondering why it bothered him when people called him a perfect banker. It happened often enough and, of course, there was every reason for it, being the son of a banker and having worked in banking all his life. It was usually meant as a compliment. Then why did it bother him? Because it hinted at a certain one-sidedness? She had thought his only interest in Compiègne could be the narrow one of banking.

Why narrow? Wasn't banking the broadest possible viewpoint in the business world? Was there a business with a wider one? Then why be bothered by the accusation? Why even call it an accusation? Damn it.

Palmer realized he had been silent for a long time. 'No,' he said then. 'Not banking.'

He proceeded to tell her the events of that day in 1944. He had just finished describing the run along the mined diagonal road when abruptly, like a mirage, the titanic roofs and towers of the Chateau of Pierrefonds swam into view below them, totally out of perspective, as if magnified in some trick optical way to a relationship out of all sense with the tiny village houses that lay at its feet.

'My God!' Miss Gregorius said. 'What *is* that?'

'More history,' Palmer said, pulling the Buick off the road and stopping. 'Louis d'Orléans built that in the fourteenth century when royalty couldn't always make up its mind whether it needed a fortress or a palace. Two centuries later, Louis the Thirteenth had as much of it torn down as he could to punish its current owner. Then, under Napoleon the Third, the architect le Duc dug up the early plans and restored it almost exactly as it had been five centuries before.'

'And it was here that you ... ah, encountered the Gestapo?'

'I'll show you.'

'You still remember?'

Palmer set the Buick moving down the road toward Pierrefonds. Telephone poles and lines obscured the chateau for a moment. Then the road curved around the massive base of the fortress-castle's hill. Palmer steered the heavy car up a stone road that climbed behind the chateau, over a bridge that spanned the wide back moat, and around by the stone towers of the rear gate where the Gestapo cars had tried to make a run for it.

The Buick's brakes shrieked. The car jolted to a halt. Dust filled Palmer's nostrils.

'It isn't necessary to recreate it that realistically,' the girl said.

Palmer laughed abruptly. 'Sorry.' He got out of the car and tried to orient himself by clumps of trees. He couldn't be sure of positions at all.

Then, after a long while, he realized she was watching him rather intently from her seat in the car. He turned back. 'I must apologize. This means nothing to you.'

'Did you kill many of them?'

'No. They surrendered.'

'You lost none of your men?'

He shook his head. 'A bloodless encounter. But we managed to pick up the names of almost a thousand collaborators and saboteurs.'

'And kill them?'

A bird began to sing in a nearby tree. Palmer blinked in the hot sun. The Cyclopean walls of the fortress loomed over him. Above them, in the hard blue sky, the great round defense towers sat in somber rows, capped by sharp conical roofs of slate.

'I don't know,' he heard himself saying.

The air around him seemed to swallow up the words as they left his mouth. He turned to look at the girl. She had opened the car door to let in a breeze, but she sat half in and half out of the car, one foot touching the dusty road, as if she had begun to join him, then stopped.

'I don't know what happened to them,' he finished saying.

CHAPTER 9

Although the day was a perfect one, with a sky whose intense blueness had been painstakingly accented by small scraps of fluffy cloud, Palmer sensed that something had gone wrong between his interpreter and him.

It didn't bother him terribly. She was, after all, an employee and he had decades ago given up the idea that he had to be beloved by his staff or that, indeed, a boss ever really was anything more than a bastard to most employees. On another level,

55

he might not care about her reactions as an employee, but as a pretty woman, her opinion of him had a certain validity.

He decided that what had cooled off between them had to do with his little Gestapo exploit, or, perhaps, not with the event as such but with some resonance it had sounded in her own memory.

'Did you have any trouble during the war with the Gestapo?' he asked abruptly. 'Or did someone in your family?'

They had lingered awhile at Pierrefonds, wandering through the chateau's courtyard, and were now driving southwest toward Morienval. Palmer intended to take a quick look at the church there – Virginia had made a point of asking him to see the place – and then head back to Paris as rapidly as possible, drop the moody Miss Gregorius, and spend an evening on the town by himself.

'No,' she said.

Nothing more was forthcoming. A few minutes later they reached Morienval and parked near the Church of Notre Dame. To Virginia, who had been to Europe alone several times in recent years, this church had somehow stood out from all the scores of cathedrals and other churches as something special she wanted Palmer to share with her. He wondered how she would be reacting now.

Not at all big, the church had the chunky massiveness Palmer associated with Romanesque, rather than Gothic. Its three square towers rose to sharply pointed roofs, lightening the solidity of the building itself. He turned to Miss Gregorius. 'Coming?'

'I'll wait here, if you don't mind.'

He walked into the church. It seemed even smaller inside because of the tremendous thickness of the walls. He picked up a booklet in English describing the church, put down a five-franc piece and learned that most of the building dated from the eleventh century, with copious restorations down through the ages.

He wandered along the nave moving slowly toward the altar behind which sun poured in through twin arched windows. The tombstones of long-dead abbesses and nuns lined the floor. His footsteps over their graves echoed and re-echoed. The silence in the low-ceilinged church was almost absolute. Palmer stopped walking and the silence became complete. Then he heard someone coming along a side aisle. An old priest appeared, evidently summoned by the sound of Palmer's footsteps.

'*Bonjour,*' he said, approaching Palmer. '*Anglais, monsieur?*'

'American.'

'Ah, yes,' the old man went on in an English so accented that Palmer found it hard to understand many of the words. The priest's hands flew in this direction and that, calling Palmer's attention to the stalls and the choir capitals. He was especially insistent that Palmer examine the arches overhead.

'*Je ne comprends pas,*' Palmer interjected into the flow of the old man's English.

The priest paused and resumed at a much slower tempo with many pauses. 'Ze arcs?' he began.

'Arches,' Palmer translated from English to English.

'Are unique. *Oui.* Century twelve.'

'Twelfth-century arches.'

'Early twelve,' the priest cautioned him, lest he fall into the error of believing them to be more modern than they were. 'Zey are oh-gheev?' He clapped his hands in impatience with himself. '*Qu'est-ce que c'est* oh-gheev?' He frowned at Palmer and, holding his palm forward, inscribed letters on it one after the other like a teacher with a reading class. 'O,' he began, 'ghee, ee, vay, eh.'

'Ogive arches,' Palmer responded.

He got a brilliant smile for his trouble. 'Ze oh-gheeves here are ze oldest in Europe.'

'*Oui, je comprends.*' Palmer started to nod and edge away from the old man.

'Ze groin-ed vault, *monsieur*, was easy to damage.'

Palmer kept nodding. The priest followed him as he started toward the front door. 'Soon zay learn to strengthen ze edge of ze groin.'

'Strengthen the edge.'

'And zay learn ze strong edge carry all ze weight.' They were at the door now. The priest raised his finger higher than his head as if to import some great theological truth to Palmer.

'And from zis come eviary thing else in architecture.'

'I see. Very interesting.'

'In Morienval, you understand, is where it starts, *oui*?'

'*Oui, d'accord.*'

Abruptly, the old man's hand shot out and gripped Palmer's to give it three strong shakes. 'God bless you,' he said then and waved good-bye.

Palmer stood outside the church for a while, aware that Miss Gregorius was probably waiting impatiently for him, but determined to try to take in as much of the view as he could so that he could truthfully respond to Virginia's enthusiasm when he got back to New York. Of course, being Catholic, she probably drew more meaning from a church than he did, Palmer thought. He supposed he wasn't terribly religious. For that matter, neither was Virginia any more. But still...

He turned and walked slowly back to the Buick, stopping once more to view the church from a slight change in angle. 'What did the priest want?' the girl asked him. Her voice sounded lighter. She seemed to have worked her way out of her mood.

'To make sure I understood that the ogive arch was born here.'

'The what?'

'Not important.' He started the car. 'Except to an architect, I suppose.' He turned to her. 'What do you think of the church?'

'It's very ... beautiful.' She paused cautiously. 'Very compact and very right in its dimensions.' She paused again. 'It's a church you can be comfortable with. It doesn't try to overwhelm you, does it?'

'No.' He eyed her and wondered why she was suddenly talking away when she had stopped almost entirely before.

'Some churches try to knock you in the eye,' she was saying, 'with their sheer size. You are supposed to go down on your knees, mentally as well as physically, you know. The church is supposed to overwhelm you. This one doesn't. You can be a human being in this church. It is scaled to the human body.'

Palmer started the Buick moving along a road he believed would get them back to Paris. 'Are you a student of architecture, then?'

'Not at all.' Trying to explain herself, she crossed and recrossed her legs. Palmer glanced sideways. Her bangs had gotten disarrayed and her face looked longer because of the great height of her forehead. 'It's just that I'm not a very religious person, you know. Nobody in my generation really is, the generation that were babies during the war, yes? And we react very badly to many things that don't bother the generation before ours or the one after. My daughter, *par exemple*, doesn't have the same feeling about cant and hypocrisy that I do. My generation can't stand to –' She stopped suddenly, aware that

58

she was disclosing too many things to an employer.

Palmer nodded. The sun had started to go down and he was no longer sure which way true west was. When he came to a fork in the road, he headed what he hoped was southwest toward Paris. 'Your generation,' he said then, 'was the beneficiary of all those lies and hypocrisy in action. My generation was one that made up the lies.'

Her eyebrows went up. 'We are of the same generation, surely.'

Palmer was about to comment and then, with a vague quit-while-you're-ahead feeling, said nothing at all. The road was taking them through the heart of the forest and Palmer knew, without precisely remembering the map, that if they were heading toward Paris they should have been out of the forest many miles before. A small lake and country house of some size flashed by on their left. '*Etangs de* what?' he asked.

'De St.-Perrine,' she said. 'The Pool of St.-Perrine. Do we have a map in the car?'

'I wouldn't think Dauber would let us go without one. Check the glove compartment.'

She found a map and consulted it for quite a while. 'Yes, here it is.'

'It was on our left. Can you tell what direction we're heading?'

'Ye-es. North?'

'Oh no.'

'North to Compiègne.'

At that moment a sign told him he'd reached the outskirts of the town, having driven in exactly the wrong direction from Paris. 'You're right,' he said then. He glanced at his watch. 'After six and all we've had is that peculiar sandwich.'

'It's seventy kilometers back to Paris. That's, ah, forty-five miles?' The car reached the main square again. The same autos seemed parked in the center and the same soldiers seemed to be enjoying evening aperitifs at the sidewalk café. 'Compiègne is not possible, stomach-wise?' she asked, then giggled.

Palmer pointed at a hotel to the right of the city hall's high-roofed wing. 'L'Hôtel de la Cloche,' he read. 'Is the clock a big historic thing around here?'

'This is my first visit.'

'That's right. I'm the Compiègne expert.'

Palmer tried to read the sign in the hotel's dining-room window. '*Dîner gastronomique?* That sounds enticing.'

'Is it possible, in such a town as this?'

Palmer parked the car. 'There are people inside,' he said. 'I figure it this way. In a small town most people eat dinner at home. If some are eating here, the food must be exceptional.' They left the car.

She stumbled on the cobblestones and Palmer took her arm. Her skin felt very soft under his fingers, but beneath the flesh he could feel bone close to the skin. She had one of those modern, show-girl figures, he decided, all legs and really on the skinny side, with probably immense breasts.

Eleanora really was a different generation, he thought as he ushered her into the restaurant. Virginia Clary, by contrast, had the short, full figure that had preceded hers in general popularity. Something about the vitamins seemed to turn out long, skinny girls in the postwar era. His own Geraldine was one. Of course, so was her mother. And Edith was most certainly not of the new generation.

They sat down in the small, plain front room, aware that several other dining rooms were available but that this one seemed to be most favored by the guests. At a corner table, four men in business suits were just finishing what was either a long bout of wine drinking, to judge by the empty bottles on the table, or a late lunch that had dragged on through the afternoon.

People alone ate at most of the other tables, propping their elbows on the clean white linen and working over their food with knife and fork in the businesslike way the French usually eat, bringing the food to terms quickly in order to let it know at the outset who was master.

A young couple in the far corner ate in the total silence common to married Europeans. Neither looked at the other, Palmer noticed, but concentrated on his plate or stared at other diners. Words were not uttered except when a waiter arrived with something new.

Palmer and the girl were given a small menu which described, in a carbon-copy version of typing, the main outlines of the food available. It seemed to Palmer that the *dîner gastronomique*, which cost a few francs more than the regular dinner, offered a greater variety.

The waiter arranged their silver, serving plates, basket of bread, napkins and butter and then addressed them in French.

'*Parle anglais?*' Palmer asked. The waiter instantly removed himself. 'What have I done?'

'Why not let me order?' Miss Gregorius asked.

'Did I insult him?' Palmer wondered.

A moment later a short, plump man in his sixties detached himself from the group of businessmen in the corner and came to Palmer's table. 'Good evening, *m'sieur-dame.*'

The little man led them through the menu without seeming to. They ended up with quite an array of courses, beginning with asparagus in a vinaigrette sauce. 'This is the time of year for *les asperges,*' their host noted in a small, footnoting voice, simultaneously enlarging Palmer's vocabulary and making a sales pitch.

'I see we can get *les asperges* several ways,' Palmer responded. 'Is the vinaigrette your recommendation?'

'Absolutely.' The manager shook his head quickly from side to side as if denying that any of the five other asparagus dishes on the menu came within a light-year of the vinaigrette's suitability.

He had a roundish face with red cheeks and sparse gray-blond hair. After he had taken their orders for soup and a main course, he left a small booklet on the table and set about the business of placing their order with the kitchen. Palmer opened the folder and found another carbon-copy of typewriting, this one headed 'L'Hôtel de la Cloche.' He turned it over to Miss Gregorius, who quickly scanned the typing.

'The first Hotel of the Clock dates from 1515,' she translated, skipping about from paragraph to paragraph. 'Kings, emperors, painters, poets, and magnates of finance like Rockefeller have rested here,' she said. 'Ah, listen. Alexandre Dumas placed several of the most moving scenes of *The Count of Monte Cristo* in a room in the Hotel of the Clock. There's a description in Book Three of the hotel itself. My goodness.'

She continued reading to herself. 'Here. The editor in chief of *Sport* magazine stated in the year 1865 that the excellent dinners at the Hotel of the Clock remind him of fine eating as it was enjoyed in the era of Charles the Tenth.' She frowned and glanced up at Palmer. 'Charles the Tenth?'

He frowned back. 'Early nineteenth century?' He tried to recollect something about the monarch. 'I think when Lafayette returned to the United States he was an emissary of Charles the Tenth.'

'You are the most learned man I have ever met,' Miss Gregorius said.

Palmer glanced at her perfectly candid eyes and decided she was not being funny. 'I have a good memory,' he said.

'Phenomenal.' The host arrived with the white wine they had ordered as a beginning. He opened the chilled bottle of Pouilly-sur-Loire and plunged it into the ice bucket. 'A few moments more of ice, monsieur.'

Palmer realized the girl was still watching him closely, as if to divine the secret of his phenomenal learnedness. It was at times like this that he lost most of his own savoir faire. Flattery rarely undid him, but when it arrived unexpectedly, and for something undeserved, it could throw him off base enough to make for an awkward moment. Did she really think him learned? Or did she associate with such slovenly dunces that by comparison he seemed learned? Or was it simply that her generation – how easily he had slipped into that idea, he noticed – had a higher regard for learning of any kind, even the spotty, unfocused command of memory that Palmer had displayed today.

'Sherlock Holmes,' he said then, 'once remarked to Dr. Watson that the average man's mind was an attic stocked with useless stuff. Holmes had stocked his with useful material, of course. Which was why he could feel so superior to the average man. But the kind of odd facts in my attic can hardly be called learning.'

Her eyes never left his face. 'This Sherlock Holmes,' she said then. 'He is English?'

Palmer had conceived and rejected four possible answers, but was saved from using any when *les asperges* arrived, each plate heaped with long whitish spears whose tints only slightly approached the faintest of greens. Miss Gregorius spooned the vinaigrette sauce to mix it and began helping Palmer to some.

The asparagus seemed to disappear quite rapidly, but not any faster than the white wine. Palmer found it particularly dry and fresh, with a chill that soothed his throat. In New York, when he had lived with Edith and the children, wine had been rare except when they entertained guests. With Virginia, in the last six months, he had learned to know and like quite a few wines. But he had never thought of himself as a great fancier of wine. A glass or two at meals was his usual ration. However, there was no disputing the fact that the entire fifth of Pouilly-sur-Loire was gone.

'Problem,' Palmer said, pouring the last of it into the girl's glass. 'I with my *boeuf* and you with your *poulet* present an obstacle *formidable*. Wine-wise, that is.'

Her eyes focused slowly on his. *'Rouge ou blanc?'* She shook her index finger back and forth very quickly, which Palmer had already noticed was a European way of saying no without shaking the head. 'Is there anything wrong with another bottle of this?' she asked him.

Palmer found that the second fifth lasted well through the soup course. He was only mildly – and rather pleasantly – surprised to learn that they had ordered an intermediate course of crepes before the main dish. The crepes arrived still perking in their pale yellow sauce, their filling of forcemeat and chopped vegetables spilling out in generous gushes. A third bottle of wine seemed necessary.

'Cant and hypocrisy and lies,' Miss Gregorius was saying.

Palmer found himself nodding. 'Quite so.'

'Which was why I grew so angry with you at Pierrefonds. I'm most terribly sorry,' she said. 'I hope you didn't notice. But I'm afraid you did.'

'Nothing. Of it.'

Palmer frowned at the queer spacing of the words as he uttered them. He watched the waiter bring a mixed salad and it seemed quite appropriate to him at this moment. The tartness of the dressing contrasted nicely with the rich, creamy flavor of the crepes. He signaled for another Pouilly-sur-Loire.

'Without an explanation, certainly,' Miss Gregorius was saying. Palmer wondered what had ever given him the idea that she was taciturn. 'But you must not construe it as anything anti-American. This whole anti-American thing in Europe bores me to distraction, it's so gauche.'

'Yes?'

'But it is an American trait, is it not, to feel absolutely right about what one is doing, to swoop in as you did and pick up a thousand names and make sure they were all rounded up? And not to remember, or even to know, what was done to the people. Those were names of people, you understand. It's so American to keep at a distance from a thing by putting words in between, yes? A thousand names. Collaborators. Fifth columnists. Saboteurs. Traitors. Words. But they were a thousand men and woman and not even to know what became of them angered me. I admit it. I've had much too much wine. I will be sacked for this, of course.' She turned to him and grinned broadly. 'Yes?'

'Canned. Fired. Let go.'

'Because this my generation insists on,' she rolled ahead steadily, 'to take responsibility for oneself is *all* one can do. But one *must* do it. *Each* one must. Only in that way does some kind of *mass* responsibility have any existence. Don't you agree?'

'Not sure I understand.'

She nodded vehemently. 'It was obvious to me at Pierrefonds that you had *never* given a second thought to the thousand people whose names you secured in that brave, Wild West fashion. It was your job to *get* the names. It was someone else's job to *find* the people. Perhaps a third man had the responsibility of prosecuting them and still another of sentencing and another still of executing them. This kind of piecemeal responsibility isn't responsibility at all.'

'It's buck-passing,' Palmer cut in.' 'Good old American game of buck-passing. S'why committees were born. Ha.'

'But it has infected Europe. Everything here is now American. Even the modes of thought. Everything is a pragmatic quagmire of Yankeeism.'

'Pragmatic quagmire.' Palmer pursed his lips and whistled very softly. A waiter appeared, probably by accident.

'*Encore du vin, s'il vous plaît,*' Palmer heard himself say. The strong nasality of his voice shocked him pleasantly. When the hell did he learn to speak French, much less pronounce it? Or did wine do that for him?

'The most learned man I know,' the girl echoed. 'I know you hate me to say it. But it's true. And besides I have offended you with all this philosophical tittle-tattle at the dinner table and now I must flatter you to make you like me again and not sack me.'

'Talk about pragmatic.'

'We Europeans are very pragmatic when it comes to living. But we like to espouse philosophies that deny the pragmatism of real life.'

'So do we Americans.'

'Surely not.'

Palmer shook his index finger from left to right very quickly with a practiced air. 'You must stop trying to put the human animal in national categories. All human animals are the same. We must live like animals in order to exist. But we shock ourselves so much that way that we have to invent fairy-tale philosophies and pretend they represent the real us.'

He frowned at the new bottle of wine. Third? Fourth? My God.

When he glanced at Miss Gregorius, he saw that her eyes were moist.

'That is the most dismal thing anyone has ever said,' she told him. 'Do you Americans really believe that?'

'Please stop you-Americaning me.'

'I'm sorry.'

'You are not going to be allowed to make me the apologist for my nation. Not unless you tell me your nation so I can bother you with it. How do you Dutch feel about that, nation-wise?'

'I am not D –' Her hand flew to her mouth and she began laughing again. 'I see,' she shrieked. 'Oh, very good. Very well put.' She dabbed at her eyes with the thick damask table napkin. 'Damn. Eye shadow. You must not make me laugh. Or cry.'

'*D'accord.*'

The main dish arrived, together with its accompanying flotilla of side dishes. Palmer ate and drank and ate again. Neither of them spoke for a long while, so necessary was it to concentrate on their food. Palmer could feel a slight chill on the back of his neck. He realized he was perspiring slightly, but didn't understand why in such pleasant weather. He sipped the wine again.

Miss Gregorius was laughing at something he said. He hadn't been aware of speaking, but surely he must have because she was laughing. Perhaps he'd been witty? Perhaps. They touched glasses.

The waiter arrived with something big and pinkish-orange on a platter. Palmer could tell that slices of some fruit – peach? pear? – lay beneath the glaze and pastry. The table slanted sideways for a moment. Palmer sipped some wine.

Eleanora Gregorius and the waiter were mopping him with napkins. There was wine on his jacket and trousers. He reached for the glass and found it overturned on the table. He could just barely touch it with his fingers.

'Second floor,' he heard someone saying, 'front room on the right. Careful. Careful.'

'Amazingly light,' Miss Gregorius was saying.

CHAPTER 10

He was sitting in the Ubco boardroom at the long table. Behind him hung the Monet of the water lilies period. Around the table sat most of his board, but not all. He had the curious sensation that he was invisible to them.

Harry Elder was talking in his hoarse, all-weather voice. He was going on at some length about something Palmer couldn't quite grasp. All the sensual physics were peculiar, he realized, and just as they couldn't quite see him, he couldn't quite hear them.

Harry grew quite angry and had to be shouted down, mostly by Hagen, who finally produced an extremely large colonial candlesnuffer and brought it down smartly over Harry's head, extinguishing him. It was another peculiarity of the scene that visual details were excruciatingly clear to Palmer. For instance, he could see when the snuffer was lifted from Harry's head that a smudge of tallow soot remained on his left cheek and chin. But he had stopped talking.

Hagen had the floor now and Palmer's hearing wasn't getting the words. He stood up to ask Hagen to speak more distinctly. He found himself, instead, sitting up in a strange bed in a darkened room. He glanced down at himself and found that he had been undressed and placed beneath the sheets of the bed. Suddenly, with no warning, he wondered what stuffy, chubby Harry Bannister would think of him at this point. Old H.B. was notorious for his puritanical approach to this sort of thing.

'Quagmire,' Palmer said aloud.

His head ached. He threw back the covers and swung his long legs off the bed. The movement made him sick for a moment. He saw that whoever had undressed him had left his underwear shorts on. He stood up and walked on bare feet to the window. His trousers, shirt, jacket, and tie had been neatly draped over a silent-valet frame. His wallet and small change lay on the top of the frame in a cuplike depression carved out of the wood. His traveler's checkbook sat beside the wallet. Palmer leafed through everything and found it in order. He glanced out the window.

The town square of Compiègne lay flooded in moonlight. The bank's Buick sat where he had parked it, a ballooning giant among the trim, tiny European cars. Two soldiers and two girls sat at the sidewalk café and played with aperitif glasses. Palmer glanced at his watch and saw that it was nearly eleven o'clock. He decided he had been asleep since about, uh, seven? Eight? 'Pragmatic quagmire,' he said aloud, and winced.

He wondered where Miss Gregorius was and whether he could face her. He realized that the smooth white wine was something absolutely alien to his own body, something with which it hadn't the slightest idea of how to cope. He would either have to teach it or forget about white wine entirely.

He wondered what the next move would be. Sitting down heavily on the edge of the overstuffed mattress, he tried to imagine the sequence of events that had brought him, undressed, into this bed. The pain in his head sharpened for a moment, then receded to a dull ache.

Why had Harry Elder been so vehement? What a brutal way Hagen had of snuffing out that vehemence. Curious dream. Pure anxiety.

He heard a noise at the door and a faint beam of light fell across the floor and touched his toes. He looked up. Eleanora Gregorius stood in the doorway, holding a glass of something.

'If that's wine . . .' Palmer began.

She giggled solemnly and came into the room, closing the door behind her. She advanced toward the bed. 'It's water,' she said, handing it to him. Then she extended her other hand with two white tablets. 'And aspirin.'

Palmer swallowed the tablets with water. He felt them stick in his parched throat for an excruciating moment. Then the water broke them loose and flooded his throat with blessed coolness. He sighed heavily and returned the glass to the girl.

'My apologies, Miss Gregorius,' he said. 'I misjudged the wine.'

'Also the time-zone change, yes?' she suggested tactfully.

Palmer nodded, grateful for this eminently respectable alibi. 'Very sound thought,' he murmured. He glanced aimlessly about him, wondering whether he ought to pull a sheet over him or pick up his shirt, or, in fact, do anything at all. It wasn't that he was embarrassed at sitting there in his shorts. It was something else and he felt too muddled to clarify the feeling.

'Terrible anxiety dream,' he muttered then.

'Oh?' She sat down on the bed beside him, but a few feet away. 'I'm very sorry.'

He turned to look at her. Her face seemed as solemn as it was possible for a round, doll's face to look, eyes wide and under-

67

standing. Then she giggled again and the expression flew apart instantly. Palmer realized she was still somewhat drunk.

'You've been downstairs all this time, waiting for me to sober up?'

She shook her head and her bangs flew into disarray. Palmer caught a glimpse of her high forehead. It suddenly intrigued him that no one was seeing the real Gregorius face at all, it being quite oval and terribly intellectual. The bangs deliberately turned it into a roly-poly toy.

'Have you always worn bangs?' he heard himself asking.

She shook her head again. Neither of them spoke for a long moment. Then, slowly, she reached up and brushed the bangs first sideways and then back into her hair. The effect was startling. 'Have many people seen the real you?' Palmer asked.

'Very few.'

'I'm honored.'

'Yes?'

A curious intimacy seemed to have sprung up in the room, as if she had undressed, too. He reached out to push back a stray lock of hair that persisted in falling back over her high, clear forehead. She took his hand and turned it palm up. She stared into it.

'Do you read palms?'

'Yes.' Her eyes grew solemn again. 'It tells me there are two of you.'

'My palm says that?'

She nodded. 'Two men with your name and your body.'

'Does it tell you whether I'll ever be able to handle white wine?'

'Yes. One of you will learn. The other, never.'

'Fascinating.'

She nodded again. 'Absolutely fascinating.' She kissed the palm of his hand slowly. He could feel the tip of her tongue search for a moment along his life line, as if drinking up some previous fluid. A shock of excitement spread out through his fingers. He could fell his groin grow tense.

She glanced at him, her mouth still on his palm. Her eyes looked wide enough to swallow him. Then, still holding his hand, she stood up and moved until she was standing directly in front of him. He put his arms around her hips and pressed the in-swelling curves of her buttocks, pulling her body into his face. He nestled against her for a moment, looking down along her smooth, slender legs to the floor. There was a sudden flash of wild color and he was watching the brilliant patterns of her dress, puddled about her feet. He rubbed his face against her tanned belly and reached up to remove her brassiere.

The room was intensely quiet. It seemed suffused with an overwhelming sense of peace. There was no ache in his head. Her skin was warm and silky to the touch. When he freed them her breasts swelled above him like two great white hills capped with flowers of a brown darker than her tanned skin.

In the distance, rolling slowly like some long railroad train, the bells of the clock tower began to sound in a steady progression, measured like the beat of an untroubled heart. He and the girl were on the bed, slowly exciting each other with long kisses and strokings. Her skin had a gleam to it in the half-darkened room, as if it gave off its own light. He gazed down the length of her, over the swell of her breasts and past the shiny pubis, flanked by the jut of her pelvic bones, down her long, slim legs. She seemed almost unreal in the luxurious way she was put together, a wet dream of a girl.

'Don't pause to contemplate,' he heard her say.

He laughed softly and then felt her moving down alongside him in a faint series of tiny nibbles. What sounded like a convoy of military trucks went by outside the window, the heavy rumble of thick-tread tires drumming on the cobbled surface of the street. She had rolled over on top of him. In the darkness her buttocks glowed like two lamps lit from within by candles.

He could hear sounds of glassware from beneath now, glassware and the clatter of knives and forks. He was inside her now, moving slowly and steadily at an angle unfamiliar to him. Her vulva seemed to pull him deeper into her with each stroke.

Faint music came across the square from the sidewalk café, the insistent thud of a rock band and the vague keening of a singer. She had moved around now and was taking immense lengths of him inside her with a voracious intensity that almost frightened him. He could see her face in the half-dark, eyes closed, expression intent, absolutely removed from thought, as if she had somehow concentrated all of herself in the great gulping thrust of her vulva.

Across the square the music stopped and a woman laughed loudly. Another record started playing. Palmer felt himself reaching climax and tried to fight it back. She opened her eyes and bent forward over him until her breasts were swinging against his face. Suddenly he felt the fire spurt up through him and he almost fainted from the joy of it. She lay down on top of him and they rolled sideways, still joined.

They fell asleep that way. After a while, Palmer was back in the Ubco boardroom again. Harry Elder was talking vehemently.

CHAPTER 11

By Sunday noon, with Eleanora at the wheel, they had driven back into Paris. Neither wanted to sightsee. They ended up in Montmartre at the girl's apartment off the Place du Calvaire not far from the Basilica of the Sacre-Coeur.

She had had a terrible time maneuvering the Buick through the eighteenth-century streets and she had found it even more difficult to locate a parking place. Finally, in her apartment, they rested and watched each other without speaking, as they had for most of Saturday night and Sunday.

Palmer found the place about as he had pictured her apartment, orderly, powerfully feminine, restful, somewhat noncommittal. He looked around the main room, its stark whitewashed masonry walls and low, top-floor ceiling. The beams of the ceiling had been stained the dark brown of bitter chocolate.

Although the room was no more than fifteen feet square, it seemed much larger and longer because at one end a sweep of modern steel casement windows had been set into the masonry, forming almost a solid wall of glass. Through it, facing southwest from the heights of Montmartre, Palmer could see the Eiffel Tower in the hazy distance, framed by a welter of Parisian chimney pots and television antennas. The tower seemed to have been painted gauzily by Ingres.

She had searched all over the apartment for something special she could offer him, throwing open stainless steel drawers and closets with severely modern flexible wooden closures. The walls were mostly bare except for a giant poster photograph of a naked boy of three pissing into a soldier's helmet. His expression was one of rapt attention. The slogan underneath the helmet, in block red letters read: *À bas la guerre.*

Across the room, on the other wall that was unbroken by

70

doors or windows, the girl had fixed with cellophane tape a series of tiny color snapshots of herself with various men or with her daughter, Tanya, or alone. In contrast to the dense solidity of the walls and the streamlined efficiency of the fixtures, this small collection of memorabilia had an impermanent air about it, as if hastily assembled and, perhaps, as hastily removed when necessary.

At last she found the hidden gift for which she had been searching, buried beneath a great fluff of bikini briefs and bras in a drawer of the built-in bureau. She produced a long-necked brown bottle with something of a flourish.

'This is terribly expensive,' she said, 'and terribly wonderful ... like you.' They laughed at this foolishness while she struggled to remove the cork.

Palmer took the bottle and finished the job. The liqueur was called Sève-Fournier and it seemed to come from a province not far from Paris. 'The only place I have found to buy it,' the girl explained, lapsing into intense solemnity, 'is near the Madeleine. Fauchon's, it's called. They sell all sorts of food and spirits. You can shop there Monday for souvenirs to send your friends in New York, yes?'

Palmer tasted the amber liqueur and found its mild taste almost impossible to describe. The sweetness was not too cloying and the afterflavor was an almost forgotten memory of cocoa. But these were only teasing hints. The real flavor escaped him, even on second taste. She poured a tiny amount into her navel and he slowly licked it clear, the Sève-Fournier mingled with the salt of her body and the yolky taste of their lovemaking.

'You're against the war,' he said, indicating the poster.

'Against all war.'

'Any.'

'Any.' She dipped her nipple into her glass of liqueur and he picked up the cue at once. Later, his legs trembling slightly from the continuing effort of the night and the morning, he walked naked to the window wall and watched the afternoon shadows lengthen across Montmartre.

'You can see from here,' she said from the bed behind him, 'the famous cemetery where Stendhal and Berlioz and all the rest are buried.'

'It's too hazy out.'

'You can also catch a glimpse of Rue St.-Vincent, where the Lapin Agile stands. They all used to meet there, you know.

71

Utrillo, Picasso.'

'All I see is a huge tree over there.'

'Then look here,' she said, touching her pubis. 'The shrubbery effect is dazzling.'

'One mustn't be cheeky with one's elders.'

'Cheeky?' She laughed. 'Fresh?'

'Very good.'

'But how much elder – older – are you?' she persisted. 'You are now, say, thirty-eight? This is only ten years older than I am.'

'Very, very good.'

Palmer came back to the bed and stood over her. 'I'm forty-seven. That's almost twenty years older than you. You really are as poised and self-confident a liar as any I've met.'

She made a face. 'Not kind. Not kind at all.'

'Are you hungry?' Palmer asked.

She smiled up at him. 'Leisurely dinner, a few bottles of white wine? You don't learn, do you?'

Laughing, he sat down on the bed beside her. 'It's like being thrown from a horse. I have to get back on again.'

'Nowhere in Paris will you find that Pouilly-sur-Loire. The man has it bottled locally. None of it gets to Paris. You can try Pouilly-Fuissé, Pouilly-Fumé, nothing is the same.'

Palmer nodded slowly. 'Nothing ever is, the second time.'

'So we try a third and a fourth, yes?' Her glance had grown very intense. 'Do you realize that Dauber has scheduled me to be your interpreter in Germany, too?'

'And that's the mark of a smart young man.'

'Dauber.' She pursed her lips outward. 'Not very.' She reached behind his head and pulled him down on her. When she spoke again her mouth was pressed against his. 'Tomorrow morning,' she said, 'you will go to your meetings and I will be there with my notebook and my pencils.'

'D'accord.'

'And that is so many long, lovely hours from now.'

'You seem to be trying to tell me something,' Palmer said indistinctly. He felt her move slowly under him, a kind of upward glide that brought her breasts around his face. 'Ah yes.'

They finally got back to his suite at the Ritz about midnight, working out the logistics in a way both of them considered quite clever. Palmer had first gotten his key at the desk and then gone to the bar, where they had had a drink. Then he'd given her the key and she'd gone up to his suite to await him. This, they felt certain, had fooled everyone.

They had switched to dry martinis primarily because it was Palmer's contention that no bartenders in Paris could make them. The man at the George V bar had made them well enough for Palmer to lose his bet, but the man at the Ritz had clinched the matter.

If he had not been drinking, Palmer realized, he would long ago have fallen by the wayside. Alcohol kept him fueled. And, what with catnaps all night in Compiègne and all day in Montmartre, he had probably had almost enough sleep. The dream about the Ubco boardroom hadn't come back to him again and he had forgotten the whole thing.

Now he was soaping her back in the shower stall of his Ritz bathroom and the idea of the dream came to him again. He wondered about it as his hands, lubricated with suds, slowly stroked her sides and buttocks. He reached around her and began fondling her breasts. He forgot about the dream.

The shower seemed to exhaust both of them. The girl threw back the covers of the immense double bed and went to sleep almost at once. Palmer leafed through the envelopes the desk clerk had given him. He had managed to hide them in his breast pocket before the girl had seen them. Now he tore open the first envelope. 'NO ANSWER MY TWX OF YESTERDAY. PLS RETWX ME SOONEST AUTHORIZATION ON PEOPLES BANK DECISION. ELDER, NYC.'

Damn Harry. What had gotten into him? The whole anxiety dream came to Palmer now as he stood near the armoire and reread the Telex message. Then he threw it into the waste-basket and tore open the second envelope. On Ritz stationery Dauber had penned a brief note to the effect that he would pick Palmer up Monday morning at nine thirty to take him to his first appointment. The note failed to mention Eleanora. Tact?

Palmer turned to look at her across the room, her long-limbed body sprawled out across the entire bed. Without being a particularly tall girl, she seemed to cover a lot of territory. He felt an ache at the base of his throat and realized that he wanted to make love to her again. After a night and a day of it she still had the power to excite him ... without even trying.

He sat down in an armchair and opened the third envelope to find another cable. 'WHOLE DAY'S PASSED. CAN'T STAND IT. COLD SHOWERS DO NOTHING. PLEASE ADVISE. SIGNED, ANXIOUS.'

Palmer's face split in a wide grin. He reached for the telephone and then realized he had the wrong company with him for a personal call to Virginia.

He sat back, wondering what kind of person he was turning out to be in his middle years. He knew most men were inconstant to their women but he hadn't been that way with Edith, not until the past two years with Virginia. Now here he was betraying Virginia. God, what an old-fashioned word, betrayed.

He had settled into a very comfortable relationship with Virginia. She had her own job and her own money. She did well and he, even with the tremendous bite the separation was taking out of current income, still had the corpus of his father's estate intact and well invested. In time they would marry. Between them there had always been a good, bantering give-and-take thing. It would make as good a basis for marriage as any. She was terribly bright, far more intelligent than anyone he knew, male or female. She was much too bright ever to extend herself so far out on a limb again, emotionally, that he could hurt her as badly as he once had. The whole affair had blown up and they had not seen each other for more than a year. In that time, Palmer knew, he had lost the power to hurt Virginia much more than he already had. To his way of thinking this made their relationship far more secure now.

He glanced at the girl lying on the bed. She seemed fast asleep, only her breasts rising and falling slowly with the deep rhythm of her breathing. Palmer wanted to go to her and kiss the soles of her feet. He felt the ache at the base of his throat again. Instead he stood up and went into the sitting room, closing the door behind him. He picked up the telephone and put through a call to New York.

It was now one in the morning in Paris and Palmer supposed that very few calls were being placed across the Atlantic. At any rate within a few minutes he could hear Virginia's telephone ringing. She answered on the second ring and when the operator asked if she was Virginia Clary, her voice grew instantly excited.

'Woods?' she cried.

'*Allô-allô,*' Palmer said. '*Comment ça va!*'

'Darling! My God, it *is* you.'

'*Mais, certainement.* How are you?'

'Missing you.'

Palmer wanted to echo the sentiment. He let too long a pause

74

go by before saying: 'I miss you, too,' which seemed honest enough. He did miss her, in a certain way. He realized he was perspiring with guilt, all of a sudden, like the shameful liar he was.

'You sound ... tired,' she said then.

'A little. I had some trouble getting into the whole European time-zone thing,' he lied, feeling grateful to Eleanora for her ready-made hand-me-down excuse. He glanced at the closed door to the bedroom, then turned his back on it to muffle his voice by sending it in the opposite direction. 'It must be dinner time in New York,' he said then in a fine display of inanity.

'Martini time. I'm having one and thinking of you. Have one with me?'

'I'll see if Room Service can stir one up at this hour.'

'I understand in France they shake instead of stirring.'

'Horrible.'

A pause. 'Are you all right, Woods?' she asked then.

'Fine. Just fine.' Why in the hell had he called her if all he could think of were the flotsam of a thousand cliché conversations?

'I'm glad. It's been unseasonably hot here, and muggy.'

Now the weather, Palmer thought. What had happened so quickly to them? 'I saw your church today,' he said abruptly, trying to divert them from more triviality. 'Yesterday, I mean.'

'At Morienval? Oh, darling, did you?'

'It's a lovely church. The priest spent a lot of time on me. I know more than I want to about ogive arches.'

'But did you love it?'

Palmer nodded. 'Yes, of course. It's, uh ... on a much more human scale than most of the churches you see.' He heard the door to the bedroom open behind him. 'It doesn't overwhelm you,' he went on doggedly.

'That's very true,' Virginia said. 'I hadn't thought of it that way.'

The girl was standing before him, her eyes wide, her hair brushed back so that her tall forehead gleamed like polished stone. Her mouth was slightly open as she listened to him. Palmer found he could say absolutely nothing.

'Darling,' Virginia said, 'that's a very good insight. Thank you.'

'For what?' Palmer managed to ask.

'For helping me understand why I love that church so much.

Did you see Compiègne and Pierrefonds?'

'Oh, yes.'

The girls' eyes traveled slowly from Palmer's face to his penis. She went down on her knees and kissed it. 'What did you see today?' Virginia wanted to know.

'Uh, Paris. General sightseeing.'

The girl prostrated herself on the floor and began kissing his feet. Palmer stood frozen to the spot, sharp, jolting waves of desire pumping through his body. 'Isn't that wonderful,' Virginia was saying. 'Do you have a guide?'

'Some people from the bank.'

'Wonderful. It's so much better with a native who really knows.'

Why did his generation talk nothing but clichés? The girl stared up at him and then caught him around the hips and hugged him with a slow, rocking movement.

'Did Harry Elder get through to you?' Virginia asked then.

'Harry?'

'Harry Elder.'

'Oh, uh, Elder.' Palmer tried to square himself away for coherent talk. 'He Telexed me twice. The whole thing's nonsense. He doesn't need me. Has he been bothering you?'

'Wanted to know where he could phone you.'

'I didn't realize Harry knew about us.'

Virginia laughed softly. 'It's hardly a secret any more. I gather he hasn't been able to reach you at the Ritz.'

'And I don't want to talk to him,' Palmer said. 'Try to find out what's got him spooked. Although I doubt he'll tell you since you work for the hated savings banks.'

'Talk to him, Woods. He sounded desperate. Of all your thieves at Ubco he's the only one who remotely resembles a friend.'

'Such talk.'

The girl was on her feet now, watching him closely. She inclined her head toward the bedroom. Palmer nodded.

'Woods?' Virginia asked.

'Okay,' he said.

'Okay what?'

'I'll, uh, call him.'

'Now? He gave me his home phone.'

'I have it in my notebook.'

'Please do call.'

'Yes.'

'Woods?'

'Yes.'

'I love you.'

He swallowed. 'I love you, too,' he said slowly. The girl smiled slightly and kissed the hand with which he was holding the telephone. 'Good night,' he said then.

Virginia said nothing for a moment. 'Good night,' she said then. 'Thank you for calling, darling.'

'Not at all. Good night.'

As he started to put down the telephone, the girl seemed to explode around him, pulling him to her and covering his face and chest with nibbling kisses.

'I have another New York call to make,' he said.

'Nonsense.'

'I know, but –'

'But with how many women are you having affairs in New York?'

They burst out laughing together. Palmer put down the telephone and let himself be led back into the bedroom.

CHAPTER 12

They had fallen asleep for the last time as a faint light began to filter through the east windows of the Ritz suite. Palmer lay absolutely still on his back, staring at the ceiling and sensing sleep wash over him like the spume from some mighty surf that had broken again and again on the shore beyond where he lay.

He felt spent, without strength or desire. His groin ached, a low-level pain that was more of a reminder than a problem. He wondered how much of this activity it took to produce prostate trouble and, feeling sleep wash over him again, decided it didn't matter.

He went through a small dream of his childhood, a time he had swum the lake at his family's summer place in Wisconsin. The water had been cold, as the lake always was in June, and his leg had cramped so badly he had almost drowned. He immediately came awake and felt the real cramp in his thigh muscle. He eased off the bed and strode silently about the bed-

77

room, kneading the inner flesh below his scrotum. He hadn't had such a charley horse in years.

The cramp went away after a while, leaving a sharp soreness behind it. Palmer lay down beside the girl again, amused at the shallowness of his dream and how closely it paralleled reality. He tried to figure out what reality the girl was living through. He knew – from her versatility – that she enjoyed this kind of intimacy with men. The tiny color pictures on the wall of her room had showed several men her age, all grinning at the camera, she with them.

He wondered what she was feeling about him. There were so many possibilities. It might all be on the purely physical level, for instance. He had never thought of himself as anything prodigious in bed – although he knew from his experiences with Virginia that the right partner worked wonders for him – but the girl seemed satisfied. When she reached orgasm it was obvious what was happening and occasionally she could climax twice before he reached his. That spoke well for the coupling, didn't it?

But it might be a career thing, too. American girls thought nothing of sleeping with the boss. European girls couldn't be expected to differ that widely. She seemed quite intelligent enough to know that this affair would do her no harm at Ubco.

What a bastard he was, thinking about her that way.

What a cold banker's head he had, just as Virginia had told him on more than one occasion, as Edith had said too. What a fishy heart, no heart at all, to be able to analyze the girl's reactions that coldly. Wasn't it possible that she felt something real for him?

It was possible, his head told him coldly, but not probable. What could she expect of such a liaison? If he remarried – which he was in no hurry to do – he might marry Virginia. She was his proper age, had the proper background. This girl would be an innocent savage in the jungle of New York City. Virginia knew her way around as well, or better, than Palmer. And the whole age gap thing was too much.

He realized his mind was wandering now. Even so, he enjoyed its aimless, foolish stumbling.

She had such a luscious body and such an oddly exciting face. She seemed to enjoy him so much. It was impossible to imagine her in the stench and riot of New York.

Palmer frowned as he stared at the ceiling. He'd been wrong

78

to ask Virginia to talk with Harry Elder. He'd been wrong to promise her he'd call Harry. He had no intention of letting any of New York's mess rub off on him during this trip. He felt about the city as if New York were a vast cesspool of infection.

He thought it odd that he could feel so completely cut off from New York, so pleasingly in tune with Europe. He supposed it was because New York had never meant that much to him. His city had been Chicago for most of his life. He'd come to New York only three years ago after his father had died. He'd merged the old man's bank into a bigger one and gotten out with a giant chunk of stock.

New York had meant problems to him from the very beginning, when he'd been pitched headlong into the kind of nasty, behind-the-scenes political fighting all banks live with. And then there had been the attempt of Jet-Tech International actually to take over the bank.

Palmer's eyes were closed now as he lay on the bed, but he was wide awake. He saw the dream again, with Eddie Hagen clapping the gigantic silver candlesnuffer over Harry Elder's head. It was a brutal image and it came back with intense clarity, even to the smudge of soot on poor Harry's face.

Virginia had been right to call his board a bunch of thieves. Three years ago, Jet-Tech had been one of the bank's biggest customers, so ballooned with Defense Department expansion plans that Palmer could no longer justify lending any of the Jet-Tech companies more funds at their present low rate. The company had retaliated by trying to gain control of the Ubco board in a proxy fight.

Palmer had headed off the grab – with the help of Harry Elder and also of Virginia, who in those days had worked as Ubco's director of public relations. But, in the process, Palmer had given away more than he bargained for. He'd had to rely too heavily on his old World War II Army Intelligence chief, General Hagen, who now headed up a group of space-age companies around Boston and had been added to the Ubco board. He'd had to give Jet-Tech a few seats on the board, too, after all. And he'd horrified Virginia so thoroughly with all his cold-blooded manipulations that she'd quit Ubco and killed off their affair, more or less simultaneously.

Why, in his dream, had it been Hagen who snuffed out Harry Elder?

Palmer's eyes opened wide and he sat up in bed. The ache in

79

his groin increased slightly and he massaged himself gingerly there for a moment. He wondered what bothered him most about remembering those days, the brutal maneuvering or the loss of Virginia?

He supposed neither of them would ever recapture the wildness of their first passion, even though they were back together again and he was separated from Edith. Everything was different the second time.

The girl had an answer for that. 'So we try a third and a fourth time.' It was the philosophy of someone in her twenties. Once one neared fifty, Palmer realized, the try-try-again idea lost most of its practicality.

What was she really like? Palmer turned to look at her. She was lying on her side facing him, one hand under her head, the other cupped under one breast. All her makeup and eye shadow had come off hours before in the shower and in their lovemaking since. She looked young enough to be his daughter.

He tried to see himself through her eyes. He'd kept his body pretty much in trim, not by doing anything about it but more through the good fortune of being by nature thin and having a metabolism that used up what he ate, even when he overate. He'd tried to keep his mind young, or at least open to new ideas. He supposed his mind had never really been young. But he did take pains to consider new things on their merit, rather than rejecting them out of hand.

Then what did she see when she looked at him? Someone she at first hadn't liked at all? The irresponsible American, the hit-and-run Wild West hero? But then, somehow, her attitude had changed after he'd visited Virginia's church at Morienval. And then, after the meal and all that wine. . . .

His hand had showed her that there were two men in him. Palmer stared down at his hand for a moment. One of the men she probably still disliked. The other she seemed to feel great passion for.

Palmer's education had been of the old-fashioned kind that included Latin and Greek. He reflected that passion, as a word, had deteriorated over the centuries. The feeling between them had none of the pain or torment of the passion that was Christ's on the cross. Passion was dying, wasn't it?

He turned back to watch her again as she lay in sleep beside him. Beneath her closed lids, her eyes lay perfectly still in the deepest of slumbers. It had been years since he'd enjoyed that dead-down-to-the-bone sleep. Perhaps one didn't sleep that way after a certain age. Too much at the upper levels of unconsciousness kept drawing one back to the real world. Even my dreams, Palmer thought, only act out real anxiety states. A schoolboy could interpret them.

He flattered himself that she trusted him. Else how could she place herself so firmly in his hands as to surrender herself to such sleep?

Palmer got up off the bed and went to the east window. The sky was light. He guessed it was nearly six in the morning. Earlier, back at her apartment, they'd thought to have her change to a dress she could wear at today's meetings. She didn't have to go back to her apartment now. All Palmer had to be sure of was that she be out of the hotel by, say, nine, so that she could come back after nine thirty and greet him when Dauber was there.

He realized he'd slept only in spurts for two days. He would have to remain nominally alert at the meetings scheduled for him today, but tonight he would definitely turn in for a long night's sleep.

Palmer sighed. He knew he would do no such thing.

CHAPTER 13

M. Savat-Thiers (10 A.M.) was immensely learned and immensely dull. But, as a top fiscal aide in the French government, he had to be listened to both by Palmer and Miss Gregorius, who dutifully translated Savat-Thiers to Palmer and Palmer to Savat-Thiers.

M. Guignon (11:15 A.M.) was younger, with a blond beard. He represented a different secretariat than M. Savat-Thiers. M. Guignon brought his own interpreter.

M. Pringloire and Mme. Auvergnoit (1:30 P.M.) were from the tourism apparatus. Both spoke English fluently.

Col. Maudlinger (3 P.M.) represented the French side of NATO, among other things. He brought four aides, none below the rank of captain, and two interpreters, one for French-English and one for English-French.

M. Jeunefils, M. Crainquemort, and M. Leury-Cohen (4:30

81

P.M.) were high-level economic and political aides closely concerned with France's relations to the Common Market. They preferred to speak French throughout, but said good-bye very warmly in English.

Dauber was waiting with the Buick outside the ministry building when Palmer emerged with Miss Gregorius at half-past five. 'You got the real red carpet treatment,' he told Palmer. 'Most of these monkeys quit long before five.'

It took a certain amount of maneuvering to lose Dauber. First Palmer had to invite him and the girl to drinks at the George V bar. Then he offered to drive Dauber to his home in St. Cloud. He and Eleanora then had to meet Mrs. Dauber, a tall, skinny girl whose upper teeth were undergoing orthodontia of some sadistically obvious kind.

'At my age, too,' she said, offering them extremely bad martinis, warm and loaded with vermouth. 'But the whole bite must change or I lose everything. So –'

She gave a gallant, jolly little shrug and Palmer got a quick snapshot of the scene after he left, with Dauber standing angrily over her. ('What in God's name ever possessed you to start yammering about your teeth, for Christ's sake!')

Palmer smiled at her. 'I think you're brave to try it. I understand from my daughter that it hurts like hell.'

'How old is she?'

'Fifteen, going on thirty.'

Everybody laughed dutifully except Miss Gregorius, who didn't quite get it or else was too rapt in her own thoughts.

Finally the ordeal ended and Palmer drove the girl back to her apartment in Montmartre to change before they went out to dinner. They mounted the first flight of stairs and stopped at a landing to embrace. Her arms almost crushed him to her and her tongue darted demandingly between his lips. They held onto each other as they mounted to the attic floor and entered her apartment.

Some mail lay on the floor inside the door. She stooped to pick it up, leafed quickly through the envelopes and then stopped at one with a red-and-blue striped *Mit Flugpost – Par Avion* border. Palmer couldn't see the stamp as she quickly ripped open the envelope. A color photo dropped onto the floor and she fell to her knees to retrieve it.

'Tanya?' Palmer asked.

The girl looked up at him from the photograph in her hand.

Palmer could see the bright-eyed little girl standing between two men, one his age and one in his twenties, it seemed.

'Your father?' he asked. 'Your brother?'

Her eyes darted from his face to the photograph, then back to him again. He couldn't understand her expression, a veiled look, not at all what he'd expect of a mother who had just gotten a new photograph of her daughter.

'Are you all right?' he asked.

She nodded and reached inside the airmail envelope, but found nothing else. Evidently only the photograph had been sent. She turned it over but there was no writing on the back except the date printed by the processing laboratory. It showed that the photograph had been processed two days before.

'That is Tanya,' Palmer persisted.

The girl turned the color photograph over and stared at the image again. 'Of course it's Tanya,' she said then.

'And the two men?'

She shook her head. 'You don't know them?' Palmer asked.

Her glance flashed up to his face again. 'Oh no,' she said quickly. 'I . . . I of course well know them.'

Palmer listened to the tortured English and wondered what had shaken her so badly. He waited. 'They are neighbors of my parents,' she said then, speaking slowly and much more carefully. 'Next-door neighbors. You see how Tanya is laughing.'

Palmer looked at the photograph again. 'They're all laughing,' he said. 'It's a laughing contest. Are you sure you're all right?' She had slumped against his leg, half lying at his feet amid the spilled envelopes on the floor.

'I'm all right,' she said after a while. 'Just help me up, yes?'

Palmer got her to her feet. 'You young people,' she said weakly, trying a smile, 'have to remember that an old woman like me doesn't have your stamina.' She sighed and brushed meaninglessly at her face. 'The whole long boring day. I kept falling asleep. Did anyone notice?'

'Not I.'

'You dozed once.'

'During Colonel Maudlinger's dissertation?' He led her to the couch-bed and sat her down. 'You need a pick-me-up. I have just the thing.' He gestured mysteriously, like a magician, and ducked his hand into the cabinet where he'd placed the bottle of Sève-Fournier when they had left the apartment the day before. The bottle wasn't there.

Palmer swung the door open and saw that the bottle was now on the other side of the cabinet. He decided his memory could not possibly be good enough for him to swear to the change in position. So, saying nothing about it, he produced the bottle and poured her a glassful.

'*Merci, chéri,*' she murmured.

'*De rien.*'

She made a face. 'French rubs off on you, yes?'

Palmer watched her collect herself and put back together the girl she had been on the stairs outside her door. Odd about that photo, he thought. Odd thing to send, no note or inscription, just like that. And airmailed the day it got back from the lab. But, oddest of all, her reaction to getting it.

'Where do your parents live?' he asked, pouring himself some of the liqueur and sitting down in a bentwood easy chair across from her.

'East of here.'

'That narrows it down.'

'Oh, sorry.' She toyed with the glass for a moment. 'As a matter of fact, I had counted on seeing Tanya for a day or two if I accompanied you to Bonn and Frankfurt. My parents live not far from Frankfurt.'

Palmer frowned. 'In Germany?'

'The city of Trier. On the Mosel.'

Palmer nodded. 'I know Trier.'

She looked down at her glass of Sève-Fournier and rotated it slowly. 'Did you have one of your spectacular adventures there?'

Palmer let a little silence settle between them. He was amazed that she had the power to anger him with such a simple bit of (possible?) sarcasm. 'No,' he said then. 'I know it in another connection. It was the summer retreat of the Emperor Constantine.'

She put down the glass and knelt beside his chair, hugging his legs. 'I apologize. You are the most learned lover I've ever had.' She started to smile. Her hand went up to her face and suddenly she was sobbing bitterly.

Palmer watched the tears spurt wildly as her face contorted and reddened. 'What is it?' he asked, holding her. 'What is it?'

She shook her head from side to side with a kind of reckless abandon, as if wanting to dash her brains out against him. 'It's nothing, n-nothing.'

He tried to lift up her face by her chin, but she ducked away from him and scrambled to her feet, running into the bathroom. She closed the door behind her and he could hear water running.

Palmer bent over and picked up the photograph of Tanya. He examined the background of the scene. It seemed to have been taken in some sort of farmyard where the brownish earth was broken into clumps, as if by a harrow.

There was a building in the distance with a rather high fence connected to it. He studied the smiles on the two men. It really did seem like a contest as to which could produce the broadest grin. Palmer decided this particular kind of pose was quite common, even among sophisticates who did it for comic effect. He couldn't pretend to know if the two men were being genuine or poking fun at themselves. The girl's smile, more tentative, seemed real enough.

Palmer retrieved the envelope in which the photograph arrived. It bore a Luxembourg stamp and postmark. He knew Trier to be only a few miles from the Luxembourg border. There was no return address on the envelope.

He turned over the photograph and studied the date stamp. The numbers seemed to have been printed very lightly by photographic means, together with a name, perhaps that of the processing laboratory. Palmer got up and took the photograph to the wall of casement windows. The days was dying quickly, but the sky was still orange behind the Eiffel Tower in the distance.

He tried to make out the name printed beneath the date. It was in some kind of script or cursive type and extremely hard to read. It looked like two words. The first was something like *Schnelfot*. That could be a kind of telescoped trade name, perhaps, meaning 'fast photo' or something of the kind. The second word had only four letters and after a while Palmer decided it was 'Jena.'

He was sitting on the window ledge, still looking at the back of the color photograph a few minutes later when Eleanora emerged from the bathroom, her face quite pale and composed. She had applied new makeup.

She stopped and looked at him. 'I think Tanya's grown since her last photo, don't you?' She laughed slightly. 'Of course, how would you know? I feel as if you've been with me forever, but it's really only been three days.'

She reached for the photograph and he gave it to her. 'Jena,' Palmer said then.

'Pardon.'

'Jena. The Carl Zeiss works used to be there.'

'Yes?'

'Now it's in East Germany.'

'Oh?'

CHAPTER 14

Palmer got out of the cab in front of the Ritz and paused for a moment before entering the hotel. He glanced at his watch and saw that it was six in the morning. The sky was beginning to lighten faintly and a few cars and people were already moving through the Place Vendôme. His eyes felt gritty, his mouth parched. He managed to get his key from the desk without any conversation from the too-alert concierge.

As he entered his suite, Palmer could hear the telephone ringing. He cursed and dropped the key, with its heavy metal fitting, on the carpet. He picked up the phone. 'Yes?'

'Oh, you are safely back.'

She sounded concerned. 'I'm a big boy,' he said. 'Did you think I might be abducted by Apaches on my way from your apartment to here?'

'We no longer have Apaches in Paris,' she said, laughing softly. 'We have students.'

'Thank you for calling. Good night.'

'Good night.'

He heard her cut off the connection at her end. Palmer held his end of the line open for a moment, listening. Nothing happened. He replaced the telephone in its cradle. Instantly it rang again. He snatched it up.

'Yes?'

'Ready with your long distance call, M'sieu Palmaire.'

'I placed no call.'

'Ready New York,' the operator continued in an implacable voice.

'Ready Paris,' said another no-nonsense voice.

'Woods?' Harry Elder asked in his rasping voice.

'Harry, why are you calling me?' Palmer snapped irritably.

'Christ, where the hell have you been? I've had this call in all goddamned evening. It's after midnight here.' Harry paused for a moment. 'You alone?'

'Yes.'

'Don't get pissed off, Woods,' Harry said. 'I dislike making this call as much as you dislike taking it.'

'Is it about all this stuff you've been cabling me?'

'Are you alone?'

'I said I was.'

'Okay.' Palmer could hear the older man draw a long, steadying breath.

'I'm at home, Woods. This isn't going through any bank switchboard. I'm paying for the call myself.'

'Marvelous.'

'There's a question of security involved.' Harry's scratchy voice, which always sounded as if it had been left out too long in the rain, grew hoarser as he assumed a more confidential tone. 'Your buddy from the good old days has been acting strange as hell.'

'What?' Palmer squinted into the darkness of the hotel suite. He assumed Harry was referring to Eddie Hagen, Palmer's commanding officer in World War II, who was now on the Ubco board. But he couldn't understand why the reference had to be so oblique. 'Go ahead,' he said then.

'He's been pressing to have the People's Bank acquisition moved up to top priority. He wants it decided on, yes or no. He's pushing me hard as hell.'

Palmer sat down next to the telephone. 'He knows we decided to sit tight. We're supposed to do nothing till a way is found to weed out mob influence in that bank.'

'Nevertheless, he's pressing. He tried to get a meeting of the action committee convened this morning, but I said I wasn't feeling up to snuff and postponed it. I can't stall too much more.'

'Why is he pressing?'

'Says it's a capital error to let the thing hang fire. Says he wants it cleared off the books one way or the other.'

'He's crazy.'

'He's got a lot of support on the board, Woods. I'm afraid he could bring it up at the full board meeting next Monday and poll a majority vote.'

'Who's with him?'

There was a pause. Palmer could hear faint musical beeping noises up and down the scale in the distance and the muffled chatter of other conversations flying across the cable at the same time as his.

'Let me give it to you straight, Woods,' Harry said then. 'It's the same old crowd who wanted to give Jet-Tech its head two years ago. Only this time they're actually on the board . . . where you put 'em.'

'What's their sentiment,' Palmer asked, 'drop the People's acquisition or go ahead with it?'

'They don't seem to care which.'

'I don't get it.'

'Neither do I,' Harry admitted, 'but the whole thing has the aroma of a week-old trout.'

Palmer sat back in his chair and stared at the growing light filtering through the curtained windows of his hotel suite. He found it hard to concentrate on anything Harry Elder had told him. It all seemed so distant from him, like ants scurrying about in an overturned honey pot.

'Woods?'

'I'm still here.'

'Say something.'

'I'm trying to think. None of what you tell me hangs together. If they go ahead with the merger, Ubco takes over a tainted bank and we pay a stiff price in bad paper and bad management. If they want to drop the merger, we run the risk of the whole mob thing coming out in the open. Some newspaper will start digging till it finds out the real reason we dropped the acquisition after – how long? – ten years of waiting.'

'That would hurt Ubco as much as it hurt People's.'

'Much more,' Palmer said. He closed his eyes. Keeping them open was beginning to be too painful. He found himself massaging the inner part of his thigh below his groin.

'Woods?'

'Yes, still here. Look,' Palmer went on, 'you've got to develop more information, Harry. Otherwise everyone's floundering around in the dark. Talk to some of the board members in private. Try to find out who's been telling them what.'

'I've done that. Nobody knows anything.'

'Or says they don't.'

Harry Elder sighed. 'Woods, you'd better jet back here for a few days, at least to attend the next board meeting.'

'Can't possibly.'

'You can't afford not to.'

'Can't do it, Harry.'

'What kind of bait did this Foundation for Economic Study give you? What's so important about their goddamned mission that you can't drop it for a few days, even a week, and still get back to it later?'

Palmer was shaking his head slowly, doggedly. 'No can do, Harry.'

'You mean no want to.'

'Maybe,' Palmer agreed. 'Maybe I'm tired of that den of thieves we've got there in New York. Maybe I'm getting old and lazy. Or maybe I'm just enjoying myself too much over here.'

'If you let your old buddy have his way,' Harry promised, 'you sure as hell won't enjoy anything back in New York. For some reason, Woods, this guy means you no good.'

'Can't believe it. We're old buddies.'

'Screw that. He's up to no good where you're concerned.'

'I might get the idea, from your broad hints, that Eddie is fronting for someone else?'

Elder produced a wheezing sound meant to be a bitter laugh, Palmer supposed. 'A group of someone else's, let's say,' he remarked. 'A group that needs this merger more than they need life itself. This bank of theirs up in Westchester is on its last legs. Woods. They've gutted it of assets and left a fairly respectable shell for the world to see. But they desperately need to be taken over by Ubco so they can run for cover under our umbrella. Too much of their paper is too far overextended. It's all got to balloon and bust unless we bail them out.'

'They're foolish to think we'd buy them under such circumstances.'

'Not foolish,' Elder corrected, 'desperate.'

'Not likely, Harry. These boys have resources you and I know nothing about. Their cash flow from gambling alone would float half a dozen smaller banks.'

'I tell you they're desperate because they look desperate, smell desperate, and are doing desperate things. Over and above that, Woods,' the older man added, 'is the ripe plum they'll have of infiltrating the Ubco structure, placing a few officers on our table of organization like fifth columnists, and then sitting back

89

to let nature take its course. We can't have that. We can't have mob moneymen in our officer cadre.'

'If what you're telling me is true, Harry, we already have at least one representative right on our board of directors.'

'That's the way I read it, all right.'

Palmer sighed. 'It's late. I'm tired, Harry. Try to stall this crisis past the board meeting. You can do it. And if you can't, I won't blame you. At least you tried.'

There was a longish pause. When Harry Elder spoke again, his voice had grown so harsh with emotion that Palmer found it hard to understand exactly what he was saying, although there was no doubt what he was feeling.

'Listen, Woods,' the older man rasped, 'I watched you tame these monkeys with the fanciest display of footwork I ever saw on Wall Street. I watched you whip them in line a dozen times since. You can't tell me you'd lie down and let them crap all over you. Christ, it's nothing to me. I'm damn near retired as it is. But I hate to see a young guy like you let the whole thing fall apart because you're too lazy or whatever to make the effort.'

Palmer started to respond, then forcibly stopped himself in order to remain calm. He didn't intend to go back to New York now and that was that. But he respected Harry Elder enough not to hang up in his ear. 'Let me think about it, Harry,' he said then in the classic put-off. 'It's not an easy one to figure. Let me mull it over and get back to you.'

'When?'

'Soon.'

'Soon is too late,' Harry persisted.

'Soon as possible.'

'Woods...' Harry stopped. 'Oh, what the hell. I did what I could. I consider myself a friend and I've done what a friend should do. What you need now is a goddamned keeper or something. Good night. Call me.'

'Good night.'

Palmer replaced the phone, stood up, and went into the other room to lie down on top of the bed. He kicked off his shoes and loosened his tie. He had appointments in three or four hours from now. The whole report of General Edward Hagen's apparent treachery might be overblown or it might be true. The inferences Harry Elder was drawing could be right or totally wrong.

It all seemed so far away from him. He stared at the ceiling for a moment and had a picture of himself in his own office on Fifth Avenue in New York looking down at the people on the street below, depersonalized dots of movements, tiny insects, not real people. He closed his eyes and fell asleep almost at once.

CHAPTER 15

M. Auteuil and M. Lancthon (10 A.M.) represented the French central banking facilities. They spoke medium-to-poor English and relied heavily on Miss Gregorius to interpret fine points of their discussion with Palmer of dollar inflow and outflow. She seemed quite alert, although Palmer could see very faint smudges of mauve under her eyes.

Maj. ffolkes-Bruyère (11:15 A.M.) spoke perfect Oxford-accented English and went out of his way at one point – in talking about dollar spending by U.S. military dependent families quartered on French soil – to refer to the fact that his mother was British.

By arrangement, Dauber met Palmer and Miss Gregorius at noon with the bank's seven-passenger Mercedes. As Palmer entered the car, he saw that Dauber had brought along someone else.

'I expect you know each other,' Dauber said, indicating the new man.

Palmer examined him briefly. He seemed about Dauber's age, mid-thirties, with a business suit of more European cut, still recognizable as American, longish hair, and what Palmer took to be contact lenses that didn't seem to fit too well. He had a long, narrow face like Palmer, but his complexion was sallow and his mouth had been compressed, possibly since birth, into an extremely thin line. Palmer noticed some sort of skin rash below his chin that shaving had wreaked havoc with this morning.

'I haven't had the pleasure,' Palmer said, helping Eleanora to a seat opposite him and next to the newcomer.

'That's right,' the man said, extending his hand. 'I'm Forellen, from the foundation.'

Palmer took the hand and found it strangely damp. 'Mr. Forellen?'

'Stan Forellen, sir,' the man said, digging into his hip pocket for a small wallet from which he extracted a business card. He handed it to Palmer.

'Stanley J. C. Forellen,' the card read. European Director, Foundation for Economic Study.' The foundation's New York address was engraved in the lower left-hand corner in extremely tiny type and its Paris office on the Avenue de l'Opéra was similarly engraved in the right-hand corner. All in all, Palmer saw, a great deal of information had been compressed onto a tiny bit of stiff vellum. He wondered how many people had good enough eyesight to read it all without a magnifying glass.

Tucking the card away in the breast pocket of his jacket, Palmer gave Forellen a small smile. 'Miss Gregorius, of our Paris staff. She's acting as interpreter on this mission. What did they ask you to do, check up on me?' He let the smile linger to make sure Forellen knew he was joking.

'Not at all, Mr. Palmer,' the man responded in dead earnest. 'By no means. They made it very clear that you had a completely free hand in everything. I mean, your briefing is right from the top, so to speak. And it's weeks fresher than mine, of course.'

Palmer listened to Forellen's voice and placed it somewhere in the midwest United States. It wasn't quite the Chicago accent Palmer knew he himself spoke, tones produced somewhere up in the head, more muffled than clear speech required, vanadium-steel consonants cutting through with terrible clarity, but vowels softened toward the schwa sound. Forellen had the impeccable consonants – his r's. especially, cut like diamonds – but he did something to his long o's that irritated Palmer, who wondered if he weren't from farther east, possibly Ohio or even western New York.

Palmer realized suddenly that, since he hadn't spoken, neither had anyone else. This was one of the problems of being the ranking person in the group, a problem Palmer had never been entirely able to solve by one of the standard means. He knew, for example, that as top dog, he ought always to keep the rest on their toes. Questions usually did the trick.

'Are you having lunch with us, Mr. Forellen?'

'If I may, sir. I file regular reports on foundation matters and I thought you might be able to give me an inkling of how your own mission is progressing.'

'So they did ask you to check up on me.'

'Oh, by no means. Not at all.' Forellen's pale blue eyes swiveled this way and that as the Mercedes navigated the thick noontime traffic. He fastened on Dauber for a moment before realizing that Dauber's loyalties were with Ubco, not the foundation. His glance locked on Eleanora's knees for another instant, then tore loose. 'It's just that I do have to report and your mission is the hottest thing we have going on the Continent.'

'Do you report every day?' Palmer asked.

The blue eyes widened for so split a second that Palmer almost missed the movement. 'Nothing like that,' Forellen said. 'Once a month is more the case, although with a mission like yours on the fire, they like weekly progress notes, if possible.'

'I see. Well' – Palmer turned to Eleanora – 'I suppose we could give him a few thoughts at lunch. I haven't been making too many notes. Have you?'

The girl's face, completely in repose, took on so sudden an air of interest in the conversation that Palmer was sure the look was spurious. Her glance flicked past him and a faint smile removed the indistinct pout her lips had in repose. 'I have a few notes left over from translating some of the longer interchanges.'

A frown wrinkled Forellen's almost squared-off forehead. 'No real notes?' he asked, trying to keep the disappointment out of his voice.

'Highly irregular, eh?' Palmer said.

'By no means. Not at all,' the man responded too quickly. Palmer could see that his mind was trying to cope with the problem of telling a visiting bigwig – who was doing the Foundation something of a favor and paying for it out of his own pocket – to mend his ways and shape up.

'Nothing of the kind,' Forellen went on, exhausting his gamut of disclaimers. 'I'm sure your memory is well up to the job.'

'I'm not as sure as you are,' Palmer said.

Dauber found this funny, for some reason, and began laughing. Palmer's surprised glance stopped him cold. 'We'll find out at lunch,' Palmer said then.

The Mercedes was moving more swiftly west now along the broad Champs-Élysées. In the distance, Palmer could see the immense white bulk of the Arc de l'Étoile. He turned to Dauber. 'Where is lunch?'

The younger man looked flustered for a moment. 'I thought – It's such a fine day, I thought –' He took a breath. 'Would you like to dine out of doors? I have a reservation at the Pré Catalan restaurant in the Bois de Boulogne. Is that – I mean, is that all right?'

Palmer's glance turned to Eleanora. 'How does that sound?'

'Quite good.'

Palmer looked out the window. His eyes bothered him slightly. The sockets still felt coated with a fine layer of emery dust. He hadn't actually noticed what kind of day it was until now. The intense blue of the sky set off the white monument ahead of them with a theatricality that seemed almost artificial. 'Wasn't rain predicted?' he asked Dauber.

'Since yesterday.' Dauber considered this humorous, too, and laughed. 'I guess you've brought the sunshine with you.'

The four of them digested this sticky sentiment in silence as the Mercedes swung wide around the Arc de l'Étoile and headed southwest on the Avenue Foch. Palmer watched the area grow slightly more wooded as they traveled farther from the heart of the city. The Eiffel Tower moved past on his left at a stately pace. He stared at it for a moment, seeing it up close for the first time, and remembering how misty it looked from the window of the girl's apartment, veiled in gauze like a nature painting of the 1890's.

At the Porte Dauphine the car moved more slowly into the Bois past a tall building with an immense courtyard. 'The old NATO headquarters,' Forellen said suddenly. He hadn't spoken for some time now and Palmer wondered what had suddenly squeezed out this droplet of information. The Mercedes nosed into the Route de Suresnes, a curving road between thick stands of chestnuts and sycamore. Their foliage, not yet full grown, was still the pale green of spring.

'What about this place?' Palmer asked, indicating a grand old restaurant with extensive lawn tables on their right. Dauber shook his head, as did Forellen. Palmer glanced at the girl inquisitively.

'Not expensive enough,' she said. Dauber's laugh had a synthetic, abrasive quality, but this time Forellen joined him, which seemed to make the moment slightly less awkward.

Palmer watched to his left as the car branched off onto a road that led around a long, narrow lake. It being the lunch hour and the weather fair, the benches were filled with people who had

94

brought their bread and wine with them. Some had propped up short fishing poles whose lines and bobber floats lay almost motionless in the still water of the lake. A striking blonde in crotch-high caramel-colored boots allowed a white borzoi to drag her with long, loping strides past the lunchers and fishermen. Palmer glanced at Eleanora and raised his eyebrows appreciatively. She grinned for an instant and made her face return to impassivity. Palmer wondered if any of the byplay between them were obvious enough to excite interest.

'Lovely park,' he said.

Both younger men nodded in unison, like a pair of wind-up mechanical birds. The girl said: 'This is the Chemin de Ceinture du Lac inférieur. It's a beautiful place to walk.'

'I see nothing *inférieur* about this *lac*,' Palmer observed.

Her hand flew to her mouth to stop the giggle before it came out. Her eyes widened enormously, as if the pressure of her laughter was going to be too much to contain. Then she calmed down and nodded sagely. 'Here we go,' she said as the car turned off on a right-hand fork into a road that ran past the Racing Club.

'Racing Club?' Palmer asked. 'Is that French?'

'*Mais, oui.* Rasseeng Cloob,' the girl said, her face so terribly deadpan that Palmer realized he was about to start laughing, which wouldn't do.

'Connected with the Longchamp racetrack?'

She nodded. 'It's here in the Bois, near the river. Also the steeplechases are here at Auteuil.'

'I see.'

'Would you care to see some racing?' Dauber cut in then.

'No.'

The younger man subsided as quickly as he had popped up with the suggestion.

Palmer watched the early summer foliage. Then: 'Didn't we meet a M. Auteuil this morning?' He kept his voice casual, chatty.

'Yes,' she said very calmly. 'The one with the large teeth.'

'Mother frightened by a horse,' Palmer murmured. He could sense, rather than see, that she had turned away from the rest of them to hide her face. He was afraid to look at her for fear of breaking up. It was amazing, to him, this conspiratorial attack of giggles they seemed to have generated between them, something he hadn't experienced in years, if ever.

The chauffeur braked the car to a halt near the restaurant and whipped out of the driver's seat to open the door nearest Palmer. Everyone stretched as they stepped out onto the gravel drive. Dauber led the way across the close-cropped lawn to a collection of tables and umbrellas and each with its own round, white damask cloth and cleverly folded napkins.

They sat down and ordered aperitifs, a martini for Dauber, a Pernod for the girl, and nothing for Forellen. Palmer asked the waiter for Sève-Fournier.

'Grand Marnier?' he asked.

'No, Sève-Fournier.'

The waiter's eyes clenched tightly, as if Palmer's strangely accented pronunciation were as piercing as brilliant sunshine. He swiveled to Miss Gregorius. '*M'sieur a demandé Grand Marnier, n'est-ce pas?*'

'*Mais, non, pas du tout. Avez-vous Sève-Fournier?*'

'*Qu'est-ce que c'est que ça?*' The waiter had grown suddenly bored.

'*Connaissez-vous cette liqueur? Sève-Fournier?*'

'*Non, ma'moiselle. N'existe pas.*'

'*Ah, non! C'est le vrai!*' Her voice had a slight edge of anger.

'*Je suis désolé, ma'moiselle.*' He bowed deeply and turned back to Palmer. 'We do not have this liqueur, m'sieur. Would you prefer something else'

Palmer, who had watched the way the two younger men followed all this with avid attention, shrugged slightly. 'It's not an aperitif anyway. I'll have Pernod, too.'

They sat in silence after the waiter left. Palmer's glance traveled slowly over the lawn of the park before them. An immense beech, its massive trunk scaly with age, spread huge limbs in every direction. In the noonday sun it cast a gigantic inkblot of darkness around it.

'The largest tree in Paris,' the girl volunteered.

'Quite old?'

'Napoleonic.' Miss Gregorius turned to Dauber. 'Yes?'

Dauber's look of alarm started Palmer laughing again. 'I wouldn't know, I'm afraid.'

The girl turned to Forellen who barely repressed a slight motion of recoil. 'Not at all,' he said quickly, 'by no means ask me. I'm terrible on history.'

Eleanora stared at the beech for a long moment. 'The armies of England and France,' she said in a faraway voice, as if quoting something read long ago in a classroom, 'totally devastated the Bois de Boulogne in 1815. The entire stand of oaks, some of which had dated back to Clovis and Charlemagne, had to be razed. In their place acacia, chestnut, beech, sycamore, and other small trees were planted.'

'Then chances are,' Palmer said, 'this particular beech doesn't antedate Napoleon.'

'But surely he was alive. On St. Helena, but very much alive.'

Palmer inclined his head in a gesture of agreement. 'Good point.' He turned to her. 'Where did I ever get the idea you were a novice in history?'

The sun struck bright auburn highlights in her hair. She avoided his glance. 'Perhaps from me?'

The drinks arrived and, at the same time, they ordered their lunch. As they sipped, Forellen fumbled in his jacket pocket and brought out what Palmer took to be a small transistor radio. The younger man laid it on the damask linen and flicked a red switch. Palmer saw that the machine was a miniaturized tape recorder, now running.

'If you don't mind, sir,' Forellen said, 'I find this the simplest way to take notes. You can start talking any time you want.'

'How about turning it off until we've finished eating.'

Palmer's voice had grown terribly cold. Forellen volunteered: 'Size of a pack of king-size cigarettes. I have a thinner one made up as a cigar case. It fits i –' He stopped cold.

Palmer switched his attention from the recorder to Forellen. 'Go ahead. You were saying it fits . . . into an inside pocket?'

'It could.'

Palmer nodded. 'But this one has a much greater capacity.'

'Yes.'

'Which makes it better for debriefing.'

Forellen's eyebrows drew closer together and a vertical slash appeared between them directly over his nose. It gave him a pinched, stingy look. 'Debriefing?' he echoed.

'I have a marvelous idea,' Palmer said, hefting the recorder in the palm of his hand. 'You take notes with a pencil today. I'll take this along,' he added, dropping the recorder into his pocket, 'and tape all the rest of my interviews. Before I leave Europe, I'll have someone – Miss Gregorius? – get the tapes transcribed and edited. You can have a copy, of course.' He smiled pleasantly at Forellen. 'By you, I mean the foundation. Back in the States, that is.'

There was a long silence. 'I know you won't mind,' Palmer

said then. 'Since you didn't seem to approve of my casual approach to note-taking, this will certainly put things on a businesslike basis. Any objections?'

Again no one spoke. Finally, Forellen's glance lifted from the level of Palmer's pocket to his face. He cleared his throat.

'Not at all,' he said. 'By no means. Nothing of the kind. Of course.'

CHAPTER 16

They had stopped by Fauchon's on their way from the last meeting of the day to her apartment in Montmartre. Palmer had arranged for a case of Sève-Fournier to be delivered to her and had taken one of the twelve bottles. They had stopped at the store's grocery department on the way and now they were lying in each other's arms on her bed.

The apartment was small enough so that even a few things out of place could make it look messy. Palmer's clothes lay carelessly draped over the table and the girl's hung from the arm of the bentwood chair. The unopened liqueur, still in its wrappings, stood on the kitchen sink. Her string bag, bulging with the loaf of bread, sausage, cheese, and pears she had bought, sat on the floor halfway from the kitchen alcove into the living room.

Palmer lay face up and the girl lay slightly at an angle to him, face down, her head cradled on his stomach. He could tell from her breathing she had fallen asleep shortly after she had reached her climax. He supposed he had, too, but that had been some minutes ago and now he was awake again, staring at the ceiling and watching the light from the dying day outside tint the white plaster pink, then salmon, then orange, and now a bloody kind of dark red.

For a moment his eyes traced the dark brown ceiling beams, up one, down another, left, right, and back again. He still felt a gritty sensation behind his eyeballs and he wished he could remain as peacefully asleep as the girl.

She seemed totally at ease with him. He wished he were that way with her.

He shifted slightly and looked at the poster of the three-year-old boy pissing into a soldier's helmet. Then he looked at the string bag of groceries. From across the room he imagined he could smell, taste, the pears. In his youth, on the family summer estate in Wisconsin, paddling his canoe on the family lake or hiking through the pine forest, he could remember the pears and apples he had eaten as if their taste were still clear and wet in his mouth. Local pears were the best, especially those stolen from nearby orchards. There was something faintly stale about those cook bought at roadside stands. Nothing beat the taste of fruit fresh off the tree.

Palmer suddenly recalled the little old man with the rosy cheeks in that restaurant in Compiègne the other night. Not everything could be remembered, but a snatch of conversation did come back about ... about the freshness of *les asperges*. 'Nowhere in Paris will they have them this fresh,' the little man had sworn. He was undoubtedly right.

Shifting slightly again, Palmer tried to keep from waking the girl. She moaned softly but remained asleep. He watched her face, lying amid the dark blond hairs of his chest and abdomen. Her bangs had fallen away from her forehead and he realized that in sleep she had taken on an intense look of questioning, an almost scholarly look, as if in search of something very important and hard to find.

Palmer wished he could sleep as she did. As a means of getting away from the turmoil and tenseness of New York, the trip had now proved itself a failure. If it weren't that Harry Elder was whispering dire warnings about Eddie Hagen, then it was the curious Mr. Forellen and his hidable tape recorders. And if it weren't either of those, then it was the color snapshot of her daughter Tanya, mailed from Luxembourg but processed behind the Wall in East Germany.

Or if none of these had ruined the peace of the trip, then it was the fact that his briefcase, which he had carefully set up as a decoy to attract attention, had indeed attracted quite a bit. And over it all was the faceless Herr Schirmer in Bonn, waiting to hear three words whispered by H.B. in New York.

He sighed and, holding her head very gently, rolled out from beneath her and lowered her head slowly to the bedspread. She stirred but didn't awake.

Palmer slid off the bed and padded silently across the room in bare feet to the bentwood chair. He worked quickly because there was very little to check. Nothing had been sewn into her undergarments or dress. He flipped open her notebook and found only what he had seen her scribble in it from time to time. He unlatched her handbag and went quickly but thoroughly through its contents. Thin Florentine leather wallet he'd seen before. Lipstick, compact with mirror inside, small notebook, empty of writing, pencil, pen. . . .

Off at the very peripheral edge of his vision, Palmer could see that the girl's eyes had opened. She hadn't stirred yet, but he was almost certain she was watching him.

He felt a moment of panic. It simply wouldn't be possible to explain what she'd caught him doing. If he looked up now to confront her, the whole thing would be out in the open and could only go one way. He might learn much more than he really wanted to know. So might she. If, instead, he finished his scrutiny of the handbag and put it away, turning from the bed and looking out the window to allow her to compose herself and pretend sleep if she wished, then the incident could go two ways. She could pretend not to have seen. Or she could still confront him with what he had done.

Palmer realized he had a third possible course of action. Holding open the bag and turned away from the bed, he walked to the table where his trousers lay, extracted a fifty-franc note from his pocket, and folded it into her wallet. Then he replaced the wallet, snapped the bag shut, and put it back on the bent-wood chair.

'What the hell did you do that for?' she asked.

Palmer straightened abruptly and whirled on her, as if in surprise. 'Did what?'

'Put money in my bag. Am I a common whore?' She had raised herself on one elbow and her eyes looked almost black with anger.

'I don't want you spending money on me,' he said. 'You spent almost fifty francs for the groceries. It isn't right and I didn't want any arguments about it.'

The fierce look disappeared. 'You're insane,' she said, smiling. 'It's only money. But for a moment –' She stopped herself and her look became guarded again. 'Never mind. I'm insane, too. I apologize.'

'For what?'

'For thinking ... what I was thinking.' She rolled on her back and beckoned to him. Am I forgiven?'

'Let me show you.'

100

'A large amount?'

He was on top of her and he could feel her legs braced against his hips, pressing inward. 'As large as I can.'

'There may be a way I can help enlarge matters.'

This time, after he fell asleep, he didn't wake for some time. When he did the room was dark. He knew she lay beside him because he could hear her steady breathing. He held his watch to his face and decided it was either ten minutes to eight or forty minutes after ten.

He felt much better now. His eyes were no longer gritty. He couldn't remember any particular dreams he'd had. The rudimentary anxiety dreams of the past few days had stopped. He wondered if he mightn't after all salvage what peace he could from this trip.

The New York problems, for instance, could simply be ignored. He seriously doubted if Hagen and his 'faction' on the board would renege on the acquisition at this point. It would be self-destructive, more injurious to Ubco than to the mob-controlled bank they were supposed to acquire. Chiefly, of course, it would injure Palmer's own reputation to have this particular dirty linen laundered in public. But he could always point out that the merger plan had been initiated seven years before he'd ever come to the bank. He'd inherited a problem, not created it. Of course, one had to be on the scene to make this disclaimer. Until he returned, if anyone wanted to slash his character into ribbons, he had a clear field. Somehow the prospect didn't seem too distressing.

If, however, Hagen and his group accelerated the purchase of the smaller bank and actually folded it into Ubco's mix of subsidiaries, there was still no lasting harm done that Palmer couldn't undo – with some trouble, of course – after he got back. Chiefly he'd have to see to it that every man in People's Bank answerable to the mob he fired and every investment on the books related to mob business ventures be liquidated. It would take time, but it wasn't all that impossible to do.

So much for New York. Palmer's eyes opened in the darkness. He could barely make out the faintly less gray rectangle on the wall where the poster hung. The European problems weren't as easy to lay aside, he realized.

He had to know what the girl really was.

That came first. He was too old and too cynical to think that she would cease to be enjoyable if he found she had an ulterior motive for being with him. We all have our ulterior motives, he told himself. Hers may be quite understandable, quite – what was the word – acceptable? Well, perhaps not acceptable as much as permissible.

But he had to know the truth about her if only to stop suspecting her of worse things.

Forellen, now, had climbed to the top of his list of worrisome people. For that matter, so had the foundation. Palmer recalled his original suspicions about the foundation and wondered if first impressions weren't always best.

He was quite aware of the number of foundations, institutes, and research centers in America whose true motives were not what they seemed. Some were set up, he knew, as tax-free shelters of one kind or another, deduction-producing entities for wealthy givers. Others were generated by twists in the Cold War and came into being simply to fulfill the needs of some secret or little-known governmental agency. Some started in life as perfectly legitimate enterprises, only to be subverted at a later date. He wondered if the Foundation for Economic Study were any of these things.

It bothered him that Forellen was so obviously a contact agent sent to debrief him of useful information before he might forget it. Was Forellen merely one of H.B.'s boys, sent to keep an eye on Palmer? It didn't seem at all likely that H.B. needed such help. And Forellen was much too awkward to work for H.B. It bothered Palmer even more that even were the foundation simon-pure and beyond reproach, it carelessly allowed some of its employees to carry on in such an undisciplined way that they were mistaken for agents. Finally, it bothered him most that the foundation could be entirely legitimate and Forellen could have infiltrated it for some other purpose.

When it came right down to making a decision about it, Palmer felt as loath to move as he had with the girl. He genuinely didn't want to know what she was. But he just as genuinely had to know.

Lying in the darkness, he sighed softly, just once.

CHAPTER 17

This time Palmer arrived at the Ritz well after seven in the morning. The lobby was as deserted as it had been at six the previous morning. But this time the telephone in his suite was ringing even as he put his key into the lock.

He let it ring while he took off his jacket and shoes. It had to be a call from panicky Harry Elder and it could wait. Palmer moved into the living room of the suite and sat down in an armchair before picking up an extension phone on the end table.

'Palmer here.'

'Ready New York,' a French operator announced.

'Ready Paris.'

Palmer waited for the noise that would signify that Harry had been connected. He glanced at his watch. It was after one in the morning in New York. Or in Larchmont, rather, where Harry lived. His telephone bill for the month would show some stiff charges. Palmer heard the added sound of presence on the line as the New York operotor connected her caller.

'What is it, Harry?' Palmer began without preliminary.

'Darling, it's me,' Virginia said.

Palmer sat up straighter in the chair. 'Good grief, hello. How are you?'

'Fine. I'm terribly sorry to wake you at this ungodly hour, darling, but Harry Elder was here tonight and he made me promise to phone you. He thinks I may be able to get you to come back, just for the board meeting on Monday.'

'I wish Harry would keep you out of this.'

'So do I. But he's desperate.'

'It isn't fair to you to pull Ubco chestnuts out of the fire. You don't work for us any more.'

'I'm so happy I don't.'

'Um. Yes.'

'Woods?'

'Yes?'

'I love you, darling.'

'I love you, too,' Palmer said swiftly. 'Is there any way you can tell Harry to go to hell and stop bothering you?'

'He keeps saying he's doing it for you. He swears he's got nothing to lose whatever happens but he hates to see you injured.'

'How loyal can one old duffer get?'

Virginia said nothing for a moment. 'That's unkind,' she said then. 'It's unworthy of you. Woods. He means well and he's the only decent human being you've got over there at Ubco.'

Palmer felt his face redden. 'Really? What if I told you Harry Elder owes me plenty for advancing his son through the hierarchy faster than he should go?'

'I'd point out that Donny Elder is a very capable young man. You aren't doing Harry a favor by promoting him, you're just helping yourself.'

Palmer stood up and began pacing the floor in his stockinged feet. 'Harry's estate is eighty percent invested in Ubco stock and he's got a damned vital interest in which way things go.'

'That's a perfect argument for listening to him, instead of ignoring him.' She paused for a moment. 'Woods, we have to stop quarreling about this. I'm sorry if you feel defensive, but the plain fact is you should come back for the board meeting.'

'I have appointments that day with West German bigwigs. It's impossible.'

'Appointments can be postponed. They'll understand.'

Palmer began to feel hemmed in by her arguments. He picked up the telephone and began pacing in wider arcs, stretching the cord to its limits. 'You don't seem to understand what this whole thing means to me,' he said.

'Obviously I'm missing something.'

'You are.' He could hear a sharp note in his voice and he tried to calm himself. 'First of all, whatever mission I'm on, basically, I'm on vacation. Secondly, I couldn't care less what Harry thinks will happen at the board meeting. I've figured out the alternatives and none of them frighten me. None can't be fixed up when I get back.'

She said nothing for such a long time that Palmer finally asked: 'Virginia? Still there?'

'Part of me,' she said in a somber voice. 'The other part is trying to figure you out. I guess it's a life work, isn't it? And maybe not worth it.'

Palmer's first impulse was to hang up. Instead he was silent for a while. Then: 'Will you do me a favor?'

'I guess so.'

'Neither of you has enough information. Can you develop some more? Can you talk to your newspaper friends, your political people? It's wrong to ask me to upheave my whole schedule because of some vague fears and rumors.'

Palmer waited. He had used a version with Virginia of the put-off tactics he'd used with Harry. They were two very different people with quite different loyalties to him. Suddenly he was sick of people being loyal to him and, thus, requiring special treatment, maneuvering, kid-glove handling. Wasn't it possible for them to let him alone, even at this distance?

'How much information do you need, Woods?' Virginia asked then in a dead flat voice. 'How much do you think is available? Are you under the impression that details of this kind are common knowledge around town? Or do you just want me to go away and leave you alone?'

'I'm sorry. But I need a lot more to go on than I've got.'

'I see.' He could hear her make a sound at the far end of the line, something like a sigh of impatience, or a sob, but he couldn't be certain. He could picture her face, though, with its huge dark eyes. He wondered if she were in bed at this hour.

'All right,' she said then. 'It puts me in a peculiar position, trying to dig out information about a competitor bank. But, I suppose that's as good a cover story as any.'

'Right,' he agreed. 'That's the idea.'

There was a pause. 'Are you all right otherwise?' she asked then.

'Fine.'

'Health and such?'

'Just fine.'

'All right. Good night.'

'Virginia?'

'I'll call you t – No. You call me.'

'I will. Tomorrow night?'

'That's Thursday. Call me Friday. I need as much time as I can get.'

'Thank you.'

He waited to hear her voice. After a moment he realized the line was dead. She had hung up at her end. He pressed down the cradle of the telephone and held it there for a while. Then he let it up. After a moment an operator said: *'Oui?'*

'This is Mr. Palmer. On that New York call I just got.'

'Yes?'

'How long have they been trying to get me?'

'One moment.' As he waited he could hear her riffling through slips of paper. 'That call was first placed at midnight,

Paris time, m'sieur. The New York operator has been trying it every hour since.'

'Thank you.'

Palmer hung up and walked slowly into the bedroom. For seven hours Virginia had been trying to get him. She was in no doubt, therefore, that he'd been out of his hotel all night and had only come back at seven in the morning.

He sat down on the edge of the bed and stared at the pattern of the rug at his feet. After a while he lay back on the bed full length. But he found it impossible to fall asleep.

CHAPTER 18

Out of sorts, tired and very jumpy, Palmer made the chauffeur-driven Mercedes wait half an hour for him while he took additional time shaving and getting dressed. The chauffeur had reported in to the downstairs concierge at nine o'clock precisely and it was well after nine thirty when Palmer got to the lobby. He headed through the outer doors and stood for a moment just outside, surveying the already thick traffic along Place Vendôme.

He had spotted the Mercedes at once and knew that the chauffeur had seen him. Now he watched the long, dark brown car maneuver hesitantly, almot painfully, through the traffic maze. It took the man at least ten minutes to get safely through and it wasn't until he pulled up at the Ritz that Palmer saw Eleanora on the back seat of the limousine. He felt an instant lift of spirits.

'My God,' he said, getting into the car before either the chauffeur or the Ritz doorman could open it for him. 'No idea you were waiting.'

She shook her head very discreetly, as if cutting off the entire line of conversation. 'Good morning, sir,' she said crisply.

Palmer sat down beside her and the chauffeur and the doorman, fought to close the door behind him. The door man triumphed. There was something unhappy, almost surly, about the way the chauffeur slammed down behind the wheel and took the great car off in a curve that led into the very center of the traffic.

'You're Miss Gregorius,' Palmer said more loudly than usual. 'I remember you.'

Again the faint headshake. Palmer wondered why she was being this cautious. 'I'm afraid we are a bit late for our nine-thirty appointment, Mr. Palmer.'

'I'm afraid we are,' Palmer agreed. The lift he had felt at first seeing her gave way now and he was back where he'd been earlier, out of sorts and quite on edge. He wondered if hetero-sexual relations were really all they were cracked up to be. He wondered why women had such an effect on his spirits. He wondered if he could do without women and decided against it, temporarily.

'You slept well, sir?' she was asking in that flat, secretarial voice.

'Rotten, thank you.' He glanced sideways at her and produced a small, wry smile.

Under the cover of her notebook he touched her hand and squeezed it slightly. Her fingers lay inert for a moment while she glanced at the back of the chauffeur's head and at the rear-view mirror. Then she turned her hand palm up and squeezed his.

'I am terribly sorry, sir.'

'Well you might.' A pause. 'What's our appointment this morning? Who are we insulting by being late?'

She let go his hand and flipped through the notebook. 'M. Casseterre.'

'Castor? As in oil?'

'Casseterre,' she repeated. 'He is described simply as executive director. Of what I don't remember. If I ever knew.'

'What does Casseterre mean?'

She frowned and brushed at her bangs to keep them firmly in place over her high forehead. 'Ah, breaker of earth? Yes? Groundbreaker.'

'I rely on you, Miss Gregorius.'

'For such trivia?'

'For everything.' He watched the look of alarm on her face. Again the faint headshake. 'All categories of information,' he added then. 'For example, your *explication de texte* on the subject of the hectare was masterful, not to say voluminous.'

'I meant to tell you –'

'And your discourse on the trees of the Bois de Boulogne ... superb.'

'About the hectare, I –'

He patted her head to silence her. 'M. Casseterre,' he went on, 'is executive secretary of one of those NATO economic off-shoots. I forgot the name of it, but the initials are all anybody ever remembers. FANJU or BANFU or something.' He tapped the glass behind the chauffeur's head. 'Hello? Stop at a tobacco shop and get me a pack of Gauloises, please?'

'Certainly, sir.'

The girl frowned at him. 'You –'

'Thank you,' Palmer cut in. They waited in silence for a few moments until the chauffeur had guided the Mercedes to a corner. He hopped out and disappeared into a store.

'You don't smoke,' she said accusingly.

He bent over and kissed her hand. 'Why the formality?'

'Without Dauber here, we must be very proper.'

'Did something happen to frighten you?' he persisted.

'Not at all. It's just – The driver. I'm not certain. I just don't, ah, fully trust him.'

Palmer drew back from her. The edgy feeling enveloped him again. Time seemed to be crawling like a garden slug, leaving behind it a trail of slime in which one could get entangled. 'How do you mean, trust him?'

She leaned forward to the glove-leather seat that faced them, shoved her hand under one of the cushions, and pulled out a metal button about the size of an American quarter. Two twisted wires hardly thicker than threads dangled from it. 'I found this when he picked me up this morning.'

'You mean you were looking for something like this?'

She nodded. 'This is the first time I've been alone and able to look.'

'And you broke the wires?'

She nodded again. Palmer glanced at the tobacco store and calculated he had only a few moments left. He felt under the rest of the cushions and then made them change seats so that he could check under the cushions on which they had been sitting. He felt the edges of other upholstery and palped with his finger-tips the stitched edges of the ceiling cloth.

'I told you. I broke the wires.'

'It could have been a decoy mike.'

'I beg your pardon?'

He shook his head. 'Nothing else that obvious in the car. Maybe it's the only one. If so, it's the work of an amateur.'

They had just returned to the rear seat when the chauffeur

came back with cigarettes and a book of flat wooden matches. 'Thank you,' Palmer said. The driver got behind the wheel and the limousine moved off into morning traffic again.

'An amateur,' he repeated softly. 'Or something we were meant to find.' He paused. 'Perhaps meant only for you.'

Her eyes widened as she stared at him. She was wearing the same dazzle-pattern print dress she had worn the first day he'd met her. It occurred to him that she couldn't be too well paid, by American standards. Well enough as Parisian salaries went, though.

The Mercedes swung into a circular driveway that led between immense stone gates to what had once been a seventeenth-century chateau of some kind. Palmer helped the girl out and stood for a moment under the porte cochere. He glanced at his watch and saw that it was nearly ten o'clock. 'Pick us up at twelve noon,' he told the chauffeur and, taking the girl's arm, ushered her inside.

They walked for about a hundred yards on worn flagstones past intricately carved stone columns that arched thirty or forty feet overhead to form the great entry hall. Thin twin-tailed banners hung from pikes high up on the walls. No breath of air disturbed them. Palmer could smell a faint odor of mildew. He wondered whether it would bother anyone but an American. He wondered if this place were often shut up and only used on certain occasions. He wondered about the awkwardly hidden microphone. They reached a reception desk. A man of at least eighty years stood up. 'M'sieu Palmaire?'

Palmer nodded. 'To see Mr. Casseterre.'

'Suivez-moi, M'sieu-dame, s'il vous plaît.'

They followed him into a tiny elevator barely big enough for the three of them. The little old man closed the outer gate and the inner door. He began punching buttons and after a moment, groaning, the machinery responded.

The narrow elevator car, smelling of lemon-oil polish and mildew, inched upward one floor. The old man opened both doors and managed to squeeze himself into a corner of the car to let Palmer and Miss Gregorius precede him. Then he led them along one dark corridor into another and, finally, to a high doorway topped by a pointed Moorish arch.

Two dark oak doors, thick with carving, swung open. They were facing another reception desk of sorts at which a younger man sat. He jumped to his feet and came around the desk.

Palmer noticed that his glance went first to the old man, then to Palmer, and finally to the girl's legs, before returning to Palmer.

'This way, sir,' he said with a faint lisp, but no discernible French accent.

Palmer led the way this time, with Eleanora behind him a step. He kept his eyes on the male receptionist but gently inserted his right hand inside his jacket to switch on the tape recorder he had preempted from Forellen.

So it was with a certain sense of edgy surprise that the first person he saw when he entered M. Casseterre' office was Forellen.

The man's under-chin acne seemed even more mangled by shaving this morning, his long face even more sallow and unprepossessing. He jumped up and indicated the other man behind the desk with a sweeping gesture. 'Mr. Emanuel Casseterre, sir,' he began. 'Mr. Casseterre, Mr. Palmer.'

Palmer shook the man's hand and found it papery dry. He glanced at him during the amenities of introducing Miss Gregorius and getting her settled in a nearby chair near the window. Casseterre had the typical blocky European figure, wide and square-shouldered, legs short and planted wide. He kept his chin high, as if to readjust his height to Palmer's, but nothing could make up for the fact that he was a full head shorter so he sat down as soon as possible. Palmer sat across from him.

Casseterre looked more Baltic than French in the face, with wide cheeks and extra creases in his eyelids that pinched them down to a half-squint. His button nose had a dark brown wart on one side from which gray hairs grew. The close-cropped hair on his head, however, was the sleek, seal brown of a dye-job or toupee. Palmer relaxed in his chair and bared his teeth faintly at Forellen.

'Are you helping me conduct my interviews now, Stanley?' he asked.

'By no means. Not at all,' Forellen exclaimed. 'Mr. Casseterre and I have worked together on so many occasions that he thought it natural to, ah, invite me to the meeting.'

'This is your last, I take it, before moving on to Frankfurt?' Casseterre began in a rumbling kind of voice. 'I am honored that you have left me as the *pièce de résistance*, so to speak.'

Palmer smiled. 'I've reached some preliminary conclusions about the problem, as it affects U.S.–French economics,' he said. 'My understanding is that your competence extends

110

through the Benelux nations and Scandinavia. It would be helpful, therefore, if we could examine my conclusions in the light of these other areas.'

Casseterre began a long, slow speech of disclaimer, expounding on how little he really knew and how unworthy he was to sit in judgment of any kind on the talented, experienced, and brilliant Mr. Palmer.

Palmer listened to the deep voice, with its almost unaccented English, and wondered why it didn't sound like that of a Frenchman speaking. He realized after a while that Casseterre was dentalizing his t's and having a certain amount of trouble distinguishing between v's and w's. Palmer glanced at Forellen and wondered if his little cigar-case recorder were rolling quietly in his jacket.

Casseterre was winding up now and heavily throwing the conversational ball to Palmer. 'Honor us, if I may say so, with some of your preliminary conclusions, if you will.'

Palmer crossed one ankle over the other knee and sat back farther in the extremely comfortable armchair. He glanced at the girl and saw that she had been writing while Casseterre spoke. It occurred to him that since she was probably able to take shorthand she had been recording the conversation. That would make at least three versions of what would be said, the one he was taping, the one Forellen was taping, and the girl's. Fascinating. Almost like being on network television.

Palmer cleared his throat. It felt parched and scratchy. He wished he had gotten more sleep for the past few days, but he realized he would not have sacrificed being with her, even for sleep.

'I think the preeminent conclusion I've reached,' he said then, 'is that there's confusion over here as to what we in the U.S. mean by a balance of payments deficit. It's a matter of definition, really, and it doesn't help matters very much that we don't agree among ourselves in the U.S. on how to define it.'

Casseterre's thick, immobile mouth parted in a faint grin. Palmer had the feeling that it cost the man a lot to produce the muscle movement. He was getting a strong feeling of contrasts about Casseterre. His bulky, powerful body and cop's face said one thing. His flowery shower of flattery said something else. His title indicated one thing. His accent told Palmer another. In the long run, words were nothing. Words were the exclusive property of humans in all the animal kingdom. So words were man's secret weapon. Words were given man to lie with.

'For instance,' Palmer went on as cheerily as he could, imitating with some success the style of a senior professor of economics before a not-very-bright class of graduate grinds. 'For instance, we have two ways of measuring our balance. You may or may not be familiar with both of them. He watched Casseterre's thug's hand raise for a moment as if to indicate he knew, then fall as if to say 'let the fool rant on.'

'One is to measure the difference between dollars held abroad by central banks and large institutions and European moneys held by U.S. banks, institutional investors, and international companies. That gives us what we call the official-settlements account. On that basis the U.S. has a current deficit of about one-and-a-half billion dollars. It's gone higher before, and lower, too.'

Palmer glanced at Forellen, who had leaned back in his chair and closed his eyes for a moment. 'You're familiar with that method of striking a balance, aren't you, Stan?' he asked.

Forellen's eyes snapped open in surprise. 'Yes, I am.'

'Good. Then there's the other basis, which most people know about. We call it the liquidity basis and it simply measures all reportable transactions between the U.S. and the rest of the world, mainly imports and exports, of course. But since we have so many nationals living around the world or moving through it as travelers, what they spend is a factor, too. On this basis of measurement, our deficit is over two-and-a-half billion dollars. It's been a billion higher than that, at times.'

Casseterre's eyes brightened at the end of the lecture. 'And which method of measurement do you favor, Mr. Palmer?'

'Informally, I tend to take whichever method produces the larger deficit. It's not that I'm a pessimist. It's just that in trying to find a cure for this, there's no sense pretending it's smaller than it is. Find a cure to redress a deficit of, say, three billion, and you have found a way to recover two billion or one billion or whatever the figure really is. But if you start out by finding a way to get a smaller amount back, it won't work if the real figure's much higher.'

'Very sound,' Casseterre said. His faintly patronizing air had begun to grate on Palmer.

'And what sort of reactions to all of this have you had from the people to whom you have been talking?' the blocky man went on smoothly.

112

Palmer frowned. 'I beg your pardon?'

'That is to say,' Casseterre revised himself, 'what sort of conclusions have you reached as a result of your talks to date?'

Palmer's crossed leg straightened out slowly and his foot returned to the floor. He sat forward in the comfortable chair and was instantly much taller. 'I don't think I can regard my conversations to date as anything but privileged,' he said.

The indirect statement confused Casseterre for a moment. His glance flicked to Forellen, then quickly back to Palmer. 'I beg your pardon?'

'Quite so,' Palmer said, taking his words as an apology. 'You're forgiven.'

'Pardon?'

'I know you didn't mean to ask what my other conversations produced. That information, of course, rests with me for now and, eventually, with the foundation.' He turned to Forellen. 'Would you call that a fair summary of the priorities, Stanley?'

'By no means,' Forellen burst out. He stopped and winced, almost in slow motion. 'I don't mean that. I mean to say it is a fair summary. Quite fair. Except –' He stopped himself, glanced at Casseterre, and plunged on almost recklessly. 'That is to say, except for the fact that Mr. Casseterre is being asked to comment from a NATO viewpoint on material you haven't really given him.'

'Oh no, Stanley. Quite the contrary. I will ask him certain selected questions, as I have during most of these conversations to date. And he has the option of answering the questions or not.' Palmer turned back to Casseterre. 'That was your understanding, wasn't it?'

'Not quite,' Casseterre demurred. 'I had hoped to be apprised more fully of your findings to date before I committed myself.'

'I see.'

'Surely,' the bulky man rumbled on, gathering momentum as he talked and managing to get a slight note of indignation into his deep voice, 'you wouldn't expect one to make random comments more or less in the dark. It wouldn't be fair to anyone to demand that sort of response.'

'On the other hand,' Forellen put in, 'Mr. Palmer does have his own working methods. He can't be expected to –'

'But he's a fair man,' Casseterre interrupted rather harshly. 'He wouldn't expect a man in a responsible position to – what's the saying you have? – fly blind.' He wheeled the focus of his

113

eyes back to Palmer and let the glance bore in heavily. 'So, therefore, Mr. Palmer, will you be good enough to favor us with some inkling of –'

'It isn't really asking much,' Forellen assured Palmer.

Palmer sat back in the chair. He knew, finally, where he was. It amazed him that he hadn't realized before what sort of meeting this was destined to be from the moment he laid eyes on Forellen in the room.

He was in the office of Mr. Hard and Mr. Soft. There wasn't an interrogation team in the world that didn't use the technique. It had been devised back in the days of the Babylonian Police Department and hadn't been altered much since. Mr. Hard didn't play fair. He was nosy and mean and his voice could get loud. Mr. Soft was your friend. He even argued against Mr. Hard. He was on your side. He wouldn't upset you for the world. Mr. Hard would and did, or tried to.

Finally, you were wobbling so far off base that you gave in to one approach or the other. Either Mr. Hard scared it out of you or Mr. Soft cajoled it from your lips. One way or the other, you talked.

Palmer got to his feet and pointed his finger at Miss Gregorius. 'Close your notebook,' he said. Then, to Mr. Casseterre: 'I'm sorry I've wasted your time.' He turned and started to walk past Forellen, which was also the direction of the door.

He gave Casseterre until the point where he reached Forellen.

At precisely that moment he heard the man's heavy, rumbling voice say: 'This is most irregular, Mr. Palmer.'

Palmer turned back to find Casseterre on his feet, blinking slightly but whether with surprise or anger or a sham of both, he couldn't be sure. 'I agree, Mr. Casseterre, most irregular.'

'Have we – Has something been said to offend you, I wonder?'

'More done than said.' Palmer started to turn away again. He was of two minds as to which way to end the discussion. He could give in and spend the rest of the hour in polite refusals to confide information. Or he could leave now and save all of them the whole boring business.

'Something that has been done?' Casseterre persisted.

Palmer beamed avuncularly on Forellen. 'Tell him, Stanley, about the good old American verb "to whipsaw." '

Forellen's face was grayish. His nostrils looked white, as if the air had thinned and he was suddenly unable to draw enough oxygen from it. 'Whipsaw?' he asked mechanically.

'It's what I won't have done to me,' Palmer said. He patted Forellen's shoulder. 'Explain it to Mr. Casseterre, like a good fellow.'

He turned back to Casseterre. 'Once again, sorry for the waste of time. Good morning.' He gave Eleanora a thumb gesture toward the doorway. They walked out together, past the young receptionist, down a flight of stairs, and into the main entrance hall a few yards from the front door. When they stepped out into the sunlight, the Mercedes was nowhere in sight.

'Damn it, I gave him till noon.'

'Never mind. We'll get a cab.'

He took her arm and led her around the corner onto a broad avenue. 'You're going to tell me some time what happened in there, aren't you?' she asked.

Palmer neglected to answer her because he had begun trying to fit Casseterre to Forellen and vice versa. 'Won't you?' she repeated.

'Won't I what?' he asked, surfacing.

'Explain what went on in there just now.'

His eyes regarded her blankly for a moment. Somehow he had assumed she understood exactly what had happened. He wasn't sure why he'd made that assumption, whether because he felt she was familiar with interrogation techniques or simply knew more about all this than she let on. But her look of inquiry seemed genuine enough as she asked her question.

'If you do,' she said then, her face reddening, 'I'll be very kind to you.'

'Kinder than you have?'

'Kind beyond all dreams of kindness. I looked up the hectare in my dictionary. I am in a position to tell you how many are in a square mile.'

'You've already explained that,' he said, waving at a cab that passed without slowing.

'Wrongly.'

'Ah!' He glanced sharply at her. 'Don't disillusion me. I want always to remember that there are one hundred hectares in every six square miles.'

'But it's wrong.'

He hailed a second cab, which stopped. They got in. Palmer frowned heavily at her. *'Monsieur le chauffeur,'* he asked the driver, *'ditez-moi le définition d'un hectare.'*

115

'*Comment?*'

'*Connais-vous le hectare?*'

The driver squirmed around in his seat and removed the regulation one inch of cigarette from his lower lip. '*Comment?*'

'*Hélas!*' Palmer exclaimed. He opened the cab door. '*Allez, vitement.*' He handed the driver the unopened pack of Gauloises and ushered the girl out onto the sidewalk again. 'We'll wait till we find a driver who knows,' he told her.

'But I tell you,' she insisted, holding her hand to her mouth as she laughed, 'I know.'

Palmer shook his head. 'I'd rather have an impartial opinion.'

CHAPTER 19

The whole day had been handed to them, more or less, Palmer realized. He wanted to spend it wandering around Paris with the girl and, when he told her, she thought they should do only the things tourists did. 'I have never seen the things I should see,' she confessed. 'I've never had a real tourist to guide around town before.'

They stopped by the Ritz first so that Palmer could change out of his business suit and into a sports jacket and loafers. The girl waited downstairs in the lobby while Palmer picked up some message at the desk and went upstairs to change.

He found a round-robin letter from his three children, a cable from New York sent via regular RCA channels rather than Ubco's Telex lines, and three telephone messages from Stanley Forellen.

He threw the Forellen messages in the wastebasket without reading them. The cable was signed by Bill Elston, one of the younger vice-presidents of Ubco, who, with Harry Elder's son Donny, was one of Palmer's own protégés. The cablegram read: 'REQUEST PERMISSION PHONE YOU BEFORE SUNDAY, PLEASE RECABLE TIME AND PLACE TO MY HOME 128 E. 56 SOONEST. HOPE SEE YOU MONDAY. WM. ELSTON.'

Palmer tucked the cable inside his business suit breast pocket. If the message had come from Donny Elder, he would have understood it better. The son would certainly be backing up his father's request that Palmer return for the board meeting on Monday.

But Bill Elston was, in a real sense, Donny's chief rival among the younger bank vee-pee's. They were the same age. Both basked in Palmer's approval because both seemed to him the brightest of the lot. Where Donny had come up the easy way in banking – as had Palmer, by birthright – Bill Elston had found it tough going until Palmer rescued him from obscurity as an assistant treasurer. Bill had had none of the advantages of birth or family money. He'd put himself through one of these vague, formless midwestern colleges like Western Reserve or Northwestern by working evenings for a firm of certified public accountants. He'd earned a scholarship to do his graduate work at the Wharton School, but nowhere along the way had he learned to dress, talk, or behave like boys with Donny Elder's background. His uncertain manners were abrasive to Palmer, whereas Donny's were soothingly familiar. But, nevertheless, Palmer had promoted him step by step with Donny because he knew he was doing the right thing.

Now, it was clear from the cable, Bill had joined the chorus of 'inside' people urging Palmer to attend the Monday board of directors' meeting.

Palmer picked up the telephone and asked to send a cablegram. He gave the RCA operator Elston's address and then dictated: 'On the move and can't phone, but your message received and duly noted. Thanks. Palmer.'

As he listened to the operator repeat the message, Palmer's glance shifted slowly about the room and noted that one of the dresser drawers was ajar.

He hung up the telephone and strode to the dresser. When he opened the drawer he saw that his stack of white shirts had been badly disarranged. He checked the other drawers and found no sign of anyone's having examined their contents. As he changed out of his business suit, Palmer thought he could picture what had happened.

The agent had known he had the whole morning to search the room, say from ten o'clock when the meeting with Casseterre began, until noon. He had barely begun his search, however, when he'd been interrupted either by a telephone warning or by someone who came to the suite to give him the news that Palmer was no longer tied down with Casseterre. Panicking, perhaps, the agent had slammed the drawer and cleared out as

117

fast as possible. This pointed either to a poor operative with jangly nerves, or a careless one who underestimated Palmer's interest in how his shirts had been stacked. Or someone who might return and set matters straight when the coast was clear.

What worried Palmer now was what these bunglers hoped to find tucked away under his shirts.

He sat down and slipped off his shoes, changing to loafers. The other thing that bothered him, he realized as he sat there, was that the jumpy, careless agents who bungled this morning's search were certainly not the smooth operatives who had first cased the suite and been trapped only by the tiny hairs in Palmer's briefcase. The style and competence of work were totally different.

He reread the letter from his children, puzzling through Woody's oafish handwriting and pleased at how clear Gerri's backhand script had become. Tom, the youngest, still printed. Most of his penmanship had been learned in New York schools, while the older two had learned to write in Chicago. On the whole, Palmer reflected, if accuracy were the main goal – and it must be – he preferred Tom's printing, even though it permanently marked him as the product of a progressive school.

'Dear Dad,' the oldest, Woody, began. 'Hot as hell in New York. Got my SAT scores and you won't like them. Hope you're killing them dead in Europe. Best.' Palmer tried to remember which of the life-shattering examinations the SAT was, and vaguely recalled that, like the others, it dictated the shape of a student's future about as thoroughly as his bloodline would have a hundred years before.

'Dear Dad,' Gerri wrote. 'He's modest. His SAT is high enough to get him in some crummy college or other. At the school dance Friday somebody offered me a pipeful of hash. I took a drag and ... nothing. Learning fascinating details of the Norman invasion of Calabria and Sicily. Will you get down that far? If so, bring me back a Norman artifact. Small! Also learning my part for the school play, *The Beauty Part*, by S. J. Perelman. You won't get back in time to see me but I'll do a special performance for you. Love.'

Palmer wondered if the play were being given the same day as the board meeting. He had the feeling the entire world was conspiring to drag him back to New York.

'Dear Dad,' printed Tom. 'Come home soon. We miss you. Love.'

118

Palmer folded the letter away and glanced at himself in the mirror. He wondered whether he dared remove his tie and walk about Paris with an open collar. He wondered why not one but two separate teams of agents were interested in delving through his laundry. He worried that one of the teams worked for H.B. protecting the fate of Operation Overdraft.

He decided none of it mattered, none of it at all, compared to being with the girl. He hurried downstairs.

CHAPTER 20

Palmer lay on his back. The girl sat astride him, riding him like a horse. From time to time she sipped some of the liqueur and, bending down over him, let it pass from her mouth to his when they kissed.

After a while she got up and moved slowly to the window, her long legs like white shafts of light in the half-darkness of her apartment's living room. She pulled back the shade and stared down at the street, covering her breasts with her right arm and hand, in which she held the liqueur glass.

Palmer watched her for a moment and realized that she, in turn, was watching something in the street and would probably stand that way, her weight on one leg, her buttocks tucked up to one side, for a long time. He sighed with contentment.

The cool, quiet, darkened room was a refuge. It had been from the beginning and now it was even more so.

He knew every crack in the white plaster ceiling and the dark wooden beams. He knew where she kept everything, pots, pans, clothing, even her aspirin and estrogen pills. He had read all the titles of her books and leafed cursorily through all her magazines. He had mulled over her one scrapbook of pictures and even tried to read some letters on her desk in French and German. He had seen what there was to see through her windows, shopped in her neighborhood, climbed the hill with her, and come down by himself at dawn. He knew where the hard part of the mattress was and how to stop it from groaning while they were making love. He knew the different ways of helping her to her orgasm. He knew how she liked to be kissed and fondled. He knew as much about her as it was possible to know in so few days.

But one thing about her still eluded him and he was afraid to learn the truth of it.

He plumped up the pillow behind his head and watched her through a frame formed by his feet. The carefully tended bangs had disappeared from her forehead. She took no time away from him in this room to repair this crucial part of her appearance.

His glance moved from her to the tiny color photographs on the wall. He saw that she hadn't put up the new picture of Tanya and the two neighbors. He doubted she would. Everything about the photograph smacked of a code message, the way it looked, how it had been produced and mailed, and especially her reaction to it.

That it was a picture of the same girl as in the other pictures he had no doubt. The assumption was probably correct: this girl was her daughter. The message couldn't have been anything elaborate. The Luxembourg postmark was meaningless as a clue except that, like most neutral nations in Europe, Luxembourg was a prime control base for espionage networks. So were Switzerland and Liechtenstein and even Portugal, for that matter. On the other hand, Luxembourg lay near Trier, where her parents lived. Where she *said* they lived. Damn it.

Palmer closed his eyes. He was determined to exhaust the possibilities of the photograph before he took the risk of asking direct questions. The picture itself didn't seem to be carrying anything complicated in the way of messages. He knew, for example, that it was possible, by a series of object categories and positions to convey almost any information in a photograph. The number of pickets in a fence or the position of someone's hand or the distance one thing was from another told the story. This photograph didn't have the unnatural stiffness of such an overcoded message.

So, eventually, one came to the only explanation possible, Palmer decided. The photograph's message was simply: 'Tanya is with us.'

Could there be more to it? Only if the men had a special significance in their true identities, or their poses in the picture. This was impossible for him to fathom, Palmer realized. But, from what little he could be sure of, the message could only be some version of 'Tanya is with us.'

Or, to put it another way, 'We have Tanya.'

A faint chill shot across Palmer's shoulder blades. The ransom-blackmail ploy was as common as dirt. Everyone used it. If he were right about her, she had received the message after she'd met him. After they'd become intimate. It was as if someone who had had Palmer under surveillance, looking for a way in to him, had finally found it in the girl and was making sure the channel remained open.

Unless, of course, she had been told in advance to become intimate with him. But, in that case, there was no need to send the photograph, was there? Except as a kind of additional symbol of their power over her.

Them. The tendency was to equate 'them' with the Eastern Bloc. Palmer knew enough about the bases of power to know that there were dozens of 'thems' operating in the world, some well known, some undreamed of. That the photograph had been processed behind the Wall seemed to indicate an East German setup. This could be true, or it could have been fabricated to disguise the real senders of the picture. To anyone who took the pains to operate successfully in the clandestine world this minor added deception was as natural as taking a breath.

That was the whole trouble, Palmer realized as he lay on the bed and watched the girl. He was rusty and not much interested in getting back in practice again. The girl was – What? An amateur? Unwilling tool? Total innocent? Brilliant professional? It took another pro of a degree of sharpness equal to the opposition's sharpness to see through the layers of deception here. In fact, to determine whether there really was deception.

An unhappy, impatient sound escaped Palmer. He saw the girl shift position and turn toward him. 'A problem?'

'You.'

She stood motionless by the window. 'I worry you?'

'I'm very happy with you,' he admitted. Even to his own ears the words had a rusty sound, as if never before uttered by him. 'It's not that.'

'Oh.' Her eyes, under the high forehead, grew large with mirth. 'Happiness is not enough? *Pauvre petit.*'

'Sarcasm is out.' He smiled at her. 'Truth is in.' He could sense the unsteadiness of the breath he took then. 'Ready?'

She leaned back against the window frame and lifted her liqueur glass to him. '*Vive le vrai. Allons.*' She sounded sad, but resigned.

He shook his head, mostly at his own unwillingness to get

ahead with the question. He had told her the truth, that he was happy with her, but he had not told her the whole truth because he was realizing it, just this second, as he stood on the brink of losing it.

The truth was that he had never been happy with a woman the way he was with her. No one else had done this for him and he was abruptly aware that with one question he could bring it down into the dust.

'I'm afraid to ask,' he said then.

She put the glass on the windowsill and came to him. For a moment she stood over him in the half-dark, her breasts like glowing globes of light. Then she sat down beside him on the bed and began stroking his chest and belly. 'It makes everything easier if you don't ask.'

'I know that.'

'You Americans have a terrifying passion for asking questions.' She patted his pubis lightly. 'And when you get the information you want, you use it in such terrifying ways. It isn't human.'

He shook his head. 'I told you not to keep you-Americaning me.'

'But when you act like one, what can I do?'

'Politely ignore it,' he suggested.

'Why?'

'Because, I –' He looked up at her. He could feel his heart knocking sideways against his chest like a trapped animal.

'Why?' she asked again.

'Because I love you,' he heard himself say.

The room was very still for a moment. Two women in high heels walked by on the street outside and he and the girl listened to the sound until it had faded completely away. Then: 'It's very hard for you to say that,' she said.

He nodded. 'I haven't in a long time.'

'That's good.'

'And when I did,' he went on, feeling himself start to babble, 'it really didn't mean anything. It was just words. If you want to know – No. I *want* you to know. I want you to know this is the only time I've meant it.'

'And that in all your immense length of time on this earth, I am the only woman?' She smiled softly and leaned over to kiss his eyes. 'You Americans,' she whispered in his ear.

'I warned you about that.'

'You Americans bloom so late in life.'

He put his arms around her and pulled her down to lie next to him. 'You Europeans,' he said, 'fascinate us Americans. You bloom early and your lives are filled with such a tantalizing number of secrets.'

He could feel her snuggle in against him, her face nuzzling into the curve of his neck below his ear, her body curving against his thigh and legs. 'Women must have secrets,' she said then.

'I didn't realize that.'

'Otherwise we are only poor imitations of women. We must have secrets even from the men we love.'

The room emptied of sound again. Palmer hated the way, in his mind, everything seemed to fall into a terrorized hush at the sound of that word. It was only a word, after all. He knew what he was going to ask next and he could no more stop himself from asking than he could stop taking his next breath.

'Do you love me?'

She kissed his shoulder. 'I love you very much.'

Someone turned on a raucous recording of a rock singer and band in an apartment across the narrow street from them. The words were English, sung with a French accent. This didn't seem at all unusual to Palmer. He listened for a moment.

'Very much,' the girl said then.

He turned sideways and gazed into her face. She had the look of surprised pain that attends some great discovery. She seemed unable to make up her mind if loving him were a good thing or a disaster. He kissed her mouth and watched the slight pouting line of thought soften and disappear.

'But still,' she said then, 'I have my secrets.'

CHAPTER 21

The *bateau-mouche*, its all-window walls and glass roof brilliant with light, sailed under three bridges in rapid succession, the Solferino, the Royal, and the Carrousel. Inside, the music sounded jolly and loud as the waiters moved smoothly from table to table serving the evening meal. Between the entrée and the dessert course, the girl had taken Palmer up on deck. They stood near the prow of the long, fat boat, silhouetted against the light from below and the fainter *son et lumière* light from the shores of the Seine on either side.

Palmer's arm circled her waist. 'The young lovers,' she murmured. A breeze played with her bangs for a moment, lifting them and letting them settle softly back in place.

They watched the needle-narrow point of the Île de la Cité. 'That is the Square du Vert Galant,' she said. 'People fish from there.' She squeezed him slightly. 'Do you fish?'

'No. Not at all. By no means.'

'Thank you, Herr Forellen.'

'Do I look like a fisherman?'

She shook her head. 'Like a lover.' She pointed to the island of which the Square was the point. 'This is thought to be the oldest part of Paris, settled before Christ and called Lutetia. They were fishermen then. Fishermen and Celts.' She looked up at him. 'There is something very fishy about Herr Forellen, yes?'

Palmer glanced at her. 'Why do you call him Herr?'

'In German, *Forellen* means trout.'

'*Mein Gott.*'

She giggled softly and pointed to Notre Dame, newly cleaned, gleaming whitely in the distance. 'This is the last monument I shall point out to you, young lover.'

'Enough of the young.'

'But you are very young tonight. This light coming up from under makes you a boy.'

'Then you must be an infant. Tonight you don't even look eighteen.'

'I am like your daughter. What did you call her? Fifteen going on thirty?' She took his hand. 'Women are not to be trusted when it comes to age.'

'Just age?'

'They will be serving our dessert,' she said, pulling him with her. 'Let's get below.'

They returned to their table in time to have their picture snapped by the ship's photographer. Another bottle of wine had been served in their absence and they toasted each other silently. Palmer watched the rest of the Île de la Cité pass by through the glass wall of the boat. 'What's this?'

'Île St.-Louis. It should be of special interest to you. Bankers first built mansions here. But later all sorts of common folk were allowed in, Baudelaire, among others.'

'We're turning around,' Palmer noted.

'But we have more than an hour to go yet. These boats give one one's money's worth.'

'I'm glad you're economy-minded.'

'I? I have to be. The only person I know who doesn't have to be is you.'

Palmer nodded. 'Would you like me to buy you a mansion on Île St.-Louis?'

Her eyes widened for a moment. Then she grinned. 'Why not several?' She lifted her glass to him. 'It's a giddy business being in love with a banker.'

He laughed as he touched glasses. 'Giddier for the banker, I assure you.'

She sat closer to him and her voice dropped to a more confidential level. 'Tell me,' she began, speaking almost into his ear, 'is it true that you've never loved any woman the way you love me?'

'*Vraiment.*'

'How delicious.' Her lips brushed against his ear. 'Tell me something else. Do you love me enough to take me in your arms at this table and kiss me violently?'

'*Peut-être.*'

Her tongue darted into his ear for a moment. 'And if I asked you to get down on your knees and kiss me all over?'

'*Avec circonspection.*'

'And take off all my clothes and make love to me?'

'*Immédiatement.*'

'In front of all these strangers?'

'*Mais certainement.*'

'Very well, then,' she murmured. 'I so command you.'

Palmer pushed back his chair and had started to go down on his knees before she stopped him, laughing, and lifted him back into his chair. 'My bluff is called,' she said. 'But you see, I was right. You're no banker. You're a lover.'

'*Sans doute.*'

'And a linguist.'

'*Décidément.*'

'And a cunnilinguist.'

He laughed so hard that the people at the table ahead of them turned around. Palmer's face went deadpan. '*Avec dévotion, ma'moiselle.*'

125

He poured more of the cheap white wine and they touched glasses again before drinking. Palmer glanced around him. 'We'll never be welcome on *les bateaux-mouches* again,' he said, adapting the old punch line.

'Why not?'

Palmer glanced at her and fell silent. Every once in a while, as now when she didn't know – couldn't possibly have known – the context of the old joke, he became aware of the chasm between them. All at once he was dismayed at the idea of trying to bridge so many abysses all at once, the difference in age, in nationality, in general background, even in the way they looked at life. It simply didn't make sense to base anything permanent on such an overextended footing.

'It's an old and not very funny American joke,' he said then.

'It saddens you that, like so many things, it will have to be explained to me.' She touched his cheek. 'You don't have to explain it. We don't have to be equal. We are lovers, not business partners.'

Palmer held her other hand. Marriage was a business partnership if ever there was one. 'In America,' he said, 'we don't understand casual affairs, not in my generation, although we have them. We always assume they lead eventually to marriage. And marriage is definitely a business contract.'

She nodded. 'I know.'

'I was forgetting. You've been married, too.'

She held up two fingers in a V sign and nodded solemnly when he stared at them. 'Yes, twice,' she said. 'At seventeen and at twenty.'

'Do you ever see either of them?'

'Dieter is Tanya's father, so we see each other now and then, usually about money. I have retaken my maiden name, of course.'

'Where does Dieter live?'

'I'm not sure.' She sipped her wine and then poured more for each of them. 'Naples? He travels a good deal.' She sipped some more wine. 'It's clear to me that the marriage contract signs the death warrant of love.'

'You were very much in love.'

'He was handsome, you understand. Thin and tall and very blond. A former ski instructor, you know the type? You resemble him quite a bit except that in your face there is character and meaning. In Dieter's there was nothing but that goose-

down look of self-indulgence. You know, the parents' darling and now his own favorite person? But, my God, how I loved him. Then.'

'So you married.'

'*Natürlich.*' She stopped and frowned, then went on quickly. 'For a while it was the same, although perhaps a bit less so. Then I found that we had stopped talking about foolish, personal love things. Instead it was plans and programs. I'll meet-you-at-three-fifteen-sharp-and-don't-forget-to-mail-the-rent check sort of thing. Schedules, advance bookings, social tit-for-tats, weekends arranged months into the future. It's August, so this must be Oslo. It's May, so this must be Capri. Dinner precisely on the dot. Dirty laundry. Clean laundry. Lists, leases, wills, joint accounts.'

She stopped suddenly because Palmer had squeezed her hand hard, almost involuntarily, as if to dam the flow of reminiscence.

'I beg your pardon.'

He shook his head. 'I've been there, in marriage country. And with three children.'

'When Tanya came' – she held her hand to her cheek – 'Dieter was no longer his favorite person and mine. He had to share me with Tanya. Everything went quickly to pot. As you see.'

They were silent for a while. Then Palmer patted her hand. 'You still regret the divorce?'

'Not really. I think a child should have both its parents, or at least a man and a woman who show it what adults are like. Patterns for adults. But I wouldn't want Tanya to think that all men are patterned on Dieter.'

'Does he see her often?'

She shook her head. 'A few times a year, perhaps.'

'And you see her more often?'

Her glance darted to him, then flicked away. 'She lives with me. It's only now, when summer begins, that I ship her to my parents in Trier.'

'Are your parents German, then?'

'My mother only.'

Palmer disliked the way the conversation had suddenly become an interrogation. He wished she would either give him full answers or tell him to go to hell. As it was, he felt himself forced to continue asking fragments of questions to match the shards of answers.

'And your father?'

'Polish-Russian.'

'When did he emigrate?'

'In the 1930's. I believe.'

'And met your mother in Germany?'

'In Trier.'

'And you were born there?'

She shook her head and said nothing. 'Not in Germany?' he persisted.

She looked up at him. 'I was born in Asolo, a village in the foothills of the Italian Dolomites, in the year 1942. My parents were on the run at the time from Austria into Switzerland. They had crossed into Italy from Lienz and were trying to make their way to the Lombardy plains and, via the Trieste–Zurich line of the railroad into Switzerland, through the Simplon tunnel. They hoped to make Zurich, where they had friends, before I was born. My mother became quite ill with a fever during the crossing through the Dolomites on muleback. In the snow. They headed through Cortina d'Ampezzo to Belluno, where they found a doctor who wanted her sent to the hospital at Padua or Venice. But Asolo was as far as she got before labor set in. The midwife assured her I would die.'

'I'm sorry,' Palmer said. 'I didn't mean to pry.'

'But you did. So now you know. Are you ready to ask me about Tanya?'

Palmer sat back in his chair. The *bateau-mouche* had sailed past its landing dock and was moving toward the Eiffel Tower on its left. He could see the structure quite clearly through the window walls of the boat, each stage bathed in light as the tower narrowed to its peak.

'What about Tanya?' he parried.

'All about Tanya.'

She looked away from him now and, after falling silent for a moment, pointed to the Eiffel Tower. 'Completed in 1889, it rises a thousand feet over Paris but exerts only fifty-six pounds per square inch of pressure on the ground, the same as that of a seated man.'

'I said I was sorry.'

She turned away from him. 'Please,' he could hear her say in a small, pinched voice, 'please ask what you want to ask about Tanya.'

'I've forgotten.'

She shook her head so violently that the long sable hair at the back of her head swirled like flames. 'It's the unspoken thing. It sticks between us. Please ask.'

He touched the skin of her bare forearm and found her cold. He rubbed her slowly on both arms. 'I'm afraid to ask.'

'You must not be. I —' She turned back to face him and he saw that she had been crying without sobbing. The eyeshadow under her left lid was starting to soften and run. He touched it with the tip of his napkin and blotted it dry.

'I'm too in love with you to care what you ask any more,' she said somberly. 'Just ask and I'll answer and there will be an end to questions.'

'Do they have her in some kind of custody?'

Her large brown eyes blinked twice, fast, and Palmer realized that she had had no idea how much he had guessed or would ask. 'Who told you she was in custody?'

'The new photograph told me.'

'You misread it, then.' She took both his hands in hers and held them tightly. 'It doesn't tell me she's in custody.' Her eyes were still wide, but an extra fold at the corners of the upper lids told him it pained her to talk about the girl. 'It only reminds me that her life is in my hands.'

'I don't understand.'

'Yes. You do understand. The word "custody" doesn't explain it. I'm sorry you used the word. It sounds as if Tanya were in prison or something. She is with my parents.' Her hand went carelessly, almost wildly, up her face and into her hair, shoving the bangs brutally out of the way, forking the hair straight back over her head until her face shone unadorned like a nun's.

'The picture tells me never to forget that Tanya is a permanent hostage. As long as I have her, they have me.' She pulled his hands back and forth for a moment. 'You have children. You must understand the way they can become hostages.'

'Who is they?'

She shook her head and turned away. 'I don't know.'

'You must have some idea.'

'None.'

'If only by what they ask you to do,' he persisted.

'They haven't asked me to do anything. Recently.'

'But before?'

129

'Small things. Petty information. Minor reports.'

'From UNESCO files?'

'And others.'

'What others?' he pushed on. 'Ubco files?'

'Stop it.'

'I —'

'Just stop it.' Her voice had dropped to a low whisper.

'So the photograph really means, "get ready to serve us again." Is that it?'

'I beg you to stop.'

Palmer turned away. The boat was moving rapidly between the Left Bank and a long, narrow island planted with trees. A feeling of queasiness began to grow into nausea. He gulped his water. It was cold and soothing. He turned back to the girl and saw that she had been watching him with an expression of concern. 'Well,' Palmer said then.

'Yes.'

'Well, nothing.' He sat back in his chair and closed his eyes for a moment to let the dizzy feeling pass. What had gotten into him? Was he so much in love with her that it hurt him to hurt her?

'Are you all right?' she asked.

'As well as can be expected.' He opened his eyes and when he saw the worried look on her face, smiled at her, or tried to. He had no idea if the grimace suggested a smile or not. His jaw muscles felt rusty.

'But it's better that we got it out, isn't it?' she asked.

'I ... normally I'd say yes. Now that it's out, I'm not so sure.'

'There must be honesty.'

He shook his head up and down several times. 'By all means. Yours is the generation that prizes honesty above everything. Mine is the generation of hypocrites.'

'You mustn't say such things.'

'I'm the only one who can,' he assured her. 'I'm the only one entitled to level the charges. Do you still love me?'

'I adore you.'

'And I adore you.' He kissed her for a second, then gave her a longer one. When he drew back he was aware that he hadn't glanced around him to see if anyone were watching. He wasn't interested. 'I don't care if you gave out Ubco information,' he said then. 'That's how crazy I've become.'

'They never asked me for it.'

'If they ever do, give it to them.'

They burst out laughing and Palmer failed to check on their neighboring tables. 'But you're wrong about children,' he said then, sobering up. 'They aren't hostages. Only if someone takes the trouble to make hostages of them.'

'No. *Inherently*, they are hostages.' She filled their glasses again, unnecessarily. 'You are a rich man. Have you never feared kidnappers?'

'There are things you do to make kidnapping difficult,' Palmer explained. 'Certain routines, precautions, arrangements. You can never be sure, but you must never let it worry you and the children so much that it spoils living.'

'A hostage,' she persisted, 'is someone whose well-being you will pay to guarantee. And if you don't have money, you pay in services.'

The boat was turning back now to repass the island of trees on its other side. Palmer pointed to the island. 'Allé des Cygnes,' she volunteered. 'But there aren't any swans this time of year. However, I have a surprise for you. Look there.'

She pointed to a statue at the very tip of the island past the Pont de Grenille. The air had grown moist. Light diffused gauzily through it. Palmer squinted. There was something grotesquely familiar about the statue.

'It isn't,' he said then.

'But it is. It's a miniature copy of Bartoldi's original. Or else it's the model from which the big one was made. Does it make you homesick for New York harbor?'

'My dear, sweet girl,' Palmer said, 'I have never visited the original, except to see it from a helicopter once.'

'Never visited the Statue of Liberty?'

He put his arm around her and lifted her to her feet. 'Let's go up top. This fog will make everything prettier.'

'One catches cold easily on the Seine.' She hung back for a moment. 'Tomorrow morning we fly to Frankfurt. I wouldn't want you to –'

Palmer shook his head sadly. 'Plans, programs, schedules, list-making.'

'*Schrecklich!*' She kissed his hand and led the way to the upper deck.

CHAPTER 22

They walked along the water's edge of the Seine for a while after leaving the *bateau-mouche*. Palmer felt completely lost in the thin fog, but the girl seemed to know where they were heading. They passed two bridges and, after the Pont Alexandre III, with its gilded gingerbread decoration, they mounted a long stairway cut into the stone embankment and left the region of misty lights and swirling patches of fog.

Traffic was still fairly active around the Place de la Concorde, although it was now midnight. They stopped at the base of the obelisk and Palmer examined the peculiar artwork incised into the stone pedestal on which the tall Egyptian column had been mounted.

She was holding his arm and now she swung him to the west. She indicated the wild, plunging pair of sculpted horses on their pedestals that framed the immense vista of the Champs-Élysées. 'We face the Arc de Triomphe there in the distance,' she said and, at that moment, the lighting on the arch a mile away, as well as that around the obelisk, went out. Palmer glanced at his watch.

'I want to get back to the hotel for a phone call,' he said then.

'Your New York lady friend?'

'As a matter of fact, yes.'

'Does she call you every night, *chéri*?'

'No. She isn't supposed to call tonight, either. In fact, I'm supposed to call her tomorrow. But I have a peculiar feeling she'll try calling tonight. Soon.'

They strolled along the Rue Royale, turned right on the Rue St-Honoré and came at last into the Place Vendôme across the way from the Ritz. She stopped and nodded at the column in the center. 'That spiral of bronze. It's melted down from the cannons Napoleon captured at Austerlitz.'

Palmer glanced at the column, then noted the neon sign of the Ubco office was still lighted. He checked his watch again.

'You're thinking of nothing but the telephone call,' she said.

'Sorry.'

'The block between the Rue Royale and the Rue Castiglione has the best shops in Paris. You didn't stop at even one of the windows and ask me if I liked anything there.'

'I thought it was your duty to do the stopping.'

'The old-style mistress worked that way,' she explained. 'Nowadays, we try not to appear mercenary.'

Palmer indicated an approaching cab. 'Why don't you hop in and ride around for a few minutes? Then come back to my suite.'

'So I don't have to listen to your telephone conversation?'

'No, it's another odd feeling I have.'

'You're full of them tonight,' she said.

'I have learned to listen to odd feelings.'

'Very wise.' She hailed the cab and got in. '*A bientôt.*'

Palmer waited for the cab to circle out of the Place Vendôme. Then he walked to the Ritz and got his key from the concierge. 'A gentleman has been waiting for you, sir,' he was informed, 'in the lounge.'

Palmer frowned and walked in the direction the concierge had pointed out. Expecting Forellen, he found Dauber seated in a deeply upholstered banquette with a copy of *Newsweek* and a dead glass of beer on the tiny marble-topped table in front of him. He jumped up as Palmer approached.

'I hope you'll forgive this,' he began instantly. 'I tried calling off and on, but you were out all day.'

'What's the problem, Dauber?'

'I wanted to brief you on your flight tomorrow morning. And I wanted to say that your Mr. Forellen has been making my life miserable all afternoon. Something about rescheduling a meeting with Casseterre.'

'Impossible.' Palmer sat down on the banquette and indicated that Dauber join him.

'I told him that,' the younger man said. 'He started off angry as hell and by his last call was sort of pleading with me.'

'Well, he's your Mr. Forellen now. I'll be in Frankfurt about the time he phones you tomorrow.'

'I'll pick you up at eight thirty tomorrow morning, then.'

'That early?'

'The flight's at nine forty and you know the way these airlines insist on hauling you out to the airport ahead of time.'

Palmer nodded. 'You'll pick up Miss Gregorius first?'

'She's on my way in from St.-Cloud. I'll have the tickets with me unless you want yours now.' Dauber started to reach inside his breast pocket.

'Hold onto them. What are the accommodations in Frankfurt?'

'Suite at the Intercontinental. Quite decent.'

'And for Miss Gregorius?'

Something changed very slightly in Dauber's face, but it wasn't anything Palmer could put a name to and, thus, complain about. 'She has a room in the hotel, too.'

Palmer stood up. 'Did you come by car?'

'Yes. I couldn't find anyplace to park except over on the Boulevard des Capucines near the jolly old American Express office.'

'Know the corner,' Palmer said. 'I also know a shortcut.' He escorted the younger man out past the front desk and along the various salons to the corridor that ran all the way back through the hotel to the Rue Cambon.

'When you come out, turn right and walk to the Capucines.' He clapped Dauber on the shoulder. 'Don't for God's sake turn left or you run into a branch of the Chase.'

Dauber laughed at some length. 'I'll remember that, sir.'

'Also, the timer on your Ubco sign is off by five or ten minutes. Have it checked.'

The younger man's eyes widened slightly. 'I certainly will.'

'Good night.'

'Good night, sir.'

When Palmer got to his room he half expected the telephone to be ringing. When it wasn't, he decided his instincts had at any rate been half right. He'd suspected it would be bad to bring the girl into the hotel with him. Imagine if Dauber had seen them together this late. His uneasy feeling about Virginia's call had been a wrong guess, but he was quite pleased with the way he'd gotten Dauber away from the front entrance of the Ritz before the girl returned.

Palmer removed his jacket and cuff links, eased open his collar and tie, and stepped out of his shoes. He telephoned room service for some Sève-Fournier and ice and got it within two minutes. He poured himself a tiny glass straight, drank it, and made another with two cubes of ice. She had been gone from him at least fifteen minutes. She should return at any moment.

He walked to the window and stared out at the column in the center of the Place Vendôme. How many cannon had Napoleon captured at Austerlitz? Did armies capture equipment any more? Wasn't war a gentlemen's agreement that both sides would devour as much machinery of the other's as possible to keep the industries of both flourishing?

Palmer sipped the iced liqueur. He was getting old and cynical. It wasn't attractive to be either, but age was at least a natural phenomenon. Cynicism wasn't. A wide-eyed idiotic acceptance of every lie and deception fed him was the natural state of man.

Anyway, he reflected, it was no longer necessary to destroy war machinery. The passage of time made all equipment obsolete. And both sides worked to shorten obsolescence time more and more. If they weren't careful, they'd end up with fiascos made obsolete before they were off the drawing boards. A fine blunder that would be, to phase out equipment before a few billions in taxes had been pounded down the rathole by making prototypes and test models and the like.

What the hell was keeping her?

Palmer made himself another iced drink and sat down in an armchair. He'd told her to take her time, hadn't he? Or had he? He'd said 'a few minutes.' What were a few? Was she deliberately teasing him?

Perhaps she'd run into trouble. A girl alone, even in a town she knew, could always run into trouble. What if she'd bumped into Dauber? No, not the way he'd been routed out of the hotel. Was she having trouble getting past the goddamned concierge?

Did she have money for the cab? Maybe she was angry with him. Maybe she didn't intend coming back to his suite. Maybe the idea of Virginia's telephone call had angered her. It was a lot to ask of a girl. But she'd overheard Virginia's previous call without getting angry.

Palmer picked up the telephone and gave the operator Miss Gregorius' home number. The telephone rang a dozen times. Palmer hung up.

He stood at the window again. The Ubco sign was out now. The lights around the column were out. Paris was falling asleep. Where in the hell was the girl?

Why should she come back, anyway? What was in it for her? It was only a matter of time before she would begin to feel exploited and used. The very nature of what she wanted out of it – or rather, of how little she wanted from him – guaranteed that she would grow tired of it soon enough. And his poking around in her past didn't help.

He sat down and thought about his children being kidnapped. She hadn't said Tanya was being held. She'd said

135

something subtly different, but it came to the same thing. Extortion, using the child as hostage. He wondered why she'd never been curious enough to find out who 'they' were. Or was she pretending ignorance just to make things easier between them?

In any event, there was no good reason for her to return to him tonight. Tomorrow morning would be soon enough to pick up the threads of their peculiar relationship. She was being paid for doing one thing, interpreting from one language to another. She wasn't being paid to take the kind of abuse he had given her on the *bateau-mouche* tonight. The fact that he loved her didn't make up for his behavior.

He clasped his hands tightly in his lap. She had to come back to his suite. He was simply misjudging the time. It was only twenty minutes or so she'd been gone. He glanced at his watch and found that it was now almost one in the morning, forty minutes since he'd left her at the entrance to the Place Vendôme. He picked up the telephone and gave her number to the operator again. This time he let it ring twenty times, counting the double rings very carefully. Then he hung up.

As he did, he heard a faint knock on the door. He ran to it and let the girl in. 'Is Dauber gone?' she asked.

'You saw him?'

'I saw you standing in the lobby with him. So I took another drive in another cab.'

He hugged her. 'I thought you weren't coming back.'

'Why wouldn't I come back?'

'I don't know. I'm getting irrational.'

She had folded her coat on the foyer settee. Now she walked into the bedroom and lay down on the bed. 'I hope you remember the command I gave you on the *bateau-mouche*.'

'I think so.'

'Then start with my shoes and make it quick.'

CHAPTER 23

The telephone rang at 2 A.M. Paris time.

They had been lying head to toe on the bed and Palmer had been kissing her toes very slowly, one by one. After a while they had fallen asleep, or at least he had. He had dreamed that they

136

were bathing in a forest brook in the sunlight, lying on their backs in the shallow stream while the warm water flowed over their naked bodies shimmering in the sun. He awoke very slowly, by languid degrees, to find that she was licking the sensitive skin of his inner thigh in long strokes, like a cat cleaning another cat. Her hands were under him, cushioning his buttocks. When she saw him come slowly awake, her fingers tightened on his rump and began to knead the flesh slowly. Her hands were very strong. The telephone startled her so much that she gave a shriek and fell sideways almost off the bed.

'*Vive Mademoiselle New York!*' she cried, clutching at his leg to pull herself back on the bed.

'I'll let it ring.'

'You'll answer it.' She reached across him, her breasts dangling in his face and picked up the telephone. She handed it to him silently, then nestled in beside him to listen.

'M'sieu Palmaire? New York calling.'

'Palmer here.'

'Ready New York.'

'Ready Paris.'

'Woods, darling?'

'Ginnie, I thought I was to call you.'

The girl gave him a terrible frown of disapproval. Her lips moved silently, miming the words 'say hello.'

'How are you?' Palmer added lamely after the prompting. 'This is a pleasant surprise.'

'Did I wake you? I know it's late as hell there. But I was sitting here trying to make sense out of all this crap I've dug up for you and getting quite fed up with it. The more I thought about it the more I decided I'd better call and unload it.'

And see if I catch you out all night again, Palmer added silently. To Virginia, he said: 'I hope you found that Harry's imagining things.'

'No.'

The girl was stroking his penis. Palmer started to panic for a moment, then calmed down. 'Woods?'

'I'm here.'

'Are you alone?'

The damned woman was fey, always had been. 'Except for ⸱e girls from the Folies-Bergère, but they don't speak English.'

'Woods, Harry was right. You must be at the board meeting ⸱nday.'

137

'Can't be done.'

'I've checked the schedules. Air France, Lufthansa, or Pan Am all can bring you out of Frankfurt Sunday afternoon and get you into JFK the same evening. You'll have a good night's rest and be ready to take on these people the next morning.'

'What makes you so certain there's anyone to fight?'

'Woods, I checked your old Army buddy, Hagen. I haven't forgotten the way he and you pulled off that coup two years ago. But since then Hagen's been strictly out for himself.'

'That's hardly news.'

'And made some interesting friends along the way.'

Gently, Palmer pushed the girl's hand away from him. She gave him a giant, fake grin and snuggled in closer to the telephone to eavesdrop.

'You remember that story of yours about Hagen in the war?' Virginia was asking.

'Which story?'

'Those orders you got from him in Sicily. When the Allies invaded and you were supposed to make contact with the local Mafia capo-dons and set them up to control the island?'

'I remember.'

'Hagen's new friends date back from that era.'

Palmer frowned at the phone. 'You're mad, my dear. Eddie Hagen has never had mob connections.'

'Never is a long time,' she said. 'He has them, as of now. Since last summer when this bid of Ubco to buy that bank in Westchester started to backfire. I think the other bank got to Eddie. They're using him to move the merger along. Get it over with while Woods Palmer is away.'

'There's nothing they could offer Hagen to make him sell me out.'

'You're talking like a baby, Woods.'

The girl nodded sagely and pointed to the telephone, as if to say, 'she's right.'

'And you're talking like Harry Elder,' Palmer retorted. 'The two of you have managed to frighten each other with ghost stories.'

'The other ghost I've uncovered is a few of the old Jet-Tech crowd, headed up by Barney Lynch on your board. They've activated a loan application with Ubco the size of the nation debt. At seven percent.'

'They're insane. We can't even lend at eight anymore.'

'They figure that in your absence, they can swing it.'

The girl began to kiss his left nipple, worrying at it like a hungry infant. Palmer felt it tense and harden. He tried to push her away, but failed.

'Woods?'

'Yes, Ginnie.'

'Harry will meet you at JFK Sunday night and fill in the rest of the details. He'll have a folder of material for you to study before the board meeting. Wire him your arrival time. I promised you would.'

'Ginnie, look.'

'Sorry to have wakened you, darling,' she said. Her voice sounded cool, but no cooler than it had when she'd said good night at the end of their last call. 'Give my best to those five girls.'

'Did I say five?'

'Maybe,' she said slowly, 'it just seems like five. Good night, love.'

The line went dead. Palmer hung up the telephone.

'She knows,' the girl ventured.

'Of course she knows. She's Irish.'

The girl pulled away and watched him warily for a long moment. 'Did you once love her the way you love me?'

'I thought so, yes. But that was –' Palmer stopped and tried to think. The entire conversation with Virginia was having a kind of delayed depth-bomb effect. His mind was tearing around among the morsels of information she'd deliberately fed him, knowing they would eventually begin to worry him.

'But that was before you met me?' the girl prompted.

'Yes,' Palmer agreed, without actually thinking about it.

She nodded somberly. 'And after you meet your next lover, you'll think of me in the same way that you now remember Ginnie?'

Palmer tried to focus on what she was saying, but the possibilities of Eddie Hagen being in cahoots with the mob had begun to churn in his mind. 'No,' he said, knowing it sounded feeble. He made a determined effort to clear his mind. 'No,' he repeated more strongly. 'I thought I loved her before I knew what it was like to love somebody.'

'Ah.'

The girl smiled beatifically and cuddled in against him again. 'It's exactly the right thing to have said,' she murmured. 'I

139

don't even care if it's a lie.'

'It's not.'

'Really?' She drew slowly away from him and got to her feet. 'Do I mean that much?' she asked, moving to the closet and taking one of his robes from it.

'Yes. You do.'

'You're convincing,' she said, shrugging into the robe. Despite her height, the hem came down almost to her ankles. She rolled back the sleeves one turn and said: 'You are worried about what Ginnie told you.'

'Not worried. Just trying to make sense of it.'

'And you're resisting the trip back to New York.'

'I'm not going, if that's what you mean.' Palmer got up and made them two drinks of liqueur on ice.

'Because of the mission you're on.'

'Because of you.'

'If you leave me for two or three days, won't I be here when you return?' she asked.

'What?' He stared at her. 'That's not the point. I've found someone who makes me happier than I've ever been.' He leveled his forefinger at her. 'Why in hell's name should I leave that person and stick my head in that miserable hornet's nest back in New York?'

'You're afraid,' she said.

'Nonsense.'

'You're afraid of seeing Ginnie again.'

He laughed unhappily. 'You keep reducing this whole thing to some sort of affair of the groin. It's not.'

She accepted her drink from him and, hitching up the robe, sat cross-legged on an upholstered settee across the room. 'Why do you Americans always –' Her hand flew to her face for an instant. 'Sorry. Why must you assume that there's something ah, impermanent, not quite real, about a relationship because most of it takes place in bed?'

'Because the world outside doesn't take place in bed. Bed is just a part of life, not the whole thing.'

She gave an elaborate shrug that shifted the robe almost off her shoulders. 'What would it do to your psyche, my love, if eventually you found out that sex *is* everything?'

He laughed a bit more happily. 'It would sure as hell surprise me.'

She sipped her drink thoughtfully. 'I think that for some

140

people, sex is everything. Nothing is greater than it and everything they do is linked to it. I think for other people, sex is secondary. You must find out which sort of person you are. I am still in the process of learning it for myself, so I'm of little help.'

'About that you're quite wrong.'

She smiled. 'But tonight's not the time for you to decide, is it? You're trying to decide whether to go back for that meeting.'

'It's decided. I'm not.'

'Ginnie sounds like a very sensible woman. She wants to see you again, of course. But if she says you should go to the meeting, you should.'

Palmer put down his drink and walked to the window without looking out through it. He stood with his back to the girl for a moment. 'What if I told you I was seriously thinking of resigning from the bank?'

The room's quiet seemed to add solemnity to his statement. He turned to see that she was studying the big toe of her left foot, playing with the cuticle and trying to rub it back. 'You are the man,' she said then. 'You make your own decisions.'

'I have taken care of Edith's separation settlement and the kids out of fixed-return income,' he told her. 'When all of that is figured in, I still have enough to live comfortably in some quiet little place.'

'In Europe,' she added.

'Yes.'

'With me?'

'Yes.'

She gave up on the cuticle and looked at him. 'You really are in love.'

'Yes.'

'And I will show you I am, too.' She pulled the robe more tightly around her shoulders. 'In a year with me you would become restless for the life of action again. You aren't ready to plant roots like a vegetable. You're too used to power to give it up that easily. It's a drug. The withdrawal symptoms will be anguishing.'

He waved his hand at her as if brushing away smoke. 'I know all about that "power corrupts" line,' he said. 'It's nonsense.'

The silence between them seemed to grow abruptly. He realized he had done with her what he often did with people whose opinion he tried to shove aside. He had fobbed her off with a

141

catchphase. It was a habit in which he had caught himself many times over the years, trying to reduce the other person's idea to a shopworn slogan and, by so doing, denigrate it completely.

'It isn't nonsense,' she said at last in such a wounded voice that Palmer's heart seemed to squeeze inside him.

Why did he do this to people? Why couldn't he, with her of all people, react in a more human, give-and-take way? Why was he slamming doors in her face? When you did what you could to help someone and got a dash of ice water in your face, you had every right to turn away.

'I didn't mean to –'

'Yes, you did,' she cut in firmly. 'You tried to shut me up by making me a cliché-monger. Is there such a word in English? But I don't crush easily. Europeans don't. We are either resilient or we are nothing.'

'I'm sorry I –'

'Don't be sorry on my account,' she interrupted again. 'When you put your hands over your ears and cry "nonsense," the only one you deafen is you.'

'I really am sor –'

This time she cut him off simply by glancing at her watch. 'It's almost three A.M.,' she said, standing up and letting the robe fall to the floor around her feet. 'I have to get home, pack and be ready quite early for Dauber. You, too, must pack. While you do, please think about what's happening in New York.'

She pulled on her panty hose and snapped her bra in place. 'Think about attending that meeting. Wherever you leave me, I'll simply wait there for your return. I won't disappear in a puff of smoke. If you want me in Frankfurt, I'll be there. If you want me back in Paris, I'll wait there for you. It will take more than a brief absence for you to lose me.'

He watched her finish dressing. Then he stirred himself. 'Let me help you get a cab.'

'The concierge will be pleased to get one for me.'

'Will you be all right alone?'

'No.'

She walked over to him at the window and her arms went around him. She kissed him once, softly, then more firmly. 'No, I'll be terrible. But we'll pick you up in the car at eight thirty this morning and then I'll be fine.'

CHAPTER 24

The porter had picked up Palmer's bags from his room by eight fifteen. Palmer's eyes felt grittier than usual and the cold blast with which he had finished his morning shower had only awakened him momentarily. It was in a sleepy and somewhat grumpy mood, therefore, that he followed the porter downstairs at eight thirty in time to see him loading the bags in the rear trunk of the Mercedes limousine, with the unnecessary help of the same surly chauffeur.

Dauber was standing at the open rear door of the car. His smile positively shone in the morning sunlight. 'Right on time,' he enthused.

Palmer grunted something unintelligible and got inside the limousine. He sat down next to Eleanora, said 'Good morning' somewhat stiffly, and then saw that Forellen had come along.

'You again,' Palmer said ungraciously. He was giving a life-like imitation of a curmudgeon, but he didn't much care at the moment.

'I'm sorry about yesterday's meeting,' Forellen began instantly, as if Palmer had pressed a hidden spring.

Palmer nodded. 'You ought to be.' He turned very deliberately to the girl. 'All set for Frankfurt?' he asked in a ghastly tone of fake jollity.

'Yes, indeed.'

Palmer nodded owlishly. 'Get in, Dauber, and let's take off.'

'Right with you, sir.' The younger man supervised the slamming of the trunk lid, then hopped in on the seat facing Palmer. The car moved off ponderously.

'About yesterday,' Forellen began again.

'You're not going all the way out to the airport with us?' Palmer inquired in the rudest tone he could summon.

'Why, I thought – That is, if –'

'I'm damned if I'll spend the whole ride out to Orly listening to your version of what went wrong yesterday with Casseterre. We both know what went wrong. I, for one, am willing to let it drop if you, for the other, will shut up about it.'

'But that's just it,' Forellen persisted, 'I have no idea what went wrong and I was hoping you'd sort of put me in the picture.'

Palmer nodded. 'I'll do more than that, Stanley.' He reached

143

forward and rapped the chauffeur's window next to Dauber's cheek so vigorously that Dauber flinched.

'Stop at the next corner,' Palmer informed the driver.

He had the curbside door open before the Mercedes stopped rolling. '*Adiós*, Stanley,' he said. 'When I get back to the States, I'll give your boss, Mr. Mather, an explanation of the whole thing. Maybe it'll filter down through channels to you.'

Forellen shot him a stricken look. 'I must say, Mr. Palmer, that I'm not used to this kind of pushing around.'

Palmer took his elbow and helped him out of the car. 'Nor am I. Good-bye.' He pulled the door shut and rapped on the glass again. The Mercedes started off into traffic, leaving Forellen staring after them.

'How the hell did he hitch a ride?' Palmer demanded of Dauber.

'He was waiting outside my apartment house in St.-Cloud this morning at eight.' The younger man shrugged unhappily. 'I'm terribly sorry.'

'How did he know where to be and when?'

'I'm afraid I let our departure time slip yesterday over the phone.'

'All right. Straight answer.' Palmer nodded encouragingly at him. 'You're forgiven. I should have warned you that he and I haven't seen eye to eye since that lunch he horned in on with us. That reminds me.' He reached in his pocket and handed the tiny tape recorder to Dauber. 'Return this to him when you get a chance. I'm keeping the tape.'

The 727 three-engine jet took off precisely on time. Palmer sat next to the window in one of two first-class seats reserved for him. Eleanora sat in the other and the space between them was taken up with her handbag, his briefcase, and a camera she had brought along. It was as if they were under such thorough surveillance, Palmer realized, that they had to be extremely careful to keep from even seeming to touch each other.

He glanced out the window at the slanting horizon of Paris. Then the plane straightened out on its eastbound run and began climbing. The long-promised rain, which seemed to have held off over Paris during his visit there, was massing now in an immense stretch of dark clouds rolling up from the south. Palmer estimated the clouds would be over the city by noon. Dauber would immediately remember that Palmer had, indeed, brought the sunshine.

He should have complimented the boy more when they left. Dauber had done a good job, considering how eaten with curiosity he must have been at Palmer's mysterious disappearances during most of his unscheduled hours.

Palmer's eyes moved slowly across the leaden bank of storm clouds below him. Farther south, as the jet climbed, he could see an ocean of clouds stretching, it seemed, to the Mediterranean. His eyes were so weary of watching everything. He could feel himself start to doze. The voice of the stewardess came faintly to him. 'Will Monsieur take coffee?' she was asking the girl.

'*Nein, danke.*'

'*Sie, Fräulein?*'

'*Ja, mit Milch, bitte.*'

Palmer's thoughts wandered. Behind his closed lids pinwheels of fatigue spun slowly. He could hear a faint clinking of silver on porcelain. The sound seemed to come from far over the Mediterranean, muffled by a universe of dark storm clouds.

They were in a small boat, rocking in the midst of the sea. Ripples spread out from the boat as if they had been tossed into the center of the sea by a giant hand. He reached out to her and his grasp on the oar gave way. The oar slid slanting into the water's depths. There had been only one oar.

'*Auf dem Hotel . . .*' the stewardess was saying.

Palmer watched the clouds closing in over their tiny boat, helpless without oars. Lightning flickered on the horizon, forking lacily down from the gray sky above to the gray sea below.

'*Und der Name ist Mann . . . Feld Oberst Mann . . .*'

The thunder was very faint, considering that the lightning seemed almost upon them. Palmer tried to remember if an open boat during an electrical storm were a safe place to be.

'*Nach Dachgarten . . .*'

Palmer stirred. The stewardess' voice faded and so did the dream. He turned slightly in his seat and fell asleep again, but so soundly that he had no consciousness of dreaming.

Her voice awakened him an hour later as she announced over the loudspeaker in three languages their imminent arrival at Frankfurt International Airport. Palmer had a moment of awareness, as he woke up, that the quality of the stewardess' voice over the intercom system was harsher than when she had been talking to the girl.

He opened his eyes and saw that the girl had been putting her papers in order, shuffling notes and schedules together in her

145

notebook. She stopped for a moment and examined at some length the glossy photograph of the two of them, taken on the *bateau-mouche* the evening before. In it she looked amused, he a bit startled. His eyes had first narrowed in anticipation of the flash, but as the photographer hesitated for a moment, his eyes had widened just as the flash went off. Palmer could see that the mole at the point of his jaw on the left side of his neck had somehow cast a shadow big enough to make it look three times its normal size. He frowned and took the photograph from her.

She gave a tiny shriek. *'Mein Gott!* I thought you were still asleep.'

'Can I burn this?'

'Never. You look so handsome. Have you been awake long?' He handed it back. 'Just woke up.'

'Good.'

'Hm?'

'I said good. That you got so much sleep, that is.'

The look she gave him said that she wanted to hold him as soon as possible. Palmer found himself wondering how long after checking in at the hotel could he invite her to his suite.

He glanced out the window and saw that the storm clouds were moving in over Frankfurt, too, as they were over Paris. They reminded him for a fleeting moment of a dream he'd had about a boat and someone speaking in German. None of it came back clearly at all.

CHAPTER 25

The limousine that met their flight at the Frankfurt Airport was a Cadillac. Palmer assumed, as he got in after Miss Gregorius and settled down for the short ride into town, that the limousine used to impress visiting dignitaries must always be a foreign make, the Mercedes in France, the Cadillac in Germany, *und so weiter.* He turned to the girl to remark on this and caught her touching her handkerchief to the eye shadow on her lower lids.

'You all right?'

'F-fine.' Her voice had a too-airy brightness about it.

'Sure?'

146

'Absolutely,' she said with great steadiness. She tucked away the handkerchief and glanced about at the standard throughway-turnpike scenery.

'It's the same as the ride from Orly,' Palmer assured her, 'or the one from JFK International in New York. Even the signs and the overpasses look the same. Only the language changes.'

'It won't be long before that is the same, too,' she mused. 'They already have a collection of road signs using only symbols. My job will be obsolete in a few years.'

'Which job? Interpreter?'

She frowned slightly. 'Is there another?' She glanced at him and grinned. 'Oh, that. But it's not a job.'

'Isn't it?'

'It's a ... an avocation. Yes?'

'A hobby,' he suggested wryly.

'No, no. What do you call it in English? What the amateur devotes his life to enjoying.'

'Ah,' he said, 'a lifelong passion.'

'That's it. A lifelong passion.'

Their glances met for a long moment. She reached for his hand and gave it a discreet squeeze below the eye level of the driver's rearview mirror. 'Is that a fact?' Palmer asked slowly. 'Lifelong?'

She shrugged slightly. 'Why not?'

'Usually one's much older before choosing a lifelong passion.'

She shook her head. 'One doesn't choose a passion. It chooses one.'

'Sounds like being hit by a truck.'

'Yes,' she agreed. 'Very much like.' They were silent for a while. 'And as for youth,' she went on then 'it's mostly a matter of how much experience one packs into one's formative years. At a certain point one has enough to know "this is right." That point has little to do with one's chronological age.'

The heavy Cadillac rumbled over a long bridge that crossed the river. 'Welcome to Frankfurt am Main,' the girl said. 'You should be at home here. It's one of *the* banking cities of the world.'

'Where the Rothschilds began,' Palmer said.

'The "five Frankfurters," Rothschild's sons?' she asked. 'You know about them?'

'Does the Pope know about St. Peter?'

She frowned uneasily. 'I beg your pardon?'

147

'It's a joke.' He watched the slightly curving River Main pass below. 'I know about the sons. Most bankers do. They fanned out to Paris, London, Vienna, and Rome.'

'Naples, I believe,' she corrected him gently.

The huge glass façade of their hotel stood to the right of the highway like a glazed waffle iron.

The driver steered the Cadillac smoothly up to the entrance. Across the street construction was under way and a sign announced that an eighteen-story annex to the hotel was going up. The chauffeur jumped out and whipped open the door a full five seconds before the uniformed doorman, who had been talking on the telephone, came running to perform the same job.

Palmer handed the girl out of the car and followed her into the lobby. A youngish man in a dark suit and white shirt came running around the check-in counter with his hand outstretched. 'Herr Palmer,' he began even before they shook hands. 'It is indeed an extreme honor to our hotel and a great personal pleasure to me, as the assistant manager, to welcome you to Frankfurt and to express the sincere hope that your stay here will be both interesting and productive.'

Palmer stifled a smile as he took the man's hand. 'On behalf of my bank and of the Foundation for which I have undertaken this mission,' he intoned solemnly, 'I assure you that I am pleased beyond words to arrive in your lovely and historic city.'

'But I must apologize from the bottom of my heart,' the younger man went on in flawless Oxonian British, 'that our esteemed manager cannot be here in person to greet you. He is unfortunately away from the city and most desolate about his absence. He especially wanted to be at the reception this afternoon and make certain that everything was totally in order.'

A phrase echoed in Palmer's head – *'Alles ist in Ordnung'* – but he ignored it. 'Reception?' he asked aloud.

'There is a reception in your honor, sir, at fifteen-thirty hours today in the *Dachgarten* atop the hotel.'

The German word reverberated for a moment. Palmer had the idea he knew the word, or had heard it recently, but his mind failed completely to come up with an answer. *'Dachgarten?'*

'Our rooftop terrace, Herr Palmer. The view of the city is completely magnificent, as you shall see.' His glance darted past Palmer to the middle of the lobby. 'I see your luggage is here. May I escort you to your suite, sir?'

'Certainly.'

Palmer followed the assistant manager who choreographed a small snake dance as he made his way to the elevator, picking up three porters carrying Palmer's bags, then the limousine chauffeur, and, finally, Miss Gregorius. 'Where is the brass band?' Palmer whispered to her.

'Would you like me to find out?'

'*Nein, Dummkopf.*'

'One never calls a woman *Dummkopf*. It's a word exclusively reserved for men.'

The assistant manager had commandeered two elevators, relegating the lesser humans to one and bringing Palmer up in the other, uncontaminated by enforced proximity to his own luggage. He had hesitated for a moment about whether to include Eleanora in Palmer's elevator, but Palmer had solved the protocol problem by ushering her in ahead of him.

His seventeenth-floor suite occupied the corner of the building. The sitting room's window wall provided a view to the west, as Palmer found when the assistant manager pulled back the floor-to-ceiling blue draperies. The bedroom's terrace faced south and Palmer could see a small tug pushing two coal barges up the river.

'Most pleasant,' he commented at last.

'I am enchanted that it pleases you, Herr Palmer, sir.'

The assistant manager then supervised a quadrille of the porters, each depositing his bag at a specified location and removing himself immediately. Upon the departure of the ultimate porter, two blond chambermaids entered, all smiles, and began unpacking bags and hanging away suits.

Palmer returned to the sitting room. The chauffeur stood awkwardly at the door, awaiting instructions. Palmer glanced at his watch and saw that it was nearly eleven o'clock in the morning. 'Tell him to take a break and be back here at two,' he told the girl. 'No, wait. There's a reception at three thirty. Tell him, ah ... Tell him to report back at seven o'clock.'

'Our supper club is the finest restaurant in all of Frankfurt,' the assistant manager put in quickly. 'There's no need for you to eat outside the hotel, if I may suggest it.'

'I'm certain of that,' Palmer assured him. 'We – I may want to do some sightseeing.'

'But, of course, sir.'

The assistant manager executed a small minuet around the

149

perimeter of a large cocktail table, indicating an immense basket of fruit there, as well as an ice bucket, several glasses, a bottle of Haig Pinch and one of Jack Daniels. 'With our heartfelt compliments, Herr Palmer,' he said. 'It shall be my very great pleasure to see you again at the *Dachgarten* and to make certain that the reception progresses smoothly, sir.'

He started to perform a vaguely entrechatlike series of departure movements. 'Where is Miss Gregorius staying?' Palmer asked then.

His eyebrows shot up. 'A thousand pardons, Herr Palmer. In the excitement of your arrival, sir, I totally forgot to explain the young lady's room' – he nodded deferentially to Eleanora although he continued to use the third person – 'is across the hall, Number 1702. It was our feeling that, in the interests of top efficiency she should be located as conveniently as possible, should you require her services, yes?'

'Very good,' Palmer nodded him out the door. 'Once again, I appreciate very much your efforts on my behalf. Will you' – he reached in his pocket and brought out a crumpled ten-franc note – 'please distribute this among the porters?'

The assistant manager's eyes widened. 'It's not necessary at all, sir.'

'I insist.'

The younger man took the bill. He seemed to be having difficulty saying good-bye. Palmer solved his problem by smiling, stepping back into the room and closing the door. He walked to the cocktail table and saw the two room keys, his and the girl's, lying beside each other. He put ice in two glasses and indicated the Scotch. The girl nodded. He removed the wired-down top of the bottle and poured two drinks, handed her one and lifted his glass. 'To the interests of top efficiency,' he said.

She touched glasses. 'To requiring my services.'

'To the Five Little Frankfurters, and how they grew.'

'To Johann Wolfgang von Goethe,' she toasted.

'The Sixth Frankfurter?'

'Of course.' They sipped their drinks. Her glance slid sideways to the bedroom. '*Nous ne sommes pas seuls,*' she murmured.

Palmer squinted at her for a long moment. 'Ah. *D'accord.*'

She drifted to the doorway of the bedroom and watched for a moment. As if on signal the two maids finished unpacking and filed out the door, ducking their heads in greeting. Palmer pressed the rest of his French change on them and they left the suite. He closed the door behind them and locked it from the inside.

When he turned back, he found the girl studying something in his flat black briefcase. 'I don't find any mention of a reception in your schedule,' she said then, closing the case and putting it on the cocktail table. 'And don't you find it odd that no one from Ubco was here to greet you?'

Palmer shook his head. 'We have no branch in Frankfurt.' He sipped his drink. 'I'm damned if I can explain the reception. I have no meetings scheduled until tomorrow, have I?'

'None. One moment.' She picked up the telephone, studied a list of inside PBX numbers printed around the edge of the dial, and finally dialed two numbers. She began speaking immediately in German, didn't seem to get what she wanted, hung up, and dialed another pair of numbers. This time she reached someone who could answer her questions. After she hung up she grinned and said: 'You seem to be the honored guest of some bureau or agency of the Bonn government. This reception is jointly sponsored by them and by one of the local business groups.'

'Chamber of Commerce idea?'

'Something like that. They expect over fifty people this afternoon.'

'*Mein Gott*. It isn't black tie?'

She shook her head. 'What you're wearing should do very well.' She patted the dark-brown lapel of his suit jacket. 'For the reception, that is,' she added. 'But the reception is hours away,' she added, removing his jacket and letting it drape over the back of a chair.

Later, in the darkened bedroom, she got up and tiptoed into the sitting room, thinking him asleep. He lay there and tried to picture her moving naked around the room. She was back a moment later with the basket of fruit, which she put down on the bedside table. 'Did I awaken you?' she asked. 'You really should nap.'

'I'm fine. Do you think sexual intercourse can replace sleep?'

She examined an orange, turning it slowly about in her fingers. 'Only in bed,' she announced then. 'Here.'

She chucked the orange at him so quickly that his hands involuntarily tried to cover his genitals. 'Easy!'

'Oh, *pauvre petit choux*.' She began fondling and kissing

151

him. 'Where does it hurt, the poor baby?'

'Never mind sarcasm. It wasn't always that small.'

'Here?' she asked, nibbling at him.

'Um ... yes.'

'Here?' she went on, taking soft bites with her lips.

'Definitely there.'

She had been bent over his groin. Now she looked up at him. 'You could be eating your orange, you know, instead of staring at me like a bloody voyeur.'

'Never thought of it that way.' He picked up the orange. A purplish stamp on the skin announced: *'Produkt von Israel.'*

'You're not really that disinterested that you're going to eat your orange?'

'Women are a mass of contradictions,' he announced. 'Wasn't that what you suggested I do?'

She nodded. 'The idea of your being completely cool to me has a salacious effect. It makes me feel like a whore, or something, a sexual object, a slave.'

'And this excites you?'

'Eat your orange,' she commanded, 'and leave me to my little frankfurter.

CHAPTER 26

At three o'clock the girl went to her room to change. Palmer washed and dressed slowly for the reception. He supposed his most somber, ministerial business suit and white shirt would do the trick. He had noticed that the French businessmen and officials with whom he'd talked over the past week had been almost a matched set of chessmen, all neat and tidy in their identical clothing.

There was, Palmer knew, a uniform for businessmen as for any other calling. One always sought, by the traditional cut of one's jacket, the unobtrusiveness of shirt and tie and the shortness of hair to somehow merge with the woodwork and assume its structural solidity. Palmer also knew that a different breed of businessman, the international figure in his wraparound sunglasses and tousled bangs, had begun to make an impression in Europe. But it was just another uniform, actually, and it only impressed like-minded people. It still couldn't impress a banker or a government official. In those two types of men, the repository of an almost racial tradition of unobtrusiveness was firmly rooted.

Palmer pulled out a white shirt from the drawer where the maids had put them. He thumbed through the remaining shirts, wondering if he ought to be sending some out for laundering or if he had enough to last through Germany and into Italy. The second shirt from the bottom had longer collar tabs than the rest. Palmer frowned and pulled it out of the pile.

It was a perfectly ordinary plain white shirt, even to the Brooks label in the collar. Since leaving Edith, Palmer had taken to sending his shirts to a laundry instead of having them done by Mrs. Gage, Edith's housekeeper. So gradually, over the past few months, all his shirts had acquired a PALM laundry mark which was missing from this shirt. Palmer looked it over, fairly certain he owned no white shirts except those with button-down collars or tab fastenings. This collar had fairly long wings spread somewhat farther apart than any of the rest.

Palmer broke the blue paper band and, holding the shirt by its collar, snapped it open full length. The cardboard inside dropped to the floor without floating. It simply dropped straight down.

Like lead, Palmer thought, putting the shirt aside and picking up the cardboard. It seemed quite a bit thicker than the normal cheap cardboard New York laundries used. It weighed more, too.

Palmer took it into the living room of the suite where the light was better. He sat down beside the cocktail table and gently inserted a fruit knife into the edge of the cardboard. After a while he succeeded in splitting one edge of the board and peeling back the top layer like a book.

The 35-mm negatives were about half a foot long. Two of them lay side by side, each with about six postage-stamp-sized images.

Palmer took a paper napkin from the fruit basket and used it to lift one of the negative strips. Grasping it with the napkin, he held the film up to the light and saw that the original material copied on the negative was a series of legal-length typewritten pages that had been bound at the top through two punched holes. His eyes weren't good enough to read any of the tiny words, but the look of the page gave him the feeling of a governmental or military document.

He sat for a while and tried to sort out the whole thing, beginning with when the shirt had become part of his baggage. He decided there was no way of knowing, actually, although he was pretty sure it hadn't been with him when he'd unpacked his own shirts at the Ritz in Paris.

Palmer wished he had a magnifying glass. He wasn't consumed with curiosity over the nature of the documents, but he felt they might give him a clue as to who was using him as a courier or, conversely, setting him up for an arrest as a spy-courier.

Probably the plant had been made in Paris the day Casseterre and Forellen had tried to whipsaw information out of him. The obviously searched-through look of his shirts that day had been either a double-bluff blind or sheer carelessness. As a double bluff, the maneuver was masterful. It had totally misdirected his attention because it pointed to a poorly executed search of his belongings, rather than the addition of a doctored shirt cardboard.

Palmer frowned and tried to think the problem through a bit further. He had felt that he was under surveillance from several quarters. Now that he was in Germany, only a few days from his Monday meeting with Herr Schirmer in Bonn, he would have to make up his mind whether to do Harry Banter's 'little errand' or not. If any of the surveillance to the date – the clumsy work or the professional stuff – was being carried out at Harry's orders, then Operation Overdraft could go hang.

There were too many possibilities for rational analysis, Palmer realized. Too many motives could be spurring on too many factions. Bannister had his own reasons for keeping Palmer under observation. If someone were employing Eleanora, he had his own motives. Even mob interests back in the States could be considered in the picture.

It wasn't like Harry Bannister to plant incriminating micro-film on a man he desperately needed. Yet, in another way, it might just be Harry's way of ensuring Palmer's full cooperation.

It wasn't like the mob to fool around with subtle touches like microfilm, when a good old-fashioned hand grenade would do the job more efficiently. But that was the old-time mob. Today's gangsters were smoother.

He decided that, either way, his first responsibility was not to be caught with the negatives. He placed the film in an ashtray,

154

added some bits of torn paper to help matters, and set the whole pile aflame. He noticed, as the film buckled and curled with the heat, that the edge of the strip where the sprocket holes were showed a Kodak emulsion name. In itself this meant nothing, although if the film had been Agfa or Perutz or Ilford it might possibly have meant a little something more.

Palmer poked about in the smoldering scraps and made sure all the film had been consumed. Then he carried the ashtray into the bathroom and flushed the remains down the toilet.

He would have given a lot to have read the documents. But he wasn't in that business, he reflected as the ashes swirled out of sight and vanished down the drain. He was simply no longer in that business, he repeated to himself.

I wonder, he thought, if that's ever possible?

CHAPTER 27

There were, Palmer noted, damned near the fifty people they had expected at the reception. The *Dachgarten* was a magnificent place for the always ill-at-ease ambience of a reception where no one knew the guest of honor, or even exactly what he was supposed to be. The long, narrow room seemed to float above the city of Frankfurt like the gondola of a dirigible, all floor-to-ceiling glass, some areas roofed over and lighted with curious turrets of cannon-snout lamps, others open to the bright blue sky.

The leading actor in the reception, aside from Palmer, seemed to be a Herr Reigensraffner, who looked almost exactly like the old silent screen star Nils Asther, very handsome, slight but not skinny, well-boned, square-jawed, with a firm, friendly mouth and the soft, understanding eyes of a professional funeral director.

As Palmer conversed with his hosts, turning now and again to Eleanora for the little help he needed – most of the Germans' English was quite good – he toyed with the idea of giving the girl a running box score on which host resembled which film personality.

There was, for example, a chubby little fellow with flabby cheeks whose impersonation of S. Z. 'Cuddles' Sakall was

155

superb, a Cassiuslike double for Martin Kosleck, a younger version of Von Stroheim, ramrod spine and all, not one but two Albert Bassermans, and even a thinned-down Harry Baur. He toyed with the idea, that is, but quickly abandoned it on the assumption that she'd never heard of or seen any of the actors in question.

The girl was one of three women at the reception, not counting waitresses. The other two were dowdy but well-groomed wives, along for the free drinks, Palmer supposed, after one too many you-never-take-me-anywhere complaints.

Next to himself and Herr Reigensraffner, Palmer supposed, the star of the show was Eleanora. Her legs were very clearly the true focus of the room's attention, even attracting the glances of the two wives. It was natural enough for the men to cluster around Palmer. They were there, after all, to greet him. But it didn't hurt at all that by clustering around him they were clustering around the girl, too.

The stellar attraction for Palmer, however, was the 360-degree view of the city. Frankfurt didn't seem anything special at first glance, having been rebuilt in anonymous Postwar Moderne after the extensive bombings of World War II. But here and there he found views that were intriguing. He hoped he could remember them and take a closer look later in the evening when they took the limousine for a ride.

The river itself, with its steady stream of barges, freighters, tugs, and lighters, was fascinating to Palmer as he peered over the heads of his hosts. Further along the river, on the same side as the hotel, he could see what appeared to be a medieval square of buildings clustered near a fairly impressive cathedral. He would have to visit the square tonight, he promised himself.

'This part of Germany, of course,' a younger Paul Henried was telling him.

'Ah, why is that?' Palmer responded, having no idea what the man had been saying.

'Because of your Air Force installations, of course.'

'In this part of the country?'

'But most assuredly, sir,' the man explained. 'I believe that from here west to the Luxembourg border and north to Koblenz you have approximately twenty-five thousand U.S. Air Force troops on duty, most of them with their families.'

'Oh, of course,' Palmer agreed.

'I would estimate, good sir,' he continued in a smooth,

156

pleasant voice, 'that from the Rhineland–Palatinate area here, west through the Mosel Valley, you are keeping upwards of one hundred Strategic Air Command bombers and perhaps a thousand jet-fighter escorts. *Nicht wahr?*' he broke off, turning to Herr Reigensraffner.

'Without a doubt.' He nodded sagaciously, and yet with that look of grave commiseration that a proper mortician assumes with the family of the bereaved. 'This, of course, means many dollars to the local economy.'

Palmer nodded. 'It's one of the things I am here to learn about,' he said.

'The leak you want to plug up, *nein?*' Reigensraffner suggested, smiling.

'Not necessarily plug up.'

'One hopes not,' the other man said. 'Without the GI's, this would be an economically depressed area indeed.'

'Surely not,' Palmer demurred. 'You're heavily manufacturing here, aren't you? Electrical equipment, autos, chemicals, and the like?'

'Here,' Reigensraffner agreed, pointing to the floor at his feet. 'But west of here, to the border, there is nothing to support the populace but the Riesling grapes and the GI's. Take away one or the other and it is a totally depressed area.'

The other man had switched his attention to Eleanora and was carrying on an animated discussion in German, with the help of some younger colleagues who had tried to annex her before. They seemed to be having a guessing game as to where in Germany she hailed from. Palmer wished them luck.

It gave him an odd feeling to know that the woman who was attracting so much close attention was his mistress. It was a somewhat unfamiliar feeling for him. While Virginia Clary was pretty, in her short, dark way, Eleanora had the true showgirl body that lured men like a beacon. A false light, Palmer thought. None of these eager types would get anything but talk from her.

It wasn't that Virginia didn't attract men. She couldn't help but, considering the nature of her personality and conversation. His wife, Edith, for that matter, hadn't been at all unattractive, in her thin, somewhat undeveloped way.

But this girl had something else. It wasn't that she was a dozen years younger than Virginia or Edith, although that helped. It was something else, some thread that ran through her

157

personality, the way she looked and what she said, that Palmer had himself noticed from the moment he met her.

She was not merely a different generation from the other women in his life and from most of the men in this room. There was also a sharp difference between her generation and the one before. Partly it was her freer attitude toward life and sex and men, which couldn't help showing. With this girl, men felt, sex was an entirely new thing.

But she was off limits to all of them. Palmer smiled almost secretly at the thought.

He glanced around the room during the lull and noted that a few of his hosts seemed to have sneaked away. There were about thirty-five on hand now. He surreptitiously glanced at his watch and saw that it was well after five. He hoped the rest would beat a retreat soon. They had homes to go to and wives waiting, didn't they? Or didn't it matter here, any more than it did in New York?

His glance fastened for a moment on a short, dark young man in a somber olive-green suit who, to his knowledge, hadn't yet come up for an introduction. He was seated at the far end of the terrace, playing with a drink that looked, from a distance, to be empty. The young man's eyebrows were very bushy and seemed to meet over the bridge of his nose, but this may have been a trick of the light or the fact that he might have been frowning.

'Even our celebrated wines,' Reigensraffner was saying.

'Surely they bolster the area's economy.'

'Not as you might expect. The margin of profit in wine-making has dropped enormously over the years, of course. In the old days a man and his wife and his children tended the vines on their hillside and spread the manure from their own cows and pressed their own grapes and bottled their own wine. They could count, of course, on selling the wine for enough to live on all year. Generation after generation this held true. The valleys of the Rhine, the Ruwer, and the Mosel became as famous in their way as any vineyard area of France. But it's all changing now, of course.'

Palmer's eyes glazed slightly. He could never remember a time in his life when someone wasn't explaining to him why agriculture was on its last legs.

'It's the youth,' Reigensraffner explained. 'They don't want to climb the steep hillsides or turn the hand presses or fill the bottles. In the last analysis, of course, they don't want to work for their fathers. They want a nine-to-five job with fringe benefits, health insurance, a trade union, guaranteed holidays, the right to strike, pension funds, bowling leagues, and all the rest. So, of course, the small vintners go bankrupt. More and more vineyards are sold, combined into the holdings of fewer and fewer companies. And these men are forced to mechanize, of course. I would hate to tell you, good sir, how wine is made today. So much of it is what we call *Schlum*, sold in supermarkets and drugstores like Coca-Cola.'

'*Schlum?*' Palmer repeated, his eyes even more heavily glazed over.

'Mud,' Eleanora murmured in his ear. She resumed her banter with the other men.

'Mud,' Reigensraffner agreed. 'It looks like wine and it tastes like mud. Oh, really fine wines are still made, of course. Most people can't appreciate them. They buy *Schlum* for a few marks a bottle and to them it's no different than the real thing.'

Palmer nodded and tried to revive his flagging interest in the wine industry. 'What's needed,' he said, 'is a marketing plan that makes clear the superiority of the good wines, that makes it socially unacceptable to drink or serve *Schlum*.'

Reigensraffner's square-jawed face cracked in a broad smile and he started to clap Palmer on the shoulder before he realized the impropriety of this and halted the gesture. '*Prima!*' he said. 'But this campaign should be mounted in markets outside Germany, of course. It's no good telling Germans this.'

'Why not?'

The older man made a complicated shoulder motion that resembled a one-sided shrug. 'Because despite all this affluence one reads about, our people can only afford *Schlum*. The moment they can afford better of course, they buy French wine.' His face went dead for a moment as he watched Palmer, waiting to see if the irony of this had sunk in.

'But then it should be obvious,' Palmer responded, 'that your heaviest marketing efforts should be directed to your own people.'

Reigensraffner's head shook slowly from side to side. 'We are strongly Americanized, of course, in so many things,' he said, 'and I trust you will not take this as meant in an unkindly way. But the fact is the bulk of our people are not much swayed by advertising. Yet.' He chuckled. 'You see I say yet.'

Palmer nodded. The party had thinned to about twenty-five

now. He saw the dark young man with the heavy eyebrows get to his feet and bring his glass to the bar, where he traded it for a full one. He moved toward Palmer now and his rather stern features seemed to be rearranging themselves into a more amiable mien.

There was a burst of laughter from the coterie around Eleanora. She glanced sideways at Palmer and her eyes lifted very slightly toward the ceiling in a how-long-must-this-go-on gesture. Palmer nodded encouragingly. 'You're the hit of the show,' he said in an undertone.

'Like you to meet...' Reigensraffner was saying.

Palmer turned back to find the dark young man smiling at him. He had one of those faces somewhat too big for his frame, with a long, outjutting chin, cleft rather deeply, and a powerful nose to match it. Palmer saw that his eyebrows were not, in fact, joined, at least not when he smiled as pleasantly as he was now. The face was not only out of proportion to the body, Palmer decided, but the smile was out of proportion to the occasion.

'This is –' the older man began.

'Mr. Mann,' the young man cut in quickly, extending his hand. 'Heinz Mann,' he added. He had evidently learned English from a Midwestern American, except that in the United States nobody's *a*'s were as flat as that, Palmer reflected, nor *r*'s as prolonged.

'A pleasure,' he responded.

Herr Mann's hand was firm, dry, and hard-skinned. His handshake was short and powerful. His eyes locked with Palmer's, giving him what Palmer often had occasion to call the sincerity bit. 'Herr Mann,' Herr Reigensraffner explained, 'is one of our leading young –'

'Personnel,' the younger German interrupted. 'Fascinating field, is it not?'

'Fascinating,' Palmer agreed. He watched the young man's black eyes swivel sideways to Eleanora's legs. This is where I lose him, Palmer thought. A moment later, the dark young man shifted sideways under cover of one of Reigensraffner's interminable oral essays on the low state of agriculture. He began talking German to the girl.

'Aging of wine is a farce these days, of course,' the older man went on. 'The all-around golden year for Mosel, Rhine, and Ruwer wines was 1959. Of course, this was true for the French, too. But we've had some very good years since, to judge by the

160

best of the wines, a Graacher Himmelreich, for example, or a Piesporter Goldtröpfchen. Yet in the same year, with the same sun, most of the vineyards are producing millions of gallons of *Schlum*. Of course, we...'

Palmer tried to hear what Herr Mann was telling Eleanora. The conversation was one-sided, since most of the other men, out of some strange deference to the newcomer, had stopped trying to attract her attention.

The dark young man bothered Palmer. He couldn't put his finger on what troubled him about Heinz Mann. Perhaps it was his lateness in coming forward, or the way he kept cutting in on the old duffer's introduction, or perhaps that he was now delivering a monologue to Eleanora.

That was it, Palmer realized, jealousy.

Mann was her age, not bad looking, quite self-assured, and obviously interested in the girl. Obviously, too, he was Somebody.

The penalty for having such an attractive mistress, Palmer decided, was eternal jealousy. No, actually that wasn't what he was doing wrong. The sin for which he was being penalized was not having such a mistress, but being in love with her. Love seemed to carry heavy penalties Palmer had never before experienced.

He longed to get her away from Mann and the other men and this room. He longed to get her back into bed.

'Fortunately, the aging of white wine doesn't take as long,' Reigensraffner ground on in ponderous tones, 'since they can be drunk as soon as a year later and, of course, in a good year up to even six or eight years after, but not much later than that. Of course, if one...'

Palmer's attention slid to his right again, but he couldn't hear a syllable of what Mann was saying. The dark young man stopped his monologue at about that point, took Eleanora's hand, bowed over it and Palmer could have sworn he heard a faint heel click as he kissed her fingers. Palmer felt another pang of uneasiness.

A rash of hand-kissing now began as the other men consulted their watches and began a series of laborious and ceremonial good-byes. Palmer felt a certain sense of relief.

'And good vintners require good customers,' the older German continued to expound. 'Without customers who refuse to buy *Schlum*, of course, vintners end up moving inevitably toward low-end product. With a clientele that appreciates good wine, the vintner can make a living by producing good wine. It's a vicious circle,' he added, 'but, of course . . .'

Palmer's half-glazed eyes surveyed the darkening blue overhead. The day had been warm and pleasant. In a little while he and the girl would be alone, perhaps for an hour before the car returned. He might . . .

'*Also!*' Reigensraffner concluded. 'Enough of wine, eh? I believe I am to escort you to several meetings tomorrow, isn't it?' He turned to Eleanora, whom most men took to be Palmer's secretary, rather than interpreter. 'They are minor appointments, to be sure. But on Monday you will be meeting alone with some rather high officials in Bonn.' He beamed at both of them.

By six Palmer and the girl were taking a shower in his bathroom. She had spent a great deal of time on his back, soaping and rubbing him first with a washrag and then with her bare hands. Her fingers now worked powerfully in the muscles of his neck and kneaded their way down his back to his buttocks. She began to fondle him from behind, the soapsuds lubricating the massage in a particularly exciting way.

Palmer leaned forward against the glass door of the shower stall and groaned with sheer animal delight. Then he got behind her and began to soap her. At one point she bent over for a moment and he felt himself entering her almost without realizing it. The posture was excruciatingly arousing. She had only to straighten up or bend over further to inflame his penis almost beyond control with her strange internal shiftings.

He rammed her up against the wall, pinned her arms at his sides, and tried to finish her off as slowly as possible. From far away, as over a faulty telephone line, he could hear the animal noises they were making, her squeals of joy, his grunting thrusts. He couldn't believe this was him.

Lying down later on the bed someone had thoughtfully remade since the earlier afternoon, he tried to think about himself. Was he really all he thought he was . . . and *this*, too? Was it possible to have lived his kind of life, cerebral, manipulative, concerned almost exclusively with the intrigues of money, and still rut like a bull in heat? Where was all this heat coming from? Surely he should be drained of it by now.

He recognized finally that his thinking had started from a false premise. The heat she generated in him wasn't a waste

162

product to be drained and discarded. That was the puritan-ethic approach. The heat wasn't *in* him. The heat *was* him.

'*Liebe Gott*, we had visitors while we were in the shower,' she announced, coming in from the sitting room with an ice bucket in which a slim green bottle stood chilling.

'Discreet, aren't they?'

'Very wise men. There's no card. Is it courtesy of the hotel?'

Palmer sat up on the bed and examined the bottle. It was a Bernkasteler Doktor of the magic 1959 vintage. 'Thank God,' he murmured. 'For a moment I was afraid it might be the ubiquitous *Schlum*.'

'Herr Reigensraffner's present?'

'Or perhaps Herr Mann.'

'Who?'

'The one with the face and eyebrows to match.'

She glanced around. 'There must be a corkscrew somewhere.'

'I got an odd feeling about him,' Palmer said. He stood up and padded on bare feet to the living room, where he started rummaging through a desk drawer and came up in rapid succession with two pens, a letter opener, a plastic phone dialer, and a corkscrew. He began removing the cork of the Bernkasteler Doktor. 'I don't think he's a civilian.'

She watched him struggle with the bottle. 'Not what?'

'I think he's military.'

'How odd.'

'Um.' The cork surrendered and Palmer poured out two glasses of the pale yellow-green wine. 'No evidence. Just a hunch.'

'A what?'

'Hunch. To lovely soapsuds.' He touched his glass to hers. 'Cleanliness is next to godliness after all.'

'To soapsuds. Remind me to show you what I can do for you with wine.' They sipped the Doktor.

'Definitely,' Palmer stated, 'not *Schlum*.'

CHAPTER 28

At ten minutes to seven, Eleanora returned to his suite, wearing a soft white crepe dress that ended a few inches higher than the one she had worn to the reception.

'Do you like it?'

'It's very chic.'

'If you don't like it, I'll change. I bought it for this trip, actually.' She whirled slowly to let the skirt flare. He caught a glimpse of her buttocks through the dark upper section of her panty hose. 'Too short?'

He tried to keep his face blank. This was a sort of test, he supposed. If he said it was too short he'd have to explain why he felt that way, which would lead to the question of his new-found jealousy. Something inside him cautioned him against giving her this powerful weapon. Something else within him hated his inbred stinginess of spirit.

'It's too short,' Palmer said, taking a deep breath. 'I'm already jealous of every man who looks at you and this dress will attract the attention of blind men. But you must wear it.'

She shook her head. 'I'll change.' She started from the room.

The telephone pealed sharply. They glanced at each other. 'The chauffeur,' Palmer said, going to the phone. 'Hello.'

'Palmer?' A husky voice, low and somewhat harsh.

'Yes?'

'Get that fucking broad out of your room, Palmer.'

Palmer's eyelids drooped slightly. He could feel himself tensing for an attack. The skin across his shoulders tightened and the telephone hurt the palm of his hand as his fingers tightened around it.

'What did you say?' he asked in a voice so cold that the girl's eyebrows went up as she watched him.

'You heard me, lover-boy.'

Palmer's mind delved wildly through the card files of memory, noting the fact that his caller was an American, probably from New York. 'Rafferty,' he snapped, 'no wonder you never made brigadier.'

The man at the other end of the telephone exploded into guffaws of laughter. 'You miserable bastard,' he shouted, 'how did you remember my voice? It's been twenty years.'

'Where the hell are you calling from, Jack?'

'Downstairs. I missed your reception, Woody-baby, but I figured one Yank was enough to hold that kettle of Krauts.'

'Come on up. By an odd coincidence we have Jack Daniels.'

'We do? Who's we?'

'I thought you got cashiered out of Intelligence,' Palmer retorted.

'But that don't make me dumb, do it?' The caller hung up.

Palmer glanced at the girl. 'Please stay,' he said, 'and please wear that dress. This is an old Army buddy, Jack Rafferty. We were in S-2 during the war.'

'I wouldn't want to make you jealous of him, too,' she said, with a faint upward twist to one corner of her mouth.

'Now, now. Don't tease an old man.'

'You must like this Rafferty. Your whole attitude has changed. You've stopped being so serious. I like you better this way.'

Palmer nodded. 'You just like wearing that dress.' He came over and kissed her gently to keep from mussing her lipstick. 'You'll like Jack. He's insane.'

'An insane Army officer is what the world needs.'

'Insane-funny.'

'Then I'll like him.' She began putting ice in glasses and fussing with the basket of fruit. 'The proper hostess, yes?'

Palmer was laughing as he opened the door. Rafferty stood there for a moment, an inch or two taller than Palmer and much beefier. Palmer was glad to see he'd worn civilian clothes. His dark hair had receded slightly over the years and his cheeks had gotten a bit puffier. Otherwise, give or take a few dozen pounds and some wrinkles, he looked about as he had the last time Palmer had seen him. He took Rafferty's hairy, pawlike hand and pulled him into the room.

'You look great,' he said, 'fat and great.'

Rafferty's eyes swiveled to the girl and stayed there. 'So do you, Woody,' he said absentmindedly. 'Who is this charmer?'

'Miss Gregorius, Colonel Rafferty. It's still Colonel, isn't it?'

Rafferty nodded, his eyes still fixed on the girl. 'A pleasure to meet you, my dear.'

She handed him a highball, by way of shaking hands. 'Jack Daniels?'

He took the glass and turned to Palmer. 'Is that all I get? Her last name and a drink?'

'She works for my bank,' Palmer said. 'She's my interpreter

on this junket. Her first name's Eleanora.'

'Junket is right.' Rafferty winked at the girl and sat down in a chair, which creaked as his weight hit it. 'What the hell is this mission anyway? It's got all the Krauts stirred up. They must have mobilized every bigwig from as far away as Mannheim and Cologne for your party. Do you rate that kind of attention, Woody?'

Palmer made an offhand gesture of disclaimer. 'Why not?'

The big man stared at him almost rudely for a moment, then gulped his drink. 'Why not?' he agreed. He turned to the girl. 'Quite a fellow, your boss. Did he tell you what the two of us got into during the war?'

'He barely had time to tell me your name.' She handed Palmer a Scotch.

'What are you doing in Frankfurt, Jack?' Palmer asked.

'Finishing out the rest of my time. I retire in August and I'll be damned if the Army's going to cheat me out of my half-pay-for-life.'

Palmer laughed. 'The Army didn't cheat you out of much. What did they pay for over the past quarter century?'

'My BA,' Rafferty responded promptly, 'my MA, and my PhD.'

'*Dr.* Rafferty?'

'Why not?'

'Good God, I see it all. You'll retire on half-pay, teach in some college back home, and keep getting co-eds in trouble. What did America do to deserve you?'

'Co-eds don't get in trouble anymore, for Christ's sake. Do they?' he asked, swiveling to face the girl.

'The pill?'

He nodded sagely. 'And they aren't called co-eds anymore, either,' he informed the girl. 'If this man is teaching you current U.S. usage, you are in very big trouble.'

She made herself a small drink and sat down near the cocktail table. 'As a matter of fact,' she said then 'I haven't done that much interpreting on this trip. Most of the people he's talked to are fluent in English.'

'Then maybe he isn't talking to the right people.' Rafferty swiveled to face Palmer and the chair creaked again, loudly. 'You've got quite a few heavy hitters on your Monday and Tuesday schedule in Bonn, though. They ought to be able to shake loose some information for you, if they decide to cooperate.'

'Then you're still in Intelligence,' Palmer suggested.

The other man shook his head vehemently. 'I'm in photo interpretation, part of Intelligence. But I'm way the hell and gone out of the mainstream. And happy as a clam that way.'

'Why?'

'Those lintheads? College boys who wouldn't know pukka gen if it jumped up and pissed in their ear.' He turned to the girl. 'Pardon me, Miss Gregorius. Pukka gen is RAF slang.'

'For accurate information,' she said.

His stare froze on her for a long moment. He glanced at his drink, which was empty, and put it down on the cocktail table. Then he looked at Palmer. 'It's no wonder we do the worst staff work in the world,' he complained. 'When you start with rotten information, all you can make is rotten decisions. Look at Vietnam.'

'You look at it,' Palmer said. 'We're kind of sick of it back home.'

'The whole original strategy was to bomb Hanoi into surrender,' Rafferty went on. 'It still is, basically, among those turdheads who are screaming to fight. But in the history of conventional aerial bombardment, when did it ever force a surrender? Stalingrad? Dresden?'

'Hiroshima,' the girl said, handing him a refilled drink.

Rafferty shook his head violently. 'That wasn't a conventional weapon. And it wasn't what forced the Japanese surrender. Their effort had gone bankrupt months before. Anyone who tells you we had to A-bomb the Japs to save U.S. lives is handing you a meadow-muffin of giant dimensions.'

Her eyes shifted nervously to Palmer. 'Meadow-muffin?'

Palmer sketched a small mound about a foot in diameter. 'It's what cows leave behind.'

Her giggle was so abrupt that both men blinked. Her hand shot to her mouth and she subsided slowly into her chair, murmuring, 'Meadow-muffin, meadow-muffin.'

'I like her,' the big man announced. He turned to Palmer. 'Heard you and Edith split.'

'For a man who's just waiting out his last few months tucked away in a corner of photo interpretation, you have an amazing grapevine. It wasn't even in the columns back home.'

'Word gets around. Especially since the word's been out on your mission for over a month.'

'Which brings us to the subject of your visit.'

Rafferty gave him a hurt look and lifted his glass. 'This is the subject of my visit. Booze and nostalgia. I'm taking both of you to dinner.'

'That's nice of you.'

Rafferty put down his empty glass and stared at it for a moment. He heaved a sigh. 'What do you hear from Eddie Hagen?' he asked then.

The last person Palmer wanted to discuss with Jack was their old commander, Hagen. They hadn't seen eye to eye on him then and they probably wouldn't now.

'What makes you ask?'

'Heard you put that little four-flushing sneak on your payroll.'

'He's a director of the bank.'

'That's tantamount to Cleopatra taking the asp to her bosom.' He turned back to the girl and accepted a refilled glass.

'You've always had this thing about Eddie, haven't you?'

Rafferty nodded heavily. The chair creaked beneath him. 'I'll tell you something else,' he said then. 'Nothing that's happened to Hagen since the war has done anything to bolster my opinion of him. He's a sneak, a liar, a creep, and, to top it off, he made brigadier and I didn't.'

Both men chuckled for a moment. The big man's glass clicked against his teeth. He took it away half empty. 'Pity I couldn't retire at half a brigadier's pay.'

'You talk too much to make brigadier.'

'I talk too much period.' Rafferty's eyes grew smaller as he stared into the glass. 'I think I'll spend my first year of civilian life writing my memoirs.'

No one said anything for a while. All three seemed rapt in their own thoughts for a moment.

'This Mr. Hagen,' the girl spoke up then, to Palmer. 'He is the one Ginnie mentioned to you?'

Palmer frowned at her. 'Not in front of J-A-C-K,' he spelled out.

'You're already having trouble with him, huh?' Rafferty surmised. 'I wouldn't wonder. You have to slam him hard, Woody. You have to come down on him like a bootheel on a cockroach. Leave nothing but paste smeared on the floor. Otherwise he'll get back up on his legs and crawl off under the woodwork and start all over again.'

'Will you give Eddie Hagen a rest?'

Rafferty pushed his empty glass across the cocktail table. 'A light one for the road, my dear.'

'You said the word was out on my mission,' Palmer said then. 'What word?'

Rafferty shrugged so massively that the chair back let out a sharp twang. 'The usual. Nothing official.'

'What's the word on the Foundation for Economic Study?' Palmer persisted.

'Straight goods. More or less.'

'But infiltrated,' Palmer added.

'Not to my knowledge.'

'What would a semiretired photo interpreter like you know?'

'That's right.' The big man examined his fresh drink's color and found it no lighter than the previous mixtures. 'Let's give that a rest, too. We have an eight o'clock reservation at the Brückenkeller.' He smiled at the girl. *'Kennst du die Brückenkeller, Fräulein?'*

'Nein.'

'Sehr schöon, sehr gemütlich.'

'Lieblich.'

Rafferty nodded. He got to his feet and the chair toppled over backward onto the floor. The big man blinked but made no move to pick up the chair. 'A quarter of a century in this lousy Army,' he said then to no one in particular. 'Twenty-five years, two wives, five children.' He drained his drink.

'And three university degrees,' the girl suggested.

'And two good friends,' Rafferty yelled, taking her arm and Palmer's at the same time. 'Let's go *machen* whoopee!'

CHAPTER 29

Despite his size and the number of drinks he'd already had, Rafferty moved quickly enough almost to out-distance Palmer and Eleanora as he led them through the lobby of the hotel and into a waiting cab. Palmer excused himself for a moment to dismiss his own chauffeur and tell him to return at nine the next morning. He thought for a moment of using his limousine for the evening, but it was better to give Rafferty his head.

Palmer remembered enough of his old associate to recall that whether he turned out to be right or wrong about something, his instincts were usually good even when he'd guessed wrong. This inevitably produced a heartfelt apology the next morning or whenever the Jack Daniels had finally been oxidized.

Palmer only half listened as Rafferty chatted with the girl on their way along the River Main to the Brückenkeller. Rafferty seemed to be trying out a series of possibly mutual friends on her and the girl was finding none of the names familiar.

The moon had come up early. As the cab slowed for a moment, Palmer noticed they were passing through the medieval square he had seen from the hotel's roof garden. He caught a glimpse of a sign that read 'Römerberg' and an instant later Jack Rafferty bellowed '*Halt machen!*' at the driver.

'Ninety-nine and forty-four one-hundredths percent rebuilt after the bombing,' Rafferty said, pointing to the low two- and three-story stone buildings. '*Aber sehr richtig,*' he added to Eleanora. 'Very accurate reproduction work. They didn't take any modern shortcuts. Strictly fifteenth-century techniques. That's the Dom over there.' He tapped the driver and signaled him to continue to the restaurant. 'You have to remember that all the emperors of the Holy Roman Empire were crowned in Frankfurt.'

'Not all,' the girl demurred. 'It's true that Charlemagne lived here after about 790. And Frederick Barbarossa was crowned King of Germania here. But the imperial coronation took place in Aachen until the middle of the sixteenth century I think.'

'You think,' Rafferty echoed. He winked at Palmer. 'Beware the girl who says "I think." She means "I know, but I don't want to make you think I'm showing you up." Anyway, a mess of Holy Roman emperors took the pledge around here.' He turned back to the girl. 'What's a smart girl like you doing in a bucket-shop like Ubco?'

She frowned slightly. 'Bucket-shop?'

Palmer gently pressed Rafferty's bulk back in his seat so that he could get a better look at the girl, sitting on the far side. 'Colonel Rafferty is denigrating the probity of our financial establishment. Bucket-shop is a term of opprobrium.'

The girl grinned uncertainly, but Palmer noticed that his friend's face had gradually gone deadpan and now looked somewhat grim. 'Unless you really meant it, Jack,' he added to Rafferty.

The colonel shook his head almost absentmindedly, as if his thoughts had already leaped ahead to a different, and more serious, subject. 'Come on,' he said then. 'This is supposed to be a fun evening, Woody.'

'I'm having fun already.'

Rafferty's glance raked him for a moment. 'Good,' he said then. The cab pulled up before an extremely old stone building and the colonel led them down a long hall and around several corners down a flight of stairs that seemed cut into bedrock. Another flight led down still further into the earth, flanked by bronze railings. Palmer could hear music from a small band.

As the three of them descended the second flight of stairs, Palmer saw that they were in what appeared to be a real cellar formed of mighty semicircular arches, some cut into the stone, some cast in cement and roughly covered with a pinkish-yellow plaster. Niches had been cut into the curving side walls and gilded carved-wood religious figures mounted in the recesses. At one side the immense oval end of a wine barrel over six feet high had been set into one wall. The flat face of the barrel end had been deeply carved with a series of scenes.

The headwaiter, whose speech was heavily larded with 'Herr Obersts,' led them to a table overlooking a still-lower level of cellars.

'How far down does this go, Jack?' Palmer asked.

'Since the year 1654,' the headwaiter replied, under the assumption that he had answered the question. 'The Brückenkeller barrel there,' he went on, indicating the immense object, 'held five thousand gallons.'

Palmer saw the strolling trio of musicians open a door in the side of the barrel and walk inside, one of them wiping his forehead. 'It now holds three musicians?' Palmer remarked.

The headwaiter blinked. 'Sir?'

Rafferty waved his hand negligently, as if dusting away anything that had been said up till now. 'Give us a very, very cold bottle of Graacher Domprobst,' he said. 'You still have the '64 *feinste Auslese*?'

'*Jawohl, Herr Oberst.*'

'Unless I hear a scream of anguish,' Rafferty said turning first to the girl and then to Palmer, 'I'll do the ordering and we'll stick with white wine. I knew a man once who could drink whiskey and follow up with red wine, but he was a card-carrying masochist and didn't last long in these parts.'

'Order away,' Palmer agreed.

'You can start chilling two bottles of Wehlener Sonnenuhr '59,' Rafferty told the headwaiter, 'because tonight money is no object, and you can bring us a few hors d'oeuvres to begin. Something light.'

'*Ganz richtig, Herr Oberst. Augenblicklich.*' The headwaiter scribbled wildly on a small card. 'The waiter will take your dinner order when you so desire, *Herr Oberst.*'

'*Sehr gut.*'

'Do you require the musicians, *Herr Oberst?*'

'*Noch später.*' Rafferty made the same whiskbroom movement with his arms and the headwaiter retreated tactfully.

Palmer got the distinct feeling that, in addition to being well known here, Rafferty's need for music with his food was also understood. At any rate, the trio of guitar, accordion, and violin arrived with the Graacher Domprobst and immediately produced a creditable version of 'East Side, West Side,' for Rafferty, who sang along with the guitarist.

'This gentleman is from Chicago,' he then announced.

The guitarist nodded sharply, once, and the trio burst into the song of the same name, with complete lyrics. Palmer smiled and sipped the cold, dry wine. He glanced at the girl and saw that she had been watching him with a kind of indulgent look, as if assuming that he was tremendously pleased by having 'Chicago' sung to him.

'I saw the sight,' the guitarist sang, 'the sight of my life. I saw a man dance with his wife in Chicago, Chicago, my home town.'

Palmer applauded at the song's end. 'This young lady,' he announced then, 'is from Paris.'

The trio seemed to have begun playing 'I Love Paris in the Springtime' almost before Palmer finished speaking. Palmer was beginning to enjoy the game. As soon as the musicians had concluded he held up one finger: 'But she hasn't seen it in some time,' he pointed out.

The trio began 'The Last Time I Saw Paris.' Rafferty nodded sagely. 'You've got the idea, Woody-baby.' When the song ended, he winked at the guitarist. 'He was born in Chicago, but he lives in New York.'

The musician shook his head, intoned 'A hell of a town, *nein?*' and led his group into the Bernstein song from *On the Town.*

'Come back with the *Fleisch und Kartoffeln, ja*?'

'You bet,' the guitarist said, leading his flock elsewhere.

Palmer saw that they were now on their second bottle of the Domprobst. 'Have you ever stumped them?'

'Not in ten years.'

'Marvelous wine,' the girl said.

An hour later, as Palmer sipped a sweet, thick wine called Abtsberg Spätlese Eiswein, he listened to the faint sound of the trio somewhere in one of the other cellar rooms working over a collection of Strauss waltzes. Palmer felt stuffed with food, but not drunk. Evidently the white German wines treated him more mercifully than the white French wines had in Compiègne. Of course, he reflected a bit hazily, if he hadn't passed out in Compiègne that night, none of this might have happened. There might never have been an occasion for her to warm to him or he to her. And the whole enveloping feeling of warmth he had with her now might never have happened.

He beamed at her with love and gratitude and longing. She didn't see any of it, being locked in a rather tense discussion with Rafferty about who had actually assassinated the Kennedys. Palmer made a face. He hated things like that spoiling his mood. This was euphoria if ever he'd felt it. He wanted to preserve the feeling.

'Not one of these paranoids who sees conspiracies under every rock,' Rafferty was telling the girl. 'And I'm the first to admit how peculiar it looks from the outside, especially to someone who really doesn't understand America. I mean, if these two murders weren't part of a conspiracy, then there's no logic left in the world, is there? But I tell you, little girl, there is no conspiracy. There is just the sad, sad fact that we have loonies running around like Oswald and Sirhan. You don't believe me,' he added morosely. 'Why should you? What the hell, why should anybody believe anything we tell them any more?' He stared at Palmer. 'You silly bastard, you were supposed to keep the home fires burning and all you did was blow our national credibility to hell.'

'Me?'

'But, look,' the girl persisted, touching Rafferty's sleeve to deflect his wrath from Palmer. 'Why has no one assassinated your President Johnson or Nixon?'

Rafferty shrugged. 'I said you wouldn't believe me. You won't believe me when I say they run the same risks the Kennedys did.

173

There's something in the whole democratic process, my dear, sweet young girl. Keep telling people the same lie generation after generation – that all men are created equal, which they ain't – and pretty soon a moron with a gun knows he's as good as the President of the United States and, by Christ, he's gonna prove it, too, don't you know, because his mother and his teachers told him so.'

The girl drew back as if slapped. 'Surely this is not true.'

'As sure as you're sitting there smart and pretty,' he told her. 'That one big lie is responsible for everything rotten in America. Lousy teachers in lousy schools. Rotten cops, Crappy politicians. Hoodlum-businessmen and businessmen-hoodlums. Loafers drawing welfare money. What the hell, who has to earn a day's pay when he can con the government out of it? Where everyone's created equal there is no incentive to do your best. The only way to get ahead is to cheat the other guy before he cheats you.'

'I have never heard so much utter nonsense from a grown man,' Palmer put in, 'since the last time I had the misfortune to listen to your half-baked ur-Anarchist ravings. When do we get to the part about property being a crime?'

Rafferty grinned at him and signaled the waiter. 'Clear up some of this before we start throwing dishes,' he instructed the man.

'Then he isn't serious?' the girl asked Palmer.

'He is seriously insane,' Palmer said. 'He's an *agent provocateur* of ideas. If you listen to him long enough you end up in the laughing academy.'

'Laughing academy?'

'Funny farm,' Rafferty explained helpfully.

'I'm sorry.'

'Loony bin,' the colonel expanded.

The two men nodded to each other. Palmer poured everyone a little more *Eiswein*. 'But he holds a doctorate of philosophy,' the girl insisted. Palmer realized that, for the first time he could remember, she was showing signs of having had too much to drink.

'And don't you forget it,' Rafferty warned her gruffly.

She stood up. 'Excuse me.'

Both men watched her legs as she left the table and headed for the ladies' room. 'You always did like them long and lean,' Rafferty said then. 'How's Edith and the kids?'

'I don't know and fine, in that order.' Palmer sipped the *Eiswein*. 'What do you think of the girl?'

'Smashing. I am going to dream about her for months to come.'

'I'm serious.'

'I know you are.' Rafferty laughed softly. 'It sticks out all over you. Mr. Icewater-in-the-Veins is in love.'

'I think she's some kind of part-time agent.'

'Most of them are.'

'It doesn't shock you to hear me say that?'

Rafferty shrugged. 'Woody, I've been over here so long I'm a goddamned European myself most of the time. We don't shock easy, us Europeans. I don't even want to know who she works for. I gather you don't, either, huh?'

'Eventually. But right now it's too much fun to spoil.'

The colonel nodded heavily. 'If you were a European like me, baby, you'd find out and it still wouldn't spoil the fun. What the hell are we here on earth for except to have fun? How much damage could that girl do you?'

'I don't know.'

'I mean, if you were still married, well, okay, they'd have your ass over a barrel, candid photos, the works. Blackmail City.'

'I was there once,' Palmer said. 'A couple of years ago. It didn't work.'

'With your money? What would?'

'Planted microfilms of secret documents?' Palmer suggested softly.

'Yeah,' the colonel agreed, 'but only of H-bomb plans or MIRV warheads.'

Palmer got the feeling Rafferty wasn't being serious. Which was just as well. Jack was his friend, but of late no longer his confidant. Any point in telling him about the films in the shirt cardboard? For some reason he couldn't put a name to, Palmer decided against the idea.

'You're a hard man to box in,' Rafferty was saying. 'You're too rich. If you were a wage slave, and married, they could really mess you up.'

'Who is they?'

'*Ich weiss nicht.* Didn't the girl give you a hint?'

'No. It might be the Eastern bloc.'

'That's the easy answer. Just like the girl thinking Jack and Bobbie were killed in the same plot. It's not hard to think like a

175

paranoid these days. So you make the assumption that the Russkis or one of their allies is paying the girl. I means, when in doubt scream "Red!" But this goddamned continent's honey-combed with espionage networks of so many different allegi-ances that I gave up keeping track of them long ago.'

'Including free-lancers who work for anybody's pay.'

'Right.' The heavy man sighed. 'Will you humor an old buddy, old buddy?'

'How?'

'What kind of trouble is Eddie Hagen giving you?'

Palmer listened to the sudden way Rafferty's speech had grown sharper and less slurred. He knew the man to have an immense capacity for drink without showing its effects, but he found it hard to believe that Hagen meant that much in Rafferty's scheme of things. 'He's no trouble.' Palmer countered. 'I'm under a lot of pressure from New York to fly back for my Monday board of directors' meeting. The girl knows the pres-sure I'm under and she thinks I ought to do it. The minute I tell you about it, you'll want me to go back too. It's a conspiracy to get me the hell back to the last place on earth I want to be, New York.'

'Look who's being paranoid,' Rafferty upended the *Eiswein* bottle and found it empty. 'This stuff'll kill you. I think it got the girl sick or something. Want me to have them send a waitress in after her?'

'Give her a few minutes more.'

The colonel stared into his half-full glass for a long moment. 'Woody,' he said then, his voice heavy again, 'did you ever wonder why I made chicken colonel in 1955 and haven't gotten that one lousy brigadier's star since?'

'I assumed the Army wasn't entirely out of its mind.'

Rafferty's mouth creased in a halfhearted smile. 'I mean really, buddy, really. You know I was a damned good intelli-gence officer. In my head there are files not even the CIA and MI 5 have. Not even the KMG. I mean, I was one of the best and you know it.'

'Was?'

'Shit, I'm rusty now. My heart hasn't been in it for years.'

Palmer shook his head. 'I never understood what a wild Irish radical like you was doing in Intelligence work anyway. You couldn't be part of the Establishment if you tried.'

'That's not why the pricks held me down in grade.'

176

'You're dying to tell me the real reason, aren't you?'

'Bet your sweet ass I am.' Rafferty hunched forward in his chair, which creaked loudly. 'How good's your memory, baby? Try Sicily, 1943.'

Palmer nodded. 'I've had reason to remember it a lot in the last six months. What part of it do you want played back? Where I went in with orders to save the top Mafiosi from being shot by the partisans?'

'I want you to think about the part where one Eddie Hagen, then a colonel and now a retired brigadier, the bastard, gave you those orders.'

'Now who's the paranoid?' Palmer retorted.

'Hell, Woody, I told the girl there was no conspiracy to kill the Kennedys. That sure doesn't mean there's no conspiracy to do some other things.'

'To do what?'

'Shit if I know.'

'Lower the voice,' Palmer said. 'You'll have us thrown out.' He took Rafferty's glass of *Eiswein* from him and drained it. 'What are you trying to tell me, Jack? That there was conspiracy between Lucky Luciano and U.S. military government to set up the Mafia as our deputy rulers in Sicily? Because if you are, it's a matter of public record in the files of Congressional investigating committees. So what?'

Rafferty's beefy, handsome face darkened slightly. 'Woody, you're putting me off, aren't you? You don't really want to hear this any more than you want to know who the girl's working for. Christ, in a way I don't blame you.'

'The point, Jack, get to the point.'

'The point is, or was, that I always wondered about that little deal with Luciano. Tom Dewey was supposed to be in on it, and maybe his deputy governor, Poletti. But what I always wondered was where Eddie Hagen got into the picture.'

'He was given orders and he followed them.'

'You're still putting me off, buddy. You're pretending to answer questions I haven't asked.' Rafferty sighed deeply and tried to relax by leaning back in his chair. 'What I'm asking about is possibilities. That's all we ever get to look at in this world, isn't it? I'm asking about the possibility that something begins in a certain way – under the exigencies of winning a war – and moves on smoothly and logically to something else and then develops into a third thing and a fourth and so on. All logical. All connected. Sicily 1943 was the beginning of a road. Isn't it possible the road didn't end there? That instead it led on, as roads do, until the end we have now is something quite different from the beginning we had then.'

'In other words, a current conspiracy.'

Rafferty shrugged massively. 'It's possible to deny specific plots. It's impossible to deny the possibility of any plots at all.'

Palmer started to say something, to deny this hazy suggestion of a conspiracy, the outlines of which neither he nor Rafferty would ever be able to describe or trace. Then he subsided. Jack was right about his motives, or lack of them. The state of euphoria was tenuous enough, hard enough to achieve and easy enough to destroy. I really don't want facts, Palmer told himself. I don't even want to hear paranoid hypotheses from as brilliant a paranoid as Rafferty.

'Okay, Woody, here comes your lady. I'll shut up.'

'Thanks, Jack. I'm floating. Don't shoot me down just yet.'

Rafferty clapped him on the elbow. 'Christ, I know the feeling, baby. Far be it from me to –' He stopped and frowned. 'But, hustle your butt back to New York for that Monday clambake. I couldn't live with myself if I didn't tell you that.'

Eleanora looked pale, but able to cope with things, as she returned to the table. Palmer got up to help her into her chair. 'Now Jack's joined the chorus sending me back on Monday.'

'Will you go?' she asked.

'But I have important business in Bonn on Monday.'

'Postpone it a few days,' Rafferty suggested.

The girl glanced up at him and her brown eyes looked faintly worried. 'He is your friend,' she said. 'You must listen to him.'

'Everyone's my friend.' Palmer sank back into his seat. 'I don't have a single enemy in the whole cockeyed world.'

CHAPTER 30

Palmer knew he was dreaming.

Otherwise it simply wasn't possible for Brigadier General Edward Everett Hagen, U.S.A., Ret. (Eddie), chairman of the board, Massachusetts Aerospace, Inc. (M.A., Inc.), and member of the board of directors of United Bank and Trust Company,

S.A. (Ubco), to be wearing a double-breasted white sharkskin jacket with a white shirt, white tie, broad-brimmed white fedora, and black-and-white golf brogues. He had just lighted a long, fat cigar and had assumed an Edward G. Robinson squint, sour-faced and malevolent.

Palmer rolled over away from the girl and woke up in a sweat that began to grow cold the moment he was cut off from the animal heat they generated between them under the covers. He lay there thinking.

Eventually, the air-conditioned room cooled Palmer down to a point where he began to shiver. He finally rolled off the bed and stumbled into the bathroom, on the way picking up his wristwatch from the bedside table. He saw that the time was now either 6 A.M. or 12:30. His eyes seemed glued together by *Eiswein*. He sat down on the toilet bowl and tried to use logic, his one remaining weapon.

Jack Rafferty had brought them back to the hotel about three in the morning, so if the time were now half-past twelve, the light of noon should be streaming in through the windows, which it wasn't. Palmer concluded he had been asleep roughly three hours when the sight of Eddie Hagen as a stereotype of a Mafia capo-don had roused him from troubled slumber.

Having determined all this to his dubious satisfaction, he also concluded that he was now wide awake. He knew the girl carried sleeping pills or tranquilizer tablets, but they would be in her room across the hall. In short, Palmer decided, what's left of the night will be white.

He padded silently through the bedroom into the living room, closing the door behind him. Then he sank into an armchair and began reading through one of the magazines hotels provide for their guests, the kind of publication that relates in terrifying detail what there is to see and do in the city where one happens to have lighted momentarily, as long as all one cares to do is stay out late watching bobbing breasts in a floor show or prowl in search of jewelry, perfume, watches, and cameras.

Palmer cast the magazine aside after a moment and began wondering what he should do with his life.

As it had for the last few years, during which he had begun asking himself the same questions over and over again, it once more struck Palmer as insane that a man his age was still unsure of what to do with himself.

In his teens he hadn't had a moment's indecision. He'd

known, almost from puberty, not what he would be, but what he damned well wouldn't be. Since his older brother, Hanley, was first in line for training at their father's bank in Chicago, Palmer knew that the one thing he would never have to be was a banker.

At the start of the war, Hanley had gone out on a PBY training flight that failed to come back to Pensacola. The bodies were never recovered. When Palmer got home after the war, there was no Hanley as a buffer between him and his father. Palmer was married by then and the only sensible thing was to submit to the old man's will.

That sort of enforced decision, Palmer realized now as he sat in the chilly hotel room and watched the sky lighten in the east, is insidiously simple to live with. If he'd fought and clawed his way into banking. there would have been long, desolate hours of questioning whether the decision was right. But to have it handed over as a birthright, and a damned lucrative one at that, made the whole thing too disarmingly convenient. Only now, decades later, having buried his father and sold the old man's bank, having come to New York where the action was, and having found enough of it to sicken him, only now was he beginning to ask the desolate questions he should have asked at the very beginning.

As if, he thought now, I have a whole life ahead of me.

That was it, of course. He didn't have that much time ahead of him – twenty years, the actuarial table said, but it was an average that included men who died both early and late, not a guarantee that each of them would live out a full allotment. He'd pissed away almost the first fifty years, one way or another. He knew it didn't look that way from the outside. One always managed to patch together a life that seemed interesting to others and dull to oneself. But, like most people, he'd pissed away his youth and was now wasting his middle years. He had enough honesty these days to realize it, but not enough insight to know what to do about it.

His inability to decide led him into all sorts of silly positions, like this business with the Monday board meeting. It seemed almost as if even total strangers were telling him he had to be there. What did either Jack Rafferty or the girl know about it? Yet both of them – and Ginnie and Bill Elston and Harry Elder – were absolutely certain his main responsibility lay with seeing the bank through this so-called crisis.

It was almost as if his mission for the Foundation was taken seriously by no one but himself, and perhaps a few numskulls like Forellen. And Mather, Forellen's boss in New York.

Palmer got up and walked on bare feet around the room, trying to locate a thermostat that would cut off the cooling. He found a control at last and turned it off, hearing the faint noise in the room – which he hadn't been aware of before – suddenly stop. He continued pacing to keep warm. It was a mark of his peculiar mood that he knew he could go into the bedroom and get a dressing gown, but he simply didn't care to.

The mission wasn't any more serious than he wanted to make it, Palmer decided. He himself wasn't taking it that seriously, using it first as an excuse for a vacation, a reason to flee New York, and now as an alibi to stay with the girl because he couldn't bear being away from her. Then why should anyone else except H.B. take it seriously?

If she were telling the truth, he could easily postpone his appointments, go to New York, and come back to find her waiting for him wherever he wanted her. He knew enough about her now to realize that she really meant it. She hadn't promised to be with him to the end of time, but a commitment of this range was perfectly understandable. And the postponement also put off having to make up his mind about doing H.B.'s 'little errand' for him.

'Where are you?' she moaned from the other room.

'Go back to sleep.'

The bedroom door opened and Palmer turned to see her, naked, leaning against the frame, using the back of her hand like a cat to push the hair away from her face. 'It's freezing in there.'

'Come sit on my lap.'

She walked slowly to him, taking short uncertain steps, because her eyes were still half closed, instead of the long strides she usually took. Her breasts shone rosy-gold in the first horizontal rays of morning sun slanting in now across the rooftops of Frankfurt. She sat down on his knees facing him and pulled his face down to bury it between her breasts. They felt almost hot on Palmer's cold cheeks. She began to rock forward and back against him and in a while she had managed to work him into her although he was still soft.

He leaned back in the chair and smiled at her. 'There's nothing like this in New York,' he told her. 'Why must I leave it even for a few days?'

She had begun to rotate slowly with his penis as the center of their small world. 'Because it's always here for you,' she said. 'I'm always yours.'

He felt himself grow inside her and he could feel her pulling him deeper into her. They were moving together now against each other. She lifted one of her long, slim legs and rested it on his shoulder. Then, after a while, she began to turn gently away from him. She moved in slow arcs through a circle until she was facing out into the room. He cupped his hands over the swell of her hips as they broadened out from her waist. Her buttocks surged back and forth, swallowing him and letting him almost escape, only to engulf him again. When he came, the angle of entrance parceled his spasm into short, sharp bursts of ecstasy, one after another, like machine-gun fire, each more beautiful than the last, until he screamed, hanging onto her buttocks for dear life. He sank back exhausted against the armchair.

When he awoke he was in bed beside her, under the covers, warm and safe, without knowing exactly how he'd gotten there. His wristwatch told him it was now seven in the morning.

She was watching him. 'You never screamed that way before,' she said. 'It frightened me.'

'I'm fine.'

'I know. But it frightened me for a moment.'

His mouth felt dry. He tried to moisten it and, after a while, succeeded. 'I've decided to fly to New York Sunday,' he said then. 'I'll be back here in Frankfurt Tuesday or Wednesday.'

She nodded. 'You screamed because it was good.'

'It was perfect.'

She nodded again. 'You should let yourself make more noise. You shouldn't bottle yourself up. Will you promise me to try?'

He grinned at her. 'Anything. I promise you anything.'

'It's this thing men have, this male mystique thing. Little boys don't cry. Grown men don't cry. And when they experience orgasm they must pretend to – ah, the slang word – to cool it. Don't cool it with me, *chéri*. Yes?'

'Yes.'

She patted his chest for a moment. 'As for New York, I think you should postpone all your appointments, today's as well as Monday's. That way we could have all of today and all Saturday and half of Sunday together. We might see the Rhine and the Mosel.'

182

'Postpone them all?'

'But, you see, otherwise all we really have together is Saturday and it isn't enough.'

'Greedy.'

'Yes, greedy. I want as much as I can of you if I'm not to see you for three days.'

Palmer's eyes closed. 'You're saying all the right things,' he murmured. 'My God, how I love you. I nearly died inside you before. It was the passion on the cross. It was so lovely, it hurt.' He opened his eyes and laughed embarrassedly. 'Listen to that. You are the resurrection and this is the life. Zap. Pow.'

'What? Zap? Pow?'

'Just forget everything except that I love you.' He pulled her on top of him and kissed her. Her mouth had an early-morning taste he loved. Then: 'Okay. Postpone everything. Let's find us a few rivers.'

She jumped off the bed. '*Mein Gott!* I think we've missed the *Schnellfahrt!*'

'I beg your pardon, Miss Gregorius.'

'The fast steamer from Mainz.' She snatched up the telephone and began pouring a great stream of German into it. '*Nein, nach koblenz, bitte,*' she was repeating. '*Rheinabwärts, kein aufwärts.*'

After a while she nodded and hung up the telephone. 'We have thirty minutes,' she announced.

'*Was ist los?*'

'The limo will pick us up downstairs in thirty minutes and get us to Mainz by quarter to nine, when the *Schnellfahrt* casts off.'

'Is that what a *Schnellfahrt* does?'

She stared at him for a moment, and then her hand went to her mouth. 'You are turning very rapidly into a dirty old man.'

He leaped out of bed and made a grab at her. 'Old?'

CHAPTER 31

The *Schnellfahrt*, Palmer learned, was only *schnell* when compared with the other big, white steamers that sailed the Rhine in both directions. Instead of stopping at every village along the

183

way, it skipped clusters of them but still paid calls at half a dozen.

They spent most of their time on deck chairs watching the river banks flow smoothly past, examining the castles along the way and the heavy and light shipping that shared the broad river with them. The boat seemed loaded mostly with Americans and little old German ladies. When they sailed past the famous Loreleifelsen, one of the few towering granite cliffs too steep to support vineyards, the ship's public address system ceased its steady trilingual sightseeing gabble and played a recording of the Lorelei song. All the old women, Palmer noticed, joined in softly, their eyes moist with their own memories.

'It's so sad,' the girl murmured in his ear, speaking quietly, not to offend the old women, but to keep from being overheard by American tourists.

'It's a pretty old song.'

'The women are so sad. You know what their lives have been. At that age, they've lost fathers and husbands and sons and grandsons in two wars.'

'Two wars Germany started.'

She drew back from him. 'Does that make a difference?'

Palmer suddenly felt as if he had stepped into a patch of quicksand. He really didn't know this girl, he realized. All he actually knew was that he needed her so badly he would do anything to keep her. 'I don't suppose it does matter,' he said, trying to dismiss the subject he'd raised.

'Then why raise it?' she countered. 'We know the Germans are their own worst enemies. But what could these women have done about it?'

Palmer shrugged. He still hoped to head them into another avenue of talk. 'Nothing.'

'But it's clear from your attitude that you hold the whole German people responsible both for the Kaiser and for Hitler.'

Palmer smiled at her and shook his head. 'It's too pretty a day. Let's just sunbathe.'

The girl took a long breath. 'Perhaps it's only fate, after all,' she said in a calmer tone. 'You hold all of them responsible, as if a woman could have done anything against the whole German military machine. But the irony is that today the whole world holds you Americans responsible for what your military machine is doing in Vietnam.'

'You Americans again.'

'Yes, again.' She pulled slightly away from him, as if emphasizing the gap between them as they lay back in their deck chairs. The sun put sharp red flashes in her hair as she moved. 'You Americans. The last time we had a fight it was also about personal responsibility, wasn't it?'

'Yes.'

'And here we are fighting again.'

'With you on very shaky ground,' Palmer pointed out. 'Either each of these little old ladies is personally responsible for the Kaiser and Hitler – and I for Vietnam – or all of us are innocent.'

'That word.' She lay back in her chair and closed her eyes. 'Nobody is innocent of anything, *chéri*. People like us ought to remember that.'

'Why?'

'And another thing,' she said, suddenly sitting back up again, 'how can one compare an ancient German *Hausfrau* with the head of one of the chief sources of financing for the American war machine?'

'*Mein Gott!*'

'Her personal responsibility is of an order far different and far less crucial than yours.' Her eyes had grown much darker as she talked. 'Can you deny that the Ubco bank is in the mainstream of the American military effort?'

'And that we both work for it?'

Her face went dead for a moment and then she smiled ruefully. 'You are a skilled debater,' she said after a moment. 'Were you Jesuit-trained, perhaps?'

Palmer watched her settle back in her deck chair again. Apparently the crisis had passed. 'Three years ago,' he said then, 'or perhaps longer, I don't remember, I was being interviewed for the job of executive vee-pee of Ubco. The man interviewing me was Lane Burckhardt, whom I later eased out as chief executive officer. He's retired now and hates my guts. I probably gave him ten extra years of life by pushing him out of the nest. Anyway, Lane was trying to impress me with the importance of the job he was offering me. He said bankers had to see things much more clearly than ordinary people. He said that the world was divided into two camps and in the camp of capitalism, the U.S. ruled the roost. And when you said the U.S., you meant the banks, because the banks finance the country. And when you talked about the big banks, you meant Ubco because it was biggest. And when you mentioned Ubco, he said, you meant him. Because he ran it.'

'And now you run it.'

'Lane's out because he actually thought he ran Ubco. He didn't, any more than I do.'

'Oh, that's an easy rationale.'

'Don't be fooled by titles. A bank is like any other business – or maybe even more so. It lives by providing what the public wants. It's true that I sit at the head of it and on my say-so, we can change the brand of paper in our toilets, or refuse a loan here or grant one there. But if in the long run I don't do what the public wants, I go down. Just like Lane. Somebody pushes me out of the nest.'

'This public,' the girl began to ask. 'What –'

'The business public, mainly,' Palmer explained. 'A bank our size does most of its work for businesses. We take checking and savings accounts for private citizens. But that's to have a source of cash flow. We live or die by how well we serve business.'

She nodded and pointed to two steep terraced cliffs rising on the right-hand side of the river. 'See there? Burg Katz is the first one. The other is Burg Maus.'

Palmer stared at the rise of the cliff, with tiny vineyards tucked away on every possible space that was less than vertical. At the top a brown double-turreted fortress loomed against the sky, its round dungeon tower rising even higher than the conical turrets. '*Katz und Maus?*' he asked.

'We'll be in Koblenz quite soon,' she said, standing up and moving to the rail. 'Thanks for the lesson in politico-economics.'

'That was a lecture, not a lesson.'

'We can continue it in the car. They're meeting us with a Hertz Volkswagen at the Koblenz dock.'

Palmer joined her at the rail. 'You did all that with one phone call this morning?'

'The concierge helped.'

'And the concierge is canceling my appointments.'

'He's a very reliable man.'

'I'm sure, but...' Palmer stopped himself. 'I can think of better things to do than discuss politics and economics,' he went on in a lighter tone.

'We'll drive slowly along the Mosel to Trier,' she promised him. 'We'll stop at every little village and sample the local vin-take. We'll sleep in tiny inns. We'll take naps after lunch. We'll wander among the grapevines. We'll take naps after dinner. You'll love it.'

'And we'll meet your parents in Trier?'

'Only if you wish.'

'And Tanya, too?'

She had turned away from him. 'There!' she cried, pointing, 'around that turn is Koblenz.'

CHAPTER 32

Friday and Saturday seemed to flow together like the Mosel itself, slow, sure, curving at a languid pace, disclosing one beauty after another. In retrospect, Palmer couldn't remember anything but isolated moments and scenes. Now, as he lay alone in his Trier hotel room trying to get some sleep against to-morrow's early-morning drive to Frankfurt and the flight back to New York, he tried to soothe his mind by remembering what he could of the past two days.

He missed the girl badly, but they had decided it was best for her to spend the night with her parents, even though their apartment was a small one. She had gotten him a room in the ultramodern Porta Nigra Hotel, across the street from the ancient Roman gate that gave it its name. Trier – or Treves as the French called it off and on over the centuries whenever they felt they owned it – had been an early Roman colony a century before Christ and boasted ruins in better condition than Rome itself.

What he knew of the city the girl had told him at dinner that night with her parents. She had seemed so much younger in their presence, like a schoolgirl eager to show off her knowledge of the city her family now called home.

But the long, meandering trip along the Mosel to Trier had begun on the dockside at Koblenz where the Hertz man, anxious in his yellow jacket, had stood by the side of the pale blue Volkswagen, waving his yellow-and-black insignia over his head to attract the attention of Herr Palmer. The girl had taken the wheel at first and quickly headed them out of the city southwest into the Mosel Valley, the river running alongside the

187

two-way road, sometimes only a few yards from its edge.

It seemed to Palmer, as he lay there in darkness, that they had crossed and recrossed the Mosel literally dozens of times, by bridge and by ferry. The tiny one-man electric flatboats were guided by overhead cables. He and the girl would stop, invariably across the placid river from where the ferry was docked at the moment. The boatman would see them and bring the craft across. It could hold four Volkswagens, Palmer recalled, or four of the high-wheel tractors that dotted the landscape. Or one Cadillac.

The tractors seemed to be the family car of the area, most of them U.S.-made, with three or four youngsters clinging to them or wagons in tow carrying immense tanks of liquid fertilizer or insecticide. Its being June, the first harvest of hay was also being brought in as Palmer and the girl motored slowly along the river. The grapevines, each trained around a pole some six to ten feet high, were still young at this time of year, the grapes themselves hardly more than clusters of tiny hard green seeds the size of orange pips.

Palmer could clearly picture his first castle, up close, the Thurant at Alken, a twin-towered ruin thousands of feet above the river. The Volks had to make the trip in low gear up the narrow dirt-road switchbacks. Through the archer's slits in the thick stone walls, Palmer and the girl watched small barges floating slowly down the peaceful, looping river below. The town had hit upon a scheme for renting apartment space in the castle as a means of keeping it in repair and free of vandalism. Private quarters were screened from visitors' view by lush gardens of rock plants and flowers.

'This is where you could live out your life with me,' the girl had said teasingly. 'Is it romantic enough?'

'What makes you think I'm a romantic?'

'Just answer the question. Would you live here?'

'Yes. I'd love it.'

'Then you're a devout romantic.'

Palmer had watched the strong wind ripple her chestnut hair. It made the flowers nod their bright red heads and set the thick layer of ivy on the ruined walls shivering like the flank of a horse. The sun overhead poured down a flood of brilliance on them and the grapes and the river. There was no Ubco, no Eddie Hagen, no films in shirt cardboards.

And the wine, Palmer thought now, lying in bed. The wine.

Not the bottled sweet stuff sent to New York, but the fresh-from-the-barrel dry Mosel that was never exported because the natives drank it all, the simple taste of the *natur* wine without added sugar, like rainwater in the desert, like innocent grape-juice, like pure love.

Palmer's second castle was hard gained after half an hour's walk through bosky forest paths to Burg Eltz, towering improbably overhead. The girl had explained that nobility had never lived in Burg Eltz. Consequently no wars had ever been fought for it. Burghers and merchants had owned it and made very certain armies stayed far from it.

By mid-Saturday. Palmer had become an expert on Mosel wines. He'd sampled them in tiny postcard-scene villages like Beilstein, in the shadow of the brooding Burg Metternich. He'd drunk them in Cochem and Karden and Marienburg. He'd tasted Zeller Schwarze Katz in Zell and Wehlener Sonnenuhr in Wehlen and Krover Nachtarsch in Krov. In Graach, which they reached too late in the day, the only place they could find was a *Weingut*, the place of business of someone who grew and made wine.

Palmer could remember quite clearly the small tasting room where, no doubt, big buyers were treated to dozens of bottles when the new vintages were ready for sale. At this point in time, however, only he and the girl were there to share a half-bottle of Graacher Himmelreich, which they drank out of long green-stemmed *Pokal* glasses with clear glass tops.

The old woman who served them turned out to be the owner of the *Weingut*, a widow whose son was now in charge of making the wine. Palmer and the girl had been introduced to the son, who spoke enough English to take them through the caves, show them the great fiberglass vats in which wine was made and the pneumatic presses which gently squeezed the grapes.

Lying in his bed in Trier, Palmer could still feel the chill of the caves, the natural cold of the earth itself without artificial air conditioning. The young vintner in overalls and gum boots had sloshed from vat to vat talking of *auslese* and *spätlese*.

'And here we have the filters, you see,' the winemaker had announced proudly. 'In the old days the wine was left to settle. Now we pump it through many layers of asbestos and it comes out so clear, yes?'

Trying to recall glimpses of life on the Mosel, Palmer particularly remembered the business of the asbestos filters because it had precipitated his only argument with the girl during the two days. That night, in their hotel room in Bernkastel overlooking the river, they were slowly undressing, tired after an evening of drinking and eating in the tourist-haunted narrow streets and cramped market squares of the old village.

'Those asbestos filters,' Palmer had mused, lying back on the bed. 'I keep remembering them.'

'Why?'

'In the U.S.,' he'd said, 'we're finding out that asbestos is a killer. Its crystals are immortal. Nothing destroys them. They settle in mucous membranes of the lungs and stay there collecting radioactive matter forever. They form these tiny pearls that can kill you after a while.' He'd closed his eyes, envisioning the idea. 'Pearls of death.'

'Why didn't you tell the *Weingut*?' she had demanded.

'I'm not sure it's harmful if you drink crystals of asbestos, only if you breathe them.'

'It must be.' She had begun pacing the room, half undressed, gesturing angrily. 'The alimentary canal has even greater areas of mucous membrane than the lungs. My God, it's all mucosa! And you kept your mouth shut?'

'But the way he told it, all Mosel wine is filtered that way now.'

'Precisely!' she exploded. 'You must report this to the authorities.'

'Are you crazy?'

'Please have the decency to take some responsibility for this,' she said. 'I can't have respect for a man who keeps quiet in such a situation.'

'You don't understand.' Palmer had started pacing the floor at cross angles to her. 'The French, the Americans, who else filters a wine through asbestos? Do you realize the upheaval involved here?'

'It doesn't matter. You must report it.'

'Don't you imagine the word has already gotten to them? It's not exactly a secret in the U.S. that asbestos is a killer.'

'No?' Her voice had grown bitter and hard. 'The only secret is that the wine trust is putting these pearls of death into the wine.'

He had laughed. 'You're off on another conspiracy again.'

'And you're determined to keep your mouth shut about it. What does that make you to the conspiracy? Accessory? Or does Ubco finance the wine trusts?'

He'd fallen back on the bed in utter dismay at the impossibility of explaining to her that not only were there no wine trusts, but that the first winemaker to stop using asbestos filters would probably blow the whistle on all his competitors and make sure the public bought his asbestos-free wine rather than their tainted product. For the first time in their affair, they'd gone to sleep at opposite sides of the bed. The freeze had thawed about dawn when Palmer awoke to find her hugging him while fast asleep.

Alone now in his Trier hotel room, Palmer realized that even when they were angry with each other, he preferred her in bed to lying alone. This was a great change for him. He and Edith had always had separate beds and, while he usually shared Virginia's immense king-sized bed, it was rarely for the purpose of a night's sleep.

The Mosel below Bernkastel, Palmer recalled now, was a valley of sharp hillsides and increasingly wider curves. The river no longer looped back on itself as frequently. The sky overhead was alive with the sound of jet fighters far out of sight at great altitudes above the brown, rocky earth. Occasionally Palmer would look up to find a thin white contrail being traced forty or fifty thousand feet in the air by a plane, entirely invisible, whose noise would not reach him for minutes to come.

'It must be a source of irritation,' Palmer had told the girl's father at dinner that night. 'To be peacefully tending one's grapes and to have these jet fighters doing practice dogfights overhead. The headaches alone would be bad, but the cultural shock must be worse.'

Her father was a small, thin man, like a jockey grown grey and shriveled. His face was narrow through the chin and mouth but it widened skull-like through the cheek and the great forehead she had inherited from him. His English was British, as hers was, and somewhat rustier, but it was the thinness of his voice, a papery rustling somewhere between a whisper and true speech, that made what he said seem so much more important.

'The economic shock of not having the U.S. Air Force here,' he had said, 'would be much greater. We are all willing to put up with the headaches because of the dollars.'

Their apartment had the same air of impermanence that the girl's had in Montparnasse. The same white-washed walls, almost devoid of pictures, the same bare minimum of furniture,

191

made Palmer realize that, like the girl, her parents seemed born birds of passage, permanently adjusted to impermanence. He wondered if one were ever born to this kind of upheaval or merely accommodated to it because one had to live.

'It's the same in the U.S.,' he had told the old man. 'We all put up with a lot of headaches because of the dollars.'

Palmer had been a little impatient with himself for putting the idea in just that way. He felt it had a faintly toadying note to it, as if he were being a bit anti-American to curry favor with these Europeans. Not that they'd expressed any anti-American sentiments, just that he perhaps expected them not to like the United States – their daughter had made no bones about it – and was anticipating this by his remark, meant to be disarming. But had it been anti-American, after all. Wasn't it true that most Americans put up with almost anything in pursuit of the dollar?

'It's the same all over,' the girl's father had said then. 'To live one must eat. People will put up with almost anything in order to eat.'

'You should know,' the girl had put in, with a faintly disguised note of malice. Palmer recognized an old wound.

At this point, with the smoothness of long practice, the mother had diverted the flow of the talk into another channel. 'You must excuse our famous Porta Nigra, Herr Palmer,' she said, boldly striking out along a non sequitur. 'Some misguided ones have decided to clean it. It will no longer be black with twenty centuries of the past.'

'The Porta Blanca,' the girl surmised.

'They're cleaning everything,' Palmer said. 'Even the Notre Dame in Paris.'

'The new generation always denies the old,' the girl's father put in. 'But today it's qualitatively different. The new generation even denies the past.' His pale eyes turned on his daughter and his face seemed to grow narrower. 'Even to the point of sandblasting away the entire testament of history.'

Stocky and plump, the mother instantly got to her feet and began collecting their soup plates by way of again heading off a possible clash between the girl and her father.

Lying in his bed now, Palmer tried to remember as precisely as he could the one interchange after dinner that had so disturbed him. He had deliberately avoided mentioning the little girl, Tanya. She was not with her grandparents and he was told she was away for the weekend visiting friends.

'After I leave you at the airport,' the girl had suggested in front of her parents, 'I think I'll go on to pick up Tanya and spend some time with her. I'm sorry you won't meet her.'

But that had been before dinner, Palmer recollected now. After dinner, after more wine from the old man's cellar, including a reverently opened quart of 1959 Goldtropfchen – 'the year of the century,' as the father had put it – Tanya's name had come up again in a side conversation between the mother and the girl. Palmer wasn't sure he'd even been meant to hear it.

'Bring her back here?' the mother was asking.

'Why can't I? Who the hell does he think he is?'

Both women's eyes had flicked sideways to Palmer and their conversation had automatically shifted into German. Palmer tried his best to follow them, but the father was droning on about the vintage of 1959 and the best Palmer could get was the name Dieter, which led him to believe Tanya was with her father over the weekend, the handsome ski-instructor type whom he resembled, according to the girl.

As he felt sleep begin now to shut down the active part of his brain, Palmer remembered with great fondness that he had learned why the girl's first name was Eleanora.

'After Duse,' her mother had explained to him privately. 'Always she was a great favorite of mine and Asolo was so close to her heart. The Duse lived in Asolo a great part of her life. Our Eleanora was born there.'

Eleanora, Palmer thought. He could feel the drowsiness moving along his arms and legs. He felt loglike, sinking into slumber.

Eleanora.

CHAPTER 33

The Air France jet was scheduled to leave Frankfurt Flughaven at nine forty-five in the morning. The pale blue Volkswagen swung into the parking lot at nine fifteen and the girl accompanied Palmer through the nearly empty terminal, parts of it still under construction. It had the same temporary look Palmer had found in so many other airports around the world.

193

The girl's eyes looked darker than usual, nearly black, with faint mauve half-moons beneath her lower lashes. She seemed distracted and unable to concentrate on even the meaningless talk between them.

'Rather in Trier than in Frankfurt?' Palmer was asking her.
He had picked up his tickets and was standing near the loading gate. His plane had already been called for departure, but he wanted to stay with her as long as possible.

'Pardon?' she asked, glancing around her unseeingly.

'I asked if you'd rather meet me back in Trier.'

'Ah . . .' She stopped and tried to concentrate. The fingers of both her hands were entwined around his left arm, as if unable to let him go. He felt them contract and relax in an unsteady, offbeat tempo that bothered him. 'Ah . . . let's meet in Trier,' she said then. 'Yes, Trier. I'll be with my parents. They're in the telephone directory. If I've had to run out of town for the day or something, they'll know where I am.'

'And you'll have my new schedule of appointments for Bonn?'

Again her eyes did a blind sweep of the terminal and her fingers tightened. She seemed to be wringing her hands, unaware that they were clasped around his arm. 'New appointments?' he repeated as gently as he could.

She nodded several times. 'I wish we could have been alone last night,' she said then. 'I missed you very much.'

'Not as much as I missed you. Will you be picking up Tanya now?'

She said nothing for a long moment. Then: 'Yes, Tanya.'

Palmer had sworn not to question her any more about the girl. 'I think Eleanora's a lovely name,' he said then. 'Is there a nickname for it? Ellie?'

'Never.'

'Nora?'

'I love you,' she said abruptly and buried her face against his chest. An instant later she withdrew slightly. Anyone watching them might have missed the movement completely. 'I can't stand this.'

'I'll cancel the flight. To hell with New York.'

She shook her head several times and her manner grew distracted again, her glance slipping away from him. Finally: 'But what do I call you. Woods?'

'It's my name.'

'Colonel Rafferty calls you Woody-baby.'

'Colonel Rafferty is an Irish madman.' Palmer frowned for a moment. 'Or is that a tautology?'

'Woody-baby,' she tested. 'Terrible.'

'I agree. You don't have to call me anything, you know.'

'I love you, Woods.' Her mouth went into a line of anguish he had never seen before. 'I adore you. I want you to feel as miserable as I do all the time you're gone. You will be miserable. Promise?'

'Promise.'

She smiled at him and her mouth regained its fullness. 'And be very nice to Ginnie. I don't even want to hear that you were cold to her.'

'How solicitous you are.'

'But, you don't understand,' the girl explained. 'I know how she feels about you. I couldn't bear you to make everything so much worse for her.'

'It sounds suspiciously as if you're giving me a license to steal.'

'To sleep with her?' Her attention had again focused closely on him. 'If you feel it will ease things for her.'

'You'll forgive me if I don't believe a word you're saying.'

She nodded. 'I'm babbling. I would hate you to sleep with her but I would understand, *chéri*. Believe me I would. She thought she had you and she doesn't. That's a terrible feeling for a woman. But I know you're coming back to me. It's a wonderful feeling. It makes a woman very generous. And, perhaps, stupid.'

They both laughed at this. 'It sounds as if going back to New York will be more dangerous than I suspected,' he said.

Her glance wandered about the terminal. He had lost her again for a moment. After a while she began talking again and Palmer realized her mind had slipped back several cogs in their conversation. 'Yes, Tanya. I hope she'll be with me when you return. You two must meet.'

'You hope? What's to prev –' Palmer stopped himself. 'I'll be back Wednesday evening at the latest. Make my appointments in Bonn for Friday. I want all of Thursday with you.'

She nodded in a distraught way. 'Friday in Bonn. Yes.'

'If you say the word,' Palmer told her, 'I'll cancel the flight.'

'No. You must go. I shall be in Trier, waiting for you.'

'Can I kiss you?'

She shook her head. 'I am dying.' She pointed to the Air France girl, who was motioning to Palmer. 'This is it.'

He stooped and kissed her cheek. 'Wednesday in Trier.'

'Wednesday in Trier. Oh!'

'Yes?' He had started toward the gate, but stopped.

'If you have time.'

'Yes?'

'Find out about the asbestos. If one drinks it.'

He laughed so loudly a fat woman carrying a Yorkshire terrier turned and stared at him. 'Wednesday in Trier,' he called, 'Eleanora!' He dashed through the gate and out onto the field. Three minutes later the 727 was taxiing for takeoff.

An hour later, Palmer was being guided through Orly from one Air France gate to another, where he boarded a 707 for New York. He had so arranged his packing that the bulk of his clothing remained in two large cases being held at the Intercontinental in Frankfurt. As he sat back in his first-class compartment seat and watched Paris bank crazily away from him, Palmer realized that he would be in New York shortly after Sunday lunch without anyone from Ubco knowing it. In his rush at the last minute he had told no one of his decision to return, much less his expected arrival time. All he had had time to do, actually, was pack an extra suit and two extra shirts, with appropriate underwear, socks, and ties.

He had, it was true, spent precious minutes on Friday, before they had left for the *Schnellfahrt*, examining the rest of his shirt cardboards and other suitable hiding places. It wouldn't do to have the luggage searched in his absence by whoever wanted the microfilm discovered and publicized. Still, Palmer supposed, new incriminating evidence could as easily be planted in his absence as it had when he was on the scene. It was his feeling, however, that with his departure from Europe, interest in him would subside for a while. At least he hoped it would.

The 707 notched in on an automatic inertial guidance system bearing known only to its computer and its pilots. Palmer sat back for the boring return flight. It was a shame, somehow, that the only exciting things about air travel anymore were when something went wrong.

He realized he had unblushingly left Jack Rafferty in the lurch. The man had surely expected to see him again and here he was sneaking off to New York without even a phone message. But, if he knew Jack, the man already knew everything anyway,

196

including the Mosel idyll and what Mrs. Gregorius had served for dinner (chicken and warm *Kartoffelsalat*).

He wondered how sincere Jack had been about the way one 'went European,' an odd idea something like 'going native,' perhaps. Surely he'd been wrong to think that 'going European' entailed a tremendously more tolerant attitude toward such matters as espionage and serving as an agent. Neither of the elder Gregoriuses seemed that laxly unprincipled, yet they and their high-minded daughter on her asbestos crusade were as typically European as anyone could be.

As he relaxed in his seat, he pictured Burg Thurant, its twin towers wrapped in trembling ivy as the wind whipped past the crag high over the Mosel. The girl had been right about him. He was a goddamned romantic under his banker's quick-frozen heart.

But even in the beginning she'd told him that, hadn't she? She'd looked at his palm in that room over the restaurant in Compiègne, after he'd been sleeping off the wine. She'd told him there were two men with his name and body. It was the cynical one, the product of espionage double-dealing and banking chicanery, that Jack Rafferty knew. But she had spotted the romantic who wanted to live out the rest of his life in a ruined castle over a sleepy river, getting old and fat on *Kartoffelsalat* and riesling.

Nevertheless, the cynical one had been alert enough to spot the unmarked shirt with its too-heavy shirt cardboard, alert enough to save the romantic's ass.

Palmer's mind shifted sideways in time to the hotel room in Frankfurt and the girl naked on his lap. He could feel the swell of her buttocks under his hands. A moment later, it seemed, the stewardess was quietly, discreetly, waking him for a meal. Since it was preceded by champagne, served with two kinds of wine and finished off with Armagnac, Palmer quickly fell asleep again and it was some five hours later that he awoke to the pilot's voice announcing an imminent landing at JFK International Airport.

He cleared customs in mere seconds, so slow was traffic at this hour. Then, carrying his small overnight case, he headed out the swinging doors into the main concourse of the International Arrivals Building. Bill Elston immediately appeared in front of him and relieved him of the bag.

'My God, I'm glad to see you, sir,' he said in an undertone.

'How the hell did you know I was on this flight?'

'I've been on the phone with Dauber in Paris since yesterday,' Elston said, leading Palmer through the lobby and into a small elderly Volvo parked in a no-parking zone.

As Palmer sat down beside Elston, he realized this was Elston's own car. Typical of him to choose a car with no looks and a long life. The man had no class at all, Palmer reflected, but you simply couldn't find anything in his judgment to fault.

'I told Dauber he had to come up with an airline and a flight number or his job wasn't worth a plugged franc,' Elston said with a certain smug satisfaction as he maneuvered the Volvo into the parkway maze that led back to Manhattan.

'What made you so sure I was coming back?'

'I wasn't sure. Harry Elder was.'

'I see.'

'He told me to meet every plane until I produced your body.'

'Or else your job wasn't worth a plugged nickel.'

A look of alarm flashed across Elston's plain, bland face. 'I hope I didn't overstep my authority,' he said then. 'You're not upset, are you?'

'I'm suffering from the bends.'

The alarmed look grew more pronounced. 'Sorry to hear that, sir.'

'The cultural bends,' Palmer explained. 'Six hours ago I was deep in the heart of Europe and loving every moment of it. Now here I am stuck in Sunday traffic. You tell me how I should feel about that.'

'I know.' Elston nodded seriously several times. 'But look at it this way. If you'd taken a later flight, the traffic would be ten times worse on this end.'

'Also,' Palmer added, 'it may be two P.M. here, but it's late evening on my personal schedule. I'm bushed.'

'I certainly understand that. But the meeting won't take very long.'

'What meeting?' Palmer demanded.

Bill Elston glanced uneasily at him. The Volvo was standing still in the middle lane of the Van Wyck Expressway, cars in all three lanes at a standstill. After a moment, motorists began to honk their horns. Palmer listened to the orchestration, short angry beeps and long harassed blats, mournful hooting and overwrought barking, a whole symphony of frustration.

'The, uh, meeting. Mr. Elder's reserved a suite at the Plaza.

He's driving in from his home now, with Donny. They should get there about the time we do.'

Palmer sat up higher in the front seat and tried to look past the car ahead. In the distance he could see some tallish buildings, not those of Manhattan but high-rise apartment houses here in Queens. The air had a grayish, creamy thickness to it, a kind of dirty yellowness that made the buildings, the trees alongside the highway, even the stalled cars in the distance look mean and pinched and somehow cheap.

The driver of the car behind the Volvo leaned on his horn and sent a great baying yawp through Palmer's shocked ears. Palmer sat back in the seat and closed his eyes tightly. He was home.

CHAPTER 34

It may well have been the worst night Palmer ever spent. At least it seemed that way while it was happening.

He couldn't really blame anybody for the way things had worked out. Harry Elder and his son, Donny, had gone about the business of briefing him as thoroughly as they could. Bill Elston had had the foresight to bring along a full agenda for tomorrow's board meeting, as well as the portfolio of supporting materials Palmer's secretary, Miss Czermat, always prepared for him whether he attended a meeting or not.

Everyone had done his work and cleared out of the hotel suite by nine o'clock. The unspoken feeling was that Palmer should spend the night there rather than at his bachelor apartment where, conceivably, one of the 'opposition' could, by a random telephone call, learn that he had secretly returned to town. Naturally, no one presumed to tell Ubco's chief executive officer where or how he should spend the night. But, thinking it over after they had left him alone, Palmer decided their message had been clear, even if unvoiced.

Palmer himself doubted if the 'opposition' was aware of his return to New York. He had begun over the past few hours to feel his own mental processes shift gear, so to speak, and grind ahead into the New York tempo. There was a New York way of thinking – angle-playing, paranoid, motive-sniffing, statement-questioning – that had first appalled Palmer when he arrived in town three years before. Once he found how easy it was for him to think successfully in the New York Style, he accepted it as a condition of life. But a week in Europe seemed to have made this way of thinking as distasteful to use as the poisoned air was to breathe.

Thus it was that at about 9:30 in the evening – 3 A.M. Trier time – Palmer sat in an armchair of his Plaza room sipping a Scotch highball and hating everything that was happening.

He had had the time, with his mind in its new gear, to examine a lot more realistically some of the peculiar things that had happened to him in Europe. Paranoia explained it all, that particular kind of New York viewpoint that begins with the question 'what's in it for me?' and concludes with the decision 'do it to them first.'

It seemed quite clear to Palmer, as he sat sipping his drink, that some of the spying was the work of the 'opposition.' He found it distasteful to use the word because it meant he accepted Harry Elder's hypothesis. But Jack Rafferty's comments that night in the Brückenkeller had probably forever poisoned Palmer's mind against old Army buddy Eddie Hagen.

So it was with great certainty now that Palmer attributed some of the espionage to Hagen's faction on the board of directors. And it seemed equally certain that they knew he had quietly returned to New York for the board meeting. Nevertheless, on the axiom 'never overestimate the enemy's intelligence,' Palmer was determined to make a sudden, late, dramatic entrance at tomorrow's meeting, hopefully knocking them all off their pins.

At this point, Palmer knew, if he tried to fit the films in the shirt cardboard into the Hagen conspiracy, he would simply confuse himself. And if he went to work on Eleanora's motives, he would destroy himself utterly.

Palmer picked up the telephone and gave the operator Virginia Clary's number. He listened to seven rings and hung up.

He gave the operator Edith's number and, after the third ring, heard her answer. He felt something lurch sideways at about the level of his stomach but ignored it and spoke as off-handedly as he could. 'Edith, it's Woods. I called to say hello to the children.'

'You're talking to a children,' the voice responded.

'Gerri? You sounded exactly like your mother.'

'Are you calling transatlantic?'

'I'm in New York for a day or two –'

'Yea!'

'And I wanted to see all of you before I flew back to Germany.'

'Boo! I thought you were back for good.'

'Some business to attend to. I'm having a great time over there. I want all of you to come over this summer. Do you think your mother would let you?'

'I don't know.' There was a pause. 'You're about as popular a topic of conversation as chancres.'

'Gerri!'

'Well, it's true. We started telling her about where you were in Europe and she racked us back so hard I thought my head would come off. Woody's not home. Tom's asleep. He has a head cold and went to bed early. Mom is out.'

'Where?'

'Hard to tell. Are you really interested? Because I think she's got a boyfriend.'

'Okay,' Palmer said. 'End of conversation. Pick a new topic.'

'Will you be here tomorrow night? The school play's tomorrow night.'

'I'll make it my business to be. What time?'

'Eight P.M. Come and laugh at my lines, please? Did you bring me anything Norman from Italy? But you haven't even gotten there yet. And applaud my curtain calls. Bring me back for seconds and thirds. Please?'

'Right. Will the boys be there? I could take you three out for dinner before the play. Or a snack afterwards.'

'Gotta clear that with You Know Who.'

'No, you don't,' Palmer assured her, remembering the 'unlimited access to children' clause of the separation agreement.

'Yes, I do. Shall I phone you at the office?'

'Only after lunchtime tomorrow. Not before. Nobody knows I'm back.'

'Gonna fall on them like the Assyrian on the fold?'

'Something like that.'

'Groovy! This is exciting.'

'Why?' Palmer asked. 'What do you know about the bank's business?'

'Not that. You coming to the play.'

Afterwards Palmer had tried Virginia's number again, without luck. He glanced at his watch and saw that it was only nine forty-five. He wished he felt the slightest bit tired. He'd been awake so long now that he ought to easily fall asleep. But there was something about remastering the art of New York thinking that destroyed sleep.

Edith's boyfriend, something else to chew on. Edith's meddling in his free access to the children. Something else to mince up fine and examine under the microscope of paranoia.

Where would Virginia be at this hour? With whom was she having a date? If Harry Elder had suspected he'd return to New York, why hadn't Virginia? Why hadn't she called him? Or had she tried his apartment earlier, not knowing about the suite at the Plaza? Did that mean Harry no longer trusted her? Is that why he hadn't told her about the Plaza meeting? For that matter, why was Harry trustworthy? Everyone's motives were suspect.

Palmer drained the rest of the drink and unpacked his overnight case. He methodically put away the shirts and underwear and hung up the suits. He found that someone had stuck the corner of an unfamiliar, extravagant Paisley scarf in the breast pocket of his gray suit. He frowned and pulled out the scarf. A note came away pinned to it.

'*Chéri*, you will knot this around your neck when we take up residence at Burg Thurant. No more collars or ties. E.'

Palmer sank back on the bed and ran the silk scarf through his cupped hand, feeling the smoothness of it. The wild colors of the Paisley scarf, oranges and yellows and purples, seemed to warm his fingers. He lay back on the bed and pressed the scarf against his face and kissed it.

Horns honking outside his window on Central Park South woke him at midnight, New York time. He remained awake for the rest of the night.

Palmer paced the suite for a while, trying to get tired again. He sat for a while and watched an old movie on television but couldn't seem to make any sense of it. Finally he turned off the sound and watched the tiny silent figures gesticulating as they moved through their paces. At 3 A.M. he ordered more Scotch from room service. At 4 A.M. he lay back on the bed and tried for sleep. At 5 he resumed pacing.

It was the thinking that he couldn't stop. Even as he sat or stood or paced, or busied himself with the silent television or the

Scotch or whatever else he found to distract himself, even then he was aware that his mind was a machine with a broken governor. It was racing ahead at unsafe speeds, churning out circular thoughts. It was a stamping press whose operator was no longer there to feed it raw sheet metal. The immense press would wind up and stamp the air. Wham! Again! Producing nothing. Producing punched air.

At about 7 A.M. he wandered into the bathroom and stared at himself in the mirror. If he showed up at the meeting looking this way, he'd be thrown out. There were blackish shadows under his eyes and under his high cheekbones. His dark blond hair looked dank and tangled in a way he knew from experience would not comb out unless he washed it first. His gray eyes had grown smaller with fatigue. He got an idea of himself holding up a false face to the mirror and peering out through its pig eyes. This would never do.

He showered and shaved and powdered his face and brushed his hair and examined the results. Better, but not really.

He went downstairs at eight thirty and drank two large silver pots of coffee with his eggs and bacon. Still better, but now he began to get caffeine jumpiness like a fine tremor through his arms. The machine was no longer lurching out of control, but vibrating self-destructively.

He gathered his agenda and portfolio and took a cab to his apartment. He didn't even glance around at it. It wasn't really a part of him. He went to the medicine cabinet and found the small plastic tube of green-and-black Librium capsules. He shook two into the palm of his hand, then tucked them into the breast pocket of his suit jacket.

It was after nine when he left the apartment in the East Sixties and looked at the day. New York had produced a beauty for him, as warm and clear as any in France or Germany. He had an hour before the board meeting began or, rather, before making his dramatic entrance there.

Palmer thought for a moment of walking east to the small house on the river at 58th Street which Virginia owned. He might intercept her on her way to work, although it was a bit late for that.

He might walk uptown a few blocks to the house where his children lived. They would be on their way to school, of course. Probably they'd already left.

He might try sneaking in to his own office at the bank, but

that seemed needlessly unsafe if he wanted to surprise anyone.

There was nothing in his apartment or his hotel suite to lure him back there for an hour. In fact, there was really nothing anywhere for him, was there? Except possibly a pleasant stroll about the city on this bright June morning.

Palmer started down Third Avenue. As he crossed with the light and came abreast of one of his own Ubco branch offices, two jackhammers a yard to his right erupted into sudden blasting noise. Their compressors, parked at the curb, filled the air with the iron clangor of diesel thrumming. Palmer winced and fled from the pain of the noise.

He rounded a corner and came up short against a major excavation in which five rock drills were hard at work on the native schist of Manhattan. A loud warning hoot sounded. Palmer could see a man in a yellow helmet press down a detonator handle. The thickly woven blanket of steel cable puffed upward from the dynamite blast it was smothering. Palmer felt the earth shake beneath him. Three 'all clear' hoots deafened him. He turned and made for the opposite side of Third Avenue. An effeminate boy lounging in the doorway of a decorator's wholesale supply store raised his eyebrows at Palmer, who kept on walking.

He had an hour to kill, Palmer told himself, unless it killed him first.

CHAPTER 35

Palmer couldn't be sure, but if he evaluated his dramatic entrance strictly as an act of stagecraft, it was a smash hit.

The meeting had been called for ten o'clock sharp. The first two items on the agenda were unimportant. Palmer entered the Fifth Avenue doors of the bank at ten ten and nodded briskly to the floor man on duty near the front. Surprised, the old-timer threw Palmer a salute but failed to whip out his usual toady cry of 'Good morning, Mr. Palmer, sir.'

However the floor man at the rear, near the elevator door, had spotted Palmer the moment he walked in. He arranged for the elevator doors to be open and, as Palmer strode past him, moving with fake energy and zip, the guard murmured a discreet

'Nice to have you back, sir' before the elevator doors slammed shut.

Palmer rode to the top and stepped out on the long carpeted corridor that led, eventually, to his own office. He could see Miss Czermat at her desk, framed by the Jackson Pollock on the wall behind her. She looked up and Palmer could hear the small shriek of surprise as she leaped to her feet. He laid his finger on his lips and waved his folder of papers at her, then took a side corridor that led to the immense conference room where the meeting was already in progress.

At ten twelve he pushed open the double doors and walked in just as Eddie Hagen was saying 'Move we get this thing in high gear and haul ass. It's dragged on long enough to – Woody !'

Palmer let the doors swing shut behind him as he surveyed the long table. The full contingent wasn't there, barely a quorum of the board, but most of the principal actors were in attendance. Eddie himself, his mouth an O, was sitting to the left of Harry Elder, who sat at the end in the chairman's place. Next to Eddie was one of the bank's senior vice-presidents, Sam Phipps. Next to him sat on 'outside' director like Hagen who didn't actually work for the bank, a man named Phil Carmody, whose primary business interests were in steel and aluminium fabrication plants.

On the other side of Harry Elder sat two more outside directors. One was Barney Kinch, the head of Jet-Tech International. It had been Barney's concern, a few years back, that had staged a proxy raid on Ubco as a means of getting more favorable financing for its tremendous spread of industrial and service activities. The grab had been thwarted by Palmer, but at the cost of putting Kinch on the board.

Next to Barney Kinch sat Edith's Aunt Jane's third husband, Tim Carewe. Palmer could never quite figure out if there were any title for the relationship between himself and Tim. Former uncle-in-law? Since Tim had divorced Edith's Aunt Jane and Palmer would soon be divorced from Edith, there was probably no name left in the language that described matters. After a career in government work, Tim had also been instrumental in helping Palmer head off the Jet-Tech grab. Now in investment banking, he was usually a rather silent, noncommittal member of the board.

Elmer Hesselman, Ubco's new executive vice-president, sat next to Tim, a heavyset man Palmer's age whom he'd stolen from a Minnesota bank six months before when Harry Elder had decided to retire from the exec vee-pee post to his present semihonorary position as vice-chairman of the board. Elmer was an 'inside' director, of course, and so was the man seated next to him, a senior vice-president named Forrester. At the far end sat Irma Hellman, who'd taken notes of board meetings for twenty years now.

Neither Donny Elder nor Bill Elston was a member of the board, of course. As he stood there eyeing the group at the table, Palmer almost wished he had the two younger men in the room with him. He knew where their sentiments lay. The feelings of most of this bunch were unknowable. Yet.

'For Christ's sake, Woody!' Hagen burst out. 'I thought you were in Bonn.'

Palmer noted how accurate Hagen's information on the itinerary was. Today he was, indeed, supposed to have been in Bonn. Palmer decided on a big, quick flashy lie.

'I always planned to attend this meeting, Eddie. You knew that.'

'The hell I did!' Hagen's mulish face went red down to his collar and Palmer realized that the lie had, at least for a moment, put Hagen at a disadvantage with whomever else in the room he had plotted. Palmer took a long, steadying breath. He'd stopped a quarter of an hour before at a drugstore on Madison to take the two Librium capsules. He already felt quite calm. He'd hit just the right note of confusion and it was up to him to keep confounding it before Hagen could counter-attack.

'Barney' – he wheeled on Kinch – 'didn't you tell him I'd be back?'

'Nobody told me.'

Palmer shook his head. Harry Elder got up without a word and gave over his seat, moving to a new one next to Irma Hellman. Palmer sat in the warm chair and opened his portfolio of notes. He saw that, for tactical purposes, the seating couldn't have been better arranged. Eddie Hagen, who seemed to represent forces that wanted the Mafia bank brought quickly into the fold, sat on one side. Barney Kinch, who represented forces that were once again pressing for immense amounts of financing at low rates, sat on Palmer's other hand. Palmer would have to keep up the pressure or they would begin to whipsaw him between them.

'I think you're both getting old,' he muttered. 'You were both

206

told of my plans and you both forgot. It doesn't matter.' Palmer waved his hand negligently in Eddie Hagen's face. 'Forget it. Oh, by the way, regards to you from Jack Rafferty. He still hates your guts.'

'What?'

'Had some interesting things to tell me, Jack did.' Palmer nodded benignly at Hagen. 'He's been doing a hellish amount of research.'

Hagen's face lost its reddish look as he sat back in his chair. He hadn't actually gone pale, but he rubbed his square chin and watched Palmer with a new thoughtfulness. 'Barney,' Palmer pounced, turning on Kinch, 'is it true that in a period when we're getting ten and twelve percent on industrial loans you have the gall to suggest we lend you at nine? Do you realize what'd happen if word got out that Ubco favored a board member's company in that bizarre a fashion?'

'I don't know where you're getting your information,' Kinch began very calmly. His silvery hair, close-cropped, seemed to bristle slightly as he rubbed the palm of his hand forward through it. 'We're not asking for anything we're not entitled to as a long-time, old-line customer.'

Palmer's eyebrows went up. 'Some of us remember Jet-Tech a lot better than that, Barney. However,' he went on with a spurious increase in speed, 'you're wasting our valuable time with this stuff, gentlemen. We have an agenda and I'm here to move it along briskly.'

Not waiting to give this terribly unfair remark a chance to generate a reaction, Palmer went ahead quickly: 'Have you disposed of Items One through Three? I gather from Eddie's special pleading tone as I walked in that he was on his favorite subject, helping the Spiritual Sicilian Brothers of the Poor. I gather you're in favor of overruling the board's earlier decision to sit tight and do nothing for a while?'

'The board didn't decide that,' Hagen grunted, 'you did.'

'In conjunction with the DA's office and the local FBI,' Palmer lied. 'The whole matter is known to them,' he went on, spinning out the story as plausibly as possible, 'and they've been busily digging into it. When they delouse that bank and we're convinced it's free of mob influence, I'll be the first to start the merger moving. Till then, if we move too fast, we'll excite the suspicion of all the law people working on this thing.'

Phil Carmody frowned heavily at Hagen. 'You never told me

about this, Eddie.'

'*He* never told *me*,' Hagen retorted. 'What're you trying to be, Woody, the Lone Wolf of Wall Street?'

'Just trying to keep all of you out of jail.' Palmer nodded to Harry Elder at the far side of the table. 'Have you heard anything from the law since I left?'

Harry shook his head ponderously and at some length. Palmer could see he was trying to stay with the lie and be as convincing as he could. 'Not a word yet,' he managed to get out.

Hagen's eyes narrowed. 'What kind of con game is this, Woody? Since when do you spill confidential bank business to the law without telling anyone on the board?'

'Harry knows,' Palmer retorted. 'Eddie, this isn't some child's game. This isn't your little Massachusetts Aerospace plaything. When you fool around with things like this, it's the big league and the chips are all blue. It would have been disastrous not to bring in the law. Don't try to tell us we shouldn't have done it.'

He watched Hagen try to digest this fast shuffle of near-fact and false accusation. Then, before he could respond, Palmer went on heavily: 'The only thing I worry about,' he said in an ominous tone, 'is that the law-enforcement people don't begin to dig into Ubco. I'm very much afraid they may try. And the first place they'll start is with the personalities here on this board.'

He glanced around the room and his gaze lingered on Barney Kinch. 'You remember, don't you, Barney, all that stuff you confessed to us a few months ago about Jet-Tech's involvement with the mob?'

'What stuff?' Kinch grinned nervously. 'What confession?'

'I'm sure the rest of us remember.' Palmer, sensing Carmody had been an ally of Hagen's until this minute, turned on the man. 'All except you, Phil. I don't think you were at the meeting when we heard how Jet-Tech buys its gift liquor by the case at prices that can only mean hijacked goods. How it resorts to black-market scarce metal sources during shortages. How it hires the Mafia to settle labor disputes. All that stuff.'

The room lay in absolute silence. Palmer could hear his own chair creak as he swiveled back to face Kinch again. 'Barney, that kind of thing would murder Ubco if the law ever dug into it. And I'm very much afraid Jet-Tech isn't our only connection with organized crime.'

No one spoke. This time Palmer could hear several chairs creak. He shuffled with slow deliberation through the papers in his portfolio, until he came to a perfectly innocent sheet of typing that was single-spaced so that, trying to read it upside-down, no one could easily decipher it.

'I don't think this is the time, yet, to divulge some of the things that have been reported to me,' Palmer said in a judicious tone. He frowned at the piece of paper and slapped the port-folio shut.

He nodded to Tim Carewe. 'You're still fresh from govern-ment work, Tim,' he said. 'How do you think Washington would react if, after reporting to the FBI the problem we're having with this mob-controlled bank, we then rush ahead and buy it without further ado?'

Carewe's nasal New England voice was more of a snort than anything else. 'Shew-uh-ly, Woods, you know the ahn-suh as well as I. They'd cream us.' He smiled slightly and his small teeth bared as if to take a bite. Palmer had the feeling he'd hear later from his sometime, onetime kinsman, who would want to claim a reward for supporting Palmer's position.

'Woods,' Harry Elder said, 'I move we table this question till further notice.'

'Second,' Carewe chimed in.

'Just a goddamned minute!' Eddie Hagen barked. His color was back up and he was sitting as high in his chair as he could, as if trying to get his head away from the choking confines of his own collar.

'It's been moved and seconded,' Palmer announced. 'We'll hear Eddie discuss it for a moment and then I'm calling the question. Eddie?'

'Just who in the hell are you trying to hustle, Woody?' Hagen began at a high pitch. 'I've known you for goddamned near a quarter of a century now and I've never seen you pull some of the crap you've tried here today.'

'Easy,' Palmer said in a soft, soothing tone. 'Calmly.'

'Shit on that!' Hagen snapped. 'Sorry, Irma, but I'm so god-damned mad I don't care if they hear me down on Fifth Avenue. Either this is a democratically constituted board of directors' meeting or it's a showcase for Woods Palmer's cheap histrionics. I, for one –'

'Cheap?' Palmer cut in. 'Don't talk about cheapness when the reputation of this bank is at stake. What have we got if we don't have our good name? What does any bank have?'

Hagen shook his head blindly, as if trying to dodge a swarm of bees. 'Nobody suggested we cheapen our reputation,' he responded in a confused way.

'You deny it?' Palmer asked.

'You bet I do.'

'You deny trying to push us into this merger ahead of time?'

Hagen's mouth worked for a moment. Then he settled back in his chair. When he spoke, he had mastered his anger and his voice sounded quietly reasonable. 'Woody,' he said, 'I don't mind being misunderstood now and again. But we have got us a colossal failure of communication here. You're accusing me of things I never said or wished for.'

Palmer recognized the judo master's trick of suddenly relaxing posture and letting the opponent's momentum trip him up. He slacked off even more dramatically than Hagen had. 'Eddie, if I did that I humbly apologize. I honestly do.' He turned to the rest of the board. 'I guess that ends discussion on the question. It seems Eddie really wasn't arguing against it after all.'

'Hold it!' Hagen yapped.

'All in favor of tabling it till further notice?' Palmer forged ahead. He counted five raised hands, noting that Barney Kinch's was not among them but Phil Carmody's was. 'Any opposed?'

Things had happened so quickly that not even Eddie Hagen raised his hand. 'Motion passes. Next item of business.' He glanced down at the agenda.

'Woody,' Hagen began again in his low, calm tone.

'Yes?'

'Let the record show that while there were nine members present, out of the full board of twelve, this motion passed with only five votes, which doesn't constitute a majority of the full board.'

'Mrs. Hellman, did you get that?' Palmer inquired.

'I did.'

'Then let the record also show that under the bylaws nine members present represents a legal quorum to conduct business and five represents a majority of said quorum.'

'I have that, too, Mr. Palmer.'

'Anything else, Eddie?'

210

'Yes. But I'll put it to you privately, where your playacting won't have an audience.' Hagen's words sounded much more bitter than anything else he'd said until then.

'Really, Eddie,' Palmer countered, 'these personal attacks of yours have to stop. This is a place of business.'

'Personal attacks!' Hagen burst out. 'Listen to the man. What's he been doing but personally attacking Barney and me since he slammed in here unannounced?'

Palmer gave him a look of surprise. 'Did I make any personal attacks on you, Eddie?' Then he frowned. 'You're not referring to what I said about the information I'd recently gotten hold of? Is that an attack on you?'

Hagen's mouth closed in a tight line. He folded his arms and sat back in his chair. Palmer turned to Kinch. 'Did you feel I was attacking you as a person, Barney?'

But Kinch had always had tighter rein on his temper than Hagen. He simply grinned at Palmer. 'How could I feel that way, Woods?'

'Exactly.' Palmer opened his portfolio. 'Let's talk about your Jet-Tech loan application. Let me give you a bit of advice, Barney. Now that you're on the board, Jet-Tech can't possibly expect special treatment. In fact we're going to have to bend over backwards with your financing from here in. Doesn't that make sense?'

Kinch's grin broadened. 'You mean my best bet is to resign from the board?'

'You said it, I didn't.' Palmer's grin was, he hoped, as wide as Kinch's.

'Is that why you put me on the board two years ago?' Kinch asked. 'To clip Jet-Tech's wings permanently?'

'Absolutely not.'

'But it's had that effect,' Kinch pointed out.

'Regrettably.'

'Then suppose,' Kinch mused, 'we take all our new financing to National City or Chase or Bank of America? Suppose we just stop doing business with Ubco any more? Jet-Tech's a fourteen-billion-dollar corporation, Woods. We meet our payments and Ubco get rich lending to us. What if we just stop doing that any more?'

Palmer shrugged. 'I'd hate to see that happen, Barney. It would hurt Ubco almost as much as it would hurt Jet-Tech. After those other banks got through charging you the rates

211

they'd have to charge, you'd wish you were back with friends again.'

Kinch thought for a moment. 'Maybe it's worth a try.'

'Talk to your comptrollers, Barney. Maybe it is.'

Kinch laughed softly. 'You don't scare easy, do you?'

Palmer smiled. 'Neither do you.'

Whereas, Palmer added silently to himself, Eddie Hagen scares like a rabbit. Palmer wondered for a moment whether everybody hadn't been exactly right about Hagen's mob connections. Harry Elder had hinted at it. Virginia had confirmed it. Jack Rafferty, stuck way over in Germany, had flatly stated it. The different ways Hagen and Kinch had stood up to Palmer's razzle-dazzle just now indicated that Kinch had nothing much on his mind except business advantage, while Hagen had a load of dirty linen he was afraid might be uncovered.

If for no other reason, Palmer decided, he was glad he'd come back to this meeting because it showed him that the two parties opposing him had not yet joined forces. If they had, his sleight-of-hand performance wouldn't have worked.

'Let's get on with the rest of the agenda,' Palmer said. 'I take it, Barney, that you're withdrawing your original point until you consult your comptrollers?'

'Fine, Woods.' Kinch smiled lazily and leaned back in his chair. 'And you talk to Ubco's comptrollers, too. See just how badly you need Jet-Tech's business.'

Palmer nodded. 'Good point. Of course, whatever they tell me, I'm going to stick to my view that we cannot, repeat cannot, be caught lending you at such a sweetheart rate.'

Kinch also nodded. 'It's a free country.'

Hagen snorted and got up from the table. 'If you don't mind, I've just remembered something important I have to do.'

'You're leaving the meeting early?' Palmer asked.

'I think almost anything I could do would be better than sitting around listening to you two purr at each other. Goodbye.' He started for the door.

'Did you have something to take up with me later?'

'If I do, you'll know it.' Hagen's stocky little figure slammed out the double doors. They could hear his footsteps even along the carpeted corridor.

Palmer relaxed for a moment. He'd won no victory over Eddie Hagen. All he'd won was a little time. The rest of the agenda looked routine: underwriting a bond issue for a new airport in Oklahoma, liquidating three Florida canning companies and refinancing the resulting merger, unloading a group of Long Island mortgages, and turning down a request from one of the smaller Arab countries for extended factoring on next year's oil volume.

He looked up across the table at Harry Elder and caught the old man's very faint wink. He hoped nobody else had.

CHAPTER 36

Palmer's office looked empty and unfriendly to him. Its immense length, leading to a twenty-foot-high window wall overlooking Fifth Avenue, gave it the appearance of some anonymous passenger corridor or tunnel in an airport. His desk was unnaturally clean of everything, including dust. They really hadn't expected him back today, he mused, as he sat down behind it. It gave him a momentary feeling of satisfaction that the 'opposition' didn't really have as good an intelligence system as he did.

He wondered if Jack Rafferty would be pleased at the way Eddie Hagen had caved in at the first sign of trouble. Did it mean anything? Was Eddie playacting? The only thing he was certain of was that no real victory had been won. He could feel the Librium draining out of him. Anxieties began to pop up in his mind, sudden questions he had been single-mindedly able to suppress with the help of the drug. He wondered what Eddie's next move would be. He wondered if Eddie were really involved with the mob or simply an innocent, outraged old friend he had now alienated forever.

There was a knock at the door and a parade of people came in, led by Harry Elder with a giant grin on his face. He was followed by his son, Donny, and by Bill Elston, who seemed the only one capable of not looking like he'd swallowed a canary.

'I've given them the final score,' Elder said, sitting down across from Palmer's desk. 'One win, one draw. Right? Batting five hundred.'

Palmer could feel his face tightening. While the tranquilizer had been pumping through his veins, he'd felt smooth and relaxed. Now everything was twisting tighter inside him again. 'Don't mislead our youth, Harry,' he said, forcing himself to use a light tone of voice. 'The win is no win. We have no way of knowing where the next contest will begin with Hagen. As for the standoff with Barney Kinch, that's a true tie. We'll never resolve it any way but to lose Barney from the board.'

Elder chuckled. 'It finally dawned on him, didn't it? I mean that you were doing Jet-Tech no favor when you put him on the board.'

Bill Elston blinked. 'The conflict-of-interest thing?' he asked.

Palmer nodded, reached forward, and pressed an intercom button on his desk. 'Elmer,' he told his new exec vee-pee, 'got a second?'

'Be right in,' Hesselman promised.

Palmer clicked off his intercom. He pointed a finger at Harry Elder. 'You keep your cynical thoughts to yourself, my friend. I don't want a clean country boy like Elmer to be infected by your dirty New York thinking.'

'Why ask him in?'

'Because he's sitting there eating himself up with questions and wondering what kind of den of thieves he's fallen into,' Palmer responded. 'Because it's wrong to let him do that.' He glanced at the two younger men, who had remained standing. 'Thanks for all your help,' he said. 'A few seconds after Hesselman comes in, you'd both better remember another appointment.'

Elston frowned uneasily. 'What appointment?'

Donny Elder laughed and punched his shoulder lightly. 'You're not for real, Bill.'

There was a heavy knock on the door and Elmer Hesselman came in, his fullback's body encased in a very sharp Italian-cut suit someone back home in Minneapolis – perhaps his wife – had told him was the way New York bankers dressed. The skimpy suit with its pinched-in waist and diagonally slashed pockets clung to Hesselman's beefy torso and arms with an impermanent air as if, with a single flex of his muscles, he could burst every seam. His round face had the pink, surprised look of a baby just waking from a nap. His blue eyes raked across all four men and returned to rest on Palmer. 'What's up?' he asked.

In the few months since Palmer had hired Hesselman, the

214

Minnesotan had already distinguished himself by, as Palmer recalled the old saying, being as loquacious as a Scotman's telegram. 'Sit down,' Palmer invited him.

'Look,' Donny Elder began smoothly, 'Bill and I have that closing to see to, so –'

'Fine. Thanks.' Palmer waved them out of the room.

He waited until the door had closed behind them, surveying them, surveying Harry Elder, beefy but not big, and Elmer Hesselman, beefy and big. He wondered whether skinny men like him had some kind of affinity for tubs like these two and Jack Rafferty. Not that they were fat. Just ample.

'How are things going, Elmer?' he began.

Hesselman shrugged. 'Okay.'

'I mean, any problems while I've been away? I'm going back to Europe tomorrow or the next day, you know.'

'Great.'

'Happy to see me go?'

Hesselman's baby face pinkened slightly. 'In a way.'

'Hear that, Harry? At least this one's honest. Why, Elmer?'

Hesselman hunched forward and smiled so slightly another man might have missed the movement. 'Less excitement.'

Palmer laughed. 'Do you mean to tell me you never have meetings like that out in Minnesota?'

'Sure.' Hesselman seemed to gird himself for a lengthy burst of words. 'We call it lacrosse.'

Both Palmer and Elder laughed for a moment. 'That's a very bloody game, isn't it?' Palmer asked.

'I think the Indians invented it,' Harry Elder suggested. 'It's the bloodiest game there is.'

'Nope,' Hesselman demurred. 'Second bloodiest.'

Palmer eyed him for a moment. 'And the first?'

Hesselman cocked his head sideways in the direction of the boardroom. His smile widened by a millimeter.

When Palmer finally got rid of both men, the last of the Librium had left him and he could feel a faint tremor in his right arm. It bothered him that he had had to depend so heavily on a drug to get through the morning. He almost never needed it, but the combination of no sleep and heightened anxiety had made him use it. What bothered him even more now was that it seemed to have aftereffects, or else that, in receding, it disclosed symptoms it had been masking, like this caffeine tremor.

He buzzed Miss Czermat and asked her to put in a call to a

Henry Mather, executive secretary of the Foundation for Economic Study. Then he got on his private outside line and dialed Virginia's private outside line at her office. It rang five times and was answered by someone who wasn't Virginia. Palmer hung up as Miss Czermat buzzed him. 'Mr. Mather on the line.'

'Henry, sorry to disturb you,' Palmer began.

'Aren't you in Bonn today?' Mather asked. His thin, weary voice seemed far too ancient for his age, which Palmer recalled as being around sixty.

'I postponed my appointments, Henry. I'm terribly sorry about it but something quite urgent came up here at Ubco and I had to dash back. Have you been getting any reports on my progress from your man Forellen?'

There was a longish pause at Mather's end of the line. Then:
'No, nothing. Why?'

'He seemed to indicate he had to make fairly frequent reports to you.'

Again the pause. 'I'm afraid I don't understand, Woods,' the papery voice responded.

Palmer began to feel a kind of itchiness throughout his body. His eyes were gritty and his throat parched. He felt unable to sit still in his chair for more than a moment without shifting position to ease the general feeling of – What? Frustration? Fatigue? After the board meeting this morning he should be feeling only relaxed and victorious.

'Do you have a lunch date, Henry?' he asked then.

'I'm afraid I do.'

Palmer sighed impatiently. He was worried at how uneasy he had begun to feel. 'Henry, may I speak frankly?'

'Of course.'

'Over this line, I mean.'

Another long pause. 'Certainly over this line,' Mather assured him.

'Can you give me an idea of how much responsibility Forellen has in your foundation?'

'He's, ah, our, ah, European director I believe.'

'Henry, is it your belief or your knowledge?' Palmer persisted.

'I'm quite sure of it. Is anything wrong, Woods?'

'His attitude. And a general aura that surrounds him.'

'Now you leave me utterly in the dark,' Mather confessed.

Palmer sighed again. Everything he said or did now seemed bogged down in molasses. All movements, all thinking cost him a tremendous effort. 'Henry,' he began, 'it's not unknown, I'm sure you'll agree, that a perfectly honorable organization becomes infiltrated by people whose motives are not those of the organization.'

This time Mather paused for so long that Palmer thought the connection might have been broken. 'Henry?'

'Yes.' The ancient voice sounded even more tired. 'I see that I can, indeed, have lunch with you today. I'll have my girl cancel my appointment. Let's make it half an hour from now at the Yale Club?'

Mather was waiting for Palmer in the club lobby at twelve thirty and led him up by elevator to the dining room, where neither at first wanted a drink. They had given their food order and the waiter had been about to leave their table when Palmer suddenly said: 'And a Scotch and soda now, please.'

Mather's eyebrows almost went up. 'One for me, too,' he ordered.

Neither of them seemed to have much to talk about during the time it took the waiter to bring their drinks from the bar. Palmer raised his and nodded. 'To the Foundation.'

'To your mission for us.'

They sipped. 'Henry, the Foundation's work is so closely related to economic research it would be surprising to me if it hadn't been infiltrated years ago by interests that needed access to your files. You've been in business – what? – since World War Two?'

Mather shook his smallish head. He had evidently once been somewhat plumper than he was now and the skin of his face hung in faint festoons from his eyes and cheekbones. 'World War One, my friend.'

'Then possibly you've been infiltrated a dozen times.' Palmer laughed slightly. 'It's conceivable that even some of your oldest employees are agents.'

'Or that even I am one.'

Palmer nodded. 'Even you.'

'Even, ah, you,' Mather pointed out. 'We do live in times like that, don't we?'

Palmer swallowed most of his drink and tried to feel any lessening of the uneasy feeling he had been suffering. He signaled the waiter for another drink and noted that his host had barely touched his. 'We do indeed,' he agreed. 'But I'm not suggesting a general philosophical concept, Henry. I'm making a specific proposal about Forellen.'

'Yes, yes, I do see your point.'

His longish, narrow hands, liver spotted, turned palms-up on the table for a moment in an attitude of helplessness, then hid in his lap. 'Woods,' he began then, 'we really, ah, don't know each other very well, but for some strange reason I feel as if we've been friends for decades. I'm not sure why except that we're from the, ah, same background, more or less, and I sense in you some of the same old-fashioned attitudes I have. I am frank to tell you that I had a tremendous feeling of confidence in sending you on this mission for us. You were highly – very highly – recommended.'

Palmer sat back. The whiskey wasn't helping too much, but possibly this inordinate amount of soft soap would. The recommendation sounded like the long, clammy arm of H.B.

'I consequently feel,' Mather went on in his whispery, thin voice, 'that I may perhaps, ah, be much more candid with someone like you – in essence an outsider to the Foundation – than ever I could with one of my own people or trustees. Do I make myself clear?'

'Perfectly.' Palmer started on his second drink.

'Has it ever occurred to you, then,' the older man continued in a somewhat lower voice, pitched at a confidential level, 'that the Foundation, relying as it does on, ah, private grants and philanthropies, would have led a precarious existence all these years if it performed a service entirely, ah, divorced from the public interest?'

'You're taking government money, that it?'

'A stipend. Enough to keep office, files, and staff together.'

'In return for which,' Palmer surmised, 'over the years you get prize morons like Forellen handed to you to hire.'

'Ah, well, yes.'

Palmer nodded. 'Do your private philanthropies understand this?'

'I, ah, believe so.' Mather's smallish, colorless eyes almost twinkled. 'As a matter of fact, I believe it's their knowledge of this that, ah, impels them to donate the sums they do to the Foundation.'

Palmer saw that he had already finished half his second drink. He suddenly wanted to be far away from this ghostly old

218

bastard. 'And that means,' he said, 'that the research you do is rubbish. Like this mission of mine.'

'I beg your pardon?'

'The results you get are dictated to you in advance. You merely fulfil government forecasts. You are the window dressing, the so-called independent assessor whose reputation bolsters the ravings of mere politicians.'

'That, Woods, is simply not so.'

Palmer listened to the quaver in the older man's voice and wondered if he were sincere or simply a good actor. 'I hope you can convince me.'

'I'm sure I can,' Mather assured him. 'For the Foundation to have flourished through every administration, Republican and Democratic, from Warren Gamaliel Harding through Richard Milhous Nixon, argues a certain posture well above the urgent demands of, as you put it, mere politicians. We are a genuine research facility, Woods. We make genuine studies like yours and determine genuine truths. There our function ends. What government and private industry do with this information is not within our province. But the information is genuine.'

Palmer began to relax in his chair. The second drink had started to smooth over the effects of Librium withdrawal. He found himself marveling at the American Way. Only in the United States would we be able to turn loose a private research group to forage for facts and then appropriate the results to be distorted, suppressed, or misused in any way we felt necessary. An entire foundation, chugging away, unearthing Truth. In a vacuum.

He smiled politely at Mather and felt almost like patting him on the shoulder. Instead, he finished his second drink and began thinking about Eleanora, as a way of getting through the remainder of the meal.

CHAPTER 37

Palmer took the time after lunch to check out of the Plaza and into his furnished apartment. He tried Virginia's private line once more and, again, another woman answered. He lay back on the bed and decided it was silly of him to have hung up without leaving a message.

He stared at the ceiling for a while, replaying the scene with Eddie Hagen in the boardroom that morning. Harry Elder had assumed that Hagen was beaten, but Palmer knew better. If Hagen represented the mob interests – as so many people had gone to great pains to tell Palmer – then there was no question that this morning had been only a delay, not a victory.

Eddie Hagen's next move could be almost anything, Palmer reflected. He could counsel his mysterious backroom interests to let the thing hang fire a while longer before trying again. Or he could suggest they write it off and try another maneuver in another part of the banking scene. Palmer stretched and heard his shoulder joints crack.

The one thing Eddie would never be able to sell his principals was to let the whole attempt die. It was inevitable that somewhere in the banking picture they would have to reach out for the cover of respectability. So much of their activity these days, Palmer knew, was purely financial. It would be impossible for them to continue growing in this field as fast as they had, or hoped to, without eventually covering themselves with the reputation and prestige of a major financial institution like Ubco.

And what more logical than using Ubco itself, which had mistakenly made a bid to buy a bank that turned out to be mob-controlled?

All this Palmer had suspected before. But the new element was what he had learned at the meeting this morning, the extent of Hagen's desperation. Somehow, Palmer had always assumed, the mob moved as ponderously and as cautiously as Ubco itself. It had not occurred to him until he'd seen Eddie Hagen in action today that an element of speed, of impending deadline, could enter the mob's maneuvering. Probably the thing that made them so desperate was the critical condition of their bank, perhaps on the brink of open bankruptcy. If the bank went bad in a public way, the mob's hopes of infiltrating Ubco were shot.

Palmer stretched again, trying to ease the cramp of his tired muscles. He found himself wondering, in a sleepy way, how badly the mob needed Ubco's merger with their bank. He wondered how deep their desperation ran. What would they do on their own, now that Eddie Hagen had struck out for them? Would they revert to classical maneuvers? Bombings? Kidnappings? Assassinations?

He smiled wearily at the idea that, in this day and age, the mob would resort to anything that awkward. His eyes closed. He stretched one more time and fell asleep.

When he awoke, he saw that he would be late for Gerri's school play. Fortunately, his apartment was only a few blocks from the school and, even more fortunately, the eight o'clock curtain was the usual ruse to get everyone seated by eight thirty. The curtain actually rose at almost nine, by which time Palmer had installed himself in a seat near the rear of the assembly hall and determined to his satisfaction that, for some reason, Edith wasn't there.

Gerri's parts in the episodic Perelman comedy ranged from small to infinitesimal, but she carried them off so well that Palmer wondered if she might do well in such a career. She had the looks for it and the carriage. And she clearly had the self-confidence.

After the show he collected her and her brothers and took them to a nearby coffee shop. Despite the fact that they had all had dinner earlier, they each ordered a cheeseburger, French fries, and chocolate milk shake. Palmer, who had had no dinner and couldn't even remember what kind of lunch Henry Mather had given him at the Yale Club – eons ago, it seemed to him – ordered a cup of black coffee.

'I gather you have your mother's permission for this,' he said at one point.

Tom looked oddly at him. When speaking to Tom, Palmer always felt that what he said had to be translated into some alien tongue before the boy would understand it. He seemed puzzled now by his father's question, but more on some private level than on any normal one of meaning. 'Mother?' he asked in an uncomprehending way.

Palmer frowned at him and turned his attention to his daughter. 'Or didn't you ask her?' he went on. 'I noticed she wasn't there.'

Gerri produced a very theatrical shrug with no conversation to support it. Palmer decided she was still high on applause. He turned to Woody, his oldest, and said: 'What did you think of the play?'

'Groovy.' The boy's voice had gotten so much deeper over the past few months that Palmer continued to be surprised at it. When he'd lived in the house with them, he realized, such changes hadn't been noticeable at all. Now, suddenly, he seemed

221

to have a basso on his hands.

He watched the three of them demolish their cheeseburgers. The two boys bargained for Gerri's potatoes, which she decided not to eat. They did, in combination with ketchup at a ratio of one part potato to two of sauce. It occurred to Palmer that having teen-age children had lost its charm.

'What did *you* think of the play?' Gerri suddenly asked him.

Palmer watched her for a moment. 'I thought you were extremely good. The play's rather, uh, sophisticated, wouldn't you say?'

She shrugged again. 'No obscenity. No nudity.'

'I think you're mistaking the meaning of sophistication.'

'I must be,' she agreed without too much interest. She carefully picked away the end of the paper wrapping on the soda straw, placed the bared end to her lips and with a single puff blew the paper wrapping javelinlike into Tom's nose. An instant later the air was filled with similar projectiles as the boys struck back.

'Easy!' Palmer snapped. 'Calm down!'

He reached out and stopped Woody from lobbing a ketchupy bit of French fry at his sister. 'College material,' he said, disgustedly. 'I'm going back to Europe.'

'You promised we could come,' Gerri reminded him.

'Yeah?' Tom asked, his eyes widening. 'When?'

Palmer noted what it took to attract his younger son's undivided attention. 'If the three of you could ever sharpen up your table manners to the point where you could be exposed to polite society, I'd be a lot surer of sending you to Europe.'

Tom sat up very straight and poked his brother into abandoning his normal slouch. 'How's that?' Tom asked.

Palmer watched them in silence for a moment. 'Groovy,' he said then.

He brought them home shortly after eleven o'clock. Apparently Edith wasn't home. Mrs. Gage, already in pajamas and bathrobe, spent a few minutes getting the children upstairs. She came back down on the run as Palmer prepared to go. 'Glad I caught you,' she gasped, out of breath.

Palmer glanced around the immense living room and saw that there had been virtually no changes made since he'd left. 'Nice to see you again, Mrs. Gage.'

He had never been much on chatting with the woman. She had always been close to Edith, even though she'd worked for the Palmers now for almost twelve years. He watched her glance skitter about the room, as if searching for dust. 'It's an easy house to keep, now that the children are bigger,' she said. 'You wouldn't kn –' She stopped herself. 'I understood you were in Europe?'

'Going back tomorrow.'

'Then you wouldn't have had a chance t –' Again she stopped herself.

'Is there some problem, Mrs. Gage?'

'No.' She hesitated for a moment and when she spoke everything seemed to pour out in a flood of flat, Illinois-accented words. 'I just thought maybe you'd know where Mrs. Palmer's been keeping. This is the second night she's been away. It's happened before, which is why I'm not worried. But the first time it near drove me to distraction. I almost called the police. But she told me never again to think of doing anything like that, that she had her own life to lead, and I wasn't paid to be her timekeeper. She said I shouldn't panic if she didn't come home and she would try to phone me first if she could. But she didn't phone and now I'm starting to get worried.'

Palmer patted her shoulder. 'I think we know Mrs. Palmer's able to take care of herself. She took pains to make sure you wouldn't worry if it happened again. She indicated it would happen again. Now it's happened. It's nothing to worry about.'

'As long as you aren't . . .' Her voice died away.

'I? Why would I worry, Mrs. Gage?'

One corner of her flat, unrouged mouth went up. 'Why, indeed,' she mused. 'And the kids are big enough to weather almost anything.'

'Right.'

'And you –' She stopped herself. This time Palmer wasn't interested in learning what she had suppressed.

'She'll be back eventually,' Palmer said, opening the front door. 'If you really have reason for concern, the children have my itinerary in Europe. You can reach me by telephone or cable. I'm sure you won't have to.'

Mrs. Gage nodded. 'I'm sure,' she agreed. 'Good night, Mr. Palmer.'

As he walked east through the warm June night, Palmer realized now why his children had been so – evasive? – about their mother. He supposed Edith was having her delayed fling, as she had promised she would. It amazed Palmer how easy it was to view this with equanimity. You'd think, he mused, that a quarter of a century with one woman would give her some sort of proprietorship of a piece of your concern or interest. But it just wasn't that way. And, he supposed, she cared even less what he did with his life. It seemed quite clear as he walked along the dark side streets now that their real separation had taken place many years before the legal one.

He saw that he was gravitating toward Virginia's house on the river at East 58th Street. It occurred to Palmer that he ought to call before making an appearance, since it was now almost midnight.

She answered on the first ring. 'You prize bastard,' she retorted to his greeting.

'I tried your office phone several times.'

'And left no message.'

'I called you last night and you weren't in.'

Her voice grew calmer. 'That's right. Oh, hell. Where are you?'

'A block away.'

'Please break a record getting here.' She hung up.

When he turned in at the mews of one-family buildings that led off 58th Street, with their gardens overlooking the river, she was standing in the doorway of her house, shading her eyes to see him against the streetlamps. Her long yellow peignoir was fastened under her breasts, Empire style, and the streetlamp's light on her bosom was almost blinding in its brightness.

She took his hand and pulled him into the foyer, closing the door behind him.

Then she let go and stepped away to take a longer look at him. Palmer had always thought Virginia too short and too full-figured for the traditional pin-up type of beauty. But there was something about the way the peignoir fell in thick vertical folds that added height to her. She had combed and brushed her long curling black hair for bed and tied it with a thin yellow ribbon. But she still had on eye makeup, Palmer noticed, and a faint touch of pale lipstick. He kissed her.

She tasted faintly of Scotch and smelled of the same perfume she had always worn, the odor of which, even from a bottle in a gift shop, was always able to conjure up her presence to him. Her body pressed against his at vastly different places from Eleanora's. It felt different, too, softer, without the hint of bone close in under the cushioning flesh.

224

When he released her at last they remained standing in the foyer, her immense eyes fixed on his face. 'My God,' she said at last, 'you're in some sort of real trouble, aren't you?'

Palmer frowned. 'Just came from seeing my kids.'

'And Edith?'

'She's taken to not coming home nights on occasion.'

'How nice for her.'

Virginia took his hand and led him into her small living room with the mullioned bay window overlooking the river. She sat him down in the armchair she had always referred to as 'his.' She made a drink for him and another for herself. Palmer tasted it and found it extremely strong. He sipped slowly, but steadily.

'Are you interested in what Edith's been doing?' she asked, sitting down across from him on the short sofa. She tucked her legs in under her and, in so doing, showed that she was wearing mules with very high heels. Palmer understood now why at first she had looked taller than he remembered.

'Not at all,' he said. 'Unless it's something that might affect the kids.'

Virginia shook her head. Her long hair settled in big unsteady curls on the fussy yellow collar of the peignoir. 'There are a few gentlemen she sees. It occasionally gets back to me through newspaper friends. Nothing bad.'

'Would you think, after all this time,' Palmer said, 'that we'd be sitting here discussing Edith? It's grotesque.'

She laughed and examined her drink. She hadn't yet sipped any of it. 'Shall we discuss us?' she asked then.

'One at a time. I'll tell you about me first.'

'Tell.'

'The board meeting went tolerably well today. I –'

'Harry Elder called to give me that report,' Virginia interrupted.

'Yes. Well.' Palmer gestured with the hand that held his drink and was startled to find that somehow he had finished all the whisky. He began to wonder why he suddenly seemed to need props like Librium and Scotch. 'I'm glad one of us got through to you.'

'Is that all you wanted to tell me about you?' she asked.

'Isn't that the main topic of interest?'

She put her untouched drink on an end table, got up, and refilled his. He caught a glimpse of her olive-skinned thigh as she strode across the room. He hadn't noticed it before but

Eleanora's skin was darker, almost tanned, compared to Virginia's brunette whiteness.

'Woods,' she said, giving him a fresh drink and sitting across from him again, 'I think we would have reached a pretty pass if my only interest in you was how you fenced around with Eddie Hagen.'

'But that's pretty much what's happened to me lately.'

She was silent for a moment. Then: 'Oh, bullshit.' The word fell plain and without emotion, as if to refute a statement she had lost interest in refuting. 'Finish your drink and go home, Woods.'

'Home?'

'That furnished flat of yours. Which you weren't in last night.'

'I was at the Plaza. Part of the security strategy.'

'You're all little boys playing little-boy games.'

He had begun to flounder. The idea of his having to go home, the thought that she wanted him out of her home, the knowledge that there really wasn't any home for him in this town even though it was now, he supposed, his home town ... all these unhappy things had begun to swamp him, coming in across his gunwales like crisscrossing waves, buffeting him from both sides. He sipped his drink and tried to make headway against the feeling of drowning.

'I think you're overreacting,' he said. 'If I've done anything to merit this sort of response on your part, it's a mystery to me.'

'I love the way you do that, Woods,' she retorted. 'You are, above all else, the compleat manager. You delegate like an angel, everything, even what is rightfully and solely yours and yours alone you delegate. Now drink up and leave.'

He shook his head. 'A complete mystery to me,' he reiterated.

'Don't force me to explode the mystery,' she warned him. 'You won't like the explanation. Don't make me spell it out for you.'

Palmer recognized the tack she was on. If he demanded the explanation, he would get it. It would be a collection of discrepancies and missed moves on his part, calls that should have been made, absences from his Paris hotel suite, rumors from elsewhere. He could respond in two equally acceptable ways, by denying everything and attributing it all to a variety of errors in interpretation or coincidences, or by admitting everything and crying for forgiveness. Either response would work because, inherent in her threat to expose his shortcomings was her desire to have them explained and forgiven.

Palmer knew all this, even in the panicky state he was in. During the early part of their affair, nearly three years ago, before they had broken up, he had played this scene with her on several occasions. Getting back together with her six months ago had been a variation on the same relationship. While the content of their crises could differ from one to the next, their motives were always the same, hers to be reassured, his to be reaccepted.

Feeling shaky and dismayed at the rootlessness of his life here in New York, it would be easy enough for him now to throw himself on her mercy. She had a lot of it for him and he seemed to have gotten himself into a corner where he needed still more.

Palmer finished his drink and realized he was drunk. He pulled himself up out of the depths of the armchair and walked to the window. He drew back the curtains and watched the lights of a smallish tanker plow slowly upstream. The black arch of the Queensboro Bridge formed a frame over the ship as it disappeared to the north, chugging smoothly and purposefully onward. Palmer wondered why it was so hard for him to be purposeful and direct. He turned back to Virginia.

'It's been a long day for me. I'm out of kilter with the time change,' he began, 'but I'm willing to tackle anything you wish.'

He could hear the softness of his consonants and knew that he probably sounded drunk. When she said nothing he took a steadying breath and said: 'Or not, as you wish.'

'What do *you* wish?'

He shook his head, mostly in exasperation at the way she could go so directly to the point. She knew as well as he that for some time now he'd had no direction and no purpose. It had little to do with the breakup of his marriage, although losing that physical grasp on reality hadn't done him a tremendous amount of good. It had much more to do with his job and the fact that he no longer had any real interest in it. Eleanora had been wrong about that: he might be used to wielding power, but he would never miss it if he gave it up.

'You really know how to disarm a fellow,' he told Virginia. 'You know I'm tired and drunk and upset and for years now haven't had a real idea of what I want.'

'You really know how to flatter a girl.'

'That's not what I mean.'

She watched him for a long moment, motionless. Then she folded her arms across her breasts. 'Woods,' she began, 'the problems of the rich are fascinating, I know. But what can be so terribly unhappy about a man who has everything, including a mistress on both sides of the Atlantic and the money to fly back and forth between them?' She paused for a moment, somewhat thoughtfully. 'Or is that too cruel for you?'

He sat down in the tufted window seat and tried to focus on what was happening. He knew, even drunk, that if she really wanted him gone she would have stopped talking long ago. The words didn't matter especially. That she kept talking did. So the question left to solve was whether he wanted to stay or not. Or, in a larger sense, whether he wanted to keep the affair going or let it die.

As they sat there, watching each other. it occurred to Palmer that he had never been able to get Eleanora to solve his problems for him. Nor would he think of trying. Whereas he had always tried to maneuver Edith, and then Virginia, into giving him answers, at least on matters that concerned them.

Palmer supposed it was the European versus the American woman's way of functioning. And very much the American male's training at the hands of his countrywomen. They made such terrible scenes if they didn't get their way that American men quickly saw the wisdom of first learning what their way was before making a decision. About the only time this had even come to a head with Eleanora had been when he confessed to her – as he had to no one else – his thoughts about quitting the bank. Palmer tried to recall her answer. Something about 'you are the man; you decide.'

He cleared his throat at last. He had no idea what he was going to tell Virginia because he still hadn't made up his mind whether he wanted to leave or not. 'All men are pigs,' he said suddenly. 'Did you know that?'

She frowned uncertainly. 'I'm learning.'

'They're pigs where it concerns women. You'll have to excuse the inelegant language. I'm sort of around the bend tonight.' He smiled meaninglessly. 'Men will do anything to get laid. It's their most universal characteristic. It's what makes them swine.' He stood up and glanced out the window at the dark river. 'They will lie to women or let them believe any sort of untruth, just as long as they can crawl in bed with them. They will scheme and maneuver and repent and despair. They'll pull any kind of trick, act any sort of part.'

Virginia sat back with a kind of cautious attention and crossed her legs. Palmer watched the pure ivory of her knees, smooth and dimpled.

'I suppose women will do anything, too,' he said. 'But their objectives are usually more permanent than a quick spasm of the prostate sphincter. I mean, men will sink to the level of pigs for something as small as that.'

In the silence he could hear a long hooting of a ship's horn, far away and forlorn. Once, then twice, then once again.

'Occasionally,' Palmer heard himself say, 'this sort of thing upsets a man almost as much as it probably disgusts women. Usually one doesn't get upset at one's own piggishness, of course. But of late, it seems I can't stop asking myself questions of such profundity that even without answers the questions alone depress me.'

His voice ran down. He came back to the armchair and sat down, not in it but on the edge of it, as if to say with his body: 'I'm about to leave, but you may have a few last words to be said.'

He himself had run out of words. He stared at the floor. When she began talking, he didn't look up at her for a while.

'I think,' she said in a low voice, 'that if men are pigs, women are geese. I blush at how gullible we are, even the brightest of us. How adept we are at kidding ourselves.'

Palmer looked up to find that she was watching him closely, her big eyes in their hollows looking as grave and forlorn as the sound the ship had made before. 'When you think,' she went on, 'on what slight evidence we build such castles of fantasy. To think of me, with all I've lived through in my life, watching you get separated from Edith, watching you come painfully out of your shell with me, convincing myself that however bad it had been two years ago, this was something new and different and valid. It wasn't a few spasms under the sheets. I thought it was for real.'

Palmer nodded. He had become curiously detached from their talk, whether through fatigue or liquor, he couldn't be sure. But he felt as if he were somewhere else in the room, watching both of them and listening to something of interest, but not of any overwhelming urgency. He felt dizzy for a moment.

'It may not be such a good idea,' he said – or rather the figure of his sitting in the armchair said, 'to talk about sex as being just sex. Apparently there is more to it.'

'And also less.'

The Palmer-figure in the armchair gestured helplessly. 'Which is why it's so hard to know oneself. So hard to judge another person. So hard to understand relationships. You do see that.'

The Virginia-figure crossed her legs the other way. 'I see that it's hard for you. It isn't that hard for me. I wonder how hard it would be for a man with normal instincts and emotions. I wonder how hard it would be for a man who wasn't a cold damned fish. And I –'

The roaring in his ears blotted out the rest of what she was saying. He watched the room slant in a peculiar way, the walls out of plumb with the floor and the ceiling much higher than before. Perhaps it was an earthquake. The Palmer-figure slid off the armchair onto its face. The rug pressed against his chin and lower lip and one cheek. He could see the individual upstanding tufts of colored wool.

'Woods!'

He muttered something as he felt her hands on him, trying to help him to his feet or to lift him back into the armchair. He shook loose and stood up. He went down on one knee with a terrible crack, paused there for a moment as if kneeling in church, head bowed. Then he pulled himself to his feet again.

'Woods, what's the –'

He shook clear of her and took a sideways step. 'I have to stop leaning on you. You've always been my leaning post.'

She stood a foot away from him and her eyes seemed enormous. He felt a chill across his shoulder blades, as if she would eat him alive with her huge eyes. She watched him turn from her and start for the door. Palmer could sense that she had raised a hand toward him, but she made no other move to detain him.

He walked out into the warm night. River mist swirled in small patches through the garden, as it had along the Seine embankment that night after they'd gotten off the *bateau-mouche*. He headed for the gate that led to 58th Street. When he got there, he turned back and saw that Virginia was standing in the lamplight in her doorway, arms crossed over her breasts.

'Good night,' he said softly.

For a moment she said nothing. Then she lifted one hand. 'Good-bye,' she said.

CHAPTER 38

He wandered for some time, the pain in his knee growing worse at first and then a little better. He tried to determine what had made him keel over on the rug that way and then, in trying to rise, what had brought him down on his knee with such force.

Palmer found himself on First Avenue in the Sixties standing outside one of those places he had always heard about but never seen, even though he now lived nearby. The place was nominally a bar or restaurant with a reputation for being a 'swinging singles' place where unmarried people in their twenties (thirties allowed?) met each other. Palmer had heard it was much frequented by airline hostesses on their nights off.

Rubbing his knee, he poked his head in the door and found the place badly lighted and almost empty, a dank cavern echoing with the thud-slop-thud of some rock group over the tremendously amplified jukebox.

'Momma-momma-momma, lemme grabya-grabya-grabya,' howled the jukebox. 'Lemme kissit, kissit, kissit, lemme huh?'

Palmer pulled himself out of the doorway and limped off along the street toward his apartment. He stopped at a newsstand that was still open and saw that there were no copies of either the *Times* or the *News* on hand, only an assortment of tabloid-sized newssheets with suggestive names and flatly obscene headlines. Palmer limped across First Avenue and headed west toward his apartment house.

He hadn't recovered from what had happened at Virginia's. He tried to analyze it as he walked along, feeling the additional exercise soothing his knee back into well-being again. The more weight he put on it, Palmer saw, the stronger it kept getting. He decided he couldn't be quite as old as he felt.

God, that had been a bad scene. He'd said everything wrong and by indirection. She couldn't be blamed for taking everything wrongly. But, of course, if he'd been able to say it straight and right, would it have ended any better?

'I've met this girl,' he would have said, 'and what I feel for her is unlike anything I've ever felt before, even for you.'

'I've met this girl, and I know that if it hadn't been for you, I might never have responded to her. I might have missed her love completely.'

'I've met this girl, and because you helped me out of my shell

231

over the past three years, I was able to love her.'

Virginia was Irish enough to have found a gun somewhere and shot him through the heart. Telling a woman she was responsible for unlocking a man's feelings so that he could love another.

'You were great,' he would have said, 'but this girl's greater. Thanks for making me appreciate her.'

Probably Virginia would have done it with her bare hands. You simply didn't tell a woman that sort of thing. And yet, if you didn't, how honest were you being?

Palmer let himself in the front door of his apartment building and saw that, as usual, the TV camera had the lobby under surveillance, a fact clearly proclaimed by a sign under the camera so that a would-be sneak thief could drape his hat over the lens if he craved anonymity. Not that it mattered, Palmer reflected as he opened the inner door, since the night man in his cubicle was undoubtedly fast asleep and not watching the monitor.

He got in the small, antiseptic-smelling elevator car and punched the button for his floor. He wondered how many of these buildings there were all over town, would-be dungeon keeps, last refuges of the frightened middle class, with windowless bastionlike façades, metallic walls and lobbies, elaborate security systems, and exorbitant rents. He knew that for the studio apartment he lived in, sublet furnished to him, he was paying some five hundred dollars a month. That for a living room, a tiny bedroom, and a phone booth of a kitchenette.

Palmer let himself into the apartment. It occurred to him as he closed the door behind him that life in Manhattan had become a strangely sterile proposition. If one had a small, warm little house like Virginia's, of course, that was something else. But the vast majority of people, at least on the East Side, seemed to live like automatons in an automated, TV-monitored wilderness of blank walls and blind glass.

He stood just inside the door of his apartment and wondered if he should have been more honest with Virginia. Real honesty for the first time in his life?

He could have slept with her tonight, but it would have been even more dishonest. Perhaps not to Eleanora, who had foreseen what might happen. But certainly to Virginia and, in the end, to him. Funny the way things twisted. The 'wronged' party would really have been Eleanora. He had pledged himself to her,

232

so to speak, and he would have been dishonoring that pledge. At least that was the old-style morality of it.

But there really was no morality to anything any more. Palmer shucked his jacket, opened his collar and tie, and sat down in a stiff, unaccommodating armchair. He rubbed his knee reflectively.

No morality, he thought, just common sense. To resume his affair with Virginia would have diminished his relationship with Eleanora. It was that simple. If all one wanted was the joyful pain of a discharging sphincter, it didn't really matter who one discharged into. If one wanted more from it all, one had to get busy and work at making it something more.

Palmer laughed slightly at himself. He had begun to sound like an aging Don Juan, bitter and alone, spouting aphorisms gained at great cost over a life of dedicated fornication.

He really hadn't tested such theories to the fullest. He'd only cheated on one wife, Edith, with only one mistress, Virginia. He was hardly an expert. But he knew the way his mind worked. He had the power of anticipation. Perhaps it was a gift, the ability to take present knowns and project them into the unknown.

Whatever he'd become in banking had been due to this gift of anticipation. Banking was a dishonest business at best, but he'd somehow slid damned near to the top of it without really trying all that hard.

Which made giving it up that much easier, didn't it?

His doorbell rang.

Palmer stood up and winced at the sudden twang of pain in his knee. He went to the intercom near the front door. 'Yes?'

'Me, Woods,' Virginia said.

Palmer buzzed the door in the lobby and, a few minutes later, opened his front door to her. She had obviously thrown a fur coat on over her peignoir. With her feet still in high-heeled mules, she looked vaguely as if she had just come from a senior prom, except that her hair had been blown in several directions at once and the yellow ribbon had slipped off. She watched him close the door behind her. Then she went to the small bar near the teak window seat and poured herself a shot of whatever bottle her hand reached for first. She swallowed the drink and when she put the glass down on the teak top, it clattered noisily in her unsteady fingers.

'Sorry to do this,' she said then.

233

'Sit down, please.'

'I stood there in my doorway for the damnedest time thinking about us and finally I couldn't take it any longer.' She sat down and reached in a cigarette box on the cocktail table. It was empty. She glanced up inquiringly.

'None in the house,' Palmer said.

'Christ.' She sighed sharply. 'Woods, is it all over? Is that what we were talking about back at my house?' When he failed to answer for a moment, she got to her feet and paced toward the window. She stopped, walked back and sat down. 'Woods?'

'I guess it meant that,' he said slowly. 'It wasn't actually said.'

'A lot wasn't said. Is there some girl you've met in Europe?'

He nodded. She stood up again, just as abruptly, sat back down. 'I can't seem to keep myself under any kind of control,' she muttered.

'You don't have to,' he assured her. 'You're among friends.'

'With a friend like you ...' she began, and let her voice die away. 'Is she our age?'

'Younger.'

'Lots younger?'

'Lots.' Palmer didn't like the sound of that. 'But not that much. She's, uh, nearly thirty.'

'Over the hill, so to speak, but not sunk in doddering senility like me.' Virginia lifted her hand to stop whatever he might say. 'Bad joke. Forget it. Is she nice? Is she bright? What's she like?'

'You mean is she better than you?'

'That's what I mean.'

'In some ways. Not in others.'

'A sort of flawed perfection,' Virginia said in a brittle tone. 'My God, how that type does appeal to the opposite sex.' She laughed in a vague way, as if having forgotten what she was laughing about. 'It's what attracted me to you, did you know that? You had looks, brains, position, everything but a heart. I was fatally attracted. I figured, what does that one little flaw mean when all the rest is perfection? The love of a good woman will thaw the block of ice and lo, within will beat a living, human heart.'

When he said nothing she laughed again, more quietly. 'So, figuring I was the good woman to do the job, I turned on the heat. I couldn't help myself. Just looking at you turned me on.'

234

She started to get up from the sofa, thought better of it, and instead crossed her legs and leaned back against the cushions. 'Do you remember all that ancient history, Woods?'

'Yes.'

'Well, it seems I'm being turned off.'

'It's not that.'

'Did I forget to pay my bill or something?' she asked him. 'Damn it, Woods, I should be the one to turn myself off if I feel like it. I did it once before with you and it was hell, but it wasn't the end of the world. This is. I freely admit it.'

'Look.' He started to sit down beside her on the sofa.

'Sit over there, please.'

Palmer went to the black glove-leather armchair and sat. Absentmindedly, he began rubbing his game knee. 'There's no question of turning on or off,' he began. 'It all comes down to a question of honesty. Of being honest with you.'

Virginia nodded. 'I don't want to hear this next part,' she said. 'You're the boy who got a gun for Christmas. You're not going to be happy till you shoot it at somebody.'

'Honesty is not a toy.'

'Good of you to notice. Honesty is not a toy.' She began picking at the cuticle of her thumb. 'Honesty is a deadly weapon. I don't want it turned on me. I'm in a very self-protective mood. If I were really smart I'd never have walked over here. I'm what you might call self-destructive-protective. I'm what you might call insane.'

She got up and stood in front of him, looking down in the darkened room into his eyes. 'You see?' she asked. 'I'm that crazy. I know what's happening but I'm damned if I'll just stand by and let it happen without digging into every bloody detail and getting myself cut up in the process.'

She turned away from him and strode to the bar. Again she poured a drink and this time she brought it back to the sofa, where she sat down. 'So she's younger than I and better where it counts.'

'I didn't say that.'

'She must be. Otherwise what is this all about? Tell me what counts? What's she better at? Fucking?'

Palmer blinked. 'Look, I think –'

'What little yummy dirty things does she do that I don't do?' she wanted to know. She swallowed her drink and shook her head. 'I didn't mean it that way. As if a gentleman would tell.'

'Why don't you sit back and listen for a minute?' Palmer suggested.

'Obviously because I'm afraid of what you'll say.' She put the glass down on the cocktail table and it clattered much louder this time on the plate-glass top. 'Anyway, what would a gentleman tell a lady in a situation like this? Damned little. A gentleman wouldn't resort to weapons like honesty.' She stood up and went halfway to the front door. 'Woods, you'll have to forgive me. I'm sorry I bothered you. I'm leaving.'

'Maybe not for a little while.'

'Now. I'm relying on you. No sudden blurtings out. No truth, for God's sake.' She stood at the door with her hand on the knob. Then she seemed to collapse against the door and grow much smaller, as if crushing against it helplessly. Palmer got up and came to her but when she felt his touch, she whirled sideways to avoid it.

'No contact,' she said. Her eyes looked immense in the darkened room. A faint gleam from the front windows was reflected in them, condensed to tiny, brilliant squares that gave her a mad, staring look. 'No contact all down the line. It's easier on you if you don't have to tell me. And Christ knows it's easier on me not to hear. Okay? Okay?'

Palmer stood clear of her with his hands at his sides as if to reassure her. 'Why do you always make it easy for me?' he asked then. 'I didn't ask you.'

'I know. I'm just a nice girl, that's all.'

'If you –'

'Don't tell me anything,' she cut in. 'I'm going as soon as I can get over the urge to cry.'

Palmer reached out to her again and again she recoiled. 'When are you going back to her? Tomorrow?'

'I think so. Yes.'

'Do you have what is referred to as an understanding?' She shook her head violently from side to side. 'Don't answer that. It's more insanity. You've known her a week. One lousy, goddamned week,' she said, her voice suddenly swelling with pain. Her eyes darted away from his face, then back. 'Let me out of here,' she whispered.

He stood away from the door. 'I'll get you a cab.'

'Never.' She froze for a moment. Then she relaxed. 'All right, please.' She nodded to the door.

Palmer picked up his jacket, opened the door and ushered her out into the hall. He pressed the elevator button and, as they waited, got into his jacket, buttoned his collar, and adjusted his tie.

Outside the street was deserted. They walked to Second Avenue, but there were no cabs to be seen. Neither of them spoke as they walked, but her mules made a crisp, snapping sound on the pavement. He took her arm to guide her over a curb and she gently disengaged herself. They were heading south along the avenue by silent agreement. When they reached 58th Street they turned east.

'I'm perfectly safe now,' she said at last, breaking the long silence. 'I can make it home from here.'

'It's all right.'

They crossed First Avenue. The illuminated clock in a nearby store showed Palmer that it was almost one thirty in the morning. He glanced at his watch and confirmed the time. 'It's late,' Virginia said in a calm, noncommittal voice. 'You can leave me here.'

'I prefer not to.'

When they crossed Sutton Place and entered the quarter block of dead end that stopped at the river, Virginia stood on the corner, facing Palmer. 'All right. Thank you. Good night.'

'I'll see you to your door.'

She turned and walked on without speaking. At her door she put the key in the lock. 'Good night.'

'I'm sorry about this, Virginia.'

'I know you are.'

'Do you?'

She nodded. 'You look miserable. It's not easy for you.'

'No, it's not.'

'To look miserable, that is.' She smiled somewhat maliciously. 'Maybe this whole thing will soften you up a lot more than you bargained for.'

'I beg your pardon?'

'Good night, Woods.'

She opened the door, went in, and closed it firmly behind her.

CHAPTER 39

Flight 010 took off on time from JFK International Tuesday morning. It was destined to arrive in Orly that evening, Paris time, but there was no convenient connecting flight to Frankfurt until the following morning. This more or less dictated a night's stay at the Ritz again, Palmer realized.

He sipped the Air France champagne as the jet angled eastward across the Atlantic. He reflected that only ten days before he had taken exactly the same flight under totally different emotional conditions.

By the time he had finished his third glass of champagne, Palmer felt somewhat sleepy. He hadn't been able to sleep at all last night – or rather early this morning after he'd walked Virginia home. Instead, he'd sat and read some of the magazines that had collected in his absence, wondering if he should take a pill of some kind and deciding against it. He worried about his new need for pills, then justified the need as being special, not to be repeated again. Yet he knew this was a lie and the knowledge bothered him even more than the sudden dependence on drugs.

The Atlantic looked solidly socked in. Palmer pulled down the shades next to his seat in first class and tried to work out some sort of balance sheet which might tell him what he'd accomplished and where he stood.

He'd meant at first to figure it out as far as Ubco was concerned, as far as his hand-to-hand with Eddie Hagen and Barney Kinch. But he found himself, instead, working out emotional charts and graphs that told him little.

Fig. 1 represented the Palmer condition of emotional bonding, *circa* ten days before. As a pie chart it showed roughly a third of his emotions engaged in the day-to-day nonsense of Ubco, a third in his children, and a third in his affair with Virginia. This could also be represented (Fig. 2) as a pictograph in which a tripod arrangement sustained Palmer's soul, each leg firmly planted in good, solid bourgeois foundations: career, children, cupid. Finance, family, fanny.

Fig. 3 was a bar-graph representation. Black ink depicted a vertical bar divided in thirds labeled appropriately, with the section devoted to family subdivided into rough thirds approximating his interest in each of his children.

Palmer's eyes were closed now as the 707 roared eastward

over the ocean. He was not asleep, in the sense that he was dreaming. But his grasp of what pictures his mind was creating was not as solid as he imagined it to be.

Fig. 4 was a new pie chart labeled 'CURRENT STATUS, PALMER BONDING.' The Ubco sector was a thin sliver, hardly enough to feed a mouse, too thin to bear a label. It required an arrow which indicated that it represented 'less than $\frac{1}{2}$ of 1%.' The wedge labeled 'Family' was diminished to perhaps a fifth of the circumference of the pie. There was no segment for poor Virginia. The entire remainder of the chart, representing more than three-quarters of the pie, was labeled 'Eleanora.'

Fig. 5 duplicated Fig. 3, but a second ink, red, had been added to establish a new vertical bar next to the old black one. Its divisions corresponded mathematically to those of Fig. 4.

Palmer struggled for a moment to construct Fig. 6, a new version of Fig. 2, the pictograph, but there was nothing that immediately came to mind to replace the bourgeois solidity of the tripod, unless it was the classic plinth of the single pedestal.

He sensed that the steward had paused at his seat. He opened his eyes and nodded yes to the proffered champagne.

Palmer realized as he sipped the wine that the chief thing bothering him was Virginia. He had mishandled everything. He had botched it. And what was worse, she didn't deserve that kind of bumbling incompetence. She deserved some much clearer thinking on his part, some responsibility for what he was doing to her, some feeling of compassion. Christ, he thought, she isn't an old enemy. You just don't behave that way to a woman you once loved.

Palmer's eyes sprang open and he sat up straighter in his seat, as if to make amends, by his upright position, for the sleazy posture he had fallen into with Virginia.

He stared at the half-full tulip glass of champagne sitting on the built-in table beside him. The bubbles moved slowly upward in two thin threads. As Palmer watched, one of the threads simply ceased to exist. There remained only one slender chain of rising bubbles. It reminded him of the extremely tiny emotional footing on which his life was now based.

He was banking everything on the girl, on Eleanora. For her he had closed out Virginia as unceremoniously as one closed out an old account. What had she said last night? Turned her off? Like gas and electric when one didn't pay one's bills?

For her, for Eleanora, he would eventually turn off Ubco, too.

He felt sure of it, or as sure as the champagne left him feeling. One of these days he would sidestep the whole mess before it got even messier and let Elmer Hesselman pick up the pieces. Elmer'd last a while, long enough. Palmer would no longer be what the SEC defined as an 'insider' and he could sell his Ubco stock before anything really came to light.

Palmer realized he was fantasizing. He leaned back in his seat and closed his eyes, surrendering to the pleasures of it. Let's pretend I'm out of Ubco, he told himself. And let's pretend the girl and I are living somewhere in Europe. On the Mosel? But there was so much more of Europe he had to see, she had to show him. Let's pretend we travel the face of the continent for years before we settle down. That would do it. She was wrong about his need to wield power. But just in case she were right, the years of travel would be a perfect way of leaving his old life and settling gradually into a new one.

She would – they would – Palmer's eyes opened wide. He was staring at the seat-belt sign, which had just gone on. The pilot's voice in French and then in English announced slight turbulence ahead and suggested the use of the seat belts, loosely fastened.

Palmer adjusted the buckle. She would – He could almost feel how narrow an emotional base his whole life rested upon. A pedestal? Fig. 6 would be a pictograph of what?

Palmer got it, finally, a picture of a carnival juggler, one of these fellows who balances a spinning plate on the end of a long pole that he rests on his chin. As Fig. 6 it was less than reassuring. He wiped it out.

It was instantly replaced by another image drawn from the carnival, the man who lifts himself in the air and supports his entire body on one index finger.

Palmer finally fell into a restless sleep.

CHAPTER 40

Dauber looked harassed as he ushered Palmer into the waiting Mercedes limousine. 'Bill Elston alerted me by cable,' he explained, without being asked. 'I've got you the same suite at the Ritz.'

Neither spoke during the long ride from Orly to the hotel, except at one point when Palmer asked if Forellen had been bothering Dauber.

'It's no bother,' the younger man assured him.

Something in his tone made Palmer suspect that Dauber had had a previous engagement tonight and was suppressing his exasperation at having to shepherd top brass around at the last moment.

'When we get to the Ritz,' Palmer said, 'keep the limo and go on wherever you were supposed to be tonight.'

Dauber's eyes widened and he started to say something. Then he gave Palmer the only genuine smile he'd produced so far this evening. 'Thank you very much.'

Palmer nodded. He went to his suite and opened his small traveling bag without unpacking it. He picked up the telephone and asked the operator to put through a person-to-person call to Miss Eleanora Gregorius in Trier, West Germany. No, he had no idea of the number but the name was listed in the Trier directory on – Palmer's brain churned through file cards of memory – Hauptalleestrasse?

The operator rang him back in five minutes to report that she had the number but that no one answered. Palmer made a note of the number and asked her to try again in half an hour.

He walked about the living room for a moment, then sat down. He had slept quite a bit on the flight over. In fact, he'd slept through the big, delicious meal, much to the chagrin of the steward and hostess who tried to tempt him later with tidbits.

The sleep had been enough for Palmer now to feel restless. He felt he ought to be up and out doing things, although there was nothing at all for him to do at – he glanced at his wristwatch – nine o'clock at night except perhaps have a bite to eat and go to bed. He sat down and rubbed his knee, which still gave him trouble from time to time.

He thought about Virginia. But he found he was suddenly trying to picture what was going on in Trier. Perhaps all three of them, Eleanora and her parents, had gone out to dinner. Perhaps they were visiting friends. They might have gone to a film or a concert. At nine o'clock in the evening – ten o'clock in Trier? – one could be doing almost anything.

When the telephone rang, Palmer winced with nervousness. The operator informed him that the number still didn't answer. Palmer asked her to hold the ticket on the call and he would get

241

back to her in a few hours. He went downstairs and let the doorman get him a cab. He directed the driver to the Montparnasse and got off at an intersection not more than a block from the girl's apartment.

He sat outside at a restaurant that faced a small park where artists had set up their easels to attract passing tourists. It seemed to Palmer as he sat there eating a poor crepe, served cool and somewhat greasy, that in ten days the seasonal onslaught of American tourism had already begun. He saw a prosperous butter-and-egg-man from Sandusky, Ohio, arguing price with an artist, after snapping a picture of him at his easel. Palmer suddenly realized that the tourist was speaking German or at least trying to get the artist to understand it.

The German tourist flood had begun, then, Palmer amended. The Americans would be close behind. It was hard to tell them apart, with their cameras and beefy necks.

He left a dollar bill next to his plate and walked in the direction of Eleanora's apartment, for no reason except to have a direction for walking. He reflected that in leaving foreign money behind him he was behaving as much like a tourist as the German with the camera. When he got to the girl's building he stood across the street from it and glanced up at the row of windows through which he had looked so often. He turned around, but saw that from the street level one couldn't see the Eiffel Tower in the distance, hazily, as if through gauze. He wished he and the girl were upstairs now.

He noticed that one of her windows was slightly open.

Palmer frowned. They had left Paris in a hurry, it was true, but she was by no means a careless person. He crossed the street and entered the building. He walked up the flights of stairs to her attic floor. Some envelopes had been slid under her door rather carelessly. He pulled one out and saw that it was a folded cardboard flyer advertising some sort of political rally against the Vietnam War.

Palmer stared at the door for a moment, thinking. Then he succumbed to what he realized had been his unvoiced desire all along. He opened his wallet and removed his Diner's Club card. Inserting the stiff plastic between the door and the jamb, he lifted up on the knob and slowly, millimeter by millimeter, eased back the catch until the door sprung open.

He entered the apartment and closed the door behind him.

He was standing on several more envelopes. The room was

dark, but there was enough light left in the sky and from the streetlamps outside, for him to see that the place was a mess.

Palmer flicked on a wall switch. The bed was unmade, sheets pulled down to disclose the mattress ticking. Drawers had been pulled open and left that way. The door of the tiny under-sink refrigerator had swung open. Palmer instinctively kicked it shut.

He made his way methodically around the room, checking and sorting and making mental notes. When he finished, some fifteen minutes later, he decided that nothing important was missing. It wasn't that he knew the apartment that well, although he did, of course. It was more that the girl kept very little here. She refused to squirrel things away and what little there had been Palmer felt he remembered. None of it seemed gone, although the drawers of the dresser looked less full. Perhaps some underwear and stockings? A blouse or two? A skirt?

Strange. He shut the open window that had first attracted his attention. He rubbed the sill next to the closed panes and found them free of dust. Then he rubbed the sill where the window had been open. It, too, was without dust. So the window hadn't been open long. A day? Very strange.

Palmer sat down on the bed and sorted through the mail. Some of the letters looked like advertisements. Others seemed to be personal. He pocketed these, intending to give them to Eleanora tomorrow.

He pulled the sheet over the mattress. He pushed the two pillows into place. He picked up one and buried his face in it. It smelled very slightly of her. He lay on the bed for a long time. Then he got to his feet and started to leave the room. The small pile of books she kept on a shelf near the bed had been tumbled about somewhat. He straightened them out. Something quite large, an eight-by-ten photograph had been stuck into a thin Gallimard paperback. He read the title, *Duse*, and realized it was a biography of Eleanora's namesake. He pulled the photograph from the book and saw that it was the one taken of them on the *bateau-mouche*.

Palmer felt a chill across his shoulder blades, as if someone had sprinkled ice water on his bare skin. He stared at the photograph. Until now he had been fairly sure that the disarray in the room had been the result of the girl's quick departure from it when they'd left for Frankfurt the previous Thursday. The lack of dust near the partly opened window had seemed to argue against this, but he had no idea how clear the air of Paris was. And the window had been only a bit open, really.

But this photograph of them. Palmer was quite certain the girl had had it with her on the flight to Frankfurt.

There couldn't have been two prints of the same shot, could there? Wasn't it more likely that she'd been back here in Paris, in this room, on a whirlwind errand so pressing that she'd opened her refrigerator door and forgotten to shut it?

And why put the photograph in a biography of Duse?

He pocketed the book and the photograph, switched off the light, and started to let himself out of the apartment. In the abrupt darkness of the place his eyes could dimly make out a line of light filtering under the front door from the bare electric bulb in the corridor outside.

It flickered. Palmer stood still and watched. The thin bar of light flickered again. Then it remained steady, a narrow, yellowish line that, as Palmer's eyes adjusted to the darkness, seemed to throw a faint illumination into darkened corners of the apartment.

The two flickers, Palmer realized, were caused by someone walking past the door rather slowly, first one foot, then the other. And without making a sound. The fact did not bother him that here, on the attic floor of the building, where Eleanora's room was the only apartment on the entire floor, someone had decided to walk past. What bothered him was that someone was trying not to make any noise.

Palmer's mind clicked into a higher gear with a sudden rapidity of which he had forgotten he was capable. He could picture the stakeout quite clearly, a classic textbook maneuver. They knew he'd spend the night in Paris. They suspected he couldn't stay away from the girl's apartment. So they left the window open to bother him. They had a man down the block somewhere in a shaded entryway or alley, waiting for the light to go on. They had the room messed up to occupy Palmer's time. They didn't even need to see Palmer at all. He would announce his own presence by switching on the light. What could be simpler?

Give the man a few minutes to make a telephone call. Give him some time to make his way down the street without being seen from Eleanora's window. Give him a few more minutes to ease his way up the three flights of stairs without making a sound. Then give him a few seconds to get in position behind the front door on the landing outside. Bad luck that Palmer had switched off the apartment light at that precise moment. It had caused the man's feet to silhouette in the bar of light under the door. Just bad luck.

Not any brilliance on my part, Palmer added to himself. He wondered how the man was armed or if he carried anything at all. He wondered who might be down on the street waiting or whether they hadn't had time to get up the hill yet.

Palmer decided he had to move quickly. The other people might just not have shown up yet. It might simply be him and the stakeout man, at least for a few more minutes. Evidently Palmer had been expected to take much longer mooning about the apartment.

Stepping back into the tiny kitchen alcove, Palmer opened a stainless-steel door and removed from it a thin-bladed boning knife with a heavy wood handle he had seen the girl use once to pare an apple. It was an unlikely knife for apple paring, being designed to cut into bone and strip away flesh.

Palmer held the knife with the blade emerging from his fist where his little finger was curled. The cutting edge was out in the approved Army combative position for hand-to-hand work. It allowed a double stroke, first forward in a slicing motion, then a backhand return which jabbed the point home and returned the weapon in position for another forehand sweep. It was not the toad-sticker position favoured for taking out a sentry from behind. It was, rather, the all-purpose frontal meat-slicing approach.

Palmer stood just inside the door. He twisted the knob with a fast wrist movement and kicked the door wide open. It banged loudly. The young man crouching in the corner of the landing blinked.

Palmer showed him the knife. It had the effect of halting the young man's forward motion, hands starting to grab. He was shorter than Palmer and possibly heavier, although he was not fast. Sweat glistened on his upper lip. He licked at it. Neither man moved for a long moment.

Palmer edged over to the stairway and took a step backward down it. Everything about the man's movements now was of critical importance. His body would tell Palmer if there were anyone on the floors below. The young man took a step toward Palmer, his face as white as suet. He looked suddenly frightened.

Palmer took two more steps down. This seemed to madden the young man. He sprang forward, clutching desperately. Palmer nicked three of his knuckles and watched a line of red spring up. The man gasped, more in annoyance than pain, and stood back. He sucked at his fingers for a moment. Then his eyes searched Palmer's face.

It seemed clear to Palmer that only someone who felt his quarry getting clean away would have tried to rush a man with a knife. Palmer turned and ran quickly down the flight of stairs, rounded the landing, and raced down another flight, fairly sure no one else was waiting to ambush him inside the house. He had only to move fast, perhaps, to get away before reinforcements arrived.

He dashed out into the street as an overnight couple in evening dress were quitting a cab. Palmer hopped inside, slammed the door and locked it. '*Ritz, s'il vous plaît, vitement.*'

It was after eleven when he got back to his suite, midnight, Trier time. He tried his long-distance call again and once again the operator could raise no answer.

He sat down in an easy chair and played with the boning knife for a moment. Its handle was about four inches long and its blade was an inch shorter. A vicious little instrument, easy enough to drop in one's breast pocket.

Palmer wondered why he felt so little sense of fear or excitement, or even the letdown that follows fear and excitement. He decided it was the fact that he seemed to have lost contact with the girl. He placed the call again at midnight and at 1 A.M. with the same lack of results. By now, in a dull sort of way, he almost expected no one to answer. But he told the operator to try the number every hour on the hour.

'I may have to awaken you, M'sieur Palmaire.'

'That's all right,' he said. He could hardly believe the hoarse, dead voice was his own. 'I won't be asleep anyway.'

He sat back in the easy chair and tried to balance the boning knife on the tip of his index finger.

CHAPTER 41

The morning flight to Frankfurt had been announced. Waiting at Orly, Palmer glanced at his wristwatch. It was now after ten, after eleven in Frankfurt. His eyes felt gritty with lack of sleep. He had no idea why the telephone number he had for Eleanora's parents had failed to answer all through the night. He'd arrived early at the airport and spent the time rechecking the number with the help of a trilingual Air France girl. It was the correct number. He also got some others in Frankfurt while he was waiting.

Now, as the flight was announced, he picked up the courtesy telephone in the first-class lounge and placed a call to U.S. Army Photo Intelligence in Frankfurt. He got through to an officious English-speaking German switchboard girl who took her time deciding that they did, indeed, have a John J. Rafferty on the premises.

'But he is not a colonel,' she informed Palmer.

'Snap it up, Fräulein,' he grated.

'He is a lieutenant colonel,' she persisted.

'And you'll be unemployed if you don't connect me *this instant!*' Palmer shouted in her ear. Immediately she got off the line and a second later he heard Rafferty's voice.

'It's Palmer, in Paris,' he told Rafferty. 'I'm leaving for Frankfurt in twenty minutes. Can you meet me?'

'Can I?' A pause. 'Can I not?'

'What's that, Jack?'

'I'll be there, lover-boy.'

'Drop dead.'

'God, does that date you.'

'I'm not in shape for repartee. You'll be there?'

'Roger. Wilco. Woody, see if they have a copy of Monday's Bonn *Zeitung* at the airport.'

'Why, for God's sake?' Palmer asked with some irritation.

'Drop dead,' Rafferty responded. 'See you *später*, alligator.' He hung up in Palmer's ear.

Palmer checked the newspaper and magazine racks of the stand next to the shops where they sold duty-free perfumes and liquor. As far as he could see, in his present raw-tempered condition, there were no German newspapers at all at the stand. He boarded the plane and sat down in first class. The stewardess offered him his choice of the Paris *Herald* or *Figaro*.

'Do you have yesterday's Bonn *Zeitung*?' Palmer asked.

Her tone indicated that she would as soon peddle week-old fish as a day-old newspaper. 'Certainly not, sir.'

'Check around. Maybe one of the crew has a copy. Maybe somebody left one aboard.'

'The aircraft is entirely cleaned between each and every flight, sir,' she let him know.

Palmer was about to snap off her head with as cutting a remark as he could muster. Instead he turned away and left her hanging over him in mid-aisle. He refused to speak to her for the rest of the flight, and by way of repayment, she refused to bid him a cheery good-bye as he deplaned.

Wearing a peculiar wool sports jacket and what seemed like black denim jeans, Jack Rafferty was waiting just ahead of the customs line. He took Palmer by the elbow and walked him past the nearest inspector, who frowned, then recognized Rafferty and waved them both through.

'Where can we talk?' Palmer muttered.

'Shut up, Lefty, and keep walking.' Rafferty piloted him out of the terminal and into a parking lot to the right marked for official and rental vehicles. He opened the door of a dun-colored Volkswagen, ushered Palmer in, slammed the door, and got behind the driver's seat. Rafferty started the engine with a hard, iron-clanging roar and in a few moments they were looping through the various exit roads on their way to town.

'Now?' Palmer asked dryly.

'You look like homemade shit,' Rafferty remarked. 'Been up all night?'

'What other acts of clairvoyance do I have to listen to?'

'There's a copy of yesterday's *Zeitung* on the back seat under my raincoat.'

Palmer picked up the tabloid paper and, although he could read almost no German, recognized it as a sensational type of publication, heavy with photographs and immense headlines. He glanced at the front page, then turned the page.

He saw the photograph almost at once at the bottom of page three. It showed him leaving a very imposing government building which to his recollection he had never seen before. The caption, as he hashed it out with some help from the proper nouns, seemed to indicate that Herr Woods Palner, with an *n*, internationally renowned banker, had completed private, or

248

possibly secret, negotiations with the ministers of economics, finance, and defense of the Brandt government.

'You look a hell of a lot better in that shot than you do in real life,' Rafferty told him.

Palmer let the newspaper drop to his lap. He stared straight ahead at the road. Morning traffic was starting to clog up on its way into Frankfurt. A fine rain was falling, but Rafferty hadn't yet started his windshield' wipers. The mouse-colored Volkswagen inched along the superhighway in fits and starts as traffic allowed.

'It does make me look a lot younger,' Palmer agreed.

'About twenty years younger,' Rafferty said. It was impossible to know from his jolly tone of voice what he was thinking.

Palmer reread the caption. 'Am I right?' he began then. 'It does say that I conferred with various bigwigs of the Brandt government?'

'On Monday.'

'On Monday?'

'Right,' Rafferty agreed. He glanced sideways at Palmer. 'I phoned the editor. He sent me a blowup of the photo.'

'Why did you do that?'

'Thought you might want it for your scrapbook. It really makes you look dreamy.'

Rafferty reached under the front seat and pulled out a brown envelope which he handed to Palmer.

Palmer examined the photograph. It showed a bit more than the poor reproduction in the newspaper. Evidently the man in the photograph was refusing to talk to several reporters, one of whom was pushing a phalluslike microphone at his mouth. Palmer reached into his jacket pocket. Next to the boning knife he had placed the folded eight-by-ten picture taken on the *bateau-mouche*. He held it beside the newspaper photograph.

'Hardly think it was the same guy,' Rafferty remarked, glancing sideways for a moment. 'But you always were a handsome son of a bitch.'

'Where are you taking me?'

'A safe place.'

Palmer frowned. In intelligence jargon a 'safe' place was one that had been painstakingly cleared of listening devices, could not be observed from a distance with telescope and parabolic reflector, and was, ideally, unknown to the enemy. 'Whose safe place?' he demanded.

'My own personal safe place. Not the Army's. Rafferty's.'

'What's wrong with this car?'

'I don't know, baby. It's been sitting this morning in the parking lot and last night it was outside my apartment all night. You tell me what's wrong with this car.'

'Christ.'

Neither of them spoke until the little Volkswagen crossed a bridge over the river and angled off into a maze of medieval houses near the Römerberg. Rafferty led the way to a side door of the cathedral and walked quickly down a flight of stairs to an underground corridor cut in stone. 'This is about what's left of the original Dom,' he told Palmer as they walked along. 'The RAF finished off everything up top. It's all rebuilt since the war.'

He ducked into a small office on whose door was the sign KÜSTER. Rafferty closed the door behind them and snapped on an ancient student lamp standing on the small desk. 'Welcome to Rafferty's snug.' He indicated a chair and sat down in another one. 'It's the sexton's office. He's a friend.'

'Of yours, personally?'

'Of mine, nobody else's. In 1946 I nabbed him blackmarketing Luckies from a Munich PX. It was a first offense and I let him go. There isn't anything he wouldn't do for me. Especially now that he's a respected sexton and all.' Rafferty's teeth showed for a moment in a fake grin.

'Pearly teeth, dear,' Palmer murmured. 'Are you about to try putting me eternally in your debt, too, Jack?'

Rafferty sat back heavily, his face creasing in folds of unhappiness. 'I'd like to see you in debt to anybody, you self-sufficient prick-bastard. What makes you so arrogant?'

Palmer placed the two photos face up on the desk. 'A man who can look that young almost overnight? You ask what makes me arrogant?'

Rafferty's grin was genuine this time. He stirred the photos about, moving them from one juxtaposition to another. 'They managed to retouch that mole of yours, huh?' he pointed out then.

Palmer nodded. 'In the one with the girl, *violà!*, there it is. In the other, poof, it's gone. Magic.'

For a long moment no one spoke. Then Rafferty sighed. 'What is that ugly thing bulging your inside breast pocket?'

Palmer removed the boning knife and laid it on the desk

250

beside the pictures. Rafferty eyed it without touching it. 'You could at least have wiped it clean,' he said then.

'Flesh wound.'

'Paris?'

'Her apartment was staked out.'

'Crude.' Rafferty drew out the monosyllable, crew-ewd, to indicate how really crude he thought the maneuver had been.

'All along,' Palmer said then, 'there had been two teams on me, some very savvy gents and some crude apes. Am I talking to a representative of either camp?'

Rafferty's heavy face creased even more unhappily. When he sat back to survey Palmer, the sexton's chair creaked forlornly. 'I am going to make allowances for the fact that your lady friend has permanently unhinged your mind. She looks as if she could.'

'And that's another thing,' Palmer began.

Rafferty held up a beefy hand. 'One goddamned thing at a goddamned time, baby. Okay?' He pushed the boning knife back to Palmer. 'First thing, you want a belly gun? I have a Beretta for you.'

Palmer shook his head. He had started off today not trusting anyone, but needing to trust somebody. He hoped it would be Rafferty. If he weren't one of H.B.'s people, he was a friend to lean on. Otherwise, he was a bad bet. Palmer stood up and walked around the small, stone-walled room, looked behind a painting of Christ on one wall, pulled back from another wall a large-scale floorplan of the cathedral itself, checked behind a bulletin board and opened two tall steel lockers which turned out to be filled with candles. No microphones.

He sat down again and regarded his old Army friend gravely. 'Don't look so offended, Jack,' he said then. 'I still love you.'

'Shit you do.' He shrugged. 'No gun? All right. Second thing, tell me where you were Monday morning.'

Palmer sat back in his chair. 'I arrived in New York Sunday afternoon. Monday morning was spent in the Ubco boardroom trying to pin Eddie Hagen's balls to a sheet of black velvet.'

Rafferty's joyous bark echoed loudly around the tiny room. 'I have to hear about that later.' He picked up the boning knife and stabbed at the newspaper photograph. 'When'd you leave New York?'

'Tuesday morning.'

'Air France Oh-Ten?'

251

Palmer nodded. 'Let me tell you who that is,' he said, indicating the picture of the man Rafferty was touching with the point of the knife.

'Dieter Ram.'

'How'd you get it so fast?'

Rafferty sighed heavily. 'The one and only time I saw Dieter was in 1962. I noted the resemblance to you and filed it away. I told you I was good, Woody. I just never told you how good.'

Palmer smiled slightly. 'Who does Ram work for?'

'Not who, what. The answer is money.'

'On this job, who?'

Rafferty thought for a moment. 'It's a question of motives,' he began then. 'Who the hell would be interested in a hit-and-run impersonation that was sure to be blown! So crude it could be blown by a single photo in a tabloid?'

'Somebody who wanted to have off-the-record, unbuttoned talks with the government's top financial people.'

Rafferty nodded. 'The intentions of the Brandt government are clear,' he said. 'They're opening doors to the east. How many doors, how widely? Not known, but there are people who must know and can't find out by asking.'

'Who?'

Rafferty's face looked pained. 'I'm surprised at you, baby. It's the Old Team. You don't think anybody else would want to know.'

'What old team?'

Rafferty stood up, paced the length of the small room, returned and sat on the edge of the desk. Palmer felt the desk shift with this considerable weight. 'You remember a good-looking guy with heavy eyebrows at your reception? You may not have no –'

'Heinz Mann,' Palmer supplied.

'Excellent. You haven't lost much over the years, huh?' Rafferty twinkled for a moment. 'Heinz was a baby when Adolf and Eva went up in smoke in the *Führersbunker* so he's politically clean. He's a colonel in the Army, a career officer with extremely good connections. They're all right-wing of one kind or another, denazified over the years by court order or by serving time or by never having been caught. And naturally their support –' Rafferty stopped.

'Go on.'

The big man waved his arms meaninglessly. 'Herr Oberst

Heinz Mann is the center of this right-wing resurgence. The Brandt thing caught them off-base. Now they're sweating it out because every move Brandt makes toward the East puts Mann and his supporters in a worse position.'

Palmer sat silently for a moment and eyed Rafferty. 'Now I know what you started to say and didn't,' he said after a while. 'We're supporting Mann, aren't we?'

Rafferty's face went slack. He glanced at his watch. 'Too goddamned early for a drink.'

'Aren't we? With CIA money and people?'

Rafferty stood up from the desk and went to the far wall where he stood next to the chromolithograph of Christ. 'Don't we always?' he asked then. 'When I said it was the Old Team, did you for a moment think I meant the Hitler team?'

'The good old U.S. team?' Palmer persisted. 'The one that masterminded the Bay of Pigs?'

'That's the one,' Rafferty agreed.

'The one that always seeks out the inevitable losers and pours tax money down the unlikeliest rathole it can find?'

'But it has to be a right-wing rathole,' Rafferty demurred. 'Franco, Batista, Chiang, Trujillo.'

'Not necessarily.' Palmer frowned at him. 'Will you stop standing next to that picture, you clown?'

Rafferty sat down in the chair. 'Hate Catholics, huh?'

'The vast U.S. intelligence network has poured money down left-wing ratholes, too,' Palmer assured him. 'Remember all those student groups the CIA infiltrated?'

'Payrolled is the word.' Rafferty picked up the boning knife and flipped it expertly at the bulletin board. It hit point first and quivered for a moment before the weight of the handle pulled it loose. It clattered to the desk top.

'But surely if the U.S. wants to know what Willy Brandt's up to, we only have to ask. He's a friend,' Palmer pointed out.

Rafferty shook his head. 'You done missed the whole point. I thought you was smart but you stupid.'

'Yes, Dr. Rafferty.'

'The neo-Nazis want to know this stuff, but Brandt won't tell them the time of day. It's worth it to Heinz Mann to put a double in your spot long enough to hear what Brandt's people tell you. No big secrets, just a mess of extremely valuable financial and economic chitchat, policies, viewpoints, small talk, forecasts, clues to the future action of Brandt's men. The same sort of stuff you've been picking up in France, baby.'

'I had some jokers on me there who wanted to siphon off what I'd learned,' Palmer said, recalling Forellen and Casseterre.

'Just another brick added to the shithouse. I assume Mann wanted the info for his own group and set up Dieter Ram to get it. But it's possible they then got pressure from the CIA, which was finding you a poor tool to work with. Ram was to collect stuff for Mann's purposes. Some of it Mann would then leak to the CIA in order to earn his regular handout.'

'You're always fast with improvised explanations, Jack. What about the Frankfurt reception? Why didn't they substitute Ram then and there?'

'That, pupil, was their best stroke. They put you on display for all to see, but not too chummily. Just enough of Palmer to show he was the genuine article. And in Frankfurt, not in Bonn. Dig?'

Palmer sat silently for a moment, listening to the resonances of Rafferty's easy explanations. So far neither of them had alluded to Operation Overdraft. Rafferty was acting pretty much as if he didn't know of its existence, but this could be nothing more than good acting.

Yet Operation Overdraft was the real reason why Palmer had been lured away from Germany and a double substituted for him at Bonn. Palmer knew this. He wondered if Rafferty knew. He wondered what marvelous sort of story Rafferty would have for weaving this contradictory fact into the scenario of cross and double cross he was spinning out now.

If Heinz Mann wanted to send in a double for Palmer in order to get from Herr Schirmer the important formula or timetable that H.B. so desperately needed, then Heinz Mann knew a lot more than he should. He knew Palmer would be running H.B.'s 'little errand.' He knew the three words that unlocked Schirmer's lips. He knew entirely too much. For him to know all this, he had to be even more closely linked to H.B. than Palmer was. It made no sense this way.

There was, of course, another possible explanation, Palmer realized. In some nonrational way, by intuition perhaps, H.B. may have decided that Palmer had decided not to run the errand, that Operation Overdraft had been bounced at the bank.

That would account for the hasty substitution of someone else, who would run the errand flawlessly, for money. But it didn't explain why the man had to look like Palmer, nor why his ex-wife had been planted a year before in Ubco's Paris office. Christ, the confusion!

Palmer realized he had been silent too long. He decided to distract Rafferty from anything but the purely mechanical line of questions the case raised. 'How did they hope to pass off Ram as an American?'

'But he was only playing American to an audience of Krauts. Did I forget to tell you he put in two years at Sun Valley in the 1950's as a ski instructor?'

'*Ach, ja*, you forgot.'

'Also somebody must have done a makeup job on him, adding a few wrinkles and such here and there.'

'That's not kind,' Palmer protested.

He sat for a moment, running over everything in his mind. 'What bothers me most, of course . . .' His voice died away.

'The girl's part in this?'

Palmer looked up at the beefy colonel. 'She didn't once warn me she'd been married to my double. She said we resembled each other, I grant her that. But nothing more.'

'No mystery,' Rafferty responded. 'To her you weren't doubles. She knew you both, ah, intimately enough – like that word? – to know there was only a strong superficial resemblance. Build, height, coloring, bone structure. From that a skilled agent, plus makeup, can make something that fools a bunch of government bigwigs. But never his ex-wife.'

Palmer's mouth flattened in a tight line. 'It was at her urging that I rushed back to New York, conveniently taking myself out of the picture. I wasn't going to budge. Not for you. Not for anybody in New York. Only for her. They had enough of a lock on her to force her to lure me away from Bonn. That simple. That crude.'

Rafferty said nothing for a while. Then he made shooing-away gestures and said, in a lighter tone: 'Typical CIA fuck-up, huh? State Department knows Willy Brandt's our pal, but State don't talk to CIA and CIA don't talk to nobody. Otherwise we'd know Willy has to open doors to the East. The Krauts can't keep living forever as our personal buffer. The only ones who want to keep the Iron Curtain slammed shut are the boys who are planning a Fourth Reich vastly superior to poor old Hitler's bungle.'

Palmer sat forward. 'Look,' he began, 'the fact that they tried to take me out last night in Paris means they have more plans for Dieter Ram.'

'Forget Ram. He's blown. He's probably on his way out of the country and into hiding. Where was your next stop supposed to be?'

'You mean for the Foundation?' Palmer tried to remember. 'I don't have my schedule with me. Miss Gregorius –' He stopped himself. The two men were silent for a moment. Palmer was watching the beefy colonel, but Rafferty was staring down at the desk. Finally his eyes with their long lashes slowly lifted to look at Palmer.

'Still stuck on her? After she made a monkey of you?'

'Her phone in Trier doesn't answer.'

Rafferty brushed the thought away with both hands, as if clearing fog from a window. 'One thing at a time and first things first. What was your next stop? And who were you talking to?'

'She has the sched – Uh, let me think. Some people from the central bank in Lausanne and Zurich and some private bankers in Basel.'

'Topic of conversation?'

'Balance of payments.'

Rafferty's heavy-lidded eyes widened slowly. Palmer could see white all around the iris for a moment. Then the lids lowered to a cautious half mast. 'My, my, my,' Rafferty murmured. 'I'd forgotten about that.'

'About what?'

The heavy man sat up straight and tapped the desk with his forefinger. 'If I were a Swiss banker and you were talking to me about redressing the balance of payments situation, what would be your first question?'

Palmer frowned at him. 'Anonymous numbered accounts.'

'Of course. How else does cash get siphoned away faster from the U.S.?'

Palmer considered this for a moment. 'The numbered account is great for absconding heads of state,' he said. 'Your King Farouks. It's good for mobsters, of course. And it's perfect for doctors and other people who get a lot of cash.'

'Fuck Farouk,' Rafferty growled, 'and screw your occasional doctor. Chickenfeed. Inevitably, you would end up talking to the Swiss about mob money. Millions of mob dollars find their way into numbered accounts. It's so bad the U.S. is using everything but thumbscrews on the Swiss to make them sing. But they won't, of course. Not till the pressure really hurts.'

As the last of his words died away in the vaultlike room, a peculiar silence fell over the two men. Neither spoke for several minutes. So complete was the silence in this tiny crypt that Palmer in his unrested condition could almost hear his own heartbeat throbbing in the inner vessels of his ears.

Finally, Rafferty moistened his lips. 'Two words,' he said then.

Palmer looked up at him. 'Eddie Hagen?'

Rafferty reached into a pocket of his ill-fitting sports jacket and handed across a tiny eight-shot .32 Beretta automatic. Palmer looked at it for a long moment. He pulled out the magazine, checked the cartridges, worked the action to make sure there was nothing in the breech, and slammed the magazine back into place. He unlatched and relatched the safety. Then he gave the gun back to Rafferty.

The colonel shrugged massively. His chair groaned in agony. To Palmer it was an appropriate comment.

Rafferty coughed. 'You mentioned two teams on your back. We can forget the amateurs now, the CIA boys, Heinz Mann, your double Mr. Ram. But the pros are still in the game, the little Sicilian brothers of General Eddie Hagen.'

'No gun.'

'Pigheaded, arrogant bastard.'

'No gun.'

'No gun,' Rafferty echoed, pocketing the Beretta. 'It was nice knowing you.'

Palmer got to his feet. 'My next stop's Trier.'

Rafferty nodded. 'Of course it is.'

CHAPTER 42

The parting was brief. Rafferty convinced Palmer to take the small mouse-colored Volkswagen. 'In back there's a Porsche engine,' he said. 'If you won't take the Beretta, the least you can do is take the souped-up VW and try not to wreck it.'

Palmer delivered the heavyset man to his office on the outskirts of Frankfurt and then took off into the maze of crisscrossing national autobahns that formed the Frankfurter Kreuz. He finally found Route 54 and headed west toward Weisbaden and Mainz, where he and the girl had taken their steamer up the Rhine just a few days before.

He was driving in a very mechanical way, keeping the speedometer needle at about 100 km, which enabled him to pass most other VW's without betraying the potential of the Porsche power plant he was carrying.

He left the high-speed roads shortly after Weisbaden. He had been driving along the base of the Taunus Mountains. Now he headed the little car along Route 50 over the Hunsruck range on a course that would bring him to the banks of the Mosel above Bernkastel, an hour or so from Trier along Route 49. He calculated that, unless he badly misread maps and signposts, he could make Trier before sundown without any trouble.

After he left the Rhine at Bingen, not far from the Mouse Tower he and Eleanora had once seen from the steamer, he noticed that the small white Mercedes which had followed him since he dropped Jack Rafferty at his office had now taken the precaution of dropping quite far back. In the heavy city and intercity traffic, it had stayed barely a block or two behind Palmer. Now it had dropped almost, but not quite, out of sight.

Amateur team, Palmer decided, an agent of Heinz Mann or the CIA, maybe even Forellen. If any of the professionals were following him, there would have been a change of cars at Weisbaden and still another at Bingen. He waited until two curves in the road hid the white Mercedes from him. Then he tramped down hard on the accelerator pedal.

He had been doing a hundred and ten kilometers, or just under seventy miles an hour. With a sudden lunge, the car shot ahead as if it had been standing still. Palmer felt his body shoved back against the padded seat as the Porsche engine poured fresh power into the transmission. The needle of the VW speedometer went off the dial at 150 km and still the car kept accelerating until it was doing well over one hundred miles an hour. As long as the curves remained fairly shallow, Palmer decided, he was all right.

He glanced at his rearview mirror from time to time and saw that he had lost the Mercedes. The amateur driver, confident that the dun-colored Volks was incapable of any real speed, had been content to follow blindly without maintaining constant visual contact.

Palmer's original idea had been to outrun the Mercedes and reach some fork in the road that could lead by another route to the Mosel. He would then take the unlikely route and let the Mercedes stumble along the likely one on a false trail. However, as his car roared up over hills and swung wide around curves, Palmer began to rethink this tactic.

He decided it didn't make a hell of a lot of difference if the Mercedes trailed him to Trier. The driver already knew he was headed that way. Being a representative of the amateur team, Herr Oberst Heinz Mann's team, the boys who had staked out the Montparnasse apartment last night, he knew Palmer would be looking for the girl in Trier. But their interest in him should be over, now that Ram's impersonation had ended, and, with it, H.B.'s aborted Operation Overdraft.

Then why shadow him from Frankfurt? Palmer frowned. He had taken another black-and-green Librium capsule before leaving Rafferty, but he was reacting poorly to lack of sleep. His reflexes were not up to par, he knew, and at this speed he was in some danger from his own ineptness.

More to the point, he wasn't thinking clearly. Part of his thinking had been done for him by Rafferty, who had a first-rate mind, but a peculiar one. That didn't automatically make the thinking acceptable. Second-hand thinking, Palmer knew, usually got him in more trouble than anything his own mind could devise.

He spotted a single-lane farm road leading off to the right. Slamming on the brakes, he put the VW into a skidding turn, bumped along for a while on the farm road and then turned in under an immense pine tree whose spreading lower branches covered the small car like a blanket. Palmer knew he couldn't be seen from the road. Or from the sky either, for that matter, if anyone resorted to aerial reconnaissance.

He switched off the engine and the sudden quiet assailed his ears with a negative force. It felt almost as if his eardrums were being drawn out by the silence, rather than being hammered into his skull by the engine's noise.

Palmer glanced at his wristwatch and waited. Two minutes passed and he heard the highpitched whine of the Mercedes shoot past. He could see nothing of it but, on this deserted road, it could only be his amateur shadower. He rolled up the windows and locked the doors from the inside. It was dark under the shelter of the pine boughs. Thanks to the Librium, he was

259

asleep within minutes.

In the dream he was back on the *Schnellfahrt* with Eleanora. The boat had cleared the bend of the Rhine at Rudesheim with Bingen on its left. The Mouse Tower lay straight ahead, a surprisingly small stone tower on its own narrow island to the left of the river's main channel. '*Die Mauseturm*,' the loudspeaker announced, '*La Tour de Souris*. The Mouse Tower.'

Palmer turned to the girl in the dream and she said in her low, pleasant voice: 'It had been a very hard winter and there was no grain. Even respectable people were reduced to begging.

'They appealed to the archbishop, who turned a deaf ear. The people were starving. Few of them hoped to live until spring. Again they appealed. Again the archbishop turned down their plea. Finally, on a cold day in February, they appealed once more to his mercy. He was Hatto, Archbishop of Mainz. On the third appeal he chuckled and rubbed his bony hands and decided to make an exhibition for his cronies and toadies. He had all the starving people rounded up and put in a barn on the banks of the Rhine. He had the doors and windows boarded up. Then he had the barn set on fire. The people inside screamed in agony. They were being roasted alive. Archbishop Hatto smiled his thin smile and turned to his cronies. "Listen," he said. "Listen to my mice squeaking." At that moment the barn collapsed in flames and from the red holocaust came a great swarm of mice with sharp teeth and fiery eyes. They attacked the Archbishop of Mainz, who took to his heels. He ran across the narrow strip of water to the island where the tower stands. He thought he was safe there. But the mice swarmed in through the slits and portcullises and devoured every bit of Archbishop Hatto. Nothing was left of him. Only the tower remains.'

Palmer awoke slowly. The darkness under the pine boughs had a greenish quality to it. He glanced at his wristwatch and saw that he had been asleep about an hour. He felt quite a bit better. He thought about the dream and realized that it hardly qualified as a dream. He had reproduced almost exactly the story Eleanora had told him in real life as they sailed past the Mouse Tower.

He rubbed his eyes to clear them, started the engine and opened both windows to air out the car. The smell of pine was refreshing. He backed the small car out and headed off along the farm road to the two-lane highway. If his hunch had been right, the Mercedes would be roaring along toward the Mosel, sixty or seventy miles ahead of Palmer, rather than a mile behind him.

He swung the car west on Route 50 and notched the speedo-meter needle in at 120 km. His gas tank was three-quarters full. All in all, and thanks to the nap, he was in better shape than he had any right to expect.

'Listen to my mice squeaking,' he said aloud.

He got a sudden picture of flames destroying the barn and the howls of the dying inside. It had been only a little while after the Mouse Tower that they had had their argument under the Lorelei cliff, their argument which was always the same argument, about personal responsibility.

She had told him he and Ubco were responsible for the war and he had told her she was responsible, too. It was almost the only thing they ever quarreled over, just as they had over the asbestos wine filters. She seemed determined to make him take personal responsibility for anything with which he was connected, however remotely.

Palmer frowned as he guided the car up over a sharp rise in the road. He wondered how much responsibility she would take for the whole amateur farce involving her former husband. It seemed clear enough to him now about the little girl, Tanya. Her father had her. Thus Eleanora had been telling the truth in a certain way: Tanya was not in custody. She was not being held against her will. Her father had her. Nothing more.

How simple. How simpleminded. If the amateur team had other plans for Dieter Ram, posing as Woods Palmer, it had badly bungled them in Paris. The man waiting on the landing should have had a gun and instructions to shoot if necessary. Perhaps that was the essence of amateurishness, the inability to face killing if killing was needed.

Palmer thought uneasily about the Beretta Jack Rafferty had tried to give him. Guns were not Palmer's weapon. Thinking was. And if he let the fact that he was carrying a gun do his thinking for him, he would end up, finally, having to use the gun. That was the trouble with guns. They had no value at all unless one used them.

Palmer slowed the car to pass through a small village, then speeded up again. Something kept bothering him as he tried to assemble the tactics of the amateur team into some semblance of a strategy. It had been the professionals who had hidden the microfilm in his shirt cardboard, of course. He had to leave that part out for now because it belonged to a different strategy.

261

He felt the same thing stir uneasily at the back of his mind. He was passing by something he should not be overlooking.

Then he realized what it was. He had accepted Jack Rafferty's thinking in one undigested lump. To him the bunglers were the neo-Nazis working with and for the CIA while the smooth professionals were Mafiosi. But what was bothering Palmer, he realized, was that he had no real reason to accept this thinking, other than that Rafferty's mind had produced it.

In fact, he had no real evidence yet that there were two teams, just a hunch he had mentioned to Jack, who had instantly produced a theory to account for two teams. If he'd known about H.B.'s Operation Overdraft, he'd have created three teams instead.

On the other hand, Palmer thought, Jack may have known more than he'd given out. He had thought there was CIA money and muscle behind the Heinz Mann group. This had to be better than an informed guess. It was more of a true confession. Their total ineptness bore a strong family resemblance to the typical CIA fiasco. Jack wasn't guessing. He knew.

Palmer sighed impatiently. He couldn't seem to get all his ducks in a row. They kept slipping away from him because he was still too tired to think properly. No, he wasn't that tired any more. His inability to think about this came from another reason. If he figured it out, he would have figured out the girl, too. And he didn't want to do that.

Palmer shook his head slowly. He should be ashamed of himself, he supposed. But until he could hear her answers from her own lips, he was damned if he cared to outguess the thing.

He reached the Mosel at Trauben-Trarbach and picked up Route 49, the same river-level road that he and the girl had followed last Friday and Saturday. It curved in and out along the river, mimicking every looping curve and lazy meander. But this time Palmer was in a hurry. He negotiated the tight curve that led to Bernkastel, but stayed on the Kues side of the river and started the last leg down through Neumagen to Trier.

When he got there he roared east over the Kaiser Wilhelm Brücke and followed a series of city streets directly to the same modern hotel, the Porta Nigra, where he had spent the night alone on the previous Saturday. Instead of checking in, however, he drove around the block and down under the hotel, parking the mousy Volkswagen next to a white Mercedes.

262

It looked like the one he had given the slip to en route, but there was no way of knowing since he hadn't been able to read the license number. He opened the hood of the Mercedes and removed the rotor from its distributor. Then, locking his own car's motor compartment, he carried his small bag upstairs into the handsome lobby of the hotel. The desk clerk remembered him and had the feeling that the same deluxe suite might be available again. Palmer called the parents' home. No answer.

Palmer unpacked in the walnut paneled room, washed, changed to a different jacket, and went out. The sunlight was fading. He stood in front of the hotel and stared across the broad double avenue at the old Roman gate which gave its name to the hotel. Floodlights illuminated the Porta Nigra, including the scaffolding that enclosed part of it now that renovations were under way.

Palmer squinted at the gate, trying to remember the direction to her parents' apartment. He crossed the avenue and began walking along the Simeonstrasse between modern shops toward the medieval Hauptmarkt. He stopped at the stone cross in the centre of the square. The girl had told him the cross had been put up in the tenth century, but so much of Trier was far older, older even than Rome.

He headed along Fleischestrasse until it turned into Karl Marx Strasse. Palmer recalled Eleanora saying something about the old boy having lived in Trier once or been born there or something. As he walked, Palmer was looking for the apartment house of her parents, a narrow modern building about six or eight stories high, with terraces all the way around it.

He spotted it, finally. The sun had left the sky now and the streetlamps were on. Palmer walked inside the entrance hall and checked the nameplates. Gregorius was Apartment 63. He was about to press the buzzer button. Instead he pressed several buttons at random. After a moment the door buzzer went off at about the same time that the intercom came alive with questions in German from some of the more cautious tenants among those he had buzzed.

Palmer slipped inside and ran the elevator up to the top floor, seven. He found a stairway and made his way down very quietly along the concrete steps. At the sixth floor exit into the corridor he paused and listened, but heard nothing. He slowly pushed the door open and walked along the carpeted hallway to Number 63. The door was locked. A metal edge of the jamb had been brought around where the bolt lay to prevent anybody from using a bit of celluloid to jimmy it open. Palmer stared at the door for a moment. Then he walked back to the stairway door and stepped outside onto the concrete landing.

There had to be another way into Apartment 63. He glanced around the bare concrete walls and steps. There were two unmarked doors beside the one to the corridor inside. The first opened into a closet complete with mop, bucket, and spare light bulbs. Palmer tried the second and found it locked. But the architects had neglected to use the same safety jamb on this door as they had on apartment entrances.

Palmer worked the plastic card in past the bolt and eased the door open. It led down a short service corridor of bare brick. He followed it around a corner and found himself looking at a thick coil of green garden hose attached to a water tap. He took another turn and saw that he was standing outside on the common terrace that led all the way around the sixth floor.

Apartment 63 would be three terraces to the right. Palmer checked the first tiny balcony to see if anyone inside Apartment 61 were watching. The lights were off. He crossed the terrace quickly and swung out around the low wooden partition that separated it from the balcony of Apartment 62. Here the lights were on.

Palmer studied the man sitting in the easy chair with the little boy on his lap. They were staring at the bluish face of a television set on which Bugs Bunny was cavorting. The little boy clapped his hands. The man began to fall asleep. Bugs ambushed a mean bulldog and ran a paving roller over him. The dog was squashed absolutely flat. Bugs folded him twice like a sheet of paper. The little boy squealed with glee. Bugs put the folded dog in an envelope, addressed it, and slid it into the nearest mailbox. The father was snoring now. Palmer crossed the terrace and swung over the barrier onto the terrace of Apartment 63.

He pushed back one of the sliding glass doors and stepped just inside the living room. Even though the room was in darkness he could see the two people sitting in the chairs.

He froze. After a while, when neither of them moved, Palmer took a step toward them. 'Herr Gregorius?'

There was no answer. Palmer stepped sideways. Neither of the people moved their heads to follow him. He snapped on a small light.

Both the father and the mother had been gagged and bound into the chairs on which they were sitting. Only an autopsy, perhaps, could determine whether they had died of starvation, lack of oxygen, or heart attack.

Palmer went to the apartment's front door and bolted it from the inside. He searched the other rooms as quickly as he could but there was nothing, neither a suitcase, a note, nor a piece of clothing, to indicate that Eleanora had ever been here.

He returned to the living room, wiping off everything he had touched along the way. He watched the two old people for a moment. Then he reached to turn off the light. Under the old man's chair lay a small rag doll with a mop of bright red yarn for hair.

Palmer stepped forward and touched the old man's gnarled hand as it lay clenched on the tubular steel arm of the chair. The flesh felt as cold as the steel. Palmer tried to unbind the old man's body. His immense forehead – Eleanora's forehead – gleamed whitely in the thin illumination of the lamp.

He had been tied into the chair with something like baling wire. Palmer untwisted the piece that held the old man's throat. His head fell forward with a waxy slowness. The gesture had a peculiar quality to it that made Palmer shudder, a quality of demonstration, as of a programmed automaton. The movement said: 'Here. Now look at this.'

Palmer looked. The hole was barely an eighth of an inch in diameter, perfectly round and blackish-red, at the nape of the neck directly below the inion's bulge. A very thin line of dried blood ran down only two inches from it, so well had the job been done. No need for an autopsy now.

Ice pick, Palmer thought.

He wanted to lift the old man's head and set it straight, but he couldn't bring himself to touch the dead flesh. He could remember something the old man had said about the clash of generations and the new one denying its past. 'Even to the point of sandblasting away the entire testament of history,' the old man had said.

He wondered as he stood there what testament either of these two old people could have given, what evidence so powerful, so damaging, that they had to be ice-picked out of existence.

Palmer switched off the light, stepped out onto the terrace, and slid the glass doors shut. He wiped them where he had touched them. The two dead people watched his departure with grave attention. He eased over onto the terrace of Number 62. A cat named Sylvester was trying to eat a small canary. Just as his jaws started to crunch down on the bird, the canary dropped a lighted stick of dynamite down Sylvester's throat and stuck his fingers in his ears. The explosion awakened the sleeping man.

Palmer crossed the terrace of Apartment 61, traversed the service hallway to the stairs, and walked down to the ground floor. He walked back to the Hauptmarkt and stood near the tenth-century cross for a while.

After a while he went into a nearby alley and threw up. He had eaten nothing since Paris the previous night. Somehow this made matters worse. He leaned against a medieval wall and tried to bring up what wasn't there.

After a while his stomach grew calmer. He remained in the alley for a while, trying to soak up strength from the stone wall. Until now he had been fairly confident that he could straighten everything out.

CHAPTER 43

The clerk at the Porta Nigra Hotel looked strangely at him for a moment, but said nothing. He handed Palmer his keys and some message slips. Palmer went to the elevator and, turning suddenly back, saw that the clerk was still watching him. His glance instantly dropped to the desk. Palmer went up to his room and double-locked the door.

The outside wall of the room was floor-to-ceiling glass in the modern style. Palmer lifted back an edge of the curtain and saw that his room overlooked another part of the hotel several floors below. He pulled both the translucent fiberglass curtains and the opaque drapery shut. Then he switched on all the lights and sat down on the edge of the bed.

Immediately, he got up and went to the mirror to try to find out why the desk clerk had looked at him so strangely. He hadn't thrown up on his coat. His face bore no smudges. He stared into his own eyes, which looked smallish and bloodshot. He frowned worriedly and watched the way thousands of tiny wrinkles sprang suddenly into existence. He rubbed his forehead to smooth them away, but they remained. So did the darkness under his dark gray eyes. So did the shadows under his high cheekbones.

He rubbed at his face again. He had stopped looking like himself, that was what was wrong. There was no Woods Palmer left. Dieter Ram was a better Palmer, a superior Palmer, the true Palmer. This one in the mirror was the shoddy, discarded version. Obsolete. Overdrafted.

He sat down on the edge of the bed and watched himself in the mirror. He looked old and tired and confused. He stood up again. One could only look that bad sitting on the edge of a hotel bed. Posture was everything. He sat down in an armchair and rubbed the polished walnut arms. They felt as cold as the tubular steel the dead man had grasped.

Palmer shivered and stood up. He sat on the sofa and decided this would be a better place to sit. He reached for the message slips and saw that both were from Rafferty, with a home number to call in Frankfurt. He didn't want to call Rafferty.

He wondered if Eleanora had been happy in bed with her husband. Was there a resemblance in sexual performance? Could there be? The new, improved Palmer was in his thirties. The discarded version was almost fifty.

If he had a single brain cell left in his head, Palmer knew, he would drive to Frankfurt and fly back to New York. Not tomorrow, tonight. He picked up the telephone and put through a call to Rafferty's home number. It rang only once and was immediately answered.

'Jack?'

'Glad you called, Woody. Some news.'

'About the girl?'

'*Vous êtes au clair.*'

'What?'

Rafferty paused for a moment, then repeated the statement in French. Palmer thought about it, sorting it out. *Au clair* could simply mean 'in the clear,' but it had an Intelligence meaning, that was different. *Au clair* was the term for a transmission that was neither coded nor scrambled. In other words, Rafferty was suggesting, the present conversation, if monitored, could be clearly understood by anyone bothering to listen in.

'All right,' Palmer said at last. 'Then what's the point of having me call you, Jack?'

'Get yourself fixed up and phone me back. Bye.'

The line went dead. Palmer sighed with impatience. He left

the room. Instead of returning the key to the desk, he pocketed it. Instead of leaving the elevator at the lobby, he rode it to the basement garage. He walked quietly past the parked cars, noting that the white Mercedes still sat next to the dun-colored Volkswagen.

He climbed up the ramp to the outside, circled the block, and made off in the direction of the Simeonstrasse by a different route. Near the old *Pferdemarkt*, on Jakobstrasse, he found a telephone kiosk and spent a good five minutes placing a collect call in his rudimentary German. Again it was answered on the first ring. He had given his name as a Mr. Woody. Rafferty accepted the charges.

'Phone booth?' he asked as soon as the long-distance operator went off the line.

'Make it fast, Jack. I'm as close to exhaustion as I'll ever be.'

'Yes, sir!'

'And no sarcasm.'

'Or you'll burst into tears.' Rafferty chuckled. 'There was a hell of an auto accident this evening on the E-Four Autobahn near Freiburg. You know the town?'

'Of course not.'

'It's in Black Forest country. Where all them elves dwell. The driver was instantly killed when his car swerved off the embankment and hit a roadside stanchion at about a hundred kilometers an hour. They found traces of a powerful antihistamine drug in his body, the kind that makes you very sleepy.'

'You're making me even sleepier. Get on with it, Jack.'

'He was carrying papers that identified him as Dieter Ram.' Rafferty paused again. 'E-Four is the highway that gets you to Basel. Zurich's only a few miles farther. It looks as if they were so sure you weren't going to gum up the works that they sent him on the next leg of your itinerary. But they couldn't foresee the auto accident.'

Palmer's eyes felt gritty. 'When is the next plane back to New York?'

'Tomorrow morning. You can't leave now, baby.'

'The hell I can't. You don't know what's –' Palmer stopped. 'Tell me something, Jack. We think we know who wanted the information in Bonn, don't we?'

'We think we do.'

'But the same people don't want the Swiss information.

You're getting two teams confused.'

There was a long pause. 'It was only a hypothesis,' Rafferty said then, almost huffily. 'I won't die on the barricades for it.'

Palmer shifted his weight to his other leg. His game knee had begun to throb with pain. 'Take this down on a piece of paper, Jack,' he said then, 'Apartment Sixty-three. I don't know the address of the building, but it's a modern seven-story apartment house with terraces somewhere near the Hauptalleestrasse in Trier. The name is Gregorius.'

'That I already knew.'

'Don't be smart, Jack. She's not here. But get the cops to do something about the two corpses wired to the armchairs.'

'Oh, Christ.'

Palmer paused for a long time. 'Her folks,' he said then. 'And here's a thought for old-timers who remember outfits like Murder Incorporated and such.'

'What?'

'It's an ice-pick job.'

'Woody,' Rafferty snapped. 'Get back to the Porta Nigra Hotel and stay there. I'm driving to Trier tonight. Don't do anything. Sit in your room and wait for me, you hear?'

'How long will it take you?'

'I'll have to get a car out of Motor Pool. A few hours.'

Palmer shrugged, then realized Rafferty couldn't see the gesture. He felt very light-headed and remembered he hadn't had anything to eat all day. But he knew he shouldn't eat anything now.

'Woody?'

'Better get going, Jack.'

'See you.' The line went dead. Palmer stepped out of the kiosk. Down Jakobstrasse a shadow moved back into a doorway. Palmer waited a second, then headed off along Kutzbachestrasse at a kind of lame jog trot. He could see the illuminated bulk of the old Roman gate ahead of him.

He paused and heard footsteps behind him. He ducked sideways into a courtyard where round tables with umbrellas had been set up. It seemed to be the cloister of an old monastery or convent. He paused again, but heard no one behind him. Limping slightly, he headed for the restaurant from which the tables were served. He walked into the well-lighted place. A waitress came toward him, wiping her hands in a small white towel and shaking her head.

'Are you still open?' Palmer asked.

She frowned and he could see that her mind was trying to shift into English. '*Nein,*' she said then. 'All closed.'

Palmer could hear footsteps entering the courtyard behind him now. He started to sidestep the waitress. '*Es tut mir leid,*' she insisted, '*aber es ist geschlossen jetzt.*'

Palmer ducked past her and made his way through two swinging metal doors into the kitchen. 'Hello!' the waitress called after him. 'Hello!'

A man in an apron was spraying a rack of crockery dishes with steaming water from a long, metal-clad hose. Palmer nodded to him and grinned broadly. He pushed straight past to the rear of the kitchen. Crates of cabbage stood to one side of a loading door. Palmer shoved at the door and it swung open slowly to reveal a cobblestoned loading dock. He jumped down two feet from the doorway and felt his bad knee twinge almost unbearably.

He began running across the cobblestones. His ankle twisted under him for a moment, but he recovered and made his way past one side of the Roman gate to the edge of a broad double avenue. He paused for a moment until a few cars had swung past him. Then he dashed across the Nordallee and entered the hotel the front way. The desk clerk had his back to the door. Palmer ducked sideways into the open elevator and went straight up to his floor.

He checked his room and double-locked the door. Then he sat down on the edge of the bed and tried to catch his breath. He had no idea who had been following him. If it were the opposition, they would probably not try anything here in the hotel. If it were the police – because the two bodies could by now have been discovered and his presence there known – then there would be a knock at the door of the room soon enough.

It would be clever of the opposition to give the police an anonymous call about a prowler answering to Palmer's description on the terrace of Apartment 63. That would be all it took to get the cops to find the bodies and put out a pick-up alarm.

Wanted, suspicion of murder. Caucasian, male, late forties, height about two meters, weight approximately eighty kilograms, eyes gray, hair dark blond, believed to be an American.

Believed to be in male change of life, or otherwise mentally deranged.

Palmer rubbed his knee. Something new and bad seemed to

have happened to it. He stood up and began walking slowly in as large a circle as he could. After a while the knee seemed to click into place and stop bothering him. He sat on the sofa this time and tried to think.

Believed to be an American, he thought, so far out of his depth as to be ludicrous. A figure of fun. The middle-aged dupe in a game of Never Love a Stranger.

But if she were really part of this, whatever it was, why had they killed her parents?

Always assuming they really were her parents and not a pair of actors hired to – But there was no mistaking that forehead, that tall brow gleaming with intelligence and the pearly dankness of death. The skull had been just under the skin. The skull was always just under the skin, wasn't it? Just under Dieter Ram's skin, what was left of it.

No more new, improved Palmer. Only the outmoded old model was left and probably not for very long.

God damn it, Palmer cried out silently, where could she have gone? We have each betrayed the other. Neither of us has been what we seemed. She an agent of Mann's. I on an errand for H.B.

His knee twinged for a moment and he started walking again, more slowly. He tried to keep thinking. His knee felt better again but he continued to walk. In one part of his mind he knew he was behaving very peculiarly, pacing his hotel room rug this way. But in another part of his mind, he didn't care at all. In that part of him all he cared about was finding her.

Somewhere along the line he had missed something. That much was certain. It wasn't possible for her to disappear off the face of the earth without a clue, some indication.

Unless she was in it as deeply as the rest. If she had been completely insincere from the beginning, then she would now do her best never to see him again. She must know by now that he had realized how she'd tricked him, lured him out of Germany and back to New York. She must feel that whatever the pressure on her, the betrayal could not be forgiven. At this thought, Palmer felt a strange, horrifying ache through his middle, as if he had been kicked. He had never before felt such a pain. It had no physical substance. It was not a real pain, he knew, but it hurt much more than real pain.

He shut his eyes tightly and hugged his midriff. Christ, it couldn't be that way. She really loved him. She really did. And what he'd done to her was far worse than her betrayal.

He sat down and tried to ease the pain away. He must never think of her that way again. She loved him as much as he loved her. That was all there was to this, or else nothing mattered and he might as well be dead.

Did she know about her former husband? That *he* was dead? Palmer's usefulness to them – whoever they were – was at an end with the accidental death of his double. But perhaps the death had been no accident. No, that was cockeyed, too. Dieter Ram had been on his way to fill the rest of Palmer's Swiss itinerary. They wouldn't kill him if they needed him to –

He opened his eyes. Something new began to shape in his mind. He had been taking his thinking from Rafferty again. It had been Jack's idea that Dieter was on his way to Basel to pose as Palmer. But this idea raised more problems than it solved.

It was much more likely that Dieter had simply been going to Switzerland to hide out. What if the pro team – the mobsters who didn't want Palmer talking to Swiss bankers – had mistaken Dieter for Palmer?

Blackmail him, yes. That was the purpose of the microfilms in the shirt cardboard. But kill him? Palmer's abdomen ached.

He tried to picture his once-harmless little mission to Switzerland as something important enough for murder. Was it possible? His mission to Bonn had been important enough for the amateur team to try a crude impersonation gambit. But in Switzerland, were the stakes that much higher ... for the pro team?

He knew, of course, that if he'd been an official of the Justice Department or Internal Revenue, the Swiss bankers would have told him absolutely nothing. His to-the-point questions would ring alarm signals and send the doors of secrecy clanging shut. But he was totally unofficial. He was a fellow banker, known to them. They did a lot of business with Ubco, some of them. Palmer was a member of the club. His informal discussions might produce some extremely interesting clues. And the mob would do a great deal to head off such a conversation, since most of their quasi-legitimate businesses in the United States were financed by anonymous investment through their secret Swiss accounts.

More to the point, Palmer realized, he wasn't just any banker. He was the one who knew the Mafia of old, from its near-death and miraculous resurrection in Sicily back in 1943. He was the one banker who was fending off a mob bid to have one of their infiltrated banks merged into Ubco, a bid to niche them securely into the framework of the largest commercial bank in the country.

That was probably the most important factor, the one he had refused to think about until now. It had nothing to do with the Swiss. It had to do with dear old New York City.

If you threw all the chips into the pot, the stakes were still not high enough for murder. But if you added that one element, then murder was the only answer. The weighty element was the fact that Palmer, and only Palmer, stood in Eddie Hagen's way, stood in the way of the mob's desperate need to gain the respectable cover of Ubco.

With that added to the picture, murder was not only indicated, it was essential. Palmer had to be removed. And Dieter had been killed because the mob soldiers sent to remove Palmer had mistaken a good impersonation for the real thing. The maneuverings of Colonel Mann, of the CIA, the mysterious interweavings of Operation Overdraft and H.B.'s inane plotting had all come together in one final orgy of misunderstanding and uselessness . . . but they had saved Palmer's life, for the moment.

Palmer glanced at himself in the mirror and produced a weak grin. Damn it, despite Jack Rafferty, this had to be the right answer! It *felt* right. Dieter had done such a good job of being Palmer that he'd died for it.

But then, who was now tailing him in Trier? Who had followed him from the telephone kiosk?

He watched the grin fade from his face. Back to Square One. He had the answer to only one thing, Ram's death, and nothing else. Certainly he had no answer to where the girl had gone to cover. He began pacing the floor again.

That was it, of course. She was in hiding. Once they'd killed her parents, she would be next. So she'd dropped under cover. But perhaps she'd had time to leave him some sort of –

Palmer stopped in his tracks, thought for a long moment, then moved to his open overnight case. He removed from it the paperback biography of Eleanora Duse. The *bateau-mouche* photograph had been placed in the book by the girl. Yes. She'd gotten back to Paris, intending to hole up there. They'd followed her. She'd had to run again. But this time she'd left a clue.

Palmer tried to remember in what page she had left the photograph. He held the book on end and tried to find a wider place where, perhaps, the photograph's extra thickness had caused a space to form between two pages. To the best of his recollection, however, the picture had been tucked into the end papers next to an inside cover of the book.

He examined the pages at the front and back of the book without finding anything written there. But there'd be nothing in writing, if it were meant as a clue only for him. It had to be subtler than that. What could one read into it? A photograph of them in a book about Duse. The message was something simple, probably. We are in Duse. I am in Duse. In my namesake. In her what?

His legs felt a little wobbly. He went to his case and found the small clear plastic tube of Librium capsules. He swallowed one with water and tried to relax on the sofa. Rafferty would be there in a few hours. He badly needed someone to talk this over with. He didn't seem to be getting very far talking to himself. Rafferty might be too quick to reach conclusions, and his conclusions might be wrong or misleading, but nevertheless he –

Palmer sat up straight on the sofa. Had Jack been deliberately misleading him? Was Jack in it with them? With whom? Mann, CIA, or was it H.B.'s shadowy apparatus?

He'd openly admitted the Mann group had U.S. Intelligence money behind it. Didn't that automatically put Jack on the neo-Nazi team?

He made a face and tried to relax again. He knew his metabolism was way out of kilter. He hadn't eaten or slept and now he was pumping drugs into his bloodstream.

He closed his eyes and made his body sit loosely on the sofa. He thought about something mechanical, about things he'd touched in the parents' apartment, touched and wiped clean. No prints. Sure of that. Steel-cold hand on cold-steel chair. Rag doll under the chair.

Tanya.

The little girl hadn't been with her father in Freiburg. Or in Paris. Or in Trier. She had to be with her mother. Somewhere.

That made it much harder for Eleanora, he realized. If she were on the run or under cover, it was easier if she were alone. Europe was full of women alone. But a woman with a small child made a description much more limited and useful to whoever was looking for her. You could check airports, hotels, train stations. Someone had to have seen and remembered the two of them.

Palmer sighed. He supposed his first move was to return to Paris and begin tracing her. He had little hope. He didn't speak enough French to do the job. He could hire someone, of course. He could phone Dauber and have him hire someone. Not a bad idea.

A photograph of the two of them in a biography of Eleanora Duse. Palmer opened his eyes and reached for the paperback. He leafed idly through it, not bothering to pause and decipher paragraphs from the French. The chapters were numbered and titled. The first, for instance, was called '*Au Début.*' He let the pages flicker past. Another chapter was titled '*Le Premier Triomphe.*' He felt himself growing sleepy.

A few more pages fluttered by. '*Réveil à Asolo.*' Palmer let the book slip out of his fingers. He knew Asolo from somewhere. A town in the Italian foothills of the Dolomites. The girl had been born there. And named Eleanora because Duse had lived in Asolo.

Slowly, Palmer's eyes swung open. Was this the clue? Did it mean she was in Asolo? He tried to get to his feet and his knee shook with the effort. He groaned and stood up. In his bag was a map of Europe. He unfolded it and tried to find Asolo, with no luck.

He assumed that it had to be somewhere north of Venice where the Dolomites came down from Austria. That made it some four hundred miles southeast of Trier. Too far. And it was six hundred miles from Paris to Asolo. In the time it would take a woman and a child to make it, they'd be found a dozen times by pursuers. Every airport, every depot, every hotel ...

Palmer wished that he knew more about Europe. The map told him a few things, but not enough. Were there planes from Paris to Venice? Undoubtedly. Trains, too. Didn't the Orient Express cover that route? Was there still an Orient Express? Hadn't it been that train her parents had hoped to reach in their flight from Austria, with Eleanora still in the womb?

He turned the map over and tried to find any further information that might help. Nothing seemed to. Instead, he was faced with the realization that, as an American in Europe, he was as limited as if he were blind.

He glanced at his watch and saw that it was past 10 P.M. Rafferty would be along by midnight, probably. Palmer didn't like waiting. He especially didn't like this feeling of helplessness. If he dared, if he spoke the languages, he'd take off now the

275

fastest way possible for Asolo.

He had no way of knowing how good his hunch was. He could discuss it with Jack Rafferty, but Jack wouldn't know any more than he. Not that he wouldn't have a definite opinion on it, of course. That was Jack's trouble. *And mine,* Palmer told himself, *is that I listen to all his ideas as if they're valuable.*

He folded the map and put it in his breast pocket. Then he took the elevator to the main floor and approached the desk man. 'Can I still get dinner tonight?' he asked.

'Most assuredly, sir. The dining room will be open until midnight.'

'Fine. Please cash this.' He removed a hundred-dollar traveler's check from its flat black folder and began to sign it.

'Ah, one hundred dollars.' The desk clerk looked uncertain. 'I don't know if I – Ah, let me see.' He fiddled around in his cash drawer, left the desk for a while, and returned with a packet of hundred-mark notes. 'Yes, Herr Palmer. May I see your passport for identification, sir?'

Palmer frowned at him. 'You still have it, from when I checked in.'

The desk clerk touched his head in shame and chagrin. 'I am so sorry, sir. Of course.' He rummaged around some more and produced the passport, copied its number on the reverse of the check, and counted out about four hundred marks into Palmer's hand. He laid the green passport book on top of the notes. 'Thank you very much, sir.'

Palmer handed back two hundred-mark notes. 'Can you give me francs for these?'

'French or Swiss?'

'French.'

The clerk's eyebrows went up very high. He made a third foray into the desk drawer and then shrugged violently. 'I am very sorry, Herr Palmer. There are none.'

Palmer took back the marks. He nodded and walked toward the stairs that led to the dining room. He circled up them out of sight of the desk, rang for the elevator, and took it down to the parking garage again. This time he stayed as far from the mouse-colored Volkswagen as possible. He left by a side door that led onto the Paulinstrasse. There seemed to be no one around.

Trier had apparently closed up for the night already. The streets were empty of traffic. Palmer wondered where in hell's name he could find a taxi at this hour. He ducked back inside the parking garage. Being one of the unattended types, there seemed no one around to talk to. Palmer wandered aimlessly about the perimeter of the garage.

Then he stopped and moved in between the two nearest cars. He peered at their dashboards, moved on to another pair of cars. He finally found a light blue BMW with the keys still sticking in the dashboard. The license plate's oval showed a TR prefix, which he took to stand for Trier. He started the car and drove up out of the garage. He retraced the streets leading to the Kaiser Wilhelm Brücke and picked up Route 49 again.

He accelerated the BMW to about 110 km and headed south-west along the level road that followed the Mosel at the base of a range of low mountains. Twenty minutes later, he slowed down for the Luxembourg border. The guard glanced at his license plate and waved him through. It was now 10:30 P.M. By 11 Palmer had parked the car at Luxembourg International Airport. He was careful to put it in the big lot, not the one meant for people waiting an hour or two. He wiped the steering wheel clean and rubbed his handkerchief over the door handles.

Then he made his way on foot toward the general aviation part of the airport. He kept walking until he found what he wanted, a smallish hangar with a few light one- and two-engine planes tied down on the tarmac. He entered the hangar and found a man working on the wheelstrut of a Cessna. 'Speak English?'

'Yes.'

'Who can fly me to Venice?'

The man looked up from the wheel. The butt of a cigarette lodged in the corner of his rather thick-lipped mouth. He had a round, young face with eyes that were meant to be very keen and knowing. Palmer waited. 'Many people,' the man said then. 'Icelandic. Alitalia. BEA.'

'Now. In the next fifteen minutes.'

The knowing eyes grew more cunning. 'No one.'

'You?'

The man laughed slightly. 'In this?' He indicated the Cessna with his thumb. 'Over the Alps?'

'For four hundred marks.'

The eyes narrowed. The lips spit out the cigarette. The man got to his feet and said: 'For how many dollars?'

'In dollars?' Palmer flipped his hand palm up. 'A hundred.' He watched the man's face. 'And a hundred to come back. You

277

wouldn't have to deadhead. Same passenger both ways.'

'You?'

Palmer nodded. He indicated his lack of baggage. 'No tricks. Just me.'

'How long to wait in Venice?'

'A few hours.'

The man began to play with a piece of wiping rag. 'Venice in three hours. Wait three hours. Or more? Back in three hours. Or more?'

'Say twelve hours for everything. Two hundred dollars for twelve hours.'

The man nodded. 'But it's an instrument flight.'

'So?'

He began wiping his hands slowly, thoughtfully. 'So it's three hundred dollars. In advance.'

Palmer laughed pleasantly. '*Au'voir, ami.*' He started out of the hangar. The man hurried after him, all pretense of shrewdness gone from his eyes. 'You're in such a rush.'

'Two hundred is my limit, instruments or no instruments.'

The man stood there, still wiping his hands. 'We'll use the Beechcraft.'

CHAPTER 44

In retrospect – many weeks later – Palmer supposed the flight could have been superb. If it hadn't been flown at night and in such a roundabout way it would probably have been quite the most scenic view he'd had of Europe.

As it was, however, with the lightness of the plane at his disposal, about the best the pilot could do was get hasty clearance from Luxembourg Airport – which seemed to be a haven for airlines Palmer had never heard of in his life – and take off around eleven thirty on a course that ran straight down the Rhone Valley between the Cévennes range of mountains to the west and the deadlier Vosges and Jura to the east.

Flying at about fifteen hundred to two thousand feet, Palmer could see very little beneath him but clusters of lights which the pilot identified with such casual lack of assurance as to make Palmer wonder if he'd know the Mediterranean when they reached it. The itinerary sounded a little like a menu in a French restaurant since they managed to fly over such cities as Dijon and all the wine towns of the Burgundy before passing Lyon and Avignon. It was more than two hours later when they touched down briefly at Marseilles Airport and refueled. It would be child's play to trace the flight. The stolen BMW, the flight plan filed with Luxembourg Airport, now this refueling stop.

On what looked like an ordinary Shell road map the pilot traced the rest of their route for them. Palmer saw that he was managing to avoid any mountains at all by the simple expedient of making a right-angle dogleg from Luxembourg due south to Marseilles and from there almost due east across the top of Italy to Venice.

'But you've doubled our flying time,' Palmer pointed out.

The pilot shrugged. His foxy eyes had grown somewhat puffy with fatigue. 'Over the Alps is insane.'

'Instead of three hours, this could take six.'

'But we stay alive.'

'Is that all the map you've got?'

The pilot's doughlike face looked even blanker than usual. 'I have another somewhere.'

'I mean, that's just a motoring map, isn't it?'

The pilot nodded tiredly. 'So?'

Palmer watched him for a moment and reflected, not for the first time tonight, that he had made a poor choice. However, there hadn't seemed to be anybody else available at Luxembourg, not for a peculiar flight like this one. As they took off again, the tiny plane bucked about considerably in the updrafts and thermal disturbances over the French and Italian Riviera. But by about 2:30 in the morning they were flying north from Genoa over some foothills of the Apennines. Shortly thereafter they headed east through the Lombardy plain from Milan direct to Venice. Palmer fell asleep at about 3 A.M. He didn't awaken until the ship's wheels screeched down at Mestre Airport outside Venice.

Communications having been what they were during the flight, Palmer for the first time asked the pilot his name, which turned out to be Klaus. The pilot didn't seem to care whether this were employed as his first or last name. Palmer paid him in marks for the outboard trip and promised to return in a few hours.

'Okay.' Klaus yawned broadly. 'If you get back by noon, the return will be very pretty.'

Palmer frowned at him. 'Get some sleep.'

'Right here in the plane. *A bientôt.*' The small eyes seemed to puff shut, rather than close, and Klaus sank back into the leather padding.

Palmer found a wiry little old man just opening the Hertz counter in the terminal. There were no clean cars available yet, the man said in halting English, but if the *signore* cared to wait until the garage man came on duty there would be an extremely clean vehicle for the *signore*.

'Anything, clean or dirty, but right now. *Subito.*'

'It doesn't look suitable for a gentleman,' the old man said.

Palmer nodded and smiled slightly. 'It's all right. I'm a banker, not a gentleman.'

Eventually, and with much bumbling about looking for it, the old man found a Fiat 850 Spider in filthy condition from having been driven through rain and mud. His nose wrinkled as he surveyed it.

'Surely the *signore* –'

'Just put in some gas and give me a map.'

'*Benzina, sì.*'

It was after six in the morning when Palmer headed the tiny open car through the maze of roads that led from the Adriatic coast, where the airport lay, over the Venice-Milan Autostrada's cloverleafs and ramps, onto Route 245, which led northwest to Castelfranco. According to the map the little Hertz man had given him, Palmer saw that Castelfranco was only about ten miles south of the elusive Asolo. In the still-dark air, he switched on his lights.

Twenty minutes later, Palmer pulled the tiny open two-seater off the road at a highway marker that showed he was on Route 13 instead of 245. He puzzled over the map again and tried to figure out where he had gone wrong. Then he saw that, rather than get further lost by trying to get back to 245, he could continue on 13 to Treviso, pick up 348 for Montebelluna, and switch to 248 to reach Asolo.

As he scanned the map, he realized he could have landed the plane much closer to Asolo if he'd only had such a detailed map before. There were airports at Treviso and Padua that would have saved him extra time. As a matter of fact, with the plane Klaus was flying, he might even have chanced a landing somewhere in Asolo itself. There had to be a strip of some kind. But of course, Palmer didn't want anyone to know his destination, not even a chance pickup pilot.

He started up the Fiat 850 again and sent it tearing off along Route 13 due north. Although it was styled like a tigerish racing sports car, Palmer found, the little Fiat had the ordinary guts of a family economy car. He managed to keep it on the road at 120 kms, but its rear engine made it oversteer on curves until Palmer learned to compensate by underdirecting the lighter front end of the car.

At seven in the morning the first rays of sun started to slant in across the Dolomite foothills to the east of Palmer. He had managed to get through the considerable city of Treviso without any problems because he was almost the only car on the road at that hour. Finding 348 without trouble, he was now halfway to Montebelluna and, he calculated, only fifteen miles from Asolo.

He punched a button on the dashboard radio and was immediately rewarded with a blast of sound from a rock group singing in English. Palmer frowned. 'Momma-momma-momma, lemme grabya-grabya-grabya, lemme kissit-kissit-kissit, lemme, huh?'

Palmer punched the 'off' button and tried to remember where he had heard the song before. He turned the radio on again in time to hear the group bellowing: 'Lemme touchit-touchit-touchit, lemme luvit-luvit-luvit all the time.' He turned them off. Up ahead his road intersected with Route 248. He swung west toward Montebelluna.

The bar on First Avenue in New York, he remembered suddenly. The place he'd poked his face in after that horrible scene with Virginia. There was some kind of international underground railway through which these same songs cropped up simultaneously all over the world. Underground was the wrong word, probably, since there was nothing clandestine about the way such songs blasted over the air. But how they made the leap from wherever they were first recorded to every radio station and jukebox on earth – instantly – was amazing.

The morning sun was behind Palmer now as he sped west through increasingly hillier country. Leaving Montebelluna, he knew he would have to watch the road signs closely now because the route to Asolo was really just a two-kilometer spur that shot off to the right at a certain point.

281

Palmer supposed that people like his daughter Gerri knew all these songs. She had probably heard this particular one so long ago – weeks, even – as to have forgotten it already. There were always six more yammering to replace it as the newest thing. Perhaps it was an 'old' song in the States or England or wherever it had originated. Perhaps the Italian radio was coming to it late. The next time he saw Gerri he'd have to ask her.

He wondered how difficult it would be to get Edith to agree to sending the children to Europe for a month or so. Their school would be ending any day now. Tom was slated for a camp in August, but there was no reason the three of them couldn't spend July with him.

No reason. Palmer checked his rearview mirror as he had throughout the trip from Mestre Airport. No one was following him. He had the road to himself, except for a hay wagon he had just passed.

It seemed probable that the amateur team had no further interest in him. If, he added silently, there actually were an amateur team and it were correctly identified as the CIA's Forellen and the Heinz Mann people who had employed his double, Eleanora's husband. If all those assumptions were correct, the farce had ended. Dieter Ram was dead.

The only loose end that remained was for Palmer to acquaint the Brandt government with the substitution and to make it quite clear that he had had nothing to do with it. Palmer didn't give a damn at this point whether the Brandt government got angry with the foundation or the CIA or the still-waiting Herr Schirmer or H.B. or the government of the United States of America. But he wanted it absolutely understood that Ubco was in the clear.

A right-hand turnoff was approaching. Palmer slowed down the 850 Spider and noted that its brakes were not terribly powerful. He checked the sign and saw that this was not the Asolo road but the one to a town called Maser. He stepped on the accelerator again. The little car surged forward powerfully enough, but Palmer felt this was due to its carrying a light load of one passenger, rather than its having a vigorous power plant, which it didn't.

All right, he thought, what's left is the pro team. If there actually were such a team and they really were mob agents bent on keeping him from his talks with the Swiss, they had by now realized that the wrong Woods Palmer had died on the E-4

Autobahn near Freiburg. The real Palmer, the old, tired, crumbling-at-the-edges Palmer, could probably be traced from Trier to Luxembourg. It was easy enough to trace him to Venice and to Asolo, if need be.

If so, the mob's agents would just about now have checked Klaus's flight plan submitted at Luxembourg Airport and reached at least one conclusion: Palmer wasn't going to Switzerland. Not directly. Not yet. A chartered plane or Air Force jet could have delivered them to Mestre Airport by now.

The next few hours would thus tell whether or nor they were still interested in him, Palmer decided. If they showed up again it meant that they still wanted him dead. For other reasons. Eddie Hagen's reasons – deep-delving reasons that had to do with the financial maneuverings of the mob in the United States, as well as with their various money-laundering tricks in Switzerland.

If this were true, Palmer realized, then he could no longer protect either himself or Eleanora. He would need help.

The correct turnoff appeared suddenly on his right and Palmer put the Fiat into a tight skid, sending it hurling up the rising road that led toward the mountain town of Asolo.

CHAPTER 45

An hour later, Palmer was ready to drive back to Venice. The whole thing had been a wild-goose chase.

The town itself, he found as he walked around its narrow, curving streets, was picturesque, with views down its own mountain to the rich farmlands below and up toward higher peaks of the Dolomites looming in the north and east. It had one good hotel, deluxe Continental style, and the rest was quite a simple village with some small but ornate *palazzi* in the Venetian manner.

Palmer had found the streets empty but filling up when he first parked the open Fiat across the street from the post office. Now, an hour later, the streets were crowded with other Fiats, inching past each other through streets barely wide enough for a donkey cart. Despite fearful impasses and traffic jams, Palmer noted, nobody honked his horn. It was as if they had all sworn a pact never to disturb the fifteenth-century peace of the town.

In the course of walking Asolo's streets and looking in such obvious places as markets and *farmacias*, Palmer had put together some idea of the town's history, if only on the basis of painfully spelling out the Italian wording of various plaques he came across from time to time. The lobby of the deluxe hotel had had a folder in English that helped. In neither the expensive one, nor any of the cheaper ones, however, had the desk clerk or concierge been able to help.

In order not to stir up anything too strongly, Palmer had concocted a story about parking his disabled car and telling his wife to take their daughter and find a hotel while he attended to the car. At none of the hotels did anyone remember a young woman and five-year-old child.

Palmer realized that there were probably a good many private *penzioni* and even more rooms-for-rent that he had of necessity overlooked. What he was hoping for was a stroke of fool luck. But there seemed little chance of it.

He sat down on the terrace of a café across the street from the small post office. It gave him a chance to rest and eat something while, at the same time, it enabled him to watch a part of town it seemed probably was a kind of center of pedestrian traffic. The waiter stood patiently by the tiny round table as Palmer scanned the menu. He returned it to the man. '*Pane e burro*,' he ordered, '*e caffè nero, per piacere.*'

Speaking the language again after all these years, Palmer remembered his earliest experience with it, when he had dropped into Sicily with the first wave of the Allied invasion, commandeered some RAF vehicles, and led his T-Force up into the hills to make contact with a certain Don G.

In retrospect now – although not at the time it happened – he knew Don G. to be one Don Giralamo Biglioto. In 1943 the Communist *partigiani* had taken over parts of Sicily. U.S. Intelligence had made another of its many classic decisions to, as Rafferty put it, pound money down a rathole. Through the intervention of that prime patriot Lucky Luciano, who hoped to reduce his jail sentence thereby, U.S. forces in Sicily were supposed to make immediate contact with the Mafia and set up the Brotherhood as rulers of the triangular island.

Palmer's T-Force had actually arrived as Don G. and his capo-dons were about to be executed by partisans from the hills. Palmer had intervened and saved Don G.'s life. By one of those sickening twists of time and human nature, some six months ago the husband of Don G.'s granddaughter had cropped up as leading executive of the Westchester bank Ubco was planning to buy, the merger Eddie Hagen had been so anxious to accelerate.

The waiter brought two twisted rolls, still warm, and a saucer with three pats of butter wrapped in tricky folds of foil that, if pulled right, sprang open to reveal the butter, ready for use. Either Palmer had ordered the wrong thing or the waiter hadn't paid proper attention because he brought both a small silver-plated pitcher of black coffee and one of hot milk.

It was pleasant to contemplate breakfast in such a place. The terrace of the restaurant had been set out under the cool shadow of one of the town's many overhanging arcades. Palmer sat more or less between two very Venetian stone columns that supported the arcade, each column decorated in long flutings, clusters of leaves, and carefully laid-out spirals of local granite. He faced the idea of breaking his long fast with quite a feeling of anticipation.

Palmer decided that since this was his first meal in more than a day, he'd take milk with his coffee. He sat there, slowly buttering and eating a fresh, flaky roll. His stomach felt sore, now that food was entering it again, as if someone had recently tromped on it. Palmer supposed it had something to do with his dry heaves last night.

He paused with the second roll halfway to his mouth, then set it down on the saucer. He hadn't thought of her parents at all or of Dieter. When he found her – he would find her somehow – he would bring terrible news with him, if she hadn't already learned it. He put down the roll unfinished.

It was obvious that this Asolo thing was a silly pipe dream. Instead of playing games, he should have waited for Rafferty and relied on his help and connections. Alone he would get nowhere. Palmer stood up, left a five-mark bill on the table and hoped that, by grossly overpaying, he could bribe his way out of not having lire. He walked across the street into the post office and explained to a man behind the counter that he wanted to place a call to the Porta Nigra Hotel in Trier, Germany.

It took over fifteen minutes to complete, at which time the clerk waved him to a nearby booth. Palmer picked up the phone. '*Bitte?*' a voice asked.

'*Her Oberst Rafferty, Amerikanische Armee, bitte?*'

'*Moment.*'

285

Palmer waited for a while. Then the voice said: *'Er ist nicht hier.'* Palmer frowned. His German wasn't up to asking the obvious question, now that he'd been told the colonel wasn't there.

'Sprechen Englisch?' he asked then, shifting his voice to a higher key.

'Of course, sir.'

'This is Major Woody in Frankfurt,' he said in his disguised voice. 'Can you tell me when the colonel is expected to return to the hotel?'

'I couldn't say, sir. Perhaps not.'

'Has he gone back to Frankfurt?'

'I have no knowledge of that, sir.'

'If he returns, tell him Major Woody will telephone again. At –' Palmer glanced at his watch and saw that it was nine thirty in the morning. 'At noon precisely.'

'Jawohl, Herr Major.'

'Danke.'

'Bitte, mein Herr.'

Palmer hung up and asked the counter clerk to place a call to the Ubco's Paris branch. For some reason this call took less than a minute to place. He asked for Dauber and got him almost at once.

'Palmer here. Anything you have to tell me?'

'I'm glad y –' Dauber stopped himself. 'Are you all right?'

'Yes. Why?'

'There was a photo.' Dauber paused. 'I don't suppose you saw the Bonn paper of day before yesterday?'

'I did. We have to make a full explanation to the Brandt government. I'll get with it in a few days. Right now, I –' Palmer switched the conversation quickly. 'Any calls for me?'

'No. If there are can I forward them to where you are?'

'No.'

'May I ask where y –'

'No,' Palmer cut in. 'Sorry. Heard from Miss Gregorius?'

'I thought she was with you.'

'I see.' Palmer stopped to clear his throat. 'Sit tight on the Bonn thing. You know it wasn't me.'

'Could you give me some sort of a clue?'

'Not worth it at this point. No need to yet. Call you in a day or so.'

'Mr. Palmer,' Dauber said on a rising note, as if to forestall his hanging up.

'Yes?'

'Are you sure everything's in order?'

'*Alles ist in Ordnung*. Why? Has anyone been asking questions? Forellen?'

'He's dropped out of sight.'

'Let me make you a bet. You've heard the last of Forellen. He won't call again. He probably left Paris the day I did.'

'He hasn't called this morning, which is unusual. Maybe you're right.'

'The boss is always right. Good-bye.'

Palmer spent another ten minutes getting the counter clerk to take marks instead of lire. He failed. Still friends, however, the two of them walked out of the post office to the nearest hotel, where the concierge changed some money. The clerk took lire, nodded in a distracted way, and left Palmer to himself.

Palmer sat down behind the wheel of the Fiat. The morning sun, higher now in the sky, had heated the black vinyl cushion covering and Palmer felt the heat in his buttocks. The tempo of life in Asolo was mounting toward its morning peak, people moving more quickly in the shadowed arcades.

It was a small town even now, Palmer reflected, even after centuries of being somewhat famous. Palmer couldn't remember 'Pippa Passes' for the life of him, except for the line 'Morning's at seven,' but since this morning knew it had been written in Asolo and contained many local descriptions. He'd even seen the Bronson House where Browning had died in 1889. Of Duse there were many mementos, too.

But none of Eleanora Gregorius.

Palmer switched on the Fiat and started the engine. He felt fairly sure Klaus would still be waiting at Mestre Airport. The pilot didn't expect Palmer till noon, an easy deadline to keep. And if Palmer arrived even later, Klaus would still be there in hopes of his return fare.

The tiny open car negotiated the U-turn with yards to spare. As Palmer drove past the café where he'd had his abortive breakfast, his waiter looked up and flashed him an immense smile and a sweeping salute. Five marks had been wildly too much money to leave. For a moment Palmer regretted the gesture, as well as the useless long-distance telephoning. He would be remembered in Asolo, not as long as Duse or Browning, but long enough for the mob's agents when they arrived asking questions.

Then Palmer decided to forget the whole thing. He waved grandly back at the waiter and steered the Fiat Spider along the narrow street that led down the winding hill road to Route 248. Within minutes, he was out in open farm country and after a while he realized from the sun's position that he was heading north instead of south toward 248.

He braked the car to a halt beside a dirt road that led into a farmyard where a single black cow drank water from an old stone trough. Palmer unfolded the map and tried to decide what was best for him, to backtrack through town and run the risk of going wrong again, or to keep north on this road till it reached one that led to 348, the highway back to Treviso. On the map the road he would follow looked narrower than the ones he had been using. It seemed to wind quite a bit, too. And it took him at least twenty miles out of his way.

The scene looked Alpine, more Swiss than Italian, with the jagged peaks as a background to the steep-roofed chalet-style cottages. 'Morning's at seven,' he repeated to himself, 'the hillside's dew-pearled.' He smiled slightly at the tricks of memory. He'd never paid much attention to his lit. course, especially the poetry. Then the rest of the opening lines suddenly came to him: 'God's in his heaven; all's right with the world.'

Silly Browning bastard. Of course, Palmer mused, for people like Browning, the world was probably just dandy in those days.

Palmer wished he had taken sunglasses with him. The sky was bright and hot now and he had to squint to see. He seemed to be unable to make up his mind what to do. Finally, he put the Fiat into another U-turn and headed back toward Asolo, vowing to watch every possible sign and make sure he took the right route this time.

Just at the edge of town the road forked. Palmer braked the Fiat to a halt and looked for signs. There were none. He could take his choice of two unmarked roads, both of which led back into Asolo.

'Papa!' a child called.

Palmer decided on the right-hand fork. He shifted into low and put the car into motion. He turned slightly to make sure the little girl wouldn't run anywhere near the car. She was small, with light chestnut bangs.

'Papa!' she called to him.

The car slewed sideways into the ditch as Palmer tramped on

288

the brake. With the transmission still in low gear, the engine coughed into silence.

The girl ran up to the open car and started to throw her arms around Palmer. Then she stopped short, a few feet from him.

'Papa?'

CHAPTER 46

From the outside, the place looked like one of those Palladian villas whose color pictures grace expensive art books. The squared-off building with its gravely balanced façade of windows and doors stood a hundred yards back from the road, separated by a field of grass. It was the grass that gave away the game.

Once there had been quite an impressive lawn there with a series of steps and landings. But no one had mowed the grass in years and the masonry lay in jagged chunks. Two small black-and-white goats, one pregnant, cropped what grass was left among the spreading patches of weeds. The villa itself had been boarded up in front, where it faced the road. The plastered walls shed big flakes of pink and ivory. Around in the back, however, life still went on, but on a somewhat smaller scale than it had when first this villa had been built for some Venetian merchant-nobleman.

Eleanora had rented a small room by the day from Signora Frascati, a thin old woman past seventy who was almost as tall as Palmer. She included kitchen and bathroom privileges with the rental of the room. Other than Eleanora and the little girl, the *signora* was alone at this time of year. She nearly always rented her rooms throughout the summer, but never this early in the year.

All of this Palmer had to learn while he stood uneasily in the rear of the villa, holding Tanya's hand and eyeing Eleanora, who had come out on the run when she heard the little girl cry for her father, only to stop short and stare.

They made an awkward group, the four of them, with Signora Frascati dominating the conversation in her heavily accented English. Palmer watched Eleanora, who seemed unable to say anything at all. She had brushed her hair completely off her forehead and looked very different, but it was her manner that was more unfamiliar than her appearance.

Palmer couldn't explain precisely what was different about her. She seemed shocked to see him. This stunned look showed mostly in her eyes, which seemed unable to stay on him for more than a moment or two before looking away, always returning within a few seconds to watch him again. Palmer had the mad idea that perhaps some unsightly, horrifying wound of which he was unaware had disfigured his face. Only something like that, attracting and repelling her glance, could account for the way she was behaving and for her silence.

Palmer felt the little girl's hand pulling out of his. He let her go. She ran to bury her face in Eleanora's thighs. Over her head, her mother stared at Palmer for a moment. Her mouth moved twice without speaking. Then she looked away again.

'Thank you,' Palmer told Signora Frascati, in what he hoped was a tone of dismissal.

'Most people,' she said, 'is too cold in June for them.' She continued her account of weather, tourism, room renting, the two goats, and assorted and related subjects.

Palmer glanced sideways at the road in front of the villa. The tiny open Fiat still sat, half in the ditch, where he had killed the engine. As he watched, a dun-colored Volkswagen went past. There was a man at the wheel, but he didn't resemble Jack Rafferty at all.

Palmer stepped out of the line of sight of the road and took Eleanora's elbow. 'Permit me,' he said to Signora Frascati. 'We have to talk.'

'*Sì, sì, Bene.*' The bony old lady turned away with a slightly grieved air and walked inside the rear door of the villa.

'Are you all right?' he asked quickly.

Eleanora nodded. 'How did you find us?'

Palmer frowned. Her eyes looked big and unhappy beneath the tall expanse of her forehead. 'I found the picture in the book.'

Her glance swiveled to his face. 'What?'

'In your apartment.'

'In Montmartre? You were in Montmartre?'

'Didn't you ret –' Palmer stopped. 'You haven't been to Paris?'

She shook her head. 'I came from Trier by bus on Monday.' She looked down at the top of Tanya's head, still buried against her. 'It's all right, *Liebchen.*' She patted the girl's head softly, smoothing the hair down. 'You gave her a fright. Dieter was so ugly to her last week. She thought you –' She stopped and her hand went to her mouth. 'Why did you come here?' she cried out.

Palmer heard a terrible note of anguish in her voice and it dawned on him that she was miserably unhappy to see him. 'You ran away from Trier,' he said.

'Yes.'

'Because I was coming back there.'

'Yes.'

'Just to avoid seeing me?'

She nodded. Palmer closed his eyes for a moment. He hadn't counted on this at all. In the sudden darkness behind his lids he heard the typical iron clanging of a Volkswagen engine somewhere along the roadway in front of the villa. He opened his eyes.

'We have to get going,' he said then. 'But you must tell me why you were hiding from me.'

Eleanora shook her head. The little girl had stopped hiding in her skirt and was staring up at the two adults now with a look of concentration. It occurred to Palmer that the girl was as multilingual as her mother. 'You must tell me. When I couldn't find you I –' He stared at her forehead and the picture of her father's forehead swam before his eyes. 'What did – Why did you run away?'

'I knew you'd find out. About Dieter. You have found out, haven't you?'

Palmer nodded slowly. 'That doesn't matter.'

'It does.' She touched the lapel of his coat for an instant. It was their first contact so far. 'You say it doesn't matter now. But eventually you'll figure all of it out, or I'll tell it all to you. Either way, it will matter a great deal. You shouldn't have come looking for me. You should have let me rot.'

Palmer shook his head. 'We have to get moving.'

'We?'

'You and I and the girl. How much luggage do you have?'

'One overnight case. The one I brought from Paris to Frankfurt so long ago.' She stopped and her eyes filled with tears but she didn't cry. 'What did my parents tell you? Is that how you came to Asolo? I made them swear to tell no one.'

'No one,' Palmer echoed.

'Especially not you.'

So it was the silence, he realized, that had finished the two old people. Someone had been tracking Palmer by tracking the girl. And when they couldn't get the information out of her parents, they had to eliminate them. As witnesses to what?

'Pack your bag. I have a little Fiat out front. There's a private plane waiting at Mestre. We can make it in an hour or so.'

'Why?'

'Some people are after me,' he explained. 'It's not the thing with Dieter. That's dead.' He stopped and eyed her face, but she didn't react to the word. He was horrified at how much bad news he carried with him. 'It's something else, something from back home in the States.'

'But they're not after me, or Tanya?'

Palmer gave her a long look, trying to read in her face some clue to the way he should take her question. Was she trying to disassociate herself from him? 'They're after you to get at me. I'm afraid I might have led them here.'

'My God,' She stared distractedly around her and found her daughter's uptilted face. 'You should have forgotten me. It would have been better for you and better for me.'

'I had no way of knowing that,' Palmer said in a suddenly quiet voice. 'I thought you were still in love with me.'

Her glance locked with his and this time she didn't look away. He tried to read her expression, but somehow he had lost the knack. He was keeping too many secrets from her and it showed on his face. She sensed it and it showed on her face. They no longer trusted each other as they once had.

Abruptly she turned from him. 'I'll be just a second packing. Tanya, wait with him. We're going for a ride in a lovely auto.'

'*Maman, j'ai de faire pipi.*'

Eleanora frowned at her and took her hand. '*Aber mach schnell, ja?*' They disappeared inside the villa. A moment later, Eleanora was back with an overnight case she was trying to fasten. 'She'll be quick,' she said, handing Palmer the bag. 'We'll meet you at the car.'

Palmer snapped the bag shut and carried it out to the road. Farm trucks were moving slowly into Asolo. They had created something of a traffic tie-up at the fork in the road. It was a silent snarl. No one was blowing his horn. He dropped the overnight bag in the tiny boot of the Fiat and slammed the cover shut. Then he got back into the car and started the engine again. He noted that he still had half a tank of gasoline. He wondered how long the jam-up at the fork up ahead would delay them. They had to get through it to reach the fast road back to Venice.

He could see Eleanora and the girl coming around the rear corner of the villa. At that moment someone in the heart of the traffic jam began to hoot his horn. It had a familiar, loud and merciless non-European sound. Palmer stood up in the seat of the Fiat and saw what the problem was. A white Mustang with two men in it, both of them featureless behind dark glasses, had tried to U-turn at the fork and double back in the direction of the villa. The driver was leaning heavily on the horn. A dun-colored Volkswagen was blocking them, unintentionally.

Palmer dropped back down behind the wheel, put it into a left-hand lock and spun the tiny open car in a quick U-turn that brought it to the front of the villa lawn as Eleanora and the little girl arrived.

'Hop in, fast!' he shouted.

They scrambled into the car and he gave the Fiat a burst of gas in second gear forward, sending it accelerating down the highway in the opposite direction from Asolo. He had it up to sixty kilometers before he shifted into third and one hundred before he shifted into high. The car was shaking wildly with the effort. The wind whipped Eleanora's hair in wild strands.

'We're flying!' Tanya shouted happily.

Palmer glanced in the rearview mirror and saw that two more trucks had clogged up the traffic jam farther. Just as well. At the wheel of the dun-colored Volkswagen had been the European executive director of the Foundation, Stanley Forellen.

CHAPTER 47

Venice was out.

They would have gotten to Klaus by now either with money or force. The plane at Mestre Airport would be a stakeout. Palmer pointed to the map the Hertz man had given him. 'Evasive action,' he shouted over the noise of the wind. 'Find the next turnoff for Venice. The road has no number on the map, but I want the name of the town.'

Eleanora reached past the little girl, who was sitting in her lap. She spread out the map as best she could in the wind and tried to orient herself. 'Possagno,' she said, at length.

'We turn away from Venice there because they expect us to turn toward Venice. That means we turn left?'

'Yes. Left to Bassano del Grappa.'

Palmer nodded. He glanced at the dashboard. The tiny Fiat was way over its normal capability, the dial showing 110 km, almost seventy miles an hour. With just himself, it might have been all right, but Palmer was afraid that, with the added weight, the auto would begin to lose vigor. He tried accelerating to a hundred and twenty and the tiny car seemed to accept the change without shivering any more violently than it already was.

Eleanora had been craning her neck to see the road behind them. 'Who is following us?'

'A Volkswagen the color of mouse fur.'

'No. There's a white car very far in the distance.'

'That could be the Mustang.'

Palmer pressed the accelerator pedal to the floor and watched the speedometer needle slowly go off the scale past 120. They were probably doing eighty miles an hour now, a speed the Mustang could practically double if it had to.

The Possagno sign showed ahead. Palmer glanced in the rear-view mirror and saw that a curve in the road hid him from the white car. He downshifted and braked, hoping the added weight of his passengers would give the light car enough stopping power. The Fiat went into a slight skid but quickly recovered. Palmer pulled it into an alley between two ancient brick buildings. The car rattled along the narrow street for a moment. Then Palmer swung it into a space, braked, and turned off the engine.

'Stay here,' he said, lifting himself out over the side of the open car. He ran back along the alley and found a spot in a doorway where he could watch the junction of the road without being seen.

The white Mustang's brakes squealed horribly. The man behind the wheel had a fixed look about him, as if he were a store dummy propped up to deceive people, the dark glasses hiding his motionless eyes. The other man craned left and right along the T-junction. He consulted a map and pointed to the right. The Mustang's front wheels howled insanely as the driver whipped the wheel to the right and accelerated sharply. Palmer watched the car roar off along the route back to Venice.

He ran back to the Fiat. 'Please,' Eleanora said. He could tell she was trying to keep her voice calm in order not to upset the child. 'Can you tell me what is happening?'

Palmer nodded slowly, calmly, and smiled at the little girl. 'We're out for a very fast ride, aren't we?'

She grinned back. Palmer saw that her left front tooth was missing. 'Very fast,' she agreed.

He started the car and retraced their route down the alley to the main road. They took the left turn and at once the road got more winding as it curved in and out of the range of Dolomite foothills. 'We'll take the road back to Venice from this next town,' Palmer told Eleanora. 'What's the route?'

'Number Forty-seven. Please tell me what is happening.'

'There are two teams. There always have been. One is in that white Mustang. Two men with dark glasses. The other is driving the car of a man I thought was a friend. Now I see that from the beginning he's never been my friend. He's only waited to betray me till it really counted.'

Her eyes looked even bigger as he glanced momentarily at her. He could see white beneath her irises. 'You met him. Jack Rafferty.'

'No.' She shook her head. 'He is your friend.'

'That's his mouse-colored VW,' Palmer said. 'And Forellen's driving it. I don't know how he got here so fast, but it has to be the same car.'

She started to say something, then stopped and patted the girl's shoulders. 'You like to drive fast, *Liebchen*?'

The girl nodded. 'Faster.'

Palmer watched the road even out as they neared Bassano del Grappa. The old town was arranged along the edge of a river. A curious covered wooden bridge of very old design led over the gap to the far side. He braked the Fiat and they sat for a moment.

'This is a very lovely place,' Eleanora said then. 'They make pottery here. But we have no time.'

Palmer reached for the map. 'They expect us to go back to Venice. We've lost them, so their next thought is that we're not going back to Venice. Once this becomes clear, they'll begin looking everywhere but Venice.'

'So we go back to Venice.'

He looked up at her and smiled. 'Exactly.'

'We can take Forty-seven to Padova and the Autostrada direct to Venice.'

He frowned. 'How well is the Autostrada policed? Are there checkpoints and tollbooths and such?'

'It's well policed.'

'Then we'll take the other route, Eleven.'

'I don't understand,' she said. 'Don't we want it to be well policed?'

'No.'

'But if there are police . . .'

'If there are police,' he finished for her, 'they are not our friends. They would be the friends of those who are following us. At least of Forellen. I'm not sure about the two in the Mustang.' He glanced at his watch. 'Did you and the girl have breakfast?'

'My name is Tanya,' the girl announced.

'Tanya. Are you hungry, Tanya?'

'No. Are you?'

'No.'

'You look a little like my father.'

Palmer's glance went over the girl's head to her mother. 'I know.' He shifted into low gear and looked for a sign of Route 47. 'On to Venice,' he said, letting in the clutch. The Fiat moved off slowly. At the next corner it passed the dun-colored Volkswagen.

Palmer shifted into a higher gear and accelerated. It would take Forellen a few seconds to stop and turn around. With his Porsche engine, it would be as impossible for Palmer to outrun him as to outrun the Mustang. Forellen's abrupt appearance in Bassano del Grappa indicated some kind of telephone or radio surveillance network, possibly with sky support.

All these things went through Palmer's head as he pulled the Fiat into a long, narrow street and forced it along the cobblestones up a steep grade in second gear, whining and shuddering as it slowly accelerated against the pull of gravity. At the top he glanced back and saw that Forellen hadn't entered the bottom of the street yet. He took a left turn at random, then a right. He was in third now, still picking up speed and almost outside the town.

He took another right and recognized the road back to Possagno. After a few moments, however, he came to a fork and

296

west was still hot with sun, but the foothills kept its rays from reaching them now that they were down below the peaks. Palmer sat in the sudden silence and watched Eleanora. He was aware, without seeing her out of the corner of his eye, that the child was watching her mother, too, but certainly not with the same sick feeling.

'Look,' he began, 'I must –'

'You must!' she snapped. 'Always you must. You are a very deceptive man. You seem calm and smooth on the outside. Kind, even gentle. But you're not. You're too used to having power and using it. When you must do something, you *must!* I cannot love someone like that.'

'Surely you don't imagine it was my idea to kill those two,' he said, pointing behind them in the direction of the fire. At this distance even the smoke couldn't be seen.

'It's not imagination that tells me the truth about you.' She turned from him and faced forward. 'It's the evidence of my eyes. Listen to me. I have no choice in what I was forced to do to you. I will never forgive myself, whatever you tell me you feel or don't feel. That is my punishment. But what you want to do to me is worse than I deserve.'

'I'm not proposing to do anything to –'

'Exile, never to see you again, is bad punishment. But now you want to wrap me in your web of violence. And my child, too. Whatever you must do, it ends in violence. No, you did not shoot the white car. But they shot at Forellen because they thought he was you. Because he was driving your car.'

'Because you nonviolently knocked him unconscious.'

She nodded. 'I know my guilts. You must believe how well I know them. But you somehow never seem to accept yours. For whatever reason they were after you and for this they died. How many others are there who have died?'

Palmer felt his insides lurch peculiarly. He looked down at the steering wheel. 'You talk about responsibility. Everything bad that happened is because I took on this mission for the Foundation. I know it. Without the mission, none of this would have happened. Having said so, tell me what more can I do about it? The situation

She shrugged. iana. This is Vittorio Veneto. Nothing more.'

'And go Palmer. lians

'To Gin tion

'That's f thous

She said nothing for a moment. 'You finished it?'

'Of course.'

'I'm sorry.'

'What else was I to do?'

She was silent. Then: 'Please keep driving. I want to get the child back to Asolo before dark.'

He drove on in silence. At Vittorio Veneto they stopped in the old main square. Palmer looked at the small, pretty little houses with their painted frescoes of the Renaissance era. Overhead the sky was a brilliant blue, but the sunlight failed to penetrate the square. He shivered.

'I'll drive you to Asolo,' he said then.

He had a terrible sense of *déjà vu*. He had made the same offer to Virginia on his last night in New York. He took the map from Eleanora's hands and consulted it for a while. Then, when it seemed clear she wasn't going to raise an objection, he drove south on Route 51 and connected via Route 13 with the road to Asolo.

'I hope,' the little girl said suddenly on the outskirts of Asolo, 'you'll stay to dinner.'

It had begun to grow quite dark. Palmer glanced at her mother. 'I'd like to do more than that.'

'What more?' Tanya wanted to know.

Palmer made the right-hand turn toward Asolo and in a few minutes they were slowed to a crawl through its narrow, arcaded streets. People seemed on the move, from work or a shop to home. They carried packages and went about their business without noticing Palmer or Eleanora or her daughter. It seemed strange and unfeeling to him that they couldn't notice what had happened. Everyone must notice. It must seem quite obvious.

'What more?' the little girl repeated.

'Oh.' Palmer stopped. 'Lots of things.'

'He wants to be your stepfather,' Eleanora said. 'But I will not marry him. Now let's forget it.'

'I already have a father,' Tanya informed him, helpfully.

Palmer shook his head. He drove to the road leading out of town and parked in front of the ruined villa. 'Eleanora,' he said then, 'you may want to forget it, but there are a few more things I must tell you.'

'I don't want to hear them.'

Again he got that sharp stab of *déjà vu*. Virginia hadn't wanted to hear him speak, either. What terrifying secrets did

Her eyebrows went up. 'Don't we? Perhaps not. Too much has been done. One thing is forgivable. Two. Ten. But when so many things are done, there isn't enough forgiveness left.'

'Within one person, too?'

'Yes. I loved you very much. That makes it unforgivable.'

'We Americans' – he paused – 'call that a cop-out.'

'Cop-out?'

'Failure to follow up on one's own actions. Failure to face up to one's own sins.' He started the engine. 'Not seeing me anymore is a cop-out. It relieves you of the responsibility of facing up to what you did.'

She stood there in silence for a long time. 'You really have no intention of driving off, do you?' she asked at last.

'Not if I can help it.'

'Then lock the car and come inside. It's silly to stand out here like a pair of adolescents.'

She waited for him to lock up. Then she handed him the overnight case. As he carried it up the slight rise to the villa, she took his other arm and helped him find his way in the half-dark through the rubble of the ruined masonry steps.

CHAPTER 49

Dinner was late. They ate it with Signora Frascati, who spent most of the meal discussing the fact that goats were not as dirty as people thought they were. 'Quite nice,' in fact. Palmer momentarily expected the pair who kept the front lawn cropped to wander in for individual plates of the *signora*'s tortellini in brodo.

After dinner Eleanora put her daughter to bed in another room, one Palmer had not been shown. She returned to the table for the *signora*'s black, bitter espresso. None of them spoke for a while and, after his first tentative taste, Palmer left the coffee alone in its tiny, cracked cup.

A sense of being in complete limbo swept over him. He was in a small, dark pocket of time that had nothing to do with what had gone before in his life and couldn't possibly connect with anything that came after. Not that he had any idea what lay ahead for him.

311

He watched Eleanora spoon sugar into her espresso. She passed the sugar cup to the *signora*. Then she stared down into her coffee. The black surface still swirled from the exertion of her spoon.

Palmer felt as if something heavy prevented her eyes from lifting to meet his glance. He dreaded having to tell her about her parents. He had no idea how badly she would take it, except that, once again, it would be an act of extreme violence connected to him. He wished he hadn't been so precipitous in Apartment 63 that night ... last night. What if there had been some vestige of life left in either of them? He hadn't even examined the woman. He'd tucked his tail between his legs and run.

He kept wishing, against the iron logic of what he knew, that he'd been mistaken, that they were somehow alive, that it had been a setup. a hoax, anything but what it obviously was. He toyed for a moment with the idea that Eleanora had hated her parents and would be happy to be rid of them. But he knew differently. There had been friction with her father, but Palmer knew she would receive the news of their murders with grief and anger. He seemed to have brought a kind of one-man plague with him, a very selective virus that killed everyone around Eleanora. It was impossible to think that she could feel about him as she once had in the innocent days of a week ago. If she had betrayed him, and of course she had, then he had paid her back as savagely, as recklessly as possible, without meaning to.

Just ten days, he thought. When her glance flicked up at him, he realized he had spoken aloud.

He shook his head and she studied the surface of her coffee again. Signora Frascati resumed her voluminous ruminations on the superiority of goats to other house pets like pigs or chickens.

Palmer knew Eleanora had been right to run away from him. Not for her reasons. What she'd done to him he had half expected and really didn't care about. The pressures on her to do it seemed more than enough to excuse what she'd done. But what he'd done to her was beyond the realm of forgiveness.

Dieter could not be left out of it, either. Palmer had no way of knowing how genuinely attached Tanya was to her father, but he *had* been her father and he *had* been killed because somebody thought he was Palmer. Whatever kind of villain Dieter had been, however shamefully he'd used the little girl, in her eyes he was her father, the only one she would ever have. She was too young to understand all the meanings of this, Palmer knew, but some day she would feel it more acutely. What would she feel then about the man for whom her real father had been murdered? Because of whom her grandparents had died?

Palmer closed his eyes at the horror of it. It was ugly and brutish and violent. Eleanora had been right. Whatever there had been between them, violence had scraped it away. How thoroughly, even she didn't yet know.

Palmer stood up from the table. 'Thank you very much, Signora,' he said, vaguely aware that he was interrupting her monologue almost in mid-word. He turned to Eleanora. 'I have a long drive back.'

She got to her feet. 'You're leaving for Venice?'

'Now.'

'I thought –' She stopped.

'So did I. But I was wrong.' He started for the door.

She followed him through the night to the car, still parked off the road in front of the villa. 'Why did you change your mind?'

'Because you were right,' he said, unlocking the VW's door.

'I see.'

'There's a lot you still haven't seen,' he said, getting behind the wheel. 'When you do, you'll realize just how impossible it is between us. You don't yet know everything I've done to you. And the horrible thing is how much I still cherish and love you.'

She stood at the open door of the car. 'Do you?'

'Yes.' He put the key in the dashboard and turned it. The starter kicked over but the engine failed to catch.

'And we won't ever talk again?' she asked.

'I have no hope of seeing you again.'

The night sky was already sprinkled with fierce chips of light In the clean air of this hill town, Palmer could see the faint band of starlight that indicated the curving sweep of the Milky Way. He watched it through the windshield for a moment, then tried to start the car again. Everything worked but the engine wouldn't catch. He switched off the key, thinking he'd flooded the motor, and let it rest for a moment.

'Something got out of hand between us,' he told her. 'I take the blame for it. Things back in the U.S. seemed to be riding with me, old grudges, old errands. All of this I brought into your life. You spoke before of something unforgivable. But you really didn't know what you meant. You will.'

313

'Tell me.'

He shook his head and tried to start the car. Again it didn't catch. He got out from behind the wheel and went to the rear of the VW to lift its engine cover. He had just swung up the lid when he felt something small and cold poke into his back at about the level of his floating ribs.

'Easy,' Forellen said. 'The rotor's missing.'

'You idiot.'

'Turn around slow.'

'You won't shoot that thing, but you could accidentally.' Palmer felt a reckless surge of energy inside him.

'I killed two for you already.'

'What is it?' Eleanora called.

'Stay out of this,' Palmer told her.

'Is it Forellen?'

'Keep out of his way,' Palmer said.

'Turn around slow,' Forellen repeated.

'Slowly, Stanley, slowly. If you'd gone to college, you'd know that.'

'You nasty, arrogant son of a bitch, turn around.'

Palmer started his turn slowly, right hand hanging loosely at his side. He felt a wild burst of anger. He didn't care how it ended. He tightened up and swung a full arc, his right arm flailing like a heavy stick of wood to catch the muzzle of the gun and knock it flying. Forellen gasped. Palmer caught sight of his pasty face and then he heard the gun go off.

There was no pain. The night sky seemed to fold in on itself like a silk scarf, the band of the Milky Way buckling and curving as Palmer fell to the rubble on the ground.

CHAPTER 50

People came and went.

They made noises, waves of sound. Rubber heels on tile floor. Silence. A roaring of blood in the inner ear. Silence. Chair scrape.

Silence.

Only sounds came through for a long time, and only now and then. A door squeaked. A window casement banged shut.

314

Sounds of rapid Italian came and went, came and went.

He heard English once. 'Blood...' Unless it was an Italian word that sounded like a word in English. He wondered about that for a while.

On the fourth day he could feel the light burning against his closed eyelids. He opened them and tears welled up, blurring his vision. He tried to wipe away the tears but he couldn't lift his hands. They were free to lift, but he had no strength to lift them. After a while he blinked his eyes clear.

The first thing he saw in the sunlight was the stand beside his bed, like a hat rack with no hats. The clear, round pint bottle with the red rubber stopper hung upside down. The red tubing went directly to his left wrist. It ended in a knurled bit of stainless steel. The rest was hidden by tape. He squinted, trying to read the label on the bottle, but it was upside down and in Italian.

They had covered him lightly with a very clean sheet. He tried to see down to the bottom of the bed. Both feet seemed to be there, but his right leg was outlandishly bloated and propped away from the rest of him. He tried to wiggle his toes and blacked out.

When he came to it was dusk of another day. Jack Rafferty, in the same miserable sports jacket, was sitting in an old-fashioned wooden armchair by his bed. The I-V stand had been removed and instead of a needle in his left wrist, there was a neat bandage. Rafferty was slowly reading through a yellow manila folder of papers, making tick marks with a pencil now and then. He glanced up at Palmer.

'Shit,' he said. 'You're alive.'

'Where's...' Palmer's voice broke up in a dry welter of throat noises. He tried to clear his throat. 'Where's girl?'

'She's okay. How do you feel?'

Palmer tried to moisten his lips. They seemed to be cracked with dryness. 'What's with leg?' His voice rasped huskily.

Rafferty poured a small glass of water from a carafe and held it to Palmer's mouth. He swallowed once, choked and coughed, then swallowed twice more. 'What's with the leg?' he asked more clearly.

'The lucky part is you were close to the gun. Once one of those Magnum slugs starts to tumble, it tears out meat like a cannonball. It went through the calf bones like an electric drill. They have the fibula and metatarsals all neatly pinned up with silver pegs and the femoral artery patched with a piece of condom or something. You bled like a stuck pig, baby. Three transfusions. One from me. You're now an honorary Irishman.'

'How lucky can I get?'

'That's what I was telling the American embassy fella. He just went away an hour ago. Been hanging around here for days.'

'Where is here?'

'Asolo. You couldn't be moved.'

'Where's the girl?'

Rafferty shrugged. 'Your solicitude for Forellen is absolutely immense. Why don't you ask me about him?' Palmer closed his eyes and shook his head very slightly. Rafferty waited. 'You asleep?'

'No.'

'Forellen's back in Paris. The CIA's gonna send the bastard to Saigon. Nobody's fucked up there in days, so naturally, they need reinforcements.' Rafferty paused. 'You okay?'

'Yes.'

'I had no idea you knew such Exalted Personages as H.B.,' Rafferty went on. 'I near crapped my breeches when he showed up here with his usual tight-lipped faggot bodyguard. They jetted the bastards here from Washington just to talk to you, baby. And you did my heart good. You were so unconscious you couldn't tell the bastards a thing.'

'Bannister?'

'Don't give me them big gray eyes, buster. His Eminence was so flustered he even confided to me that you were on a mission for him. And he knows me long enough to know I hate his faggoty insides. In fact, I think H.B. is the reason I never made it to one-star general. Hah.'

'One reason, anyway.'

'Apparently you screwed up whatever it was he wanted you to do,' Rafferty went on. 'Some guy was supposed to be debriefed and nobody ever got to him with the right trigger words. He's committed suicide.'

'H.B.?'

'No such luck. This inside pigeon took himself an L-tablet or something. Now he'll never be debriefed, except maybe by St. Peter. Does H.B. talk to St. Peter?'

'All the time.'

'Just so you'll know the official excuses, there are bandits in these hills. One of them shot you trying to steal your car. The

316

At first he was only allowed off the bed ten minutes at a time, three times a day. Within a day or two, however, he was out of bed more than in. They brought him the Rome *Daily American* and a two-week-old copy of the Paris *Tribune*. He did the crossword puzzle.

He telephoned his children one night and found that no one had told them anything so, of course, they hadn't been worried. He invited them to Italy for the month of July. They said they'd check it with their mother. He told them to have Miss Czermat get their passports quickly. Hesselman called from New York to see if he needed anything. Palmer said no. Dauber visited him for an afternoon and brought dozens of back copies of news magazines. His Rome manager arrived and stormed about the hospital, criticizing everything, and demanding they move Palmer to Venice or Milan. Palmer said no.

Toward the end of June, on the twenty-eighth, a Tuesday, the Mother Superior came to see him very early in the morning to tell him he could be discharged at once. He could really get around quite well on one crutch, now, and they very much needed his room. He got dressed and paid his bill in traveler's checks. The nun who handled the bookkeeping asked if she could call him a taxi to take him to Venice or wherever he wanted to go. Palmer said no.

He asked to use the telephone and placed a call to his children. It was nine in the morning in Asolo and 3 A.M. in New York. Fortunately, Mrs. Gage answered the call. It was one of Edith's nights out, apparently. When his children calmed down, they said their mother had made no objection to their spending a month in Europe. Palmer instructed Mrs. Gage to send them direct to Venice, nonstop on July 1 and he would meet them at Mestre Airport. Gerri wanted to know if he had any objections to travelling south into Norman country. Palmer said no.

He packed the accumulation of his weeks in the hospital into the small black vinyl bag his Rome manager had brought him. Besides the extra linen he had had the nuns buy him in Asolo there were several booklets about the town itself. Palmer leafed quickly through them. Asolo's fame had begun in the fifteenth century as a court for a Venetian girl, the widow of the King of Cyprus. Napoleon had slept there, one night in 1797. So had George Sand, with Chopin, in the 1830's just prior to Browning's arrival. 'Morning's at seven; the hillside's dew-pearled.' Palmer gave the booklets to a nun. She asked if he needed help with the small bag. Palmer said no.

He found the Mother Superior in her office and gave her a contribution which made her cry. Then he tucked his crutch under his right arm and limped out into the brilliant sunshine. He had no idea where he was in Asolo, but as he walked slowly through the arcaded streets, he recognized the post office and the café across the street. His bad leg was functioning quite well. He hadn't had liquor or drugs in weeks. It took him about half an hour to reach Signora Frascati's ruined villa. There were three goats now, the newcomer being a tiny infant on stick-thin legs. It made a noise like a cat and kept trying to get milk from its mother.

Palmer hobbled up the broken steps and went around to the back of the villa. The two women were shelling peas. The green pods split crisply beneath their fingers with small popping sounds. The raw peas rattled like pebbles against the blue enameled collander, pale green on dark blue.

Eleanora jumped to her feet. The collander went flying and landed with a clang against the stone wall of the villa. Signora Frascati stooped and began laboriously picking up the raw peas.

'They said you wouldn't be out for a few more days,' Eleanora said.

Palmer nodded. 'They needed the bed.'

She hastily carried her chair over to him. 'Sit down.'

'Thank you.' He did.

'Do you have a place to stay?'

'No.'

'There is a room here.'

He glanced at her. She seemed quite nervous. The length of her dirndl skirt was unfashionable anywhere but Asolo. Her legs looked slim and suntanned. 'Why didn't you come to see me?'

'No.' She started shaking her head and seemed unable to stop. 'No. I made up my mind. If I came it would never tell me anything about us. But if you came to me . . .' Her hand went to her mouth. 'I'm sorry.'

He shifted on the plain wooden chair. 'And if I just dropped by to say hello? Nothing more?'

Her brown eyes darkened for a moment. Then she took the crutch away from him and leaned it up against the wall of the villa far out of his reach.

'Too late,' she said, smiling.